Tara Pammi can't rememb⟨ ⟩
when she wasn't lost in a b⟨ ⟩
romance, which was much more exciting than a
mathematics textbook at school. Years later, Tara's
wild imagination and love for the written word
revealed what she really wanted to do. Now she
pairs alpha males who think they know everything
with strong women who knock that theory *and*
them off their feet!

Rosie Maxwell has dreamed of being a writer
since she was a little girl. Never happier than
when she is lost in her own imagination, she
is delighted that she finally has a legitimate
reason to spend hours every day dreaming about
handsome heroes and glamorous locations. In her
spare time she loves reading—everything from
fiction to history to fashion—and doing yoga.
She currently lives in the North-West of England.

Also by Tara Pammi

Contractually Wed
Her Twin Secret
Vows to a King
His Forgotten Wife

Also by Rosie Maxwell

An Heir for the Vengeful Billionaire
Billionaire's Runaway Wife

Discover more at millsandboon.co.uk.

BABIES TO BIND

TARA PAMMI

ROSIE MAXWELL

MILLS & BOON

All rights reserved including the right of reproduction in whole or in part in any form. This edition is published by arrangement with Harlequin Enterprises ULC.

This is a work of fiction. Names, characters, places, locations and incidents are purely fictional and bear no relationship to any real life individuals, living or dead, or to any actual places, business establishments, locations, events or incidents. Any resemblance is entirely coincidental.

Without limiting the exclusive rights of any author, contributor or the publisher of this publication, any unauthorised use of this publication to train generative artificial intelligence (AI) technologies is expressly prohibited. HarperCollins also exercise their rights under Article 4(3) of the Digital Single Market Directive 2019/790 and expressly reserve this publication from the text and data mining exception.

® and TM are trademarks owned and used by the trademark owner and/or its licensee. Trademarks marked with ® are registered with the United Kingdom Patent Office and/or the Office for Harmonisation in the Internal Market and in other countries.

First published in Great Britain 2025
by Mills & Boon, an imprint of HarperCollins*Publishers* Ltd,
1 London Bridge Street, London, SE1 9GF

www.harpercollins.co.uk

HarperCollins*Publishers*, Macken House, 39/40 Mayor Street Upper,
Dublin 1, D01 C9W8, Ireland

Babies to Bind © 2025 Harlequin Enterprises ULC

Baby Before Vows © 2025 Tara Pammi

Pregnant and Conveniently Wed © 2025 Rosie Maxwell

ISBN: 978-0-263-34492-9

12/25

MIX
Paper | Supporting
responsible forestry
FSC
www.fsc.org
FSC™ C007454

This book contains FSC™ certified paper
and other controlled sources to ensure responsible forest management.

For more information visit www.harpercollins.co.uk/green.

Printed and Bound in the UK using 100% Renewable Electricity
at CPI Group (UK) Ltd, Croydon, CR0 4YY

BABY BEFORE VOWS

TARA PAMMI

MILLS & BOON

CHAPTER ONE

RENZO DICARLO SAT fuming in his tinted Maserati, watching the different occupants of the house—women of varying ages—come back from work, dates, or whatever else they got up to at the end of the day.

The two-story Victorian home, located in a village near London, wasn't where he had expected his quarry to be.

The house was sturdy and beautiful, with a redbrick facade and elegant wrought iron railings that led to a deep blue front door. Even in the waning light, he could see the vibrant garden full of flowers and neatly trimmed shrubs.

At least she had chosen a quiet little village, relatively safe, instead of a city like London or New York. He should be thankful for small mercies, Renzo supposed.

Given the excited chatter the PI he had hired to locate her had spewed about the local folklore being rich in history, he shouldn't be surprised.

Mimi Shah had always been bookish, standoffish, and more interested in documenting other people's lives. Also utterly uninterested in the public life that her world-renowned actress mother constantly courted.

That she would prefer to share a home with a bunch of working women, instead of choosing to tell his family about the child she was carrying, grated on him.

But then, everything about Mimi Shah had always grated

on Renzo. Even though, in theory, she was the exact opposite of her stepsister, Pia, his sister-in-law of six years. The intensity of his own reaction to Mimi had never made sense to Renzo.

Just then, a pregnant woman stepped out of a beat-up car that had rounded the small courtyard in front of the home.

Her gait was off-balance as she bent to gather her bags, smile strained as she thanked the driver.

Renzo gripped the steering wheel tight as he watched her make her way towards the worn steps to the main door. With a hand bracing over her lower back, a cloth grocery bag in one hand, and her usual black backpack hitched on her shoulder, she took a deep breath and started the upward trek.

The way he was parked, he could see her body sketched carefully by the fading light. As if just for his benefit.

His jaw tightened.

She was slender to the point of gauntness, so her belly looked even more protruding on her thin frame. But it was her face that held his attention. All sharp angles and serious eyes, as if her stubborn nature had etched itself into her features.

Compared to her stepsister, Pia, Mimi Shah could be called average. Especially since, he realized with new insight, she made it a point to blend into the background.

Pia had been stunning—the kind of beauty that grabbed everyone's attention immediately. By the balls, he would say, thinking as a man who, for just a second, had also been caught in the trap. But that was the high point of knowing Pia.

Each minute, each day after that, the beauty would start to sag and fade under the claws of her personality. The spoiled, attention-hogging, immature woman that emerged within minutes of meeting her had forever put him off.

Pia had been vapid and shallow and manipulative and exhausting, but his brother, Santo, had loved her. Had found something in her to like.

Renzo thumped his head against the headrest of his seat, a sudden pike of grief skewering him.

How he wished Santo had never met Pia.

How he wished Santo had been stronger and asserted himself more around Pia, so she didn't play with his heart like it was a rag doll.

How he wished Santo had cut off all ties with her after the first time he'd discovered she had cheated on him.

But no...

His older brother had been as loyal and loving as only he could be. Always willing to see the good in everyone around him—whether it was his wife or their father, who fluttered around women as if he was a bee sniffing around flowers for pollen. Or Renzo himself, even when he got too cynical and ruthless for Santo's liking.

How Renzo wished he could have stopped Santo, and even Pia, from getting into the car on that stormy night and taking that dangerous curve while they were probably still in the middle of the argument he'd witnessed as they drove away.

Months later, the grief was just as fresh and just as sneaky, coming at him in a sudden blinding wave to nearly choke him. And it was one of those waves now that filled him with anger and frustration and resentment for this woman who was carrying his child.

His child...

Not Santo's. As everyone would have assumed, since she was the surrogate mother for Pia's baby.

A laugh burst through his mouth, filling the car with echoes of bitterness.

He was the father of the child that Mimi Shah was carrying—a secret only he and Santo had known. His brother had begged him to donate his sperm for their next IVF treatment, desperate to give Pia the child she wanted. Desperate to make one grand attempt at saving his marriage.

It hadn't mattered much to Renzo.

He was not a man who had ever felt particularly paternal. Maybe that came from having a father who was the epitome of selfish desires and indulgences. Or maybe because he'd carried too many responsibilities from a young age. Or perhaps, having been burned by Rosa, the girl he'd loved once, and having seen too many unbalanced relationships around him, he could never trust a woman to share his life in a way that would enrich it.

He'd happily donated his sperm because the child, whether it was carried by Pia or her stepsister, Mimi, would belong to Santo. And because a baby would bring happiness to Santo and maybe contentedness to Pia. Even his mother, he knew, had hoped for the latter.

Now Santo was gone, and Pia was gone, and her stubborn stepsister, Mimi, who had agreed to be their surrogate, was carrying his child.

Imagine his shock when the world-class fertility clinic director had reached out to him about the defaulted payments for the IVF treatment—it was just like his brother to forget people needed to be paid—and sent him all the paperwork that entailed.

He had paid for the past multiple rounds of extraction and the IVF and discovered a small discrepancy in the records.

Imagine his shock when he grilled the clinic director, exerting all his considerable influence, and discovered that his sister-in-law, Pia, hadn't even gone through the last round of extraction, but that it had been her stepsister, Mimi.

So now, Mimi, the woman he didn't like for reasons he didn't understand, and who didn't like him either, he was pretty sure, was carrying his child.

And while she hadn't known it was his and not Santo's, she had kept the pregnancy a secret for several months.

Cristo, he hated lies and manipulations and mind games. He'd had enough of them with their father and sometimes his entire family. But the fact of the matter was that whether he'd wanted a child or not, he was having one.

Soon.

And he couldn't let the status quo stand.

He got out of the car, knowing he was about to change both their lives in ways they couldn't even imagine.

But he wasn't his father. He didn't neglect his responsibilities, even if they were thrust on him by a cruel twist of fate.

This child was a DiCarlo.

Mimi Shah stared at the man standing on her doorstep, one shoulder pressed against the frame as if he expected the door to be shut in his face and was not taking any chances.

If she didn't despise drama with every cell in her and if she hadn't been prepared for him, she'd have done just that.

Renzo DiCarlo, the famous hotelier billionaire of Venice, had finally found her.

The man had always made her skin prickle—sometimes in anger and sometimes in undeniable attraction that she had managed to hide. In the six years of Pia and Santo's marriage, Renzo had always made it clear that her stepsister, their family, and Mimi were all nuisances he was putting up with for his brother's sake.

Panic uncoiled in her stomach like a snake unfurling from its nest. Perhaps that was an exaggeration aided and abetted by her wonky hormones, but not by too much.

Her hand automatically drifted to her belly, and his haughty gaze followed the gesture. It made her look defensive, she realized too late.

One thick eyebrow rose in a challenge, even as he somehow very elegantly draped himself over the doorframe without actually stepping foot inside.

Every hackle that Mimi possessed rose.

She wasn't foolish. She had imagined this very particular scenario a hundred times over the past few months. And here, she had been foolish. She had thought herself ready to face him and all that would follow.

With one mobile brow, he upended her hard-won composure and her resolve to stay calm and collected. Refusing to engage in his mind games, she moved away from the door without issuing an invitation.

His sudden laughter behind her made the small hairs on the nape of her neck prickle. Something loose and warm trickled through her veins, like the cork had been let out of a fizzy drink.

She rubbed her belly again, this time as a comforting gesture for herself. God, the last thing she needed right now was to still be attracted to this man. It would be like kneeling in the middle of a battleground and bowing her head to the enemy.

Again, a bit exaggerated but wholly based in truth.

"This is a…cozy room, Ms. Shah." Cruel humor touched each word, along with a hefty dose of disbelief. "Nothing in the luxury repertoire of the DiCarlo hotels could match this."

"It's my home, Mr. DiCarlo," she said, matching his exaggerated sweet tone. "And no, nothing you own would make me feel as happy or as safe."

A sense of hurried alarm seized her as he surveyed the large, airy room with a leisure that grated on her nerves.

She had enough savings, from her work as a documentary maker and event videographer, to afford the biggest room in the Victorian house that one of her friends rented out. But she was also seven months pregnant, working all hours, and tired.

The room, as a result, was extremely untidy—not that she was a tidy person even on usual days. Piles of books, camera equipment, and baby bits made the room shrink to almost half. Her temporary wardrobe on a portable wheeled rack—mostly black tights and loose, colorful sweaters—took up one wall.

Boxes and boxes of baby things that she had been collecting for months—gently used clothes, toys, blankets—took up all the floor space. And then there was her knitting stuff, because it was the only way she had been able to calm her mind in the last few months, given that she couldn't even have a glass of wine.

More importantly, she had been nesting, preparing to be a mother as well as she could on her own. The realization sent a warm feeling down her spine, washing away the little flicker of embarrassment.

This was her haven, her home, where she was in control, and she felt safe. After months of fertility shots, Pia's emotional outbursts, and the mountain of lies they had been sitting on, and then the car accident and the news of her pregnancy, she had needed to be alone. While she had wholeheartedly agreed to be the surrogate for Pia, her stepsister didn't make things easy for anyone.

Had needed to find her center again after a horrible few months. Had needed respite from her mother's opinionated commentary and her stepdad John's grief. This sunny room had given her a sense of control back after months of being near Pia for the IVF treatments.

"I can see that you've been busy preparing for what's ahead."

For just a moment, she'd forgotten Mr. DiCarlo's presence. Something the man wouldn't be used to, she thought, mouth twitching.

She turned around, just in time to catch the myriad of emotions crossing his face as he peeked at the boxes. Neither did she miss the thin thread of reluctant admiration in his tone.

Leaning against the opposite wall, she managed to check him out in turn. She refused to feel even a flicker of shame about this, too.

Twenty-six, pregnant, and apparently—thanks to one of the twisting side effects of her pregnancy—unbelievably horny. But even if she were none of those things, she could still appreciate, especially as an artist, the sheer sensual appeal of a man like Renzo DiCarlo.

Interestingly, he was the less classically handsome DiCarlo brother.

Santo had been like a marble bust with sharp cheekbones, a straight nose and thick lips. She'd just had her heart broken by someone when she met him for the first time as an art professor in one of the summer courses she'd been attending in Italy. It hadn't taken her long to realize that his perfectly boring good looks did nothing for her, though.

And soon after, Santo had turned Pia's head.

Santo and Renzo's younger brother, Massimo, had boyish good looks with twinkling eyes and a surly temperament.

But this man's appeal was something Mimi had come to appreciate only as she'd gotten older. As she'd begun to understand her own sexuality.

Renzo DiCarlo was made of imperfections—a bump in the middle of his nose, a scar through his eyebrow, a strange little dimple near his upper lip that was like a permanent indent.

As if an absent-minded sculptor, a woman surely, had gotten lost in the beauty of what she'd been creating and left a little thumbprint in his flesh.

Then there were his deep-set gray eyes and the constant dissatisfied expression that he wore. As if nothing in the world was up to his standard.

He should have been unremarkable—he had flaws enough for that—but he was more than the sum of his individual features. He had an appeal that blazed hotter than Santo's boringly perfect features ever could.

It was the air of authority and confidence he carried. And something about that air of "I can deal with anything the world throws at me" had always turned Mimi on. Even when she hadn't understood why her stepsister's new brother-in-law, who looked at them as if they were little better than garden pests, made her belly tighten and her core dampen.

She was a woman who liked to be competent in her own life, and who took matters into her own hands. Nor did she understand to this day why his confidence made her knees weak.

Maybe it was the novelty of a tall, dark, Italian billionaire being in her sphere at all. Maybe because she'd never known her own father. Her stepdad, John, like Santo, never asserted himself. Or maybe it was the age-old instinct of wanting the smartest, sexiest, strongest man around to satisfy that deep-rooted survival instinct.

Renzo DiCarlo was all of those things.

She'd stopped trying to make sense of it ages ago. It wasn't as if anything could happen between them. Then there was the fact that, within minutes of interacting with him, like now, the attraction took a back seat. The man possessed an uncanny knack for riling her up.

So she simply stood there and admired the breadth of his shoulders and how the white dress shirt neatly hugged his tapered waist, and when he went to his haunches to open the flap on the boxes of baby stuff that were everywhere, the sleek hardness of his thighs. The air inside the room was filled with his bergamot and citrus scent.

When he finished his scrutiny and turned his attention to her, it felt like a highly charged laser beam had honed in on her. Every inch of her skin came alight at his thorough, thoughtful perusal. His gaze lingered over the dark circles under her eyes—thanks to being unable to sleep well with her belly—the stress lines around her mouth that she saw deepen in the mirror every morning, the uneven flutter of her pulse at her neck, and lower.

Although mercifully, his gaze didn't linger there long.

He leaned against the wall next to the door, mirroring her stance. But while fresh tension suffused her, he looked casual with his foot propped on the wall behind him, hands tucked into the pockets of his trousers.

"Enough posturing, Mr. DiCarlo. Let's discuss why you are here."

Another rise of the damned brow, another challenge.

Mimi sighed. "I'm tired and in no mood to play the host to you."

"Let's sit down then."

"Shouldn't take that long," she said stubbornly, even though her lower back was killing her.

Anger flashed in his eyes, but when he spoke, his voice was smooth. "I'm more than happy to skip all the dramatics and jump to the Q and A session if you promise to give me truthful answers."

She bristled at his condescending tone. "I have no interest in lying to you."

"Except the giant lie of omission that we're both evading."

"I won't insult you by offering pathetic excuses. I'd do the same thing again."

"Which is exactly what?"

"Hide the fact that the last round of IVF worked and that I'm pregnant. With...their child." Her throat prickled, but she pushed on. "Retreat from everyone I know. Escape to this quiet village. All of it."

Something glittered in his gaze. "Am I to understand that even your parents are unaware of this...development?"

"Yes. They flew to Australia right after Santo and Pia's wake for Mom's latest movie shoot."

"And may I inquire why this secrecy was necessary?"

Mimi stared at him, pleasantly surprised by the genuine curiosity in his question. She felt infinitely better knowing that she could at least read him clearly. "It was a lot toward the end. My stepsister wasn't..." She hesitated, grief and guilt scraping their claws through her.

The grief she understood. As contentious and problematic as their relationship had been, she had loved Pia. And the loss was going to change her. Had already changed her in irrevocable ways. But the guilt wasn't healthy or good for the baby, her ob-gyn had told her over and over. That Pia was gone while Mimi was alive and healthy with the child she desperately craved...it hung over her like a dark cloud whatever she tried.

"Ms. Shah?" Suddenly, Mr. DiCarlo was standing close, his large hand clutching her elbow. "You've turned alarmingly pale."

Mimi pulled away, the sudden strangely familiar scent of him filling her nostrils. She could feel herself swaying on the balls of her feet, eager to fall into his strong arms, eager to let someone else carry the weight of her burdens for one glorious moment.

"I'm fine," she said, swallowing.

With a muttered curse, he pulled back and dragged the straight-backed chair from her desk. It thumped against the bare wooden floor as he placed it in front of her. "I won't think less of you if you sit down."

"I don't give a damn what you think about me."

"*Davvero?* Then why are you being so goddamned stubborn? You're heavily pregnant and weaving where you stand, and I'm supposed to think you're better than Pia?"

The intense frustration that colored his words, and the mention of her stepsister, sliced a little fracture in Mimi's prickly defenses. The moment she sat down, the twinges in her lower back eased, and a rough breath whistled out from between her lips.

A different kind of discomfort, something close to shame, danced in her chest. He was right. And she hated that she'd let him provoke her into acting like an immature child. When he squatted to look into her downturned face, alarm skittered through her.

The last thing she expected of Renzo DiCarlo was that he would kneel in front of anyone, much less her.

Don't let it go to your head. It's only because you're carrying the DiCarlo child, the sensible voice she trusted whispered.

"That's a miracle right in front of my eyes," she said, trying hard to dispel the mounting tension at his nearness.

"What is?"

"I didn't think the massive size of your ego would allow your knees to bend like that."

For just a fiery moment, something like sheer admiration flickered in his eyes. "I would advise you take that as a warning rather than a miracle, Ms. Shah. Trying times ahead and all that."

Mimi swallowed, both the alarm and her doubts. She wasn't going to let him wind her up with vague threats.

Pain danced freely in his gaze. His throat bobbed up and down. "I recognize the guilt in your face as well as if I were watching myself in the mirror. You're not responsible for their accident any more than I am."

Mimi nodded. Suddenly, he didn't seem like an enemy so much as another grief-stricken bystander. "Do you start to believe it at some point?"

A hollow smile curved his lips. "I'm still waiting for that day. But you…"

"Yes, I know. I have to think of the baby."

"I was going to say you were not even there that day. But I was present. I saw them leave." He rubbed a long finger over his temple. "They had been at it again, arguing like dogs. It was raining in dense sheets. I cherished the silence after they left. Until I got the call."

"I'm so sorry," she whispered, hearing the anguish in his tone.

"Me too." Then Renzo DiCarlo reached for her hands, and it took every ounce of willpower Mimi had to not jerk away like a frightened kitten in front of the big, bad wolf. "I'd like to understand why you hid the pregnancy from everyone."

"I… Pia wasn't the easiest to deal with."

"That's an understatement if I've ever heard one."

Shockingly enough, the dryness of his tone made Mimi giggle. "The last few months before the accident, it snowballed. Like you said, she and Santo were fighting regularly. But she desperately believed that the baby would miraculously fix everything. Only they were building more and more lies between them." Her breath came in a shallow gasp as she herself had skated over a dangerous lie. "At the funeral, it became too much. John and Mom and your family and you… I realized I needed to think of myself. I'd spent months being her emotional support even as I was the one going through the invasive fertility shots." The words rushed out of her. "I needed calm. Not John's heartbreaking grief. Or your arrogant commands. I…needed respite from everyone and everything, and time."

"That sounds fair."

"So glad you think so," Mimi said archly, responding to that condescending tone again.

"Ahhh…this is going to get so much harder for both of us if you react like that to everything I say."

She fought the urge to roll her eyes at him. "Then maybe don't speak in that tone to me."

"I don't know—"

"Like you're validating my choices with your agreement."

"You're a little porcupine under all that sensible softness, aren't you?"

Mimi flushed, hoping he wouldn't realize how much she liked his compliment. How much she liked that he saw her strength beneath her easy compliance. How desperate she had been all her life to be seen, especially next to her sister's brilliant beauty. That it was this man was more than alarming.

"Only one more question remaining."

Mr. DiCarlo uncoiled to his full height, one hand on his waist. He looked so deep in thought that the question came at Mimi like an arrow heading straight to her weakest point. "Why did you decide to keep the baby?"

"What?" she said inanely.

"Is it because it was Santo's?"

Hot color suffused her cheeks. "You don't know what you're saying."

"I know you nurtured a little affection for Santo. That you were the first one to meet him, the one who became his friend over that long-ago summer in Milan. Then Pia came along and stole him from you."

"And you think I kept the baby because I was in love with him?" Outrage colored her words. "So I not only was in love with my stepsister's husband but eagerly agreed to give over my body and my freedom for nine long months just to have his baby? That's a little twisted, don't you think?"

He shrugged. And even that movement was somehow elegant. "You agreed to be surrogate for a woman I know firsthand was incapable of thinking about anyone but herself, Ms. Shah. Although, it was only in the last year that I realized Pia's emotional vampirism extended to you too."

"She was my sister, and I loved her," Mimi declared, enraged.

But beneath the anger was that flicker of warmth that he had seen how exhausting Pia could be with her incessant competitiveness and petty jealousies and complex mind games. "I'm not hung up over Santo, for God's sake. Honestly, it didn't take me long to discover he wasn't my type."

"What 'type' was Santo?"

"You want me to list my dead brother-in-law's faults?"

"I just listed your sister's." His throat bobbed up and down again. "My family has already turned him into a saint, Ms. Shah. I'd rather remember the real man, flaws and all."

"Santo was irresponsible. No, that's not right. He didn't

take responsibility for anything, but rather had this romantic view of life that had nothing to do with reality, and he didn't stand up for what was right. It became clear to me over the years that he and Pia lived far beyond their meager incomes, and that's all because of you. In hindsight, I think it was a miracle that their marriage lasted as long as it did."

When she looked up, Renzo DiCarlo's firm mouth was slack with shock. Mimi sighed. "I didn't mean to—"

"It seems you're a good study of character. Everything you said about Santo is completely true."

Mimi was as shocked by his honest admission as he seemed to be by hers. "Then you should acknowledge that I needed to nurture something for the man who adored my stepsister like I needed a hole in my head." She took a breath to even out her tone. "Whatever else they fought over, Pia and Santo desperately wanted this baby. They went through so much to have it. *I* went through a lot. So, no, I didn't think of not having it."

"I want to believe you."

Mimi shot to her feet. God, the man was infuriating. "If you're done insulting me, I'd like you to leave."

"We're not done."

"Fine. You're here to hash out some kind of custody arrangement, right? So can we please get to it? I've had a long day and would like a shower and dinner and my bed, in that order."

"Do you want me to order takeout for you?"

"No, I couldn't eat a morsel with you hovering over me like some…rabid raptor, waiting to pick off leftover pieces."

He laughed, a husky sound that swathed Mimi in silky waves. "You have quite the tongue on you, *sì*?"

"I'm sorry, Mr. DiCarlo, for not being as mousy and accommodating as you expected me to be."

He sighed then, and that too was distracting. Because it seemed to come wrenching out of the depths of him. It pulled her out of her own head for just a second. He had lost his brother and now had the unwanted news of that brother's child.

God, what a mess...

"I have something to tell you," he said after a long pause, "and I think you should sit down. I'd hate for you to be upset in your current condition."

"Again, it's very simple," she said through gritted teeth. "Don't tell me upsetting things."

"Remember the mountain of lies that you said Pia and Santo built between them?" Bitterness twisted his mouth. "I'd rather we don't begin this relationship buried under those ourselves."

"We don't have a relationship, Mr. DiCarlo. Neither are we going to build one." She took a deep breath. "We can arrange for visitation rights for you, if you want that. One of my housemates is a lawyer, and she assured me that I don't owe you even that. But since it's your brother's child, I—"

"It's not Santo's child. It's mine." His gray eyes held steady like flinty stones that had seen millennia pass. "Just as it's not Pia's. But yours. Wholly yours."

CHAPTER TWO

Mɪᴍɪ's ᴋɴᴇᴇs, ɪᴛ sᴇᴇᴍᴇᴅ, were very much capable of giving out.

Mr. DiCarlo's strength and scent surrounded her as she was directed to the bed. Her breath played hide-and-seek with her lungs as his words began to sink in.

"Head between your knees," he barked like a general giving orders to his soldiers.

Mimi followed the commanding voice instinctively and bent her spine, as much as her belly would allow. Oxygen returned to her in large gulps, and she breathed it in like a gasping fish.

Although it was the warm weight of his large hands on her knees and the solid shelf of his shoulder that her forehead was resting on that became her anchor.

Two more seconds and I'll pull away, she told herself. It didn't slip her near-hysterical mind that she was finding respite in the same man who was causing her stress.

Renzo DiCarlo in her life, playing such a big role, chipping away at her armor, endangering her resolve to never depend on anyone.

It couldn't be the truth. He was lying for some twisted reason of his own. He couldn't be the father of her child, could he?

However hard she tried, she couldn't avoid the truth. Not even to stave off the moment's panic.

Renzo DiCarlo was the father of her baby.

Her baby.

Our baby, a voice said in her head, in his infuriating tone and accent. Great, now he was inside her head too.

Mimi jerked up and away from him, crawling back on the bed in a very ungainly manner until her back met the metal headboard. Looking anywhere but at him, she counted her breaths like they were teaching her in the birthing class, willing her heart rate to subside.

A glass of water appeared in her vision. She took it, gulped the entire thing down and returned it to him, hands still shaking.

"I'm sorry that I upset you," he said, sitting down by her legs. That his remorse was genuine didn't stem her confusion. Neither did that delicious scent of his.

Far too close, she wanted to scream. He was being attentive because of her condition. Not because he cared about her. God, she needed to get that tattooed on the back of her hand as a reminder to stay sane over the following months.

"Any possibility that you're in full-scale delulu-land because you've lost your brother?" she said in a small voice. Still not looking at him. "Grief does the strangest things to us."

"Believe me, Ms. Shah, if I could forget the rainy afternoon where I had to…into a cup, I would." Even his self-deprecating scoff stole through her veins like some kind of magic spell. "I checked every record at the fertility clinic. Santo told me his sperm count was too low to be of use. He found out after the first failed attempt at IVF. He begged me to keep it between ourselves, as their marriage was already shaky. I complied because I saw how much he wanted it to work for him and Pia. As usual, there was no length he wouldn't go to to give Pia what she wanted."

"And nothing you wouldn't do for your brother?"

"Santo would have been a good father. He told me Pia wouldn't even consider adoption. So yes, I agreed." Another sigh escaped him.

Mimi had the ridiculous thought that she was using up all of Renzo DiCarlo's sighs, a lifetime's quota of them.

"I'm assuming you were railroaded into a similar agreement," he said.

"She didn't...railroad me." Tears prickled behind her eyelids, and Mimi fought them back. "She cried and yelled and complained about her body being ruined by the fertility shots and how it was still failing her." Another thought struck her. "It was cruel of Santo to let her think the fault lay with her."

Mr. DiCarlo didn't jump to his brother's defense, and she liked him for it. A lot. "She begged me to help. Like you said, she wasn't an easy person to love, but I saw how the failed IVF attempts wrecked her. Anyway, I said yes to the extraction too."

"Ah, emotional manipulation was the best weapon in Pia's arsenal."

Mimi didn't deny it, even as a hot protest rose to her lips by habit. She had a feeling her state-sponsored therapist would love Renzo DiCarlo. He got her to break the pattern her therapist had been urging her to break for months now. She would not revise her complex history with Pia in her head because of the overwhelming guilt she felt.

Sighing, she looked up.

This close, the appeal of the man was a one-two punch. He was so large, so solid, so rawly masculine that she felt like she would drown in him. "Can you please give me room? I feel like I can't breathe."

Concern etched into his face, he moved down the bed,

ending on a pile of washed underwear she hadn't put away yet. The sight of her maternity bras and loose granny panties made mortification rise through her in a swell.

Cursing, she grabbed them from him and shoved them behind her back.

"Are you embarrassed, Ms. Shah?" he said in a curious voice. As if he was testing something out between them.

"Annoyed by your interrogation is more like it," she said, sounding like a prickly cactus.

He didn't rise to the bait. If anything, his expression turned more serious. "I understand why you hid for all these months. But whatever anonymity you had until now will come to an end. It's a miracle the media hasn't found you out."

"Why the hell would the media care about me?"

"You're carrying a DiCarlo baby. Sooner or later, the press will find out."

"How?" she demanded.

"Because I will feature in its life, one way or the other. And because I will claim it as such." His words rang with resolve. "It's not a negligible thing. Now the whole world is going to wonder why you hid, and why I didn't welcome you and this baby into our family wholeheartedly all these months. Santo and Pia's marriage was a performative circus that dragged us all into the spotlight. Now this is like throwing fresh meat to hungry hyenas."

"First of all, the baby isn't here yet. Second of all, you're a freaking billionaire. What the hell do you care what the media says about you or your family? Aren't you all supposed be egocentric kings of your own little fiefdoms?"

"I care what our name stands for, since I built it up from scandal and ruin." Mr. DiCarlo grinned as if to take away the gravity from that. Unfortunately for Mimi, it increased his appeal a thousand times. "Are you quite this colorful in your language with everyone, or do I bring out this particular talent?"

"It's you," she said, refusing to hold back. "I'm a sensible, caring woman with everyone else in the world."

"How special that makes me feel," he said dryly.

Mimi's mouth twitched despite everything.

It was a rare sight to see Renzo DiCarlo so thoroughly put-upon, after all. When he looked at her, that tiny flicker morphed into full-blown laughter that made her chest ache and her ribs spasm painfully.

"Ouch," she said, palming her belly as the baby went into high gear and kicked.

His hands reached for her belly instinctively, and he froze so fully that it was like a watching a pouncing predator come to a deathly stillness. "Is that…" he cleared his throat, his eyes intense on hers "…the baby kicking? Is it safe? Do you need—"

"Yes, it's kicking. I laughed and must have jostled it too much," Mimi said, pulling her hands back so their fingertips didn't touch. "It's very normal. If anything, I'd be surprised if the kicking didn't happen once every hour at least."

Hawkeyed as he was, he didn't miss her pulling away. But his large palms stayed on her belly, covering so much more ground than hers could.

A strange intimacy wove around them, and Mimi fought it with every ragged breath. Attraction to him because of some age-old instinct was one thing. But being bound to him in any way because of the baby—her entire rational being revolted against the very idea.

She wanted to tell him to remove his hands, but the words refused to form. Something about the look in his eyes forbade them.

Now she felt stupid for retreating. It felt as if she had ceded ground. Which was ridiculous because this was a baby, not a battlefield.

And moreover, Renzo DiCarlo wasn't interested in being a father any more than he was interested in tying himself to her in any way.

She needed to remember that.

It was like bubbles popping. Or like the flutter of tiny, fragile wings under his large, callused hands. Until it was a stronger tap that made his own breath punch out of his lungs.

Renzo stilled, stunned, eager to feel more of the tumbling, zapping feeling. It was unlike anything he had ever experienced. Awe filled him as the baby seemed to subside even as he waited, with a thundering heart.

Suddenly, the complete scope of what was happening in his life shone in technicolor. This was a child kicking its tiny feet or legs against its mama's belly, making itself known.

With his brother gone, this was fully his child now.

His child...

An innocent, pure life that he was going to be responsible for, unlike the foolish, privileged, spoiled members of his family. No, that was two more lives he was responsible for now. And the second was pure and innocent too, in ways he hadn't been exposed to in a long while.

She'd been hidden by the very large shadow that her stepsister cast, and with his vision blurred by what Rosa, the girl he had loved, had done so long ago, he hadn't seen what kind of woman Mimi Shah was. And it unsettled him, as if his radar wasn't in top shape.

He looked up and met the mutinous brown gaze and nearly burst out laughing.

A strange reaction to the most bizarre encounter of his

life, but there it was. He had braced himself for anger, fury, frustration that he was going to be yoked to a woman he couldn't tolerate, that he was going to be forced into a role he didn't want...

Anything but this sheer wonder at what they had created. Convoluted though their route had been.

"Can you please move your hands away? It's possible you have some rights to this child, but I'm not... I don't think we should, that is..."

He removed his hands immediately, bemused by her unusual floundering. "That is?"

"We're practically strangers."

"We've known each other for nearly six years, Ms. Shah."

And in those years, she had always pricked his curiosity, even with Pia's drama front and center. Now he brought all those little nuggets he had stored away into the spotlight.

She was a promising documentary maker. Even Pia had sung her praises. She supported herself without asking for handouts from her parents. Which was a quality he immensely respected, given all his siblings expected to be kept in luxury for the rest of their lives through his hard work. She was self-composed, and didn't date, at all.

And Pia, being Pia, had used Mimi's dating history to persuade her to be their surrogate. Santo had felt discomfited enough by the fact that he had mentioned it to Renzo.

She was as allergic to being the center of attention as he was. For some twisted reason, he had expected her, and her parents, to talk sense into Pia, to control her irrational stunts and her extravagant demands, to make her behave.

Which was nothing but stupid. He knew firsthand how hard it was to save someone who didn't want to save themselves, who believed their privilege afforded them anything they wanted. Like his father. And his sister and Massimo. And Santo, to a certain extent.

Now he pushed the intense dislike of Pia he had used as a shield against Mimi all these years aside and let the reality of their situation settle into his gut.

He was attracted to this firecracker of a woman with her bright, big eyes, sharp features and unusual but slow-dawning beauty. It was an attraction all the more dangerous and potent than any instant lust because it had snuck under his skin and stayed there, building in pitch all these years. He even liked her blunt wit and her refreshingly honest personality.

"Is there a boyfriend on the scene, Ms. Shah?" he said, making his tone as snarky and pointed as possible to provoke her. Better to clarify everything with her up front. "What does he say to your becoming a surrogate first, and now a single mother?"

"There isn't one," she said with a vehemence he thoroughly enjoyed. "And if even there was one, I wouldn't let a man dictate what I can or can't do for my sister."

He grinned, things falling into place.

Sì, he would have considered marriage at some point.

He was only thirty-five, though, and that prospect had been relegated to the far-off future. Maybe to when he was past forty and wanted a family, when he slowed down with his luxury resort empire and his fast life. Maybe because he would have—with his genes—turned into a self-centered, indulgent old man fixated on his legacy and how far and how fast he could spread his dwindling sperm.

Instead, here was this ready-made family being offered to him on a platter.

If he could wrap his head around the idea of having this fierce, sensible, ultra-competent woman as his wife.

She was prickly, and not the sophisticated, soft society wife he had vaguely imagined when he had allowed himself to go there and would probably not agree to any proposition he made in a hundred years, just to spite him. But she was also loyal and eminently practical, and her competence aroused him more than any other woman's ever had.

Mimi Shah was perfectly tailored to be his wife and the mother of his child.

A concept he would have laughed at months ago, when Pia and Santo had been alive and well. But now...everything had changed. His entire world was upside down, and he had to adapt to it quickly. The child, unlike him and his siblings, would have a happy, secure childhood with two sensible parents.

A sudden thrill shot through him as the mere fragment of the idea consolidated into a plan in his gut in mere moments.

Her soft gasp pulled him into the present, away from his schemes. And this time, when he looked at her, he looked past her belly, if such a thing were possible.

Large brown eyes with amber flecks studied him with a discerning expression. Her silky brown hair with its golden highlights was falling away from its untidy bun on top of her head. Long lashes cast crescent shadows onto too sharp cheekbones. And then there was her mouth, small and lushly made and a lovely dusky pink.

Desire came at Renzo, soft and slow and sneaky at first, then fisting his stomach tight, flushing his insides with sudden heat.

Ms. Shah pulled back, eyes widening. "I don't trust the look in your eyes." Fingers gripping the quilt, she pulled it over her belly, as if the worn-out fabric could somehow protect her from his wicked intentions. "Whatever you're thinking, the answer's a big fat no."

Renzo laughed again. Thrice in the matter of an hour. It had to be some sort of record. *Cristo*, but the woman was sharp as a dagger, and he would have to keep his senses alert just to keep up with her.

The sheer thrill of the future unrolling in his mind made his spine tingle. At least he would never be bored with her and their life together.

"It's interesting that you read me so well, Ms. Shah. And I must say it's mutual."

"What do you mean?"

"I think there's more than all the very fair reasons you've quoted for hiding this pregnancy for so long. Especially from me."

She shook her head, although it was half-hearted.

"You knew how big Santo and I are on family, given our father is a scoundrel who thinks nothing of shaming our mother. You knew that I wouldn't let a DiCarlo child be born out of wedlock. You knew I couldn't let a child of my blood be termed a bastard by the media. You knew, and you just didn't want to face that reality." He raised his palms. "Not that I'm blaming you."

Chin tucked down, dwarfed by the quilt, she suddenly looked small and young and innocent. "If we forget whose egg and whose sperm went into the making of this baby, I would be its aunt."

"Even if it had been Santo's, with him gone, you know I would have insisted on a wedding. Deep down, you knew that. Seems you know me better than you think you do."

For a pregnant woman who had been through so much loss in recent months, she didn't buckle down and take the easy route. Even though exhaustion drew dark smudges under her eyes.

Tenderness and a fierce protectiveness danced in Renzo's stomach, provoking each other to something even more potent.

She squared her shoulders, chest rising and falling under her brown sweater. "You don't like me, and I don't like you. We've had first-row seats to an epic disaster of a marriage between people who confessed everlasting love to each other. I know you're as allergic to love as I am. There's nothing to gain by going down this path, Renzo."

His name on her lips felt like an invocation, an invitation to something new and rich. He swallowed the thick coating that desire left in his throat as his overactive mind supplied images of her breathing out his name in better scenarios. "It would work precisely because we are not Pia and Santo. Neither of us wants false promises of undying love and devotion, turning this into a daytime soap opera. Neither of us wants anything to do with love."

She didn't deny his claim, even to blindly win the argument. His admiration for her integrity increased a hundredfold. Then, suddenly, her eyes brightened. "You're well-known for your bachelor status, your fast life, your 'inability to commit to a woman for longer than a month,'" she said, quoting a tabloid article about him.

"And how would you know that?" he said silkily.

Color returned to her cheeks. "It was the one thing about you that made Pia happy. That you weren't going to bring her competition into the family for a long time. If ever."

"Circumstances change. Bachelor billionaires are toppled every day," he said, wanting to make her laugh.

Her mouth remained pursed. "You can't force me to marry you."

"No, but I can't leave you unprotected either. And I don't mean just physically from the press. Every aspect of your life will be investigated and magnified. To the point of interrupting your work and affecting future career prospects if you choose to live separately with this baby."

"Now you're using scare tactics."

"I'm not a complete bastard, Mimi," he said, frustration in his tone.

"I don't see why the media would be so interested in me and this baby. I'm a nobody. I kept my deadbeat father's name instead of taking my mom's just so I don't get caught up in her minor celebrity. Even when John asked me to take his last name, I refused. Being connected to Pia, who wanted to be a model as a teen, would have brought me attention too."

"Imagine at how this pregnancy looks to the outside world," he said, a thread of impatience in his words. "Unless you want to expose the whole sordid truth of how Pia and Santo asked us for our contributions while actively lying to each other, it will come out that this baby's mine. Then the speculation will start. About who you are and how you managed to trap me into domesticity. I'm known to be very circumspect with my affairs and my precious billion-dollar sperm."

She laughed. It made her lips curve wide, her eyes sparkle and her nostrils flare and turned her, in one blink, into a stunning, breathtaking beauty. The ridiculous thought that he had won a prize drifted through his head.

Renzo stared, his stomach clawing with sudden sensual hunger. For all that tabloid media drew a larger-than-life caricature of his romantic exploits, he hadn't rebuilt his family's finances from near debt by playing fast and loose with his time. When he did manage to have sex in the middle of his busy schedule, it was with some nameless stranger who wanted to scratch the itch temporarily like him. Nothing more.

But this hunger was different, and he wanted to give in

to it, just to know it better. He wanted to taste that laugh of hers and swallow it for his own.

"Well, if I had known it was your precious, billion-dollar sperm, I'd have made sure my eggs rejected it," she said, sighing.

He smiled.

Her gaze stuck to his mouth, another soft gasp huffing out between her lips. *Cristo*, he was thirty-five years old. How had he not known the simple, soul-searing pleasure of being the object of this woman's desire until now? Of course, he was a tall, good-looking Italian billionaire in his prime. Women did go gaga over him, but this was different.

This woman's gaze was different.

It had everything to do with who he was with her rather than what he was in the outside world. Thrilling and addictive couldn't begin to describe it. Especially for a man who'd learned the hard way that his last name was mostly a curse and only a minimal blessing at times.

"I want the best for this baby. Can I assume you do too?"

The thin thread of reluctant trust in her question made the desire clouding his head dissipate. He nodded.

"Can we also agree that being at each other's throats in a marriage that neither of us wants would not be the best for the baby?"

"Do you plan to be at my throat day in, day out, *bella*?"

"In six years, we could hardly bear to be in the same room for more than five minutes, Renzo."

"And how much of that was because of our drama-prone siblings? Do you actually remember us arguing about anything that wasn't related to them?"

Grief shone in her eyes, as sudden and painful as it had struck him earlier. "I don't want to blame them for everything that went wrong. That seems like an awful thing to do."

"And yet the reality is that we're both facing the consequences, life-altering ones at that, of choices they made, and have been conversing about it like mature adults."

"So you don't hate me then?"

"*Hate* is too strong a word for what I feel," he said, choosing his phrasing carefully.

"Let's agree, then, that we both, for some unfathomable reason, provoke the worst in each other?"

"Is it that unfathomable, though?"

The stubborn minx nodded without meeting his eyes. "You're right that I would hate to be the center of a media spectacle. Neither can I be locked in a marriage just to get the media off my back. Not even for this baby." She tapped his wrist with her fingers and then retreated, as if that was all the contact she could allow herself.

"Any woman would jump at the offer of luxury and protection that I'm offering," he said, knowing it would only provoke her temper.

Instead, she looked almost…sad. "Maybe. But I don't like to put myself in situations where I'm rendered vulnerable."

"You have a low opinion of me. What is it that you think I will do to you?" He thrust a hand through his hair, unsettled by her distrust in him. It was an alien feeling for him to have to prove himself.

"It's not that I distrust you, Renzo. It's that I have no reason to trust you. You're a powerful man who's used to getting what he wants, a man who changes partners every month. A man who will go to any lengths to do the right thing by your family, no?"

"Why is that a negative point?"

She smiled. "What if, when things go south in this supposed marriage of ours—as they inevitably will—you take this child from me? What if you push me out of its life because I didn't bend to your will?"

Anger pierced him in a sudden spike. "I have never abused my power or privilege like that in my life. I'm not my..." He swallowed the words as her eyes shone with curiosity. "We will sign an agreement that custody will be shared equally in case of separation." He studied how her quiet resolve made the amber flecks in her eyes shimmer, how even when she was tired, her skin gleamed, silky smooth. "You clearly have something in mind to make it more palatable, *sì*? Spit it out."

"This marriage can happen only if you agree to a quiet divorce in, say...a year. Hopefully, the interest over Pia and Santo will die down, and the child will be legally a DiCarlo without doubt. I'll even agree to live in Italy if you still want an active role in its life."

"You think I will not?"

"A lot of things change in a year, Renzo. This way, if you wanted to back out of the marriage, there's no hassle. I'll sign a prenuptial asking for nothing at the end of the year. Except, of course, whatever you wish to contribute to the child's life. I understand you well enough to know that you'll help me financially."

Irate as her distrust in him made him, Renzo couldn't fault her for being thorough and protective of their child and its future. "How magnanimous of you, Mimi," he said, letting her name roll and writhe on his lips. "Letting me be your husband for a whole year."

"See there!" A throw pillow came at him and hit him smack in his face. "Two minutes into this discussion and you're already mocking me."

Renzo picked the pillow off his lap and made a show of fluffing it while his mind whirred. It seemed his almost-fiancée and he had way more in common than he had assumed. She needed to feel in control of her life as much as he needed to feel in control of his own. While he had accepted this about himself long ago, he understood why he had felt an instant affinity toward her and was angry life had made her feel that way too. "How old are you?" he blurted out.

"Twenty-six."

Damn it, she *was* young to be a single mother. To face the damned media and the world on her own. To face him all by herself. And yet, so far, she had acted with more maturity than even Santo had ever shown.

"So…" Another tap of her fingers at his wrist. "Do you agree?"

Feeling like a child thwarted by his favorite toy, Renzo turned his hand and trapped her fingers beneath his. "Since we're discussing terms and you mentioned divorce, should I hope that sex will be involved in this year-long agreement?"

Her pulse skittered as he moved his hold to her wrist. Her fingers were slender. The nails were painted a pretty pink, though it was chipped on two fingers.

When he glanced up, it was to find her looking like a deer caught in the big bad wolf's headlights. The tip of her tongue snuck out to lick her lower lip, and his gut tightened. "I didn't…think about that," she said, each word coming slower than the one before. "The last thing I expected today was a marriage proposal from you."

"And yet the proposal itself has nothing to do with thinking about having sex with me, *si*? After all, like you mentioned, we have known each other for six years."

Her breath roughened, and it was like sweet music to his ears. Hot color rushed to her cheeks. "You're…playing with me." Then her eyes did that widening thing that turned them into shiny pools that could reflect entire universes.

Another gasp escaped her. "You know that I'm attracted to you, don't you?"

Something about the utter mortification settling into the planes of her face both angered and softened him. *Dio mio*, they were barely engaged, and already she was turning him upside down. "It's not that much of a leap, Mimi. Most women I meet are attracted to me. It is what it is," he said with an aggrieved air.

Another pillow, another thwack to his face.

"You're the most arrogant man I've ever met," she said, half joking, half serious.

He returned the pillow to her side with what he considered to be utterly gentlemanly behavior. "Is it arrogant if I want all the facts stated and acknowledged, *bella*? You've clearly decided that I'm the villain you have to protect yourself from. Then I would have this out in the open too. Do you want me to be a loyal husband? Because it might be hard for a powerful, virile man like me to go without sex for a whole year."

"You're making it crass on purpose."

"I'm wondering if I'm allowed to seduce my very beautiful wife during the year or if that's breaking the rules she's setting for us."

Her throat moved in a hard swallow. With her eyes wide and her breath coming in short pants, she looked very young, very vulnerable. "You aren't joking."

He liked how, disbelieving as she appeared, she made it a statement. "It seems our siblings have played one last joke on us, *si*?"

"My blasted attraction to you has nothing to do with them."

"And yet, you or I would have never even acknowledged it to ourselves, no?"

"I did. Long ago. But it didn't mean I would act on it." She grinned at him, and he liked that he had finally defused the tension that had been swamping her at the idea of marriage. "But I probably have better control over my decisions than you."

"I'm counting all your allegations against me, *bella*. One day, I will take sweet revenge."

And before he did something that showed his hand too much, he pushed back to his feet. "I guess we'll see who caves in first." Soft light from the lamps kissed the strong planes of her face. "One thing I'll promise you is that I'd never hold your lust for me against you. Just a hint, though. A little begging should convince me to give in easily enough."

"When hell freezes over, DiCarlo," she shouted at his back.

Renzo threw her a grin over his shoulder and pulled out his cell phone.

It took him a half hour to make all the required phone calls. Food, security, and a doctor on call twenty-four seven, not far from the Victorian home. He hated the idea of leaving her in such advanced state, but he had no choice.

There was a lot he had to arrange and rearrange, to prepare for the baby's arrival, to prepare for his wedding. For their wedding. It had to be soon, before the news of her pregnancy broke.

"I'll be back in a week at the most. A new cell phone will be delivered within the hour along with food and…"

The silence behind him made his neck prickle.

When he turned, it was to discover that she'd fallen fast asleep. Her neck arched up, her palms on her belly, her legs crossed beneath her, she looked…intensely vulnerable.

His feet moved as if he were flying, and in two blinks, he was standing by her. Leaning over her. Feeling a desperate yearning for something he didn't understand.

He gently pushed at a stray tendril that fell over her eyes and tucked it behind her ear. But that was all he could allow himself.

This tenderness…it was because she was so young, so uncorrupted by the world, he told himself. And like any decent man would, he felt protective about her because she was carrying his child.

Nothing more.

Then, with one last look at her sleeping form, he closed the door behind him and made his way to his car.

CHAPTER THREE

W<small>HEN</small> M<small>IMI</small> <small>STEPPED</small> off the sleek black water taxi a mere week later, she was momentarily blinded by the glint of the sun reflecting òff the domed roof of Santa Maria della Salute.

She blinked rapidly, trying to process the magnificent sight before her.

No, no hallucinating here. The building in front of her clearly wasn't the understated chapel that she was supposed to meet Renzo at, but a grand, awe-inspiring basilica.

The vapid smile she'd pasted on for any passersby slid off her face. Fury filled her as a poshly dressed woman in a white shirt and black trousers approached her, a notepad in hand.

Mimi bit off the scream that wanted to escape at being thrust into the starring role of this circus. Renzo DiCarlo was…was an arrogant, egotistical, scheming bastard, and she shouldn't have trusted him at all.

But their easy discussion at her temporary residence in a village near London and the mature, sensible way he'd handled her little lie of omission, *and* their situation, had lulled her into believing him to be a trustworthy man.

So when he'd suggested on the phone—the man had his secretary check on her three times a day along with the frequent updates he received from her bodyguard-slash-nurse—that she travel to Venice so that they could get married in a quiet civil ceremony, *so that they could hurry up and legitimize their unborn child*, she had agreed like a meek little puppet.

Naive fool that she was, Mimi had even convinced herself that being married to him wouldn't be too bad. And that it even might be nice to have a dependable partner in the early months after the baby came.

Now she was standing in front of the same crème de la crème of the Venetian society the DiCarlo family lorded over, seven months pregnant. For just a second, she wished the doctor hadn't given her the permission to travel so easily, or that Renzo hadn't been able to arrange a private jet with two medics on board.

But she was here now, and it was pointless to wish otherwise.

The white marble steps were already lined with people. Guests dressed in designer finery milled about, their conversations a symphony of accents—Italian, English, French.

Then she caught sight of the DiCarlo family—his sleek, sharp-featured sister, Chiara, and diminutive mother watching her with cool amusement, his father surveying her like a king inspecting a commoner, his brother, Massimo, looking pretty and sullen as usual, and his cousins whispering behind perfectly manicured hands.

Her heart pounded as she felt their scrutiny, their judgment. Most of which was based on Pia's behavior with them, with Santo. Which meant she was losing before she was even starting on this path.

No, she wouldn't give them the satisfaction of seeing her crack. Also, this wasn't a real marriage, and her in-laws' approval was the last thing she sought.

At the bottom of the steps, a throng of paparazzi jostled

for position behind red rope, their cameras flashing like strobes as Renzo exited the taxi behind her. The air grew thick with the click of shutters and the hum of curiosity.

Mimi realized with a dawning horror that her name was already being shouted alongside Renzo's.

"Mimi, look this way!"

"Signora DiCarlo, how does it feel to bring the uncatchable bachelor Renzo DiCarlo to the altar?"

Her breath caught.

Signora DiCarlo.

They had already changed her name, and it felt as heavy as the weight of the hundred or more pairs of eyes on her. Thank the universe she had trusted her gut instinct and dressed in a loose-fitting lacy black dress.

She definitely wasn't going to spend her hard-earned money on a new dress for a wedding she didn't want.

Her bridegroom, of course, was dressed in a black Armani tuxedo that made him look like he'd just stepped off the pages of a wedding magazine.

Jet-black hair slicked back, olive skin gleaming in the sun, Renzo looked like a dream—a wet dream come true. Definitely hers, given how she'd indulged herself in the last week with images of him.

Her cheeks heated with the knowledge of what she'd done, like a neon sign painted over her face.

Reaching her, Renzo hurriedly pressed the back of his hand to her forehead. "You look…flushed." Concern drew deep grooves around his mouth. "Are you feeling unwell?"

Mimi fought the urge to slap his hand away.

But he was apparently as perceptive as he was high-handed. He tilted his head as if he needed a different point of view to consider her. "Ah…you're angry." Then he stepped close, closer than she was comfortable with, and pressed a quick kiss to her temple. The gesture discombobulated her, like everything about him did. And that scent of him sent her hormones haywire again.

"What the hell are you doing?" she whispered, her gaze lingering on his Adam's apple. Then, needing to do something with her hands, she fiddled with his straight bow tie. He bent his head, and Mimi's tummy did that roll and swoop again.

The sight of Renzo DiCarlo subjecting himself to his bride-to-be's scrutiny was the stuff of legends, and that he was playing the part so dutifully with her was enough to make even her sensible head go dizzy.

"Did you know that you have a very open face, Mimi? You telegraph everything you think, every emotion that moves through you, in your eyes. The last thing we need is to give the press more fodder about us."

"I'm the one giving them more fodder?" she hissed under her breath. His scent was seriously messing with her composure. "You promised me a quiet civil ceremony. This… is hardly that. And how powerful and influential do you have to be to reserve this place in a matter of one week?" She didn't give him a chance to reply to her rhetorical question. "You didn't even have the decency to tell me ahead of time. Do you realize how humiliating I find this? All these people staring at me, judging me, wondering which trash pile you pulled me out of…"

She didn't understand why tears pricked behind her eyes. Usually, she didn't give a rat's ass about how she was perceived by anybody. But something about this situation made all her hackles rise.

Renzo frowned. "You can hardly blame me for this after the stunt your mother pulled in the last week."

"What?" Mimi blinked, her frown as genuine as her bafflement. "My mom's in Australia."

He took her hands in his, and again, she had to fight the urge to jerk away like a scared kitten. He was doing it for the press. She could hear the *click-click* of cameras.

"Did you talk with your mother in the last week?"

Mimi pressed a hand to her brow. A slow dawning of what could have happened made her words stutter. "Yes. She…she surprised me with a video call. It was one of those times when she remembers that she's my mother. I didn't think before I picked up—I was tired. I forgot to hide my belly. I'd been preparing all week to tell her about it. But she saw it, and the whole thing exploded. In the end, I had to calm her down."

Renzo's fingers moved from her palms to her wrists, stroking and soothing her fluttering pulse. "What did you tell her?"

"Not much." Mimi tried to think back to the call. "She went off on how I lied to her and didn't think of how this would affect her. Wouldn't let me get a word in… I think all I said was that you and I are dealing with it. That's it."

He looked up, her frustration mirrored in his gaze.

A groan escaped her as she suddenly realized how her very dramatic mother might have construed that sentence. "Oh God. What did she do?"

"It's fine. I'm dealing with it, and it's not your fault."

"Please…just tell me. There's a reason my mother and Pia got along so well. She's always been under this impression that I have no good sense when it comes to men. And even at the best of times, her protectiveness of me is performative."

"She issued a statement to some local tabloid that the Di-Carlo men have a history of mistreating her daughters—starting with Santo, of course, and now me. I don't know if she said it in those exact words, but the gist of her statement was that I got you pregnant and discarded you because that's what my family does with women."

The granite-tight set of his jaw said how much he abhorred being tarred with the same brush as his father. And Mimi knew, from all the gossip Pia had shared about Santo and his family, that Renzo was meticulous about keeping his love life and his business affairs utterly private. Only after he'd left had she realized how much her comment about him using his power to separate her from the child would have hurt him.

It had been a defense mechanism on her part, that claim. Because one-on-one, the attraction between them had been too much to handle. As had been his shocking marriage proposal. In her heart of hearts, she knew Renzo DiCarlo would never use his power to hurt her or anyone.

For God's sake, the man was marrying her to stop being called the same names as his philandering father. Even though he owed her nothing, even though the media croaked regularly that he was a confirmed bachelor. "What a mess," Mimi said, horrified by how her mother had, in the end, messed it up for her.

"Of course, someone here picked up her statement. I told you—they're constantly looking to revive Pia and Santo's tragic love story, as they've begun to call it. This smoke was exactly what they needed."

Mimi closed her eyes and took a few deep breaths. "Right. So you decided to do damage control by throwing a wedding in front of the basilica and inviting half of Venice."

"I had to," Renzo said in clipped tones. "I can't have anyone thinking I discarded you. Honestly, this is not a bad idea. Now the entire world can think this is a regular conception and that I'm not ashamed of either you or this baby." He regarded her curiously. "Isn't this better than all the speculation about who you are and why I hid you away for so long?"

"No, this isn't better. Nothing is worse than me standing here, seven months pregnant, walking toward you in front of all these people in a mockery of what a real wedding should be."

His hands moved to her shoulders, and he pulled her close. "I called you last night. You didn't take my calls. You just kept texting me that everything was fine and you would show up."

"I was out with my friends, and then I came back early because I…" Mimi swallowed the small bite of the truth. If she told him that she'd been feeling uneasy all day yesterday and today, God knew what he'd do. "I was tired, and I'd had enough of your high-handed instructions. Honestly, I wanted one last quiet night before all this drama. Now it looks like my circus radar was justifiably going haywire."

"It's not as bad as you think. You have that glow about you, and your…" He stepped back as if to get a better view of her and laughed as he fully took in her black dress. "Ahhh… I get it now. Last little rebellion."

Despite the twisting in her stomach, Mimi smiled. How was it that he was the one man who saw her inner motivations so clearly? And that the fact that he could see her always made her smile?

"If you care about how you're perceived in all this, I can have the wedding attendant put you in a designer dress in two minutes, and then you don't have to be embarrassed."

"No. There's no way I'm pandering to these guests who don't even know me, the stupid media, or you. I'm getting married in this dress. Take it or leave it."

If she thought she would darken his mood with her stubbornness, Mimi was proved wrong.

Renzo's grin only deepened, and he gave her a short bow, as if she were a queen making the most solemn declaration for him to execute.

"There's one more thing we need to discuss," he murmured.

Groaning again, Mimi muttered, "Jesus, Renzo. At least take pity on the fact that I'm two months away from giving birth. What else is in store for me?"

"When I tried to get in touch with your mother, I got John instead. I told him of my plans, and he insisted on being here for you today."

Her heart scuttled into her throat as Mimi searched the crowd for the tall, lean figure of her stepdad. That tight clutch of tears returned to her throat as if it had never left. "John's here?"

Renzo nodded, his sweep of her features intense. His knuckles danced over her wrist in soothing strokes, as if he knew the mention of her stepdad would push her that much closer to the edge. "I told him that it was up to you whether you want to see him here today. I know you haven't seen him since the wake, and I understand how hard this might be for you."

The depth of his perception when it came to her emotions…it took her breath away anew. And the warmth it enticed in her belly scared her.

Mimi pressed her forehead into his chest, uncaring that she was messing up his pristine suit. Or that he could mistake it for her softening toward him. In that moment, she needed his support to stay standing.

Not a surprise that John would offer to be here for her. To give her away, in what was nothing but a farce, because he wouldn't want her to be alone. Even though he knew now that she was having the baby that was supposed to be his daughter's, though he'd never shown any preference between her and Pia.

He had loved them both the same from the moment her mother had married him. And Mimi had tried for his sake, more than anything, to be a good sister to Pia, who, like her, had never known her other parent, having lost her mother in childbirth.

That cunning sneak grief came at her again, making her tremble on the warm day. With Renzo's arms around her shoulders now, she wasn't alone with it.

"Shh...*cara*. You don't have to see him if you don't want to," Renzo whispered.

Mimi wrapped her arms around his waist loosely, pretending for one moment that this was real. That his care for her was real.

"Does he know how this pregnancy came about? Did you tell him that the baby's...ours?" she asked, for once hoping he had taken control of the situation. She didn't have it in her to go through it with her stepdad, didn't have it in her today to be strong for him.

"Yes, I told him the entire twisted story, and it will stay with him. I want the world to know that this is our child. I don't want any confusion—now or later. I loved my brother, but this is our life now. And there's no need to feel any guilt for making the best of the cards we've been dealt."

"It's not that simple for me," she muttered.

"What about this bothers you?" Something about the way he asked that question, his voice low and threaded with a hint of genuine concern, made Mimi unravel a little more. If she wasn't careful, he was going to turn her into a home-trained little puppy who did whatever he wanted every time he spoke in that husky tone.

"I don't like this much public scrutiny. And then there's

the fact that I'm at a disadvantage here, Renzo. This whole wedding circus makes it look like I trapped you. You're known for your bachelor status—for enjoying your freedom, for enjoying the fast life. Now it looks like you have no choice but to marry me because I'm cooking your bun in my oven. All my life…"

She swallowed the words that wanted to rush out after that. No need to bare her entire vulnerability to his eyes.

"All your life what?" he demanded.

She shrugged, not meeting his eyes. Not willing to set aside her concern to simply soothe him.

Even though his frustrated grunt urged her to do just that.

"Then how about we do something that shows the media and everybody else here that you're not trapping me into anything? That I'm standing here because I want to be here."

She looked up at him, and her breath left her in a rush at the glint in his eyes. Whatever it was, Mimi knew she was going to hate and love it at the same time. "Like what?" she said, making it clear that she didn't trust him.

Renzo's grin turned wicked. His hand moved to her waist, pulling her closer in a way that made her hyperaware of every camera trained on them. And somehow, he even managed to shift a little to the side so that he didn't nudge up against her belly. And then he clasped her jaw in a firm grip. "Something like this."

Mimi stared, transfixed, as he dipped his head and touched his lips to hers.

His were cool and soft while hers were burning hot with a longing she couldn't push down. She'd have thought it impossible for her body to even register any more stimuli…but she was minutely aware of the puffs of his breaths against her lips, the indents of his fingers against the nape of her neck, and the low rumble his chest made under her own fingers when she rubbed her lips lazily against his…and then there was the way he draped himself over her, with those broad shoulders shading her from the entire world, as if the moment was too private to be shared…

And then even that level of awareness fell away, and she was spun into pure golden sensation as the kiss deepened.

"Open, *bella*. Let me taste you."

The sensual shock of his words made her gasp, and he took immediate advantage, swiping his tongue inside her with a mastery that made her groan. On and on he kissed her, in long sips and little nips and lazy bites, stealing every inch of air from her lungs and every ounce of sense from her head.

Mimi sank into the kiss, lazy heat unspooling through her, unraveling her. And when he turned the soft nip into a sharp pull of her lower lip, dampness filled her panties, and she lost the little balance she had.

She fell into him, and he steadied her, but not before her belly brushed his…erection. A lash of pure primal heat held her captive.

God, to be wanted by this man was unlike anything she'd ever known.

His low curse feathered over her skin as his lips drifted down her jaw. Large hands rounded her shoulders gently, belying the heat and intensity of the kiss. "I only meant to give them a little glimpse into this. Now it won't look like I'm being dragged to the altar against my will."

"How very sacrificial *and* performative of you, Renzo," she said, something she couldn't control creeping into her tone.

Surprise made his mouth slacken while his gaze searched hers. Whatever he saw there, he sighed. Not that it stopped him from rubbing his thumb pad against her lower lip. "You're a hard negotiator, *cara*."

She swiped the back of her hand across her lips as if to erase the kiss, though the heat of it lingered stubbornly, mocking her. "I didn't ask you for anything."

"And yet I want to admit that only point one percent of that was for the press. The rest was for me. For us." He frowned, as if he didn't like the taste of that word on his lips. *Us*…a feeling Mimi completely understood. "I simply wanted to test a theory."

"What are the results?" she said, her voice sharp enough to cut glass.

"That we could have an altogether entertaining marriage if we so wished," Renzo replied smoothly, his wicked grin unwavering.

Mimi's fingers curled into fists at her sides. "You're unbelievable. One blistering kiss and an unplanned baby does not guarantee marital bliss. And please, warn me next time so that I can prepare myself appropriately for the performance. Although I should tell you, the acting gene missed me."

"If I told you I was going to kiss you senseless, then you'd have put your defenses up and ruined the spontaneity. That would hardly convince anyone, don't you think?"

"I would still like to be included in the plan, please."

Renzo chuckled, the sound infuriatingly rich and self-assured. "That's a fair ask. Next time, I'll tell you how much I want to kiss the hell out of you." His gaze moved to her belly. "Like you, I don't like surprises, and we've had enough to last a lifetime."

"We never agreed on the sexual side of this arrangement," she huffed in meager protest.

"*Sì*, but I'm a patient man, and the chase is half the fun."

"You're not chasing me," she sputtered, the very idea making her body hum.

"Of course not. I'm talking about you chasing me, sliding one rung down at a time from your high-and-mighty ladder. Begging me to give you what you need."

Empty air huffed out through her lips as Mimi wondered at the sheer audacious ego of the man. "I'll never beg you for kisses or sex, not if you were the last man on earth. In case I didn't make it clear earlier, you're not the man I'd have chosen to have a child with."

His smile dimmed, replaced by something unreadable. And Mimi had the most ridiculous notion that she had grazed the impenetrable arrogance and confidence that he wore like a second skin. But then the walls were back up, and he was the smooth, charming Renzo DiCarlo again. "I promise to not crow when you lose, *bella*. Should be easy since I will be too deep inside you to care about winning. Your surrender will be the true reward."

Before she could respond, he turned on his heel, his stride confident as ever as he walked away, leaving her standing there, fuming.

And Mimi swore to herself that she wouldn't surrender to the arrogant Italian, even though the vow felt just a little hollow beneath the lingering heat he had provoked in her body.

CHAPTER FOUR

MIMI STOOD BY the window in the vestry, staring at the light as it fractured across her dress. Her hands twisted nervously at the fabric, the silence in the room feeling heavier with each passing second.

The space was small and plain, in contrast to the magnificent architecture of the grand cathedral. Soft wooden pews lined the walls, a narrow stained-glass window casting muted hues of red and gold across the floor.

Despite her resolve to not soften towards her confounding bridegroom, she found herself utterly grateful to him. He had given her the quiet retreat she desperately needed, tucked away from the bustling preparations outside.

Both to catch her breath and to have a private chat with her stepdad.

The door creaked open, and Mimi turned, her chest heavy with emotion.

John stood there, his tough face etched with fatigue and concern. Usually a simple man, he looked out of place in his designer suit, and yet he was here. He'd traveled thousands of miles just so she wouldn't be alone.

"You look beautiful, Mimi," he said gruffly.

Mimi's eyes filled up, probably turning her into a raccoon, but she didn't care. "I'm... I don't know what to say. I didn't expect you to want to be here. After the last few months…" Her words choked and died in her throat, her stepsister's name refusing to come to her lips.

He stepped inside, letting the door click shut behind him. "You think I wouldn't be here for your big day?"

Her hands automatically went to her belly as she blinked the tears back. "I did this for her, John. This was supposed to be her baby. And it all fell apart."

He closed the distance between them and took her hands in his, his own eyes filling with tears. "Of course you did this for her. You were a good sister to her, Mimi. Never doubt that, okay?" His grief slashed lines through his face. "She made it so hard some days to love her, but we loved her. And she knew that, Mimi. She knew how much she was loved. So we'll remember that, yeah?"

Mimi nodded, his words chipping away at the grief and guilt, making her burden lighter. On an impulse, she threw her arms around his solid form, feeling like that little girl who had gazed up at him in wonder the day her mother had married him, and he had told her that they were a family now. "Thank you for coming. I can't tell you how much your words mean to me. How much I struggled these past few months."

He patted her back awkwardly, shocked no doubt by her sudden display of physical affection.

She'd never been one to show it. Pia's warning on the day of their parents' wedding, that he was her dad and not Mimi's, had killed any inclination to do so.

"None of that now, Mimi. You hear me? Not in your condition." He pulled back. Feeling self-conscious, Mimi released him. "Your mother wanted to be here too."

She nodded, not putting much stock in her mother's wishes.

John cast a look around as if he was searching for eavesdroppers, then leaned closer. "Everything really alright, love? You sure about this? Renzo—he's…" He stopped himself, his words faltering. "He's always struck me as a solid fellow, more reliable than Santo, at least. But marriage is a big thing."

"A solid fellow?" Mimi said in disbelief. "He's…far too arrogant and has always looked down on our family."

"Yes, but then, his gaze was colored on his brother's behalf, no? Pia didn't make it easy for anyone, and Santo enabled her, and…it's good that Renzo's stepped up to look after you and the baby after how you both got here."

"I can look after myself," she said perversely.

John's smile was like a rainbow in a cloudy sky. "Of course you can, Mimigirl. You've always had a sensible head on your shoulders, but sometimes it's nice not to be alone. Nice not to go through life all by yourself."

"Is that why you married Mom?" Mimi had no idea where that question came from. "Because you were lonely?"

John looked stunned and then shook his head. "No, I married your mom because I love her, Mimi. I know it might not look like that, the way she carries on and orders me around, but your mother…she cares, in her own way."

"I'll take your word for it, John," Mimi said, out of all pretense.

"Say what you need to, Mimi," he said, shocking her. "Get it out of your system. All this beating around the bush didn't help Pia one bit, did it? Believe it or not, your mother's cut up that you didn't tell her about the pregnancy."

Mimi stared at the resolve in his eyes. "You want me to talk about why I've never felt the remotest connection with the woman who raised me?"

John blanched but nodded. Apparently, the day's shocks would keep coming. "You know, I've never held it against her that she sent me off to boarding school or that she prioritized her career over being a mother. That she brought me home only after she and you married. But she...she never tried to connect with me on any level, John. And yet with Pia..."

"Easier with Pia because they cared about the same things, no? Clothes and acting and all the silly, superficial stuff. Your mother can't handle anything deep. You, Mimi, are the most self-composed, intellectual, thoughtful woman I know. I wouldn't be surprised if your mom didn't know what to do with you."

"That's an easy excuse," she said, even as shock tumbled through her. Then there was the fact that when it came to Renzo, all that composure went out the window.

"Why do you think she caused such a big ruckus when she found out you were pregnant?" John said softly. "She wanted to be here so badly, but I discouraged her. I didn't want her to make things more awkward for you and Mr. DiCarlo."

"It only complicated matters for me," she said morosely.

John's shoulders slumped, and for a moment, he just stood there, beaten down. Finally, he said, "She wants to make it up to you, Mimi. And believe me, it's never too late for that. Never too late for admitting that we are wrong. I'm so sorry, love."

"What do you mean?"

"I know Pia made things hard for you. Until a few years ago, I didn't see it, Mimi. I didn't realize how insecure my daughter was and how you became the target for that."

"It's fine. It's all in the past."

"It's not fine, and it's not in the past when the hurt she caused you is still...there." He rubbed his palms over his eyes. "I see now how alone you must have felt. What with your mom's head in her own career. I should've stepped in more. I should've done better by both you and Pia."

"You were there for her when she needed you most," Mimi said quietly. "And now you're here for me. That's what matters."

"You did always have the best heart out of all of us, darling." His hand lifted, hesitating for a moment before resting on her head. "I understand why you didn't tell your mama or me. But we're here now. We can help you raise the baby. I don't want you to make choices because you think you have to. This marriage, is it what you want?"

The question made her heart stutter. "It's not a love match, but it's what is necessary right now."

John studied her for a long moment, then sighed. "Alright, then. But remember, you always have a home with me and your mother. We love you, Mimigirl." He held out his arm. "Now, will you please give me the honor of walking you down the aisle?"

Tears prickled at the corners of her eyes as she looped her hand through his arm. "Thank you, John. For coming, for…everything."

He patted her hand, his rough palm warm against hers. "Always, love. Let's get you married, then."

Together, they turned to the door, the quiet solace of the vestry giving way to the bright, extravagant facade her immediate future seemed to demand.

Mimi hated to admit it, even to herself, but Renzo had been right again.

No one, not even the couture-dressed guests with their brilliant diamond chokers and beautifully cut features, could question his commitment to this union, this baby, to her.

Inside the basilica was even more overwhelming than its exterior.

Gilded domes soared high above, adorned with intricate mosaics that seemed to shimmer with an otherworldly light. Marble columns lined the nave, their veins catching the flicker of countless candles.

Rows of chairs filled with impeccably dressed guests fanned out before the altar. The space hummed with a different kind of energy now, the chatter quieter but no less intense.

The air was heavy with the scent of incense and beautiful white roses alluringly draped over every possible surface and the whispers of the gathered elite of Venice.

At her appearance, no doubt.

Mimi took a deep breath and straightened her spine, clutching John's arm as they began their slow walk down the aisle. Each step seemed to amplify that pulsing twinge in her lower back, but she decided to ignore it for now. No wonder her body was making up new cues in concert with her agitated, anxious mind.

But the ache, along with the weight of her seven-month pregnancy pressing down on her body, was a constant reminder that this wasn't a fairy tale. As much as Renzi Di-Carlo had fabricated it just so.

And then, like a fish taking bait, she caught his gaze.

Renzo, so impossibly handsome that she still thought she might be dreaming, stood with a confidence that seemed to anchor the opulent surroundings, that seemed to mock her own misgivings about this wedding.

He had more to lose than she did by tying himself like this, didn't he? His freedom as a bachelor, his fast life. He hadn't even sent her the prenup agreement she'd insisted on.

Did he trust her that much? Or was his wealth so vast

that whatever cunning scheme Mimi might run later didn't worry him?

The grandeur of the basilica dimmed in comparison to the sheer intensity of his gaze. He wasn't looking at the gilded arches or the sea of society's finest but at her. The echoes of the kiss they had shared glimmered in his eyes.

Her chest tightened and she forced herself to focus on each step she was taking toward him. The marble beneath her feet gleamed under the soft light, the polished surface cool through her thin shoes.

Soon, she was there and suddenly, she felt trapped. Her breath felt equally so in her chest, making her dizzy.

Renzo's expression softened immediately, his hand reaching out to clasp hers with a tenderness that made her breath come easy. It was maddening how quickly that look calmed her.

John pressed a soft kiss to her temple and, with one glance at Renzo that made him nod, released her into his care.

"You're almost there, *cara*," Renzo whispered as she moved to his side. Immediately, the already familiar scent and heat of his body enfolded her as if in a gentle embrace.

And for a fleeting moment, the grand trappings of her surroundings fell away. There was no high society, no fairy-tale wedding. Maybe not even her large bump.

There was only Renzo, and the remembered heat of their kiss, and the terrifyingly audacious hope that maybe there could be more than just the baby to bind them.

The water taxi pulled to a stop in front of the Grand Rialto DiCarlo, the pride of Renzo's empire. Renzo stepped out first, nodding at the concierge who scrambled to open the door for Mimi.

His gaze swept the crowd that had gathered along the cordoned-off street, their cameras flashing like strobe lights.

The spectacle grated on his nerves. More on Mimi's behalf than his own. He'd grown up surrounded by luxury and paparazzi. Every inch of his life had been under their greedy scrutiny.

He knew personally what it was to be judged as a DiCarlo first, and barely as himself. Whereas his new wife... hated that kind of spectacle and had been protected from her mother's fame at the boarding school.

His wife... Renzo frowned at the stirring of excitement at the phrase.

Dio mio, it was one thing to accept fate and adapt accordingly, and a whole other to pant after his wife, who showed no such inclination toward him.

He extended a hand to Mimi, helping her out of the boat. Her face was pale, her posture stiff. The exhaustion of the day and the strain of carrying their child were etched into every line of her body.

Guilt pressed down on him like a heavy anvil hanging around his chest. He could have made this day easier for her, but his vanity about people's perception of him had gotten the better of him. Was he any better than his father then, if his self-worth needed validating?

"I can show my face at the reception for a half hour. Is that good enough?" she said, his little trooper.

"No. To hell with the reception and the guests. I'll take you straight up to our suite. You should rest," he said, leaning closer to her so his voice wouldn't carry.

"Are you sure? I don't want you to say I didn't hold up my end of the bargain later."

"*Cristo, cara.* I'm not the devil. I can see your exhaustion clear in your face."

She glanced at him, her lips pressed tightly together as if she wanted to argue but couldn't muster the energy. "Okay. Can I ask you for a favor, though?"

"What?"

"In an hour, could you send someone to check on me?" When he frowned, she colored. "Just as a precaution."

"Half an hour and I'll come up myself. Let me get rid of everyone."

He thought she would refuse his offer, but she gave a meek nod.

Every inch of him went on high alert. For Mimi to agree to any proposal of his without a protest was not normal in any way.

Without another word, he placed a hand at the small of her back and guided her through the lobby, ignoring the curious stares of the staff and the opulence he usually took pride in.

The elevator doors slid open with a soft chime, and Renzo stepped in, pulling Mimi gently along. She winced as she stepped inside, her hand brushing the curve of her belly.

Renzo's brows knitted. "What's wrong, *bella*?"

Before he could finish, she stumbled, clutching his arm. Her weight nearly toppled him, and his hands shot out to steady her. "Are you alright?" he demanded, his voice sharp with worry.

She didn't answer immediately, her face contorted in pain. And then, a sound he didn't expect—a faint splash against the polished floor.

Renzo looked down, his mind blanking for a fraction of a second as he registered the darkened leather of his shoes and the small puddle spreading outward.

Mimi's breath hitched, her wide eyes lifting to meet his. "Oh God," she whispered, panic lacing her voice. "My water…broke."

The words hit him like a punch. His heart thundered in his chest as he took in her stricken expression. "What does that mean?" he demanded, even as his insides shook at the implication. He'd demanded and received a crash course in pregnancy and baby delivery from his mother mere hours ago. Water breaking meant...the baby was coming.

"It's too early, Renzo," she said, her voice trembling. Pale and small, she looked incredibly fragile. "The baby—it's not due for two more months. If it comes now..." Horror painted itself across her features in greedy strokes.

His insides swooped with fear, but he beat it back. "Shh... *bella*," he interrupted, his hands framing her face. "Look at me."

Her eyes were glossy with unshed tears, but she obeyed, her breath coming in shallow gasps.

"We'll handle this," he said firmly, his voice steady even as fear clawed at him. "Everything's going to be fine, Mimi. I'll be there every step of the way with you, and I won't let anything happen to you. Okay? Just breathe, *cara*."

She nodded, her fingers gripping his lapel as if it were the only thing keeping her upright. "You're here with me, and you'll make it right," she chanted, her eyes already far away.

Renzo's heart steadied at the naked conviction in her words. He reached for the emergency button in the elevator, his other arm wrapping around her protectively.

The grandeur of the hotel, the cameras outside, even the weight of the day—it all faded into insignificance. All that mattered was getting her to safety and ensuring their child came into the world as it should.

And keeping his wife's faith in him intact...because suddenly, it had become the most important thing in the world.

CHAPTER FIVE

THE NEXT TWENTY-FOUR hours were the worst of Renzo's life.

All of his arrogance—that he could control his destiny, that he was the lord and master of his fate—crumbled into so many pieces under the weight of his new wife's panic.

They had rushed to the hospital, where the world-class obstetrician confirmed her fears—the baby was coming early, and it might not be able to breathe on its own.

Words had been choking in his throat as they checked her vitals and helped her slip out of the ghastly dress that had drained all the color from her face. Although a few minutes later, he changed his mind about the wedding gown. The pale white hospital gown made her look washed out, reducing her to a shadow of worry and stripping away all the attitude and toughness that defined Mimi.

"I… I've been having these twinges in my lower back, you know, for the last two days," she said, her voice trembling. "Which is why I came back early from my girls' night out. They've been there for a while now. I guess I didn't notice that they were gathering momentum. They did hurt, and I should've told you, and I should've gone to the hospital, but I didn't think much of it, and I…"

Her fingers dug into his chest, trembling, and Renzo wished he could take even a fraction of her pain away.

"What if I neglected all the signs my body was giving me? What if I rushed to the hospital two days ago and—" Her voice cracked, the words dying on her lips.

It was the moment Renzo felt the weakest in his entire life. His wealth, his influence, his intelligence—none of it could help him now. All he had were his words, his faith, and the enormous admiration he felt for this woman.

This woman who never let herself weaken in front of anyone needed his strength now.

"Stop, *bella*," he said, gathering her to him. He made his tone as stern as possible to get through the panic, to help her find the steady ground she needed right then. "You cannot blame yourself, Mimi. The specialist has assured me that this happens sometimes for no good reason. Everything was fine at the last checkup. Only the baby seems to have shifted now. Nothing you did, nothing you thought, contributed to this. Do you hear me? If anybody is to blame, let me take it upon myself then."

Her tearstained eyes widened as his words turned into a rough growl. "What if all this is because of the stress I caused you? Because I convinced you to marry me, and then I surprised you with this giant farce of a wedding?"

"No," she interrupted, shaking her head, fair to the last. "This started way before this morning," she said, her voice exhausted, drained of all fight.

Renzo dismissed the attendants, the physician, the nurse—everyone. Then he lifted her, settling her in his lap. "Listen to me, and listen well, Mimi. You did nothing wrong."

He placed his palms over her belly, willing their baby to understand his words as well as its mother. In the matter of mere hours, his entire perspective had been turned upside down. "This baby could have been the unluckiest, losing the parents that wanted it so much before it even came into the world."

He tipped her chin up and wiped at another rogue tear from her soft cheek. "Do you know what convinced me to marry you?"

"Your obsessive need to play controlling hero in my life?" she said, a sliver of her irreverence coming back into her eyes.

Cazzo, if they got through his together, there was so much more to look forward to. Not a single day with this woman would be boring. But neither would she chase excitement or fame or sacrifice everyone else's happiness around her just to indulge her own whims.

"The faith, the strength, and the sheer joy I saw in your eyes when you talked about how much you already loved this innocent life. Such clarity of purpose in one so young…"

"Keep talking, Renzo. I believe I'm beginning to see why the media adores you so much," she said, hiding her face in his throat. But he heard the wobble there. And it tore at him that he couldn't fix everything for her.

"You didn't care that you hadn't planned for this baby, that it came out of a twisted set of circumstances. You simply remembered how much this baby was wanted by Pia and Santo—and so you would want it and love it." He blew out a choked breath. "I surprised myself when I proposed marriage to you. Did you know I don't even eat breakfast without planning and optimizing it?" These were not words he'd ever thought he would utter, but they came easily now.

"I don't know what to say," Mimi whispered against his neck.

"After losing Santo, your faith made me believe too. Gave me a purpose again, a way to honor his wishes even though he's gone. You got this far, Mimi. Now I want you to calm down and let things unfold, okay? The stress you're feeling now—the guilt you're putting on yourself—cannot be doing you or the baby any good."

Her cold hands cupped his cheeks, and he realized with a start that this was the first time she'd touched him willingly. It felt like a milestone in an avalanche of them rushing at him. "Thank you for making me listen," she whispered. "If something—"

He silenced her with a kiss, knowing they needed something more than words. A deeper connection. *Cristo*, he needed her taste and her faith in this moment as much as she needed his. The soft press of her lips against his jolted through him.

She tasted of tears and toothpaste and pain, but Renzo refused to let her go. Suddenly the idea of a world without Mimi in it, without this baby in it, felt like a nightmare he couldn't imagine.

Slowly, she relaxed in his arms, and he continued to stroke his hands down her back. Her breasts pressed into his chest. Her softness engulfed him.

It was only the awful situation that they were in that had her cuddling into him like a kitten, but he enjoyed it just the same. Whatever this woman chose to give would be a prize, he told himself, his thoughts fragmented by her nearness.

Like the flutter of butterfly wings, her lips moved under his, and she began to kiss him back. Softly, tentatively, as if afraid to shatter the fragile peace of the moment.

He opened his mouth to capture her every huff and groan. Fingers twisting in his chest, she clung to him as if he were her only lifeline.

Heated desire filled him, but more primal, more urgent than anything he'd ever known. As if every cell in his body understood the raw poignancy of the moment, as if desire could be more than just his body's need.

With a rough groan, he plundered her mouth, seeking more faith, more strength, more warmth. As if her own need for validation in this hard moment mirrored his, Mimi matched him stroke to stroke, fervor to fervor, until breathing itself became secondary. They lost themselves in the deep, drugging kiss for long moments, worries and the outside world shut away.

She pulled back and stared at him, pink mouth trembling. "Thank you for today, Renzo. I...couldn't have coped without you."

"No need to thank me for doing my duty, *bella*," he said, knowing how much it cost her to say that. He pressed his forehead to hers, his voice a gentle murmur. "We're going to be okay. You, me and the baby."

Then came the long process of labor, which had lasted several hours. She was the one in pain, and yet Renzo thought he might climb the walls of the clinic in his worried frenzy.

Finally, after what felt like ten eternities to him, his son had been delivered, though they took him away immediately. All he'd gotten was a passing glimpse of him since Mimi had lost consciousness and they had been trying to revive her. He thought his soul might have cracked a bit at the sight of her bloodless face. And yet, next to the horror was the wonder, as if both emotions could exist side by side.

A baby boy, his heart kept shouting at ear-splitting volume, as if it meant to wake up him from the numb stupor he had descended into.

A son who was months early and needed help with breathing. And his wife, his brave, fragile wife, was buried deep under the effects of anesthesia.

Did he want to see the baby? the specialist had asked him. But Renzo had refused—not that he wasn't dying to see the tiny life that had come into the world despite all the odds stacked against him. The baby Santo would have loved more than life itself, like he had always loved Renzo. The baby Pia had wanted with a desperation he'd never seen in her.

The baby he already loved more than he could have ever imagined.

But he wanted to see him with Mimi by his side. He wanted to savor this new, raw, incredible experience with her, together. *With his new wife...*

It was a foolish, sentimental thought, that rational voice he usually nurtured reminded him in its usual mocking tone.

But he ignored it.

Legs kicked out, Renzo was slouching in the plush chaise lounge as Mimi stirred awake in the oversized bed, the faint rustle of her breathing uneven at first. He tugged at his tie hanging loosely around his neck, a nervous gesture he usually had under control.

The vulnerability painted across her features made him shoot to his feet a little unsteadily. Worried about when she might wake up, he hadn't moved or slept a wink, and his eyes felt gritty.

"Renzo?" she said in a dry voice.

He switched the small lamp on at a low setting and poured water from a jug.

Face pale, with faint gray shadows beneath her eyes that made sharp blades of her cheekbones, Mimi looked drawn and waxy. Her usually shiny dark hair was matted and damp around her temples.

A grimace crossed her face as she pushed up on the bed. "The baby?" she said, clamping her fingers on his wrist.

Something twisted in his gut, making him feel as if an invisible line had been crossed. No, he'd been dragged across it by fate, and now there was no going back. Only forward.

He was a husband and a father. Two things he'd never thought he'd be. Two things the men in his family were abysmal at being.

"Renzo?" Mimi whispered, though her tone rose in pitch.

He sat down on the bed next to her and handed her the glass. "He's doing as well as possible," he said.

She shook her head, stubborn to the last. "Tell me. Is the baby…" She swallowed audibly, and tears ran down her cheeks.

Out of the depths of numbness, fresh anger coursed through him, and he welcomed it. Anything was better than the black void of waiting he'd been drowning in for hours.

"Enough, *bella*. I will not have you sick again. Enough tears. Drink the water, and maybe I will tell you."

She bristled, exhausted as she was. "You're mean. Deep down, I always knew that." But she took the glass from him and guzzled down nearly half of it.

It spilled around her mouth and down her neck. Which, in turn, made her gasp.

Renzo grabbed a napkin and wiped away the excess. Her pulse fluttered weakly under his fingers, the bones of her clavicle jutting painfully.

She grasped his wrist, her fingers ice-cold on his skin. He fought the urge to nuzzle deeper into her touch. "Please, tell me."

"We have a son, Mimi," he said, the words pushing past the chokehold in his throat. "He's healthy, although they tell me he cannot breathe by himself because he was early, like you said. Everything else is pretty good. They have to keep him in the neonatal unit for the next few weeks. Once his stats improve, we will take him home. You and I will take our son home."

Fresh tears filled her eyes, but she blinked them back. A small, precious smile fought through the tears, curving her lips. "A son…" Her smile bloomed deeper, sending color to her cheeks. Her chest rose and fell with her shallow breaths. The same awe he had felt danced in her eyes. "What does he look like?"

"Right now? Like an oversized, wrinkled grape with a thin layer of fluff on his body."

Just as he had intended, she gasped, burst out laughing and then smacked him. "Watch how you speak about my son."

"Our son, *bella*," he corrected her softly, though the emotion behind it was intense and overwhelming.

Possessiveness he had never known swamped him, fisting his insides. Without an outlet, it made him as angry as a bull.

Growing up, he'd watched his father dally and flirt and conduct scandalous affairs with one woman after the other, neglecting their mother, neglecting his children, neglecting the hotel chain his grandfather had handed him on a platter.

Making their family a target for tabloid press and fortune-hunting women. Not that he had any doubts about some of the women's claims about their father.

Self-preservation then had been the only armor he had had left.

He hadn't let anyone close—not Santo, not his sister, Chiara, and definitely not their mother, who had always been close to breaking. Hadn't let anyone see how hurt and isolated he felt even surrounded by all of them.

Worse, as soon as he'd reached eighteen, he had to become their protector. Including their father, to curtail his behavior, to save him from his own excesses. Their mother, from completely shattering. Because no one else was going to. He had worked hundred-hour weeks with his grandfather's help, guiding the company back into profits, building it bigger and better in the last few years with new branding and acquisitions.

Power, he had realized, was the only way to control his father, the only way to exist outside of weaknesses, one's own or others'.

He had tailored his life to never want anything from anyone, whether it be kindness or help or even affection. The women he'd dated had known that and had called him a ruthless, heartless monster. But he hadn't felt anything more.

And yet now, this woman and their child seemed to have razed all his armor to dust. Making him feel all sorts of emotions that he didn't know how to process, or how to exist with.

"Our son," Mimi said clearly, her gaze holding his, conveying something he couldn't put into words.

Renzo wondered if they would develop their own language now that they shared this magnificent tiny life. Like his grandparents did.

"Please tell me more about him," she said, tugging fretfully at the IV tube.

Renzo leaned forward, letting some of his weight drop onto her legs. The small intimacy immediately filled her cheeks with a burst of color. "He has a full head of jet-black hair and the DiCarlo nose."

Her lips turned down at the corners. "He looks nothing like me?"

"He has your ferocity and your strength, *bella*. They told me premature babies like him struggle with their sucking reflex, and he does too. But when they get him to clamp on the bottle, he's fierce at drinking it up. They said it's a great thing that he has such a good appetite."

Fresh tears rolled down her cheeks, and she swiped at them with the back of her hand. "More, please."

He chuckled and took her hand in his, the naked hunger in her eyes calling to something in him.

He wanted her to look at him with such bare desire, wanted her to depend on him for everything. There was something extremely arousing, extremely motivating about winning the regard and respect of a strong woman like her. A woman whose strength of character shone like a diamond's facet.

Merda, but only he could turn winning his wife over into a challenge for himself. But there it was, a sparkling new goal. One that set his entire being on fire.

"What else, Renzo?" she demanded, tugging at his fingers.

She had long fingers with chewed-up nails and chipped nail polish. The strangeness of her hand in his gave Renzo whiplash for a second. They had been through a life-altering event together, but she was still pretty much a stranger who didn't believe in his commitment.

The uncertainty of it prickled against his skin, demanding action. Demanding he arrange his future, *their future*, to his satisfaction. He never doubted his decisions, but everything they had gone through in the past few days had only hardened his resolve that Mimi and their son belonged with him. Permanently. His little family would operate on mutual respect and fidelity and their love for their precious son.

No, it was just a case of figuring out what she wanted and giving it to her.

He patted her hand and let go. The very vivid visual of

this strong, beautiful woman surrendering everything to him was enough to keep him going.

"Renzo? What's wrong?"

"I'm wondering if I should tell you a little truth. It doesn't paint me in a good light."

"Are you having second thoughts about being a father?" Alarm danced in her eyes, but she rallied fast enough. As if she were used to dealing with disappointments from others. The very thought stoked his ire. "Doesn't matter. A child's birth is such a big event in one's life that it's normal to doubt yourself. I'm okay if you want to annul the whole thing…"

"*Merda, cara!* You really think very little of me, don't you?"

The vehemence of his curse made her blanch, but she didn't back away from him. "Commitments like these are hard for certain people. I don't want to trap you."

"Noted," he said, half growling the word at her.

She leaned forward and rested her forehead on his shoulder. "I… I would be crushed if you walked away now. And not just because you're a powerful, arrogant billionaire who can arrange the world just so for me right now."

He laughed, his breath hitching at the soft graze of her body against his. How could this fragile woman be so strong? "Flattery will get you everything."

"Tell me, please. I don't want secrets between us when it comes to…*him.* Or how we feel about this whole parenthood thing. Like you said, we're doing the best we can, and there's no script for this. No right or wrong way to feel."

"I haven't seen him yet," he admitted, a hundred emotions coursing through him. But none that he could hold on to. He felt like he was constantly caught up in a river current, barely staying afloat. "Everything I told you, I was simply repeating what Massimo told me."

"Why didn't you see him, Renzo?"

He kept his eyes averted from her, not wanting to tele-graph something he didn't have under control. "You were unconscious, and it felt unfair that I see him first when you were the one who carried him all these months and cared for him. So I asked Massimo to tell me. He seems excited that he's not the baby of the family anymore."

She tugged his chin up, and the smile blooming on her face was…so brilliant that it should have blinded him. "Shall we go now and see our son?"

He laughed and drew her closer. As if they had gone through the same ritual a thousand times, she tucked her head under his chin and wrapped her arms around his waist.

Renzo felt the desperate need to kiss her again. To taste her sweetness and her desire and *her*…just one more time.

He beat back the urge. Their relationship was supposed to be built on trust and mutual respect, not his hunger for her. Yes, he was attracted to her, and that would only make their marriage pleasant. Maybe become part of their foun-dation too. But he couldn't become a slave to his own needs and mess this all up. He couldn't let anything but rational-ity rule his head.

"*Sì*, we should. But the nurses will have to check you first. They worried that your blood pressure was too low earlier. You fainted when they tried to get you to sit up to go to the bathroom."

She turned her face up to him and scrunched her nose. "Please tell me I didn't embarrass myself."

He sifted his fingers through her tangled hair. A soft groan escaped her chapped lips, sinking deep into his flesh. "Even if you had, it's okay." Tenderness engulfed him. "Did you have a name for him in mind?"

She tensed immediately, and he stroked his palm down

her back. The need to soothe away every ache from her—whether it was of body or mind or heart—engulfed him.

He had always been the one to take charge of his family affairs, even though Santo had been older. From ordering their father to control his unending flings to making sure their sister married the man she loved, to taking charge of their dying hotel conglomerate and growing it to the billion-dollar luxury resort empire it was today…he had taken control of all of it.

Not once had he bemoaned the duties that fell to him.

Then why should this overwhelming need to relieve his new wife's burden be anything different? Especially since he'd already decided that this marriage would be as real as he could make it between them. She was under his protection, and his patterns were far too deep-rooted to deny them now.

"It's your call, Mimi. Whatever you decide, I'm okay with it."

He felt her shuddering exhale, her slender body swaying in his arms. Her words were a muffled whisper against his chest. "They wanted to call him Luca if it was a boy. It was one of the few things they immediately agreed on."

He tightened his arms around her, grief twisting his stomach. This day would have been so different if Santo and Pia had been alive. And yet he couldn't imagine a different reality.

Did it make him a selfish bastard that he didn't want to?

"You like it?" he said, clearing his throat. There was no point in letting the ghosts of the past dictate their lives now.

"I do," she said simply.

"Luca it is then," he said.

She burrowed deeper into him, chanting their son's name over and over again.

CHAPTER SIX

MIMI HATED THE idea of leaving the close-by hotel when Luca had to stay in the hospital.

Her suite at a nearby DiCarlo hotel, which was a two-minute walk, was close to paradise.

But it was nearly a month since Luca had been born. The team of doctors had assured Renzo that her own medical needs had been stabilized and that she should continue recuperating in a *more restful and comfortable environment*.

Although she thought it was Renzo who wanted her in a more comfortable environment.

Because her new husband was an arrogant, high-handed billionaire who thought he knew the best for her, he'd deemed that Mimi would leave the nearby hotel and move into his penthouse. And hadn't seen fit to inform her until the last minute.

She had thought they were going for a quick boat ride.

Instead, it was only as the sleek wooden motorboat eased toward the dock that Renzo deigned to inform her she was leaving the hotel.

Trapped in the awe-inspiring sight ahead of her—the building was a striking blend of modern luxury and Venetian tradition with its smooth sandstone facade gleaming in the setting sun—she had stared open-mouthed. It was close to the Grand Canal but far removed from its touristy chaos.

The soft slap of water against the dock mingled with the distant hum of gondoliers' songs and the occasional clatter of footsteps on cobblestones. The air carried a blend of salt from the lagoon, the faint metallic tang of the boat's engine, and the floral sweetness wafting from planters lining the building's private landing.

It annoyed her that he was making her decisions for her, and yet there was too much to take in. Especially after being ensconced amid the cloying sterility of the hospital and the hotel for a month.

The staggering luxury of his home only increased her discomfort as they rode the private elevator to the penthouse. When the doors opened, she got lost in the view once again.

The city stretched out before her through floor-to-ceiling windows, a breathtaking mix of shimmering water, Gothic architecture, and the golden glow of streetlights reflected on the canals.

Renzo dropped her little overnight bag on the sleek coffee table, his tall frame at ease in the starkly modern surroundings. "Welcome to your new home, *bella*," he said calmly, holding his hand out to her. "I would carry you over the threshold, but I think you're not in the mood."

So he knows that I am angry?

Mimi stared at his hand with its long fingers and square nails. As familiar as her own. The memory of how gently and carefully those large hands could hold their son tugged at her heartstrings even now.

The sight of their tiny son cradled against his broad chest was fast turning into her favorite thing in the world. For some foolish reason that wasn't based in reality, she had assumed that Renzo would falter at holding such a fragile newborn or that, like some of her friends' partners, he would balk at being a hands-on father.

But nothing was off-limits in his role as an attentive, first-time father, and if possible, her ovaries had melted at how easily he slipped into the role. The idea of building a true connection to him and nurturing their new family for real had seeded deep inside her heart, despite her struggles to keep herself outside the fake dream she was living in.

As a husband, though…she didn't know what to expect from him.

She knew that he had been rocked to his core that Luca had been born early and that there were complications with his birth. But all along, he'd been there for her, every step of the way, every hour.

In the last few days, however, he had retreated.

The smushing hugs and the quick kisses at her temple and the wrapping his arm around her…he had touched her less and less. And the realization that she missed it hit her smack in the face.

Was it because she wasn't a near-hysterical, needy woman anymore? How could she be angry that he was making decisions for her and yet want him to hold her as if she were precious for as long as possible?

He'd also been gone more and more, work diverting his attention from her and even Luca.

It was exactly what she had prepared for, what she had known would happen, and yet it left her restless, distressed even. Ridiculous because this was real life, and he owed her nothing more than what he'd already given her.

"I know you're angry with me, *cara*." Renzo's voice gentled as if he were dealing with a wounded animal that might take a bite out of his hand any moment. He moved to stand by the windows, watching her with those sharp, assessing eyes. "But you're so exhausted that you're weaving where you stand. Won't you come in?"

She didn't miss that he had modified the command into a request. Feeling like a recalcitrant child, Mimi walked in, her footsteps barely audible on the polished wood floors.

The living room was a study in understated luxury—sleek Italian furniture, a low glass coffee table, and abstract art that somehow complemented the ancient city spread out below them. A wide terrace wrapped around the penthouse, with glimpses of the glittering lagoon visible even from inside.

Exhausted wasn't the right word for the feeling in her body. She felt…empty. Hollow. Her chest ached with grief she couldn't explain.

"I've arranged for everything you might need," he said, gesturing subtly around the penthouse. "There's a chef on call who will deliver freshly made meals four times a day. A nurse if you feel unwell, a lactation specialist to help you pump. And then there's the housekeeper, though she won't disturb you unless you call for her. There's also a nutritionist, a mobility coach, and—"

"Are you that desperate for me to get back into shape?" she said, infuriated by his directions. The effort he'd gone to should have comforted her. Yet the clinical perfection of it all—the penthouse, the arrangements, the instructions—only deepened the sense of isolation. "Am I to transform myself into the perfect trophy wife suitable for the name DiCarlo?"

"That's the most ridiculous thing I've ever heard," he said, nostrils flaring. "The doctors recommended that you would spring back better if you incorporate light exercise and stretching. I wanted you to have an expert so that you don't hurt yourself. As for turning you into something you're not…"

"I don't want your bloody experts, Renzo," she snapped.

Did he have to remind her that she'd never fit into this sophisticated life? And why the hell did that hurt so much? "Take me back. You had no right to bring me here without consulting me."

He moved closer, tension radiating from him. And for a reason she couldn't fathom, Mimi ate up the tension. She liked that he was at least discomfited by all this. God, was she turning into a drama queen like her mother and Pia? Why did she feel this unnerving urge to shatter his self-composure?

"I tried to bring it up," Renzo said. "You refused to discuss it."

"Because I want to stay back at the hotel where I'm close to him." Her voice broke on a catch, her breath coming in harsh pants. Every inch of her ached, her muscles felt heavy, and yet nothing could touch the monumental void in her chest. She knew she was clinging to her infant son and yet, suddenly, it felt like there was no place for her anywhere else.

"I don't want to be here." She covered the few steps between them, thrusting herself into his space with a belligerence she'd never displayed with anyone in her life. "Or was the hotel bill becoming too much for you?" It sounded ridiculous to even her own ears.

His sigh, more than anything, made a spark of shame flicker in her chest. "You will not provoke me tonight, *bella*." He lifted his hand to her face, seemed to think better of it, and pulled away. "It isn't good for you anymore at the hospital, Mimi. The nurses told me you were constantly obsessed with his stats. They said you raised the alarm a few times because you were worried that his breathing might have changed. You even wander over there in the middle of the night."

A prickling heat behind her eyes made the vision of him shimmer. God, she was so tired of crying. How could her tear ducts make more of them? "So they were spying on me for you?"

His hands clasped her upper arms, his grip firm and yet somehow gentle. Tight lines fanned out from his eyes and his mouth. The shimmering vision solidified, the deep trenches exhaustion had carved into his face becoming clearer.

While she'd been obsessing over Luca, Renzo had been working long days and nights, only stopping to spend time with her and Luca. And not for one moment had he shown even a glimpse of impatience or tiredness. His strength, both mental and physical, seemed to be relentless. The small spark of shame in her chest burned brighter.

"No, *bella*. They are worried about your mental health, as am I. Luca will come home one of these days, and I'm sure you want to be recovered and well for him, *sì*? Staying there isn't helping you, Mimi."

"What if something happens to him while I'm gone? While I'm sitting here in the lap of luxury sipping some disgusting green juice?"

Renzo tilted his head, his brows drawing together. "That's only your fear speaking. You said yourself how much you trusted the neonatal specialist."

"I will go mad here, Renzo. I can't—"

"Give me three days and nights, *cara*." The tips of his fingers pressed against her clavicle on both sides. And the touch, more than his words, pulled her from the edge of hysteria. "If you can't bear it, I'll take you back. And in the meantime, we will visit him three times a day. *If* I am assured that you're eating and sleeping properly."

His offer surprised her and for just a second, she could

think outside the worry constantly clouding her thoughts. And he had so many more people to worry about than just her and their son.

The realization snapped her out of the deep abyss she'd been dwelling in for days now.

She had never in her life, not even for a moment, become a burden or the source of worry for anyone. Not her mother, not John and not even Pia. If anything, she had gone out of her way to be self-sufficient, wary of trusting anyone enough to show her doubts or worries.

And yet with Renzo, she had been behaving miserably. As if he were her enemy instead of her partner, while all along, his patience and strength had been constant.

She'd forgotten how hard it was for her to lean on someone. For some reason, Renzo made it extra hard. She wanted to hide away all her vulnerabilities. She wanted to never lose his respect, never let him see the yearning to belong somewhere.

The yearning to belong to him, which had only gotten stronger in the last couple of weeks.

Some of it was her hormones riding her hard, but some of it grew because she'd had a taste of what it would be like to be utterly his. To be the center of his laser-eyed focus, to be able to lean on him, to know him like no one else did.

She nodded, not raising her gaze above his throat. "That's fair," she said softly. "I'll go unpack."

Which was an inane excuse, because she had nothing to unpack. But she needed to get away from him and his painfully perceptive gaze. Needed to find her balance.

She walked past him toward the hallway he'd gestured to, her bare feet silent on the cool floor. Without noting any details of the bedroom, she went straight to the closet. Of course, it was the size of an entire flat.

She undressed quickly and pulled on a silk robe hanging in the closet.

It dwarfed her, but she didn't care. All she wanted was a bath and then sleep, so that she could shake off this dark mood and wake up refreshed to see Luca.

Feeling much better already, she strode to the en suite bathroom and stilled.

Stunning as the rest of the penthouse, it was a marble paradise with a rainfall shower and a freestanding tub that seemed to belong in a spa.

Renzo was kneeling by the tub, his fingers dipped into the steaming water. In his other hand, he held tiny glass bottles that he was perusing intently.

Pulled up tight, his black trousers highlighted the wiry strength of his thigh muscles. The same strength her own body was beginning to not only recognize but crave melting into.

Mimi looked away, only to find her attention snagged by his profile. A sharp, too-long nose, a high forehead, and a mouth that could have been shaped by any one of the art geniuses from this part of the world…he was too magnificent to look at, too larger-than-life to be real.

Marriage had always been firmly in the No column for her in the near future. Especially after Pia had played with her emotions. When with Pia around, she always doubted a man's attention toward her. The two boyfriends she'd had had been more excited about her connections to Pia than about her.

And yet…this man was her husband. A "duty" he took very seriously. The title and their bond seemed as irrevocable as the changes in her body, mind and soul that giving birth to their son had wrought.

And she couldn't deny that for all his high-handedness,

there was a rough kindness hidden beneath the arrogance. A loyal heart and a sensible head that made up the thrumming power of his personality.

The exact kind of man she'd have eventually wanted in a partner, *if* she wanted to go that route. Nor did she fool herself that it was his physicality that tugged at her every time she looked at him. All the female nurses and staff, while extremely professional, hadn't missed the easy sensuality he wore like a second skin. A couple of them had teased her, even congratulated her for "landing and leashing" such a man.

And yet had anyone—man or woman—seen him like she did? Gotten glimpses of who he truly was beneath the designer suits and the luxury CEO mantle? Seen the flashes of overwhelming love in his eyes as he looked at their son, a responsibility he had never foreseen?

Now, with the rising steam making enticing curls of the short locks of his hair, cuffs pushed back to reveal corded forearms, he looked...touchable, real. As if he existed on the same plane as her.

Mimi fisted her hands by her side, fighting the urge to sink her hands into that thick hair. She wanted to touch every strong plane and hollow divot he was made of, muss up his perfection, somehow reduce him to the same level of distraction as he did her. Some of it was sexual, and some of it sprouted somewhere else that she was far too scared to examine.

"What are you doing?" she said, to fracture her own fascination.

He turned. A small smile tugged at his lips, deepening that misplaced dimple. "Drawing you a bath. Do you prefer lavender oil or rose?"

Mimi fiddled with the knot of her robe, suddenly aware of the deep V at her chest. "I can do that myself."

"I don't doubt that, *cara*," he said, before upending the tiny bottle into the bath. Instantly, the room filled with a cloud of scented steam. "Rose it is. I think I smelled it on your skin before." His voice turned into a gravelly whisper. "It suits you well."

Tendrils of warmth uncoiled through her lower belly. The sensation was so sharp, so different from the aches and pains that accompanied childbirth, that she gasped.

"Come, check if the water feels right," Renzo said, still kneeling on the floor, the cuffs of his white dress shirt damp. His olive skin glowed with the sheen of the steam.

She reached the tub and hesitated, her body feeling altogether alien. Which was saying something after the last month.

His gaze traveled up, lingering when the robe parted to reveal a good amount of her bare thigh. Awareness sparked through her, a tiny, flickering pulse.

She had pumped before leaving the hospital, but already, her breasts ached with heaviness and milk. But there was more, too—a pleasurable ache, as if her body was determined to remind her that she was a woman who had her own needs, that she was more than just a mother.

Still, she felt self-conscious outside the familiar surroundings of the hospital, without their son as the bridge. The fog of the last few weeks lifted suddenly. She felt like she had been dropped in the middle of some unknown land with a stranger who affected her in ways she didn't understand. And yet he wasn't a stranger either.

She rubbed her chest, confusion welling up over all the things she wanted from him.

Renzo's throat moved as his gaze climbed higher. It

snagged for an extra moment over her lips before colliding with her eyes. "You have that look again, *bella*." Distaste colored his tone.

"Like what?"

"Like I'm your enemy. Like I am the big bad wolf who might swallow you up."

"I don't consider you my enemy. But I..." she fiddled with the knot at her waist "...have been making you the target of my...frustrations and fears. And that's unfair. I'm sorry."

Surprise made his chin dip, and a smile played with the corners of his lips, though he didn't let it show. "Your honesty, as always, astounds me."

"As for the second," she said, his gaze making her bold, "I'm aware that you could very well be the big bad wolf, Renzo. And that you might swallow me up if I'm not careful." *Physically, yes, but in other ways too*, she didn't say.

He laughed and it sent a million tingles through her nerve endings. Mimi stared open-mouthed at the sheer beauty the smile carved into his face.

His chest was still shaking when he said, "Do you plan to hide yourself away?"

She shook her head, slowly bending toward the lip of the tub. "The ideal scenario would be to swallow you up in return. Since I have no idea how to do that to a man like you, the next best thing is to enjoy the inevitable, I guess. Which, with your enormous experience, is what you've been saying, I imagine."

He held her gaze and touched her hand. "A man like me, hmm. Am I so different from other men you've known, then?"

Mimi stared at him, aware of the pulsing tension his casual question carried within. But she couldn't quite put her finger on the source. "Of course you are. And not just because you're wealthy or powerful or look like that."

"What is it?"

She shrugged, unwilling to lay everything out for him. The fact was that he was unlike any man she'd ever met or dated, and he made her feel things she'd thought she would never feel.

"I keep thinking I know you now, *cara*," he said, a bite of disgruntlement to his tone, "and then you go and surprise me all over again."

"I just want to make it through the next year without ending up at each other's throats, Renzo. Whatever else happens in the meantime…" She shrugged, unable to put it into words.

A line tied his brows, but he said nothing more.

She swallowed, bent low and checked the water. It was hot but just right. Before she could move back, he pulled her hand underwater.

Mimi squealed with surprise, then laughter as he let go and splashed her. She half fell into his lap and retorted with her full might. Within seconds, his face and neck and chest were drenched.

Laughter burst up from her chest, breaking through the tightness of grief and ache, making her shake. She continued her onslaught, wetting them both thoroughly in the process.

With an exaggerated sigh, he wiped his face with one hand, while his other arm rested right under her breasts, pressing into her with the perfect amount of pressure. God, how she adored being held by him like this, like she was precious to him. Like he couldn't go another minute without having her up against him.

Like she wasn't just his son's mother.

His cheek pressed into hers as he tucked his chin onto her shoulder. "It is good to hear you laugh, *bella*."

She nodded, refusing to look into those penetrating eyes.

Slowly, he hefted her until her butt was resting on the lip of the tub, and he waited until she had her balance.

Once he was sure, he got up and moved around the bathroom, pulling out his shaving kit and shedding his damp shirt.

Mimi watched the smooth planes of his muscled back without blinking, those tendrils of warmth encasing her again. His chest was lean and sculpted with a smattering of wiry chest hair that she wanted to run her fingers through. Then there was the way his black trousers hugged his butt and his thighs.

God, the man was sexy enough to make a corpse feel things. And she was very much alive, her body coming back to itself with delicious little pangs.

He shaved in quick, deft movements, washed, pulled on another crisp white shirt. As if remembering her presence, he turned and frowned. "Get into the water. It will get cold."

"I will, after you leave," she said, pulling the lapels of her damp robe together. The motion only caused his gaze to slip down, noting how the silk hugged her breasts.

His eyes darkened, and satisfaction that she pleased him made her flush. God, was there anything this man didn't make her feel?

"I watched you give birth to our son. There's nothing to…" He stopped himself and shook his head. "Forgive me. Two more minutes and I'll be out of your hair."

She nodded, soft heat streaking her cheeks.

Intimacy swirled around them like an invisible dome, trapping them inside. Plus, it was intensely pleasurable to watch Renzo dress. He did it with a meticulous efficiency, like he did everything else. Still, the thought that *only she* was getting a behind-the-scenes show filled her with perverse, unjustified satisfaction.

Until another thought struck. "You're going out," she said, following him into the bedroom, her voice sharp enough to make him pause.

A black jacket lay on the chaise behind him, and the gleam of polished leather shoes by his feet told her everything she needed to know.

He looked up, his fingers busy fastening the cuff links on his shirt. "It's a business dinner. Something I can't skip tonight."

Mimi stared at him and nodded slowly. Her throat tightened, and she let out a shaky breath. "Those Japanese investors that your assistant was talking about."

Surprise painted his features. He finished his cuff link with a decisive snap and stepped toward her. "I'll only be gone for a few hours. Unless you need me here. Or there's something I haven't thought of."

His gray eyes held hers for several beats, willing her to say something. Anything.

"No," Mimi said, sounding more decisive than she felt. "You've arranged everything I could possibly need. There's nothing more."

His Adam's apple moved. "I'll see you in the morning then," he said, picking up his jacket.

The door closed behind him with a soft click, and Mimi stared for long minutes at the space he had just occupied. The room felt cavernous without him, the quiet pressing down on her like a weight.

Would it be just the investors he was seeing? Or would

he seek other forms of entertainment? And if he did let loose after the last stressful month, did she have any right to question in what form he sought that relief and release?

She had admitted the inevitable conclusion of their attraction, but that didn't mean a virile, attractive man like Renzo would wait for her, did it? Nor would a sophisticated man like him limit himself to her. It wasn't as if their vows actually meant anything. Not unless she asked him for exclusivity and fidelity in their marriage.

She clenched her hands in the folds of her robe, her heart warring with itself. How much of her whirling thoughts was the truth and how much was her self-preservation kicking in?

He had clearly admitted to wanting her, to wanting to make this marriage real. Would he be so cheap as to pursue another woman while she was recovering from childbirth?

At least she could have asked him to stay and keep her company on this first night away from their son. He had wanted her to ask him. She was sure of that too.

But her stubbornness, and the knee-jerk instinct to protect herself, had stopped her.

This marriage wasn't about love or comfort or their individual needs.

It was a convenience, a practical solution to their complex situation. Already, the pregnancy and the delivery had made a maudlin fool out of her. But enough was enough.

Luca was getting stronger every day and would soon come home. It was better all around if she started planning her life separately from her husband's. For that's what they would lead.

And yet as she shed her robe and sank into the deliciously hot water, her heart ached desperately for him to hold her just one more time. To give herself into his capable arms completely. Her entire being yearned to make this marriage, their relationship, real on every level possible.

CHAPTER SEVEN

RENZO RETURNED TO a dark, silent penthouse barely an hour later.

He did have out-of-town investors to wine and dine, people he had fobbed on his two assistants in the past week because he hadn't wanted to leave Luca or Mimi at the hospital.

Even if he had stolen away for an evening, he wouldn't have been good company.

Tonight's dinner was important.

And yet he had known he'd made the wrong choice the moment he'd stepped foot into their Hotel DiCarlo Palazzo, overlooking the Grand Canal.

His wife needed him but was too stubborn to admit it or ask him for anything. And he…was just as stubborn, wanting her to come to him, wanting her to seek something, anything, from him. *Cristo*, the woman could twist him up, inside out, without even trying.

Events of the last few months had been the most intense and draining experiences of his life. He couldn't begin to imagine how much more it must have cost her. Losing her sister, deciding to keep the baby, taking care of herself and then standing up to him even as she married him.

There was no doubt that his wife was an exceptional woman. And strong-willed to the core.

But she was also young and fragile, despite her every effort to act the opposite of the latter.

He glared at the large empty bed in the master bedroom, then proceeded to the two guest bedrooms. Only darkness greeted him in both. Frowning, he pushed the heavy doors of his study open.

His chest gave a painful twinge as his eyes found her small form tucked deep into his heavy armchair, fast asleep. He switched on the desk lamp, his breath coming in rough exhales as he recognized the gray sweatshirt she'd draped over herself.

It was his.

With her hair in a braid and wisps framing her face, she looked small and innocent.

The sight of her sleeping form, her nose and chin tucked against the fabric, did things to him he didn't understand. He roughly thrust a hand through his hair, a wave of tenderness shaking him from the inside.

Feeling things for her wasn't in his equation for this marriage. And yet he didn't know how to stop.

Bending, he gently scooped her into his arms and lifted her.

Instantly, she nuzzled her face into his neck as if they had taken part in this very same ritual a thousand nights before. Her trust in him, in such a vulnerable state, when she was such a prickly little thing usually, pacified some age-old instinct in him that only she called forth.

The lush rose scent, deepened by her skin, filled his lungs by the time he brought her to the bed in his bedroom. He had barely tucked her under the duvet, one knee by her side, when those beautiful brown eyes flickered open. In the moonlight filtering through the French windows, her lashes cast shadows against her cheeks, her skin smooth and gleaming.

Her fingers fisted his shirt, lush lips puffing out air. Slowly, she became aware of her surroundings. "Renzo?"

"Sleep, Mimi," he said, pressing a quick kiss to her forehead. *Dio mio*, he couldn't control the simplest urge around this woman. "The armchair in my study is hardly convenient for a night's sleep."

A soft, maybe even dreamy, smile curved her lips. "You can't help chastising me, can you?"

"You can't help fighting me, can you?"

"Not fighting in this case, Renzo," she said, her smile touching her eyes now. "It's the only room in the penthouse that smells like you. Citrus and bergamot." She blinked as if realizing what she had said. Then sighed.

Her warm, minty breath coated his chin. And if he could just nudge her chin up, he could taste her again. The last time they had kissed had been when Luca had been born, and her kiss had tasted of salt and tears and sweat.

Renzo had loved it.

But he wanted to kiss her again, when she was soft and dreamy like this. When she was fuming and mouthy with him. When she fought him at every inch.

He wanted to know how his wife tasted in every mood, like the shades of a rainbow. *Dio mio*, he was a gone case.

"I...didn't want to be alone," she whispered, and yet there was a new clarity to her tone that he hadn't seen since that day he had found her.

He tugged his gaze upward. "Understandable, *bella*."

"All the beds, including this one, were cold and sterile. One of the guest bedrooms smelled like perfume." She scrunched her brow. "Is this where you bring your lovers, Renzo?" She stiffened, looking around her, as if she could find a lover of his lurking under the bed. Ire flashed in her eyes, but when she spoke, her voice was steady. "I understand you have a life, but bringing me to your stud pad is hardly appropriate."

He smiled. "My bed is cold and sterile probably because I haven't slept here in a month. A laundering service comes in and changes everything once a week. And no, I've never brought a lover here. This is my sanctuary." He waited for his answer to sink in. "As for the guest bedroom, my sister was here a few days ago. It's possible she slept in there."

"Chiara was here? In Venice?" She tried to hide it, but an instant wariness clouded her eyes. "I thought she and her husband lived in Milan."

"She came up to see Luca and you. Without informing me of her decision."

His wife's swallow was audible.

Renzo cursed himself and his whole family inwardly. Every single one of them, including his usually kind mother, had taken their cue from his distaste and dislike of Pia and her entire family.

Only now it dawned on him that both Santo and Pia were responsible for their volatile marriage, not just the latter.

He wouldn't be surprised if Chiara had snubbed Mimi a hundred times during holiday and family gatherings in the last six years. And his own arrogant judgment was responsible for it.

"I didn't see her at the hospital," Mimi said in a small voice.

"She never came to the hospital. I sent her away."

"Oh. Why?"

"Neither you nor Luca is ready for anyone's visits or scrutiny, *bella*. Not even my family. I told your mother the same."

She threw herself at him like a child, her arms going around his waist. The scent of her hair, the press of her body turned him rock-hard. *Merda*, but he was a selfish, needy bastard.

She had given birth a month ago, and here he was, lusting after her body. The thought was so jarring that he frowned.

His lust for her was more than just for her body. It was for her mind, her soul even. He wanted to own this woman like he'd never owned anything else. He wanted her to belong to him without doubt, and he wanted her to want to belong to him.

He wanted her every waking thought to be consumed by him. He wanted her loyalty, her strength, her desires to belong to him.

"Thank you. That might be the best present you've ever given me."

"I haven't given you anything," he said, clamping his fingers gently around her nape. Her curves were soft and warm against him, notching the tension in his muscles tighter. "Not even a wedding present." He'd heard one of the nurses tease her about what gifts he had given her on the occasion of their son's birth and seen the sudden dismay before she made up a lie about a necklace.

A wedding present hadn't been necessary, he reminded himself. Nor had he had the time for it. And knowing her, she would have hated the pretense of one. And yet…some foolish, apparently sentimental part of him wished he had given her something. Anything. A small token that was meant just for her and not the fact that she was carrying his child.

She shrugged, cheek resting against his chest. "Don't need anything more than this right now. More than the three of us."

He stroked her back lightly, swallowing at the heat of her body sending tingles up his hand. He cleared his throat, hoping to dislodge the need coiling inside him. At some point, real life would intrude on their bubble, and he had to prepare her for it.

"At some point, we'll have to do a press release about him. Maybe a photo shoot. And my family will insist on visiting. My mother especially…" He swallowed the sudden lump in his throat. Still, his words came out scratchy. "She is eager to see her grandson. Please…" he nearly choked on the word, but he couldn't forget that he had a duty to others too "…consider the fact that she's just lost her firstborn."

Of late though, he was beginning to resent the emotional cost of managing his mother's grief, his sister's disappointment in her marriage, and his father's spurious guilt, which would undoubtedly launch him into impulsive behavior and another scandal.

This cocoon he had been in for the last few weeks, with only Luca and Mimi and some work as his focus, had been a luxury he hadn't known he needed.

Her breath warm against his neck, Mimi looked up. The smile was gone from her face, replaced by that shadow of a grief he knew too well. "Of course. I…like your mother. Maybe in another week? Hopefully I'll be less of a wreck then."

"You like my mother?" Renzo blurted out before he could stop himself. "In a week is more than I hoped for." He ran his knuckles down her soft cheek. "I was ready to give you another month."

"She was always kind to me. And with Pia, she never added fuel to the arguments or the drama. I understood her perspective that she wanted Santo to be happy and thought he was being trod over."

"How are you so wise at such a young age?"

She laughed, and Renzo thought it was the most beautiful sight he had ever seen. "Practice, my pupil." And then she giggled at her own joke. "You're forgetting that I'm also very strategic. Your mother had four children. She might be a fount of important advice about babies. And I want Luca to know his family, to be surrounded by so much love that he never doubts it."

"And you wonder why I insisted on marrying you?" he quipped. The sheer longing in her voice as she talked about Luca knowing love was...unmistakable. "You're already a fierce mother to him."

This time, the smile he wanted didn't bloom. Nodding, she pulled back, her gaze skating everywhere but at him. And Renzo wondered where he had made a misstep in the last minute. "As for you being a wreck, it won't get better unless you rest properly."

"Wait, I forgot to ask." She released his shirt and looked up. "What happened at your meeting? Why are you back so soon?"

"It got rescheduled," he lied automatically.

"Lucky for me." Her teasing only tightened the tension in his body. When he tried to pull his arm away, her clasp firmed.

"I need a shower, *bella*."

Pulling herself up with her grip on his arm—which of course made her grimace—she leaned close, tucked her face in his chest and took a deep breath. "You smell fine to me. More than fine, in fact. You smell great. Always do."

He shook his head, a short huff of exasperation escaping him. "Mimi..."

"Stay with me, Renzo." Then, pushing the wild strands of hair out of her face, she patted the space beside her on the bed. "I was being stubborn and foolish earlier. I don't want to be alone in this cavernous apartment. No, that's not specific enough." Her brown eyes shimmered with resolve. "I want to go to sleep with your arms around me."

When he simply stared at her, her shoulders rounded in defeat. "You want me to beg? Is that it?"

"Of course not," he said, moving up on the bed. If he lay down on the bed with her, he wasn't sure he could hide his need from her. His body would betray him with one press of her slender curves against him. And he loathed the idea of coming on to her when she was in such a fragile state, when she was asking him for companionship and comfort.

He loathed how out of control he was near her. And this would not do. Not if he wanted a successful, amiable marriage. He couldn't be at the mercy of his desires. Not now, not ever.

When she was ready for their relationship to move on to the next step, that was different. But as her husband, he could not deny her what she sought from him now.

"I have a few hours of work to get through." He pressed a finger to her lips when she'd have protested. "But I'll stay here until you fall asleep. Then shower and work, *si*?"

"*Grazie*, Renzo," she whispered.

Averting his gaze from hers, he scooted up the bed and pulled her into his side. Her palm came to rest on his abdomen, and it took everything he had to not fidget, to not scoop her completely into his arms. To not slide into the bed fully and spoon her from head to toe until she was engulfed in him.

Dio mio, he wasn't even fond of cuddling, had never even tried it. But already, he liked holding her this way, even without satisfaction for his body's torment.

He set his other hand to stroke her forehead. Soon her breathing deepened.

Tilting his head back against the headboard, he closed his eyes, running through all the work and family stuff piling up for him.

All the bullet points on his list evaded him, though. For he had never known the sweet contentment that filled him with Mimi's hands tightly wrapped around his.

It shouldn't have been so easy to settle into a rhythm over the next month, but they did. In just three days, Luca would be two months old. And each day, he was getting stronger and that much closer to coming home to them.

Four weeks since Mimi had moved to the penthouse, and it might as well have been four decades for how easily she and Renzo seemed to slot into each other's lives with minimal adjustments.

Or maybe she shouldn't be surprised, Mimi thought, given Renzo turned out to be the most accommodating man on the planet.

Contrary to all that she'd feared about sharing a space with him and his overbearing personality, the man went out of his way to make sure her every need was attended to, before even she realized she had it.

For someone who had looked after herself most of her life, it was…disconcerting to be such a focal point of someone else's attention. Not that she was very different from an important project, and Renzo was managing her with his usual ruthless expertise.

It bothered her more with each passing day. She didn't know what she wanted—and how she hated not knowing herself—but the very polite, very rational shape their relationship had taken grated on her, day and night. As did the increasingly static nature of her day.

Each morning, a hot breakfast—optimized for her maximum well-being—would be waiting for her the exact moment she came into the kitchen, after a shower and a round of stretches with her coach.

The latter was honestly a luxury she wished she could afford the rest of her life. She didn't care so much about losing her mommy pooch, as she'd taken to calling it, but she loved how light and less sore her body felt after the stretches.

Dressed in a designer suit, jet-black hair slicked back, Renzo would be chugging some disgusting protein shake. He never left for work without greeting her in the morning. Usually, she pushed her breakfast around the plate, trying to think of something witty or funny to say.

Then they went to the clinic together, where he asked the specialist for updates on Luca and then translated every word to her with the patience of a saint. He then kissed her on the cheek before leaving for work, the exact same place every day.

As if X marked the spot. As if the world might cave in if he deviated or lingered a second too long.

Then somewhere around noon, she drifted to the guest suite reserved specifically for her at the clinic, ate lunch half-heartedly, napped as if she'd run a full marathon, then went to see Luca and hold him for a little while.

Just as the sun began to set, the chauffeur brought her home. She showered, stretched, ate dinner, caught up on her favorite murder mysteries on TV and then went to bed. And somehow, every night, Renzo showed up right as she struggled to fall asleep.

He uncuffed his shirt sleeves, undid his tie, and crawled into bed with her, but never held her fully. As if someone had stuck a huge rod in his back that stopped him from bending it.

Some nights, he looked haggard and disheveled, like last night. Other nights, he would be brimming with energy, having secured some deal or achieved a milestone, and Mimi would fall asleep to the gravelly tone of his voice.

As if he had crafted her very own lullaby with that deep, chocolate-melting voice.

That he kept his promise to her soothed some neglected part of her soul, but it was limited to his one hand in her hair and his hard, corded form next to her if she needed it.

Just last night, she had nuzzled her face into the outside of his thigh, after a particularly nasty nightmare about Luca. Of course, he had pulled her up into his arms, whispered words she didn't understand in that musical lilt, pressed soft kisses to her forehead until she calmed down and drifted back to sleep.

It was as if he had turned into her personal sleeping drug, and she was already addicted to him. Mimi's cheeks heated. The hard clench of his sleek thigh muscle as she nearly tried to climb him was imprinted on her forever.

These were her thoughts as she stepped into the spacious breakfast nook another same, slow morning.

The nook was her favorite space in the massive penthouse. From her perch on the leather seat, she could see the canals' shimmering waters reflecting the pastel facades of historic buildings. Gondolas glided by, their rhythmic strokes a quiet counterpoint to the distant toll of church bells and beyond, the horizon opened to the sparkling expanse of the Adriatic Sea.

The history lover in her was dying to explore all the corners of the city. It struck her, as if she were walking out of a mist, that she was free to explore. While it soothed some elemental part of her to be at the clinic all hours, to be close to Luca in case he needed her, she was also slowly going mad. It was the reason her sleep was so fitful, for she simply drifted from one day to the next.

She'd always worked, even when she'd been finishing her bachelor's in filmmaking. Wary of spending a minute more than necessary at her parents' house, caught amid Pia's or her mom's drama, she had filled her days with work, studies and friends. If nothing else, she'd pack up her camera equipment any given weekend and wander around new cities and towns, shooting everyday places and people. She had to do that now.

If she hoped to remain sane over the next few weeks, it was important to retain and nurture those parts of herself. God, she adored her son with a breathless wonder that would never dim, but she needed to look after her own well-being too. Much as it was nice to be coddled by Renzo, that wasn't his job.

"I want to explore the city. Can you find me a map?" she blurted out, refusing to overthink it. She had to start something today, to break the rigid monotony stretching endlessly ahead of her.

Across the marble-topped table with its vase of rust-colored chrysanthemums and golden sunflowers, Renzo, in his stark black suit, looked stark and uncompromising. And all the more beautiful for it. And her libido, a sneaky, snaky thing, uncoiled and took notice.

He straightened in the leather seat, a line forming between his brows.

It was one of those little details about him that seemed to elevate the man from merely good-looking to something otherworldly. Like that misplaced little dimple near his upper lip and the little scar that bifurcated his left eyebrow just so.

A host of imperfections crafting him into a perfectly stunning man.

One of those devilish brows hitched up at her leisurely perusal of his face. Cheeks burning, Mimi took a hasty sip of her coffee and nearly hissed when the hot brew hit her throat.

"Is there something particular you want to see?" he said after long, suffocating minutes of staring at her.

"Do you have only one boat?" she snapped, reacting to that high-handedness like a child.

His frown deepened. "No. I own six boats, *cara*, and they are all at your disposal. Transportation, as you should know, is not the problem."

"Then what is?"

"I can't have you roaming the city by yourself. For one thing, you're new to it. For another, you will be recognized and mobbed, and you are..."

"I'm what? A foolish, bug-eyed tourist who can't look after myself?" It was her turn to raise her brow, and she did it magnificently. "Also, I really don't have that memorable a face."

"You're my wife and a DiCarlo. There will always be someone who's interested in you." He put his fork down with exaggerated patience and then set that gaze on her. Mimi felt like a target in some survivor game. It was crazy how dizzy his gaze made her. "You're picking a fight with me. Why?"

That perceptive statement took the wind out of her sails. And she knew, in her sloshing belly, that he was right. That she wanted more from him and didn't want to. Didn't even know how or what to ask for. "I just want to do something for myself," she said, neither confirming nor denying his claim.

"Something for yourself…" he repeated, as if tasting and testing the words on his lips.

"Is it such an alien concept?" she said softly, irritation building in her chest. "I'm going stir-crazy waiting for Luca to come home. I need to do something to break the monotony, to get back to my work. And Venice is such an interesting city. Just for collecting some footage. And all I'm asking you for is some guidance as to where to start."

"You don't want to take it easy for a little longer?"

"Can you imagine sitting around at home for days on end without nothing to do? Caught in this strange limbo where life isn't moving forward?"

The concept must have sounded so bizarre to him that he nodded. "I see what you mean."

"I'm not used to doing nothing. Wandering the city's just an idea."

"If you can wait until the weekend, I will show you around."

Her hackles rose immediately. "You don't have to babysit me. Nor do I want to force my company on you."

A sudden flash of anger danced in his eyes, but of course, he didn't let it rise. And she wondered, for the hundredth time in the last couple of months, what would happen if Renzo lost control. If he let his emotions, and desires, rule him instead of his head. "In case you've forgotten, we are married, *cara*. Spending time with you is hardly an imposition. If anything, it's one of the requirements of this marriage, *sì*?"

And there it was, that word, *imposition*.

She *was* an imposition on him, his lifestyle, his space, no matter how much he denied it. It was only duty and honor that dictated his behavior.

She had been an imposition on her mother who had only

wanted to purse her acting career without a child holding her back. An imposition on her MIA sperm-donor father who hadn't wanted anything to do with an unexpected baby.

She had been an imposition on Pia when all she had wanted was for father to remain hers.

God, just when she thought her hormones had flatlined and she could return to normal, these…twisted feelings snuck up on her.

But she knew, as surely as the longing in her body, that things were changing each day, and she was running to catch up to her own feelings. "I appreciate your offer. But I would like to do it alone," she said, keeping her tone steady.

His jaw ticked as seconds slowly rippled by.

"You do realize I don't need your permission, right?"

"You're forever trying to push the boundaries between us, *si*?" he said silkily.

"I'm trying to stay behind those boundaries, Renzo. You're the one who…"

He leaned forward, the predator ready to pounce. "I'm the one what, *bella*?"

Mimi shook her head. She was being unfair to him. Just because it was possible that he had lost all the interest in her that he had claimed before their wedding. Maybe seeing her give birth had put him off, she thought with a hysterical edge.

Falling back into her seat, she closed her eyes, arresting the ridiculous tears that came knocking.

Firm fingers on her shoulders made her straighten and then moan as they kneaded her muscles with the perfect pressure. That delicious, decadent scent of him coated her throat, making her body tingle. She was so helpless against his simplest touch.

"How about we make a deal?" he said. Something droll

danced in his tone. "It seems the best way for us to navigate this…partnership."

Her eyes flicked open. The dimple by his upper lip beckoned her touch, the perfect bow shape of his lips alluringly close.

He was upside down to her gaze and just as gloriously gorgeous. There was a part of her that wanted to commit this spiraling attraction, this simmering desire for him, as her own body and mind trying to find the normal again after the life-changing event of her son's birth.

But Renzo DiCarlo, she had to admit, would always render her knees weak, make her body hot and drown her heart in foolish longings. The first two she was fine with. It was the last that gave her pause.

His eyes seemed infinitely deep as he said, "That way, you can feel like you're in control of this."

"What kind of deal?" she said, feeling as if she were splayed out for his amusement.

His fingers moved up to clasp her cheeks. "You join me for an intimate dinner with two of my closest friends, and I will let your bodyguard, Enrico, take you to an antique notebook shop that's been standing for nearly a hundred years. You're interested in history and culture and art, right?"

"You're a tease," she said, her breath a wispy thing.

He laughed, and the lines fanning out across his sharp features looked like a map to a treasure. Her very own private treasure, if only she could reach her hand out towards it. "You're easy to tease, *cara*."

"Just two friends?"

"Sì."

"Okay. This antique notebook shop, can you arrange an interview for me with the owner? Perhaps I could document the history of the shop."

His eyes gleamed as if he had known she would ask exactly that. "Will you promise to stick to that one place for today?"

"Fine."

"Good girl," he said with a tap to her cheek, then released her.

Dampness bloomed between her thighs, and Mimi gasped at the sheer pleasure of the sensation curling deep within her. It had been a while—a long while—since her body had reacted with such a jolt of need that she felt dizzy.

Renzo's hand waiting to pull her up was less an anchor and more another stimulus.

Straightening, she watched him as he finished his coffee, collected his suit jacket, pressed another kiss to that spot on her cheek and hurried out.

She didn't want to read much into the fact that he had known how much she would like to visit the antique notebook shop. But she had a feeling he'd been holding that card for a while.

With the intention of...persuading her to meet his friends? Or to simply give her the pleasure of the visit? Could her ruthless, powerful, busy billionaire of a husband have given thought to what would make her happy?

And more importantly, why did her heart flutter like a caged bird at the thought of Renzo caring about her?

CHAPTER EIGHT

THE EVENING OF their dinner with Renzo's friends snuck up on Mimi, leaving her staring blankly at the meager selection in her wardrobe.

She was never going to be as good as the elite set that Renzo called friends, but she didn't want to embarrass herself or him by proxy.

Of course, she should have known that her very efficient husband would not only foresee her little problem but arrange a prompt solution. Multiple outfits, along with sophisticated accessories and shoes, had been delivered right to their penthouse an hour before he'd informed her he would pick her up later that night.

Suddenly, she understood what an embarrassment of riches meant.

Silk A-line dresses with cashmere shawls in warm earth colors greeted her eyes. Her heart beat out a staccato rhythm as she realized he'd noted she didn't wear too-bright, dazzling clothes.

His powers of observation and his perception, his ability to see her as she was…astounded and aroused her equally.

Bright colors and daring outfits had been Pia's domain. Since there had never been a chance that she could outshine her stepsister—nor did she want to declare a challenge that she was trying to—Mimi had always picked earthy, jewel tones. Also, as a documentary maker, it helped to blend into the surroundings, to put her subjects at ease and to gain their confidence on hard subjects.

And now, staring at herself in the full-length mirror, Mimi amended the narrative in her head.

From the moment she'd understood Pia's nature, those muted colors had felt safe. But now, it was what she preferred, she told herself.

She would always be the woman behind the camera, watching life wield its magic in the most mundane moments and recording it for posterity. It didn't, however, mean that she played it safe or that she was afraid of standing out.

Grief struck her like sudden lightning flashing across the sky. Would Pia have been more reasonable if Mimi had learned to assert herself early on in their relationship? If she had refused to give in to her every whim so easily? If she'd just believed in herself a little more and been stronger? If her mom had taken her side and disciplined Pia's extreme demands and tantrums?

Would Pia have been alive today?

Groaning, Mimi fell onto the bed, next to the neat piles of her new wardrobe.

Would these thoughts ever stop haunting her? Could she and Renzo ever make this work for each other with such guilt and grief hanging over them? Was that what she wanted for the future—Renzo as her partner, her lover, her husband for real?

Suddenly, she felt far too fragile to expose herself to Renzo's friends and their scrutiny. In addition to his.

Then her gaze fell on the last outfit.

It was a single-breasted tuxedo-inspired pantsuit in a emerald green, crafted from a luxe crepe material. The jacket had a plunging neckline with satin lapels and a cinched waist. It looked like it had been made for her, in body type and color and fabric.

High-waisted slim trousers with a subtle flare to them immediately accentuated her long legs as she pulled them up over silk panties.

She tied the dramatic black silk sash belt at her waist and sighed. The belt added a hint of femininity to her structured look, which was her exact preferred style. Her usual bold red lipstick added a splash of color, and she finished with a slightly smoky eye. Her long hair—her crowning glory— she left in its naturally glossy waves down her back.

Put together, she looked effortlessly glamorous, two words she would have never applied to herself. And all thanks to Renzo's thoughtfulness. *He can't have you embarrassing him*, whispered that sneaky, distrustful voice that had always urged her to back down with Pia.

With a shake of her head, Mimi shut it down. The last thing she'd ever wanted in life was to become this…negative person who never trusted good things happening to her. But clearly she had. And that wouldn't do, not for her, and not for Luca.

Renzo had been more thoughtful and attentive than she'd ever imagined, and she wasn't going to ruin it with old patterns of thinking.

It was time to move forward, away from the grief and guilt, time to embrace her own desires and wants.

The private launch glided smoothly through the Venetian lagoon, its polished mahogany hull gleaming under the moonlight.

Mimi sat on one of the cream leather seats, the buttery-soft material cool beneath her fingers. The interior was a masterclass in luxury, with brass accents on the handrails and a small built-in bar stocked with sparkling water and champagne.

Outside, the rhythmic hum of the engine was a soft counterpoint to the gentle lapping of water against the hull.

Lanterns strung along nearby buildings cast shimmering reflections on the water, creating a kaleidoscope of colors that danced around them as they passed.

But the magnificent beauty all around her paled in front of the man sitting across from her.

She should be used to Renzo's sensual appeal, and yet her belly sloshed with fizzy tingles near him. Even if she could fight the attraction on a physical level, the fact that she was beginning to like him and admire him was another thing altogether.

Overdelivering on his promise, he had had her bodyguard, Enrico, escort her to the most interesting places in the city all week—off-the-wall places imbued with history and art. She couldn't deny the gut feeling that he had chosen those places specifically with her in mind. That he knew her.

It was exactly what she'd needed to find her footing again, to spark her own creativity back to life. She'd shot so much B-roll and had been editing and playing with it when he returned to the penthouse at night. There had been no cuddling in the bed, and she had lost even that little contact with him.

For the last two nights, though, he hadn't returned home at all, and she had eventually slipped into a restless slumber.

Now, with his long legs stretched out casually, his focus was anything but relaxed. From the moment he had seen her step out of the penthouse elevator, something had come over him. He hadn't even paid her a compliment, and it pinched.

Pity she had never learned the art of decoding powerful, breathtakingly handsome men like Pia had.

But she wanted to understand this one desperately.

His dark eyes rested on her even now, intense and searching, making her feel more exposed than the low neckline of her jacket ever could.

"Is everything okay at work?" she said, her voice thankfully breezy. She'd had a lot of practice with burying her emotions under a calm facade, and yet she was sure it was becoming a barrier with Renzo that she didn't want to keep up. "You didn't come home for two nights."

"Are you thinking of the penthouse as home now, *bella*?"

"That's not an answer to my question."

Renzo's eyes narrowed slightly, but instead of replying, he looked out toward the horizon. The rhythmic hum of the engine filled the silence, accompanied by the faint scents of brine and of roses from the gardens lining the canal.

Mimi let the moment stretch, wary of pressing further but wanting to know.

He rubbed a long finger over his temple, his hesitation crystal clear. "Massimo got into trouble with some rival fraternity club at uni and ended up in jail."

Her mouth fell open, and she snapped it shut. "Is he okay? Did you get him out?"

"Not the first night, no."

"Oh." She frowned, confused. "Pia used to go on about how powerful your family was. Which I now realize is mostly you. But you weren't able to get him released?"

A half smile touched his lips but didn't reach his eyes. At least the reason behind his brooding was partly clear. "Pia was right. I slogged to build up the DiCarlo name to what it used to be during my grandfather's reign. But Massimo, like my father, has gotten used to that privilege far too much. From everything I learned, he was the one who started that fight after several warnings from the provost. Beating someone up as if he were a street thug..." A vein pulsed in his temple. Exhaustion coated his words when he spoke again. "He deserved to rot in jail for both nights and learn a lesson, but Mama's tears were endless. I got him out after thirty-six hours."

Mimi's stood up suddenly, eager to touch him. She nearly toppled into him before he steadied her with his hands on her hips. "I'm sorry that you had to make such a hard decision," she said, sitting by him. "But I'm sure it's for his own good."

"Such implicit trust, Mimi?" His lips quirked into a tight smile. "Even my own family won't afford me that. Papa..." the one word dropped into the silence with all the weight of a thousand-pound anchor "...whipped them all into a frenzy about how harsh and ruthless I was growing. Apparently, all this power is going to my head. And Massimo should be forgiven however many mistakes he makes because he's of the tender age of twenty-two."

Her heart ached for the sliver of hurt in those words. "I don't care what they think. But I do trust you, Renzo. Luca's fortunate to have a father like you. Santo would have loved him, but you will also teach him how to be a good man."

He looked so stunned that she felt heat creeping into her cheeks. "If I haven't made that abundantly clear already, I'm sorry." She tapped his knuckles gently. "Our son is very lucky. As am I, at least temporarily." She hated adding the last bit but forced herself to. It tasted like dust on her tongue.

He gave a curt nod and again, that tension rolled back in like a relentless cresting wave.

"Will you be gone for more nights?" she asked, trying and failing to not sound like a clingy wife.

"Probably not." He pushed his hand through his hair, though the movement lacked the usual grace. "But there's mountains of work to get through, and you seem to—"

"Why do you never lie down fully beside me? Why do you always leave, whatever the time of the night?" She was needling him. And he didn't deserve it, tonight of all nights. But she couldn't stop.

Perhaps it was the way the moonlight caught the hard lines of his jaw, or the fact that their little cocoon was gone, and she was stepping into his world. She wanted some token of connection between them before they were swallowed up by the world and even Luca.

The realization both startled and freed her.

He stared at her, as shocked at her questions as she herself was. His mouth worked, as did his Adam's apple, framed by the white collar of his shirt. Mimi had the most maddening urge to press her mouth there.

"Are you allergic to sleeping by someone?" she taunted him to cover up her own nerves. "Does no woman on the planet get the full Renzo DiCarlo treatment?"

Another half smile and then a roll of those hard shoulders. "You want the truth?"

"Yes, please." She laced her fingers in her lap. "Whatever it is, I can take it."

"I didn't want to make you aware of my...ever-present desire." Self-deprecation coated each word. "I'm furious with Massimo for having no control over his temper, and yet my body behaves like a teenager around you. After everything you've been through these past few months, it feels crass to even hint at what I would like to do to you. Even subconsciously."

It was the last thing she had expected, and she felt like a floundering fish out of her depth. But they had come this far, and she wasn't going back. "What do you want to do to me, Renzo?"

His gray eyes flashed with such simmering heat that her

belly flip-flopped again. "So that you can call yourself the victor in this battle?"

"What? No. Of course not." She was so eager to make him understand that she nearly crawled into his lap. "Renzo… I've been worried that I was clinging to you and stifling you with my demands and forcing my hands onto your rock-hard abdomen every night. I even wondered if whatever attraction we had before wore off on your side because you saw me give me birth, and then I had to take off points from you for being that shallow. God, all these days…all I wanted was to beg you for just one more kiss, and—"

She got her wish without having to beg.

His soft, cold lips trapped hers in a hard, hot kiss that made a hundred champagne bottles fizz open in her belly. Large hands cupped her hips and easily lifted her until she was sitting sideways in his lap. The shocking evidence of his half-mast erection made her gasp, and he swooped in, tasting, licking every corner of her mouth. As if he meant to plant his flag there and declare it his kingdom.

He cornered the tip of her tongue and sucked at it with such expertise that her toes curled in her pumps. The twin feelings of being tethered to the ground while flying overcame her. She clamped her arm around his shoulders, trying to burrow into him.

"Come, Mimi. Play with me," he said in that commanding voice that could melt her insides like they were made of chocolate, and she lost the last layer of inhibition.

Sinking her fingers into his hair, Mimi kissed him with all the pent-up desire she had been feeling for months now. Each rub and slide of their lips sent a spark shooting through her, teaching her about her own body's new contours and fresh needs. The taste of him--whiskey and sin—filled her to overflowing. She felt like a new woman in a new body, even one with a little wear and tear.

For the first time in her life, she was doing what she wanted, without a thought to anyone else's wishes.

Just her needs. Only her desires.

Wanton heat bloomed when she shifted in his lap and his thick, hot erection rolled against her hip. The sound that burst out of his throat was like a feral animal's, and it sent savage shivers through her. That she could arouse this powerful, gorgeous man to such heights of desire…made power thrum through her. Her arousal deepened into something more, stoked by the affection and admiration she felt for him. He was the first person in the world who had paid real attention to her, who cared what she wanted and saw her like no one ever had.

Every guttural sound he made, every harsh breath that escaped those sinuous lips, she bottled it all up like a female dragon hoarding her treasure.

"And here I thought you were an innocent minx I would corrupt with my desires," he murmured at her ear before licking the shell.

Shivering, she rolled her hips against that thickness again. In return, that dampness bloomed between her thighs. It drenched her flimsy lace panties, and that in itself was another new, decadent sensation. "It's your own fault for making assumptions." An ache pulsed at her core, fanned into a bigger flame with his roving, stroking hands and teasing lips, begging to be put out.

God, she couldn't remember the last time she had been this turned on by a simple kiss. Although there was nothing simple about how Renzo devoured her. Like everything else about him, his desire was overpowering, addictive.

Biting out a curse, he pulled back and pressed his forehead to hers. "Contrary to our pre-wedding kiss, I don't want the bloody world and the media to witness this one, *bella*."

"Hmm…" Mimi said, still riding the delirious high of his kiss.

When he grinned—which rendered him even more gorgeous—she looked around. The launch was approaching the private dock of the Grand DiCarlo Venezia. It rose like a palace from the water, its grand facade illuminated by soft golden lights.

But even the sight of the imposing hotel couldn't dim her awareness of the man holding her like she was fragile while his kisses were filthy.

"And here I thought you were all about the performance, Mr. DiCarlo."

Groaning, he gently pushed her to her feet while surreptitiously arranging his trousers. "I think you should hold off on giving me a rating, Mrs. DiCarlo."

She giggled, and his gaze swept over her face. A small but utterly genuine smile played about his own lips.

On impulse, Mimi threw herself at him and kissed that smile, desperate for a taste of it. "Your smile…it does things to me," she whispered, then hid her face in his neck. "Even worse than your voice." His laughter was a rumble against her body, both comforting and arousing. "I think I know what I want for a wedding present."

His fingers gently nudged her back. "What?"

"More of what we just did. I…like how I feel when you kiss me."

His thumb traced her cheekbone. "How much more?"

"A lot more. All of it if we can manage it." Then, because she couldn't be anything but honest, she said, "I'm nervous, but I also want this. For you and me."

"Ahhh…*cara*. Fate picked you to torment me, *si*?" In

one second, the passionate lover transformed into the caring partner who had held her hand through hours of labor. His mouth was at her temple again. "I don't want to rush you into anything yet, *bella*. We have a lifetime for all the filthy, wicked things I want to do to you."

"Do we?" The words tumbled out of her before she could stop them, propelled by an urgent desperation to know if things had changed for him. "Our agreement was for one year."

A harsh laugh escaped him. "It's never anything less than a battle with you, is it?"

"Renzo, wait—"

"Let's not argue in front of the whole world. I refuse to follow in Santo and Pia's footsteps. Everything that happens between us remains between us, *si*?"

It was a sentiment Mimi could get behind, so she swallowed her protest and nodded.

The hotel was a masterpiece. The hum of the boat faded as the launch docked at the private pier, and Mimi's heart fluttered with nerves.

She'd known Renzo's company owned luxury resorts, but seeing one up close like this was overwhelming. "This is one of yours?" she asked, her voice low.

"Ours, *bella*," he said, standing as the boat came to a stop. "The jewel in the crown of the DiCarlo empire."

He extended a hand to her, and for a moment she hesitated before taking it. His touch was warm, grounding, and despite his tight jaw, she felt a flicker of gratitude for his steady presence through everything. "Before you argue with me, the penthouse is home now, *si*? Small steps are okay with me."

"Are they? Because all I want to do is to leap into the fire and damn the consequences."

His inhale was sharp.

She turned to face him. "I've never known this…wildness before, Renzo. Everything I did and didn't do, right up to what kind of man I dated and let close, it was colored by… Pia and my mom." She swallowed the knot of shame that came with the confession. "I let them live rent-free in my head, dictating my every thought and action, and that's my fault. But this…you and me… I want to act on what I want, moving forward. And that courage comes from trusting that you want this too. That you want me and that there are no twisted reasons behind it." She pushed away the sudden surge of emotion pulsing behind her confession. "You have no idea how…liberating it is. So thank you."

His gaze flashed with understanding. Covering her from prying eyes with his wide frame, he stole a hard kiss that spun her senses into liquid sensation. "Did I tell you how magnificent you are, *bella*? When you walked out of the elevator, all I wanted to do was devour you. In that, we're equals then, *si*?"

Throat tight, she simply nodded.

As they stepped onto the dock, she straightened her shoulders. Still, nerves twisted in her stomach. With his hawklike attention, Renzo must have noticed, because he leaned closer, his voice a low murmur. "We don't have to stay long. Just tell me if it becomes too much at any point during the evening."

"No," she said, lifting her chin. "I want to meet your friends. I want to know more about your life."

"And will you share more about yours?"

She colored at his sneak attack. "You already know everything about me."

"Only what Pia told Santo and then Santo me. And we both know that's far too many filters and distortion on the way."

Biting her lower lip, she held his gaze. "I've led a very uninteresting life."

"Let me be the judge of that," the man said, relentless like a dog with a bone.

Mimi sighed. The last thing she wanted to do was to dig up the painful past. "I could be persuaded to share a few things if you kiss me like that again."

His expression softened slightly, a flicker of approval in his dark eyes. "It's a deal, *cara*."

Mimi's eyes widened as they entered the hotel, the grandeur of the lobby threatening to devour her.

It was a dazzling blend of history and modernity. Intricate Murano glass chandeliers hung from vaulted ceilings, their light reflecting off polished marble floors. Gilded mirrors lined the walls, doubling the elegance of the space.

She inhaled deeply, nerves tightening as she spotted the small crowd gathered just beyond the main reception. A hostess ushered them toward a private salon.

As the heavy double doors opened, a burst of laughter and chatter spilled into the hallway. Inside, nearly thirty people mingled, the air alive with energy and curiosity. Her pulse quickened as numerous guests turned in their direction.

This wasn't an intimate dinner with two of his closest friends.

This was...something else.

Renzo's entire body stiffened at her side. His hand fell away from her back. When she glanced up, his dark gaze was locked on the center of the room, where his sister Chiara stood, a champagne flute in hand and a satisfied smile on her lips.

She walked up to them, impeccably dressed in a silver gown that shimmered like liquid moonlight, looking anything but repentant.

"Chiara?" Renzo muttered, his voice low and sharp. And then he switched to rapid Italian, but the gist was clear to Mimi.

He was furious with his sister. Particularly about the guests she had included, although Mimi didn't understand exactly who.

"You were taking too long, Renzo, squirrelling her away as if we might all eat her up," she said, her voice dripping with sweetness that didn't quite reach her eyes. She turned to Mimi, her smile sharpening. "You look more than fine to me, Mimi. We all began to wonder if there was a reason my brother was hiding you."

The insult and the insinuation were faultless.

Mimi forced a polite smile, though her stomach twisted. This wasn't a warm welcome—it was an ambush. As Chiara gestured toward the crowd, Mimi's gaze swept the room. Older men and women with sharp eyes and polished appearances mingled with younger women, several of whom stared at her with barely concealed amusement or disdain. At least two of the women, she guessed, had been invited because they had shown interest in Renzo at some point.

Was that why he was so angry?

It was bad enough that they all knew her through Pia and her grasping, manipulative, self-destructive ways. Now they thought Mimi had gone one step further and trapped Renzo with a pregnancy.

The media and the whole world were one thing, but facing actual people who immediately jumped to horrible conclusions about her was another. Either she ran away and let them cement those assumptions or she stayed and showed them who she was. After that, their judgment was on them.

Even two weeks ago, Mimi would have run away, would have called it his world. But now with Renzo by her side, she owed it to him and their son. And to herself.

"You had no right to do this," Renzo said to Chiara, voice clipped.

Mimi laid a hand on Renzo's arm as she felt the tension radiating from him. "It's fine," she said softly, even though her heart pounded. "I did agree to meet your friends. There are more than I expected here, that's all."

His head snapped toward her, his jaw tight. "I will not expose you to unnecessary stress."

"I can't hide forever, Renzo," she said, her voice firmer than she felt. "Plus, just because I'm averse to drama doesn't mean I'm scared of it," she said, loud enough for Chiara to hear.

The woman raised a brow, much like her brother did. The gesture was now so familiar to Mimi that the tension fled her muscles. "Let me make my own impression, Renzo. I need to do this." Pia's shadow loomed large enough without her cowering away from Renzo's family.

For a moment, he simply stared at her, the anger in his eyes warring with something softer. Finally, he gave a tight nod, though his hand slipped to her waist, pulling her closer as if shielding her from the room.

God, how her insides melted at the possessive, protective gesture. No one had ever quite looked out for her like this man did, and Mimi found new meaning in the vows they had both taken in front of these very people.

Chiara's eyes flicked to her brother's arm, her smile tightening. "Come now, don't let us keep you from the fun. Everyone's eager to meet the woman who's managed to drag Renzo to the altar."

"You have made a grave mistake, Chiara. Coming for me is one thing. Coming for Mimi…" He shook his head.

A flash of fear danced in Chiara's sparkling eyes before her mouth pursed. "You talk as if you would choose her over us, Renzo."

"It's not even a choice, because she has never embarrassed me. You have that honor, Chiara. I have repeatedly warned you that Mimi's off limits."

"Is she that fragile then?"

"If you don't respect my wife, then maybe I can wash my hands of clearing your husband's business debts, *si*?"

CHAPTER NINE

BY THE TIME they returned to the penthouse, Renzo's mood grew darker. With a softly whispered "Need a shower," Mimi disappeared into the bathroom the moment they had stepped inside.

He couldn't blame her for not wanting to be around him.

His entire family, including his various cousins and their wives, had been out in droves, taking their cue from Chiara, ready and raring to not only judge Mimi but find her wanting. Even the polite ones. Their nod to her had been as the woman who gave birth to the new DiCarlo heir.

In contrast, his wife had been the model of elegance and grace. Never rising to the bait, smiling at a rude, intrusive comment about her pregnancy and even managing a laugh when one of his younger cousins—motivated by temperament and not intention—had asked her about how she leashed Renzo.

His father had curled his upper lip when she'd asked Massimo if he was okay. As if she was some stranger showing greedy curiosity about their family.

Massimo, at least, had the sense to ask her about one of her documentaries.

Mama, realizing how furious Renzo was, had showed her kindness by cutting through rude conversations, asking about Luca and her parents, and offering to babysit whenever they wanted alone time.

Forget alone time with him. He wouldn't be surprised if Mimi wanted to run away from the lot of them tomorrow morning.

The beautiful skyline flashed in front of his eyes, on and off, as he walked the living room like a caged animal. A wounded one at that.

How dare his sister invite Rosa, of all women? As if Renzo were still a bachelor. As if it didn't rile him up no end to see the woman who'd discarded him years ago without second glance.

What the hell had his sister thought to achieve?

He had done so much for them—for Papa and Chiara and Massimo—and never complained about it. He had had to grow up faster than any of them, make hard decisions for their family, take on the mantle of the family finances.

He had always been so proud of being the one who saved his family, who restored the respect and might to the Di-Carlo name again. Somewhere along the line, it had become his identity, his ego. And yet suddenly, it felt too heavy to carry—built of others' expectations of him, of his own ambition and achievements—but also empty.

As if he had built his castle on sinking sand.

Cristo, but he missed his older brother like a hole in his chest. Santo hadn't wanted anything to do with the flaming hot mess that had been the family's company or the responsibility of bringing their father to heel. Or to deal with their younger siblings' privileged problems.

But he had been a steady, calming support behind Renzo as he took on the task of fixing the family's finances. His marriage to Pia had frustrated Renzo no end, but his brother had loved her. Had been completely loyal to her.

Had that been at the root of his resentment toward her too? That Pia had constantly needed Santo, that she took him away from Renzo and deprived him of the little he had of his brother?

Had his own anger for her been fueled by his own self-ish needs?

Because Santo had been the one person who had seen beyond what Renzo could do for him.

Now Renzo wished Santo were here to help him understand the force of his anger. It wasn't like his family's she-nanigans and poor impulse control were new to him. And yet it had never bothered him this much before.

They tarred Mimi with the same brush as Pia despite his vehement declaration that it wasn't true. But worse was their lack of consideration for him. Their lack of empathy or understanding for everything he had shouldered not just in the past year but for more than a decade now.

Only Mimi, even at loggerheads with him in the begin-ning, even as she distrusted him, had understood the raw-ness of his grief at losing his brother, his friend.

Hands shaking, he poured himself a finger of whiskey and downed it in one gulp. It didn't soothe him one bit. Which meant he had to leave the penthouse. He didn't want to be near her when his anger was a cold burn in his body, a sticky coating in his throat.

"Renzo?" Mimi's tentative tone came from behind him.

Whiskey sloshed over his hand as he poured himself an-other finger and threw that back too before he turned.

His wife stood framed by the arched doorway, hands clasped in front of her in a nervous gesture that went straight to his heart. But the rest of her…was a feast to his senses.

His erection throbbed painfully at the mere sight of her, and all he wanted was to press her against the wall and bury himself deep inside her. Work his anger and frustration and this shrapnel of hurt out on her luscious body until he could escape it all.

With emerald-green silk shorts and a camisole in the same color draped against her curves, she looked…like a delicious meal he wanted to wolf down. Her face glowed with that freshly scrubbed look. With her long, wavy hair in a braid, she was eons away from the woman who had been full of elegant grace all evening.

But just as sexy, and only his.

Suddenly, he understood another little nugget at the source of his general resentment. Something about this woman brought back all the needs and desires he'd conditioned himself to not feel. Love and affection and companionship and understanding…all things he'd been determined to not need, he wanted them now.

He grabbed his discarded jacket and held it in front of him. "You need anything?" he said brusquely.

Her gaze widened. "Don't tell me you have investor meetings at this time of the night?"

"I don't."

Her arms went around her midriff, and Renzo knew that she was bracing herself against him. "Did I say or do something wrong? At the party?" She blinked. "I mean, I know I spent too much time chatting with Massimo, but he was helping me remember all your cousins, and he's easy to talk to once you—"

Renzo cut her off. "He was good to you, then?"

"What? Yes, of course," she said, looking shocked. "He's no worse than any privileged young man, Renzo. But he's not a lost cause. At the risk of interfering in your family matter, I think he got the message this time."

"It is your family too, *bella*."

"Luca's definitely. Really, Renzo, you can't expect them all to just like me when we have six years of—"

"*You* behaved like a decent person."

"I did. But I have nothing to lose like they do."

Nothing to lose…was that how she still saw their relationship? Had she no stake in it? Renzo breathed out a rough exhale, feeling as if an invisible hand had punched him. "What the hell do they have to lose?"

Mimi sighed. "I mean, you threatened Chiara right in front of me. And all night, you hovered around me as if you were a mama bird, and—"

"I don't like that analogy one bit. Not even accurate, because the last thing I feel toward you is maternal."

She laughed then, and it took everything he had in him to not pounce on her and carry her away to the bedroom like a conquering overlord. And then he would pillage and plunder her and…get her to admit that this marriage, their relationship, was important to her. That it wasn't a level-headed transaction she could walk away from when the time was up.

"My point is… Massimo told me you haven't brought a girlfriend to any party or family function in a long time. They've not heard of you admiring a woman, even in passing."

"Because I never wanted to advertise my affairs and embarrass my family like Papa does."

"Yes. But all they see is you being so protective around me. They all feel threatened. How can you not see it? You hold their fates in your palm, and they think I'll sway your head."

"They think you're like Pia," he said, brow clearing. "They don't know that the last thing you would ever want is that kind of power over anyone. The simplest things in life are most important to you."

Her eyes widened, shimmering with a wild energy. Unde-terred by his dark mood, she kept moving toward him. Bare shoulders stiff, the end of her braid dancing with her move-ments, eyes drinking him in. When she reached him, the scent of her soap and skin replaced the oily anger in his throat instantly. Releasing him from the coil of frustration and fury.

"Exactly," she said. "But it will take them time to see that. You can't just demand that they respect me, Renzo."

"If I can pay their kids' private school fees and sup-port their privileged lives, then I can demand that, yes." He shook his head. "Plus, you're the mother of my child. That should automatically get you their respect." He sounded like a grumpy, arrogant, ruthless asshole like she'd called him a long time ago.

She reached him, her folded arms grazing his. "Leave it be, Renzo. At least for tonight."

His jacket slipped and fell to the floor with a silent hiss, and his breath...suspended in his throat.

Her brown eyes held his, that crystal-clear clarity he found maddeningly arousing simmering there. She said, "I was hoping you'd stay with me tonight."

"I won't be good company, *cara*," he said, his blood heat-ing at her nearness. "I can't be...what you need tonight."

Leaning closer, she rested her chin on his folded arms and looked up at him. "What if we don't have to talk?"

Renzo's breath left him in a shuddering exhale. He snuck his fingers under her hair, circled the fragile arc of her nape and pulled her closer. That she came without resisting, giv-ing him her weight, made every muscle in him bunch with need. The lush curves of her breasts pressed against his chest, and he groaned.

"I don't think it's a good idea, Mimi."

She pouted, dragging his gaze to her lips. "You know,

you can just say you don't want to have sex with me. I can take it."

His hand slipped down her back to her waist, and he pulled her roughly towards him. She was tall enough that his erection dragged against her belly. He felt his hips instinctually buck against the cushiony softness of her belly, seeking more.

A breathy gasp fell from her lips, her fingers locking around his neck. She pushed into his body with an eager, open abandon that made renewed heat punch through him. *Cristo*, she was going to bring him to his knees... "My control is thin tonight."

The tip of her tongue swiped over her lower lip, making it glisten. "You're distressed," she said, her gaze searching his. "About more than just their bad behavior."

"*Sì*." He scoffed. "Although *distressed* is the wrong word."

"Right," she said, opening her mouth and then closing it.

Renzo watched, fascinated by everything she did. Slowly, her shoulders straightened. "These last two months, you've been so good to me. And as your partner, I want to do something for you today. I mean, I'm cleared for everything."

"Cleared for what?" he said, doubts pricking at his throat like thorns. *Cristo*, what was wrong with him tonight?

Her throat rippled with her swallow. "Rough sex might still not be the greatest idea, but..." She opened her glistening lips in an O and made a popping sound. "I haven't gone down on a man before, but I've always been a fast learner. If you don't mind walking me through it."

If the world had turned upside down at that moment, Renzo would have been less shocked. In one swooping movement, he lifted her and perched her on top of the glass table. Then he buried his face in her neck, inhaling her scent deep into his lungs.

Emotion he didn't understand overwhelmed him.

It was both comical and touching how she wanted to soothe him, to give him an escape from reality. No one, not even his mother, had ever wondered if he needed respite and relief from all the burdens they placed on him.

Cupping her shoulders, he pulled back and considered her. Then, slowly he undid her braid, until the soft tendrils kissed her cheeks, making her look even more innocent than usual. "You thank me one moment and insult me in the next, *bella*. When did I give you the impression that I expect sexual favors for being a decent man?"

"You're more than a decent man, Renzo," she said, pushing a lock of hair back from his forehead. He didn't miss the possessiveness in the gesture. "Also, wanting to do something good for you after everything you did for me...isn't that how we build this relationship? Beyond just loving Luca?"

Her hands stayed on him all the while, and *that* definitely soothed his raw edges. Maybe their relationship was transactional in nature at the fundamental level, but this way, they had the right expectations of each other. Maybe this was the only way their relationship could thrive and grow.

Still, it pricked him that her desire came from something so...polite and decent at the source. He wanted her as mindless with desire as he was for her.

Shifting closer to her, he spread his hands on her silky-smooth thighs. Her eyes grew wide and molten as he nudged her knees apart.

Bracing herself on her palms by her sides, she bowed her long neck then arched up to look at him. "Renzo?"

"When I said my control was thin, I didn't mean I would get rough with you physically, *bella*. I would never hurt you, Mimi."

"I know that," she said breathily.

"I meant that I'm in a devouring mood."

Her silk top pulled across her breasts, calling his attention to the tight nipples beading against it. "What do you mean?" Her breath gushed out in a pant as he swiped a knuckle over one proud peak.

Under his hand, her hip was lush and thick. He let his gaze wander over her, from her smooth golden skin to the lushness of her curves as a result of the pregnancy. Everything about her…glowed, inside and out.

And Renzo had the recurring thought that she wouldn't have crossed the orbit into his life if not for the surrogacy. Colored by his own prejudices and his ego, he would've never given her another glance. Never acknowledged the simmering connection between them.

And yet, as he looked at her now, staring up at him with achingly naked desire, sharp resentment at his own inadequacy pricked him.

She was too good for him, too smart, too self-sufficient, too…capable. That was at the root of his frustration, his anger. She made him wonder if there was anything he could offer her that would bind her to him. Other than their son.

Nor was he so full of honor that he would give her up.

"Renzo?"

"You're eager to soothe me? To talk me off the ledge of this dark mood?"

"Yes. I'll do anything."

"Then let me bury my face between your thighs and taste you."

It was the last thing Mimi had expected her brooding husband to say.

The word *husband* still tasted strange on her tongue, but she was beginning to like it more every day. And tonight, at the party, she had a true taste of what it was to have a man like Renzo DiCarlo be her husband in the real sense.

A partner, a protector, a caregiver, and a fierce ally if someone else came for her, even if that was his family.

Cracks had splintered in the hard shell she'd built around her heart. Suddenly she felt helpless against all the longings he set loose inside her. With each sly comment and innuendo-riddled glance, Mimi had only found herself growing stronger.

With Renzo by her side, no one could touch her. But she also realized that they were curious about not just her or Luca, but the hold she had on her powerful husband.

True to the vow he'd made to her at their wedding ceremony, despite her own reluctance to be a part of it, Renzo had kept every word.

With each brush of his body against her, with each little touch—his hand on her lower back, his arm around her waist, his fingers dancing over her nape—she'd found herself falling deeper and deeper into her own desire.

"Do you want to go into the bedroom?" she asked, sounding like a frightened virgin. Which she was not. But from the first moment she had laid eyes on him years ago, Renzo made her feel defensive. Even now, he provoked the wildness inside her, pushing her to prove something to him. And to herself.

Or was it that he made her feel so safe that she could let out all the desires and wants she'd buried deep beneath rationale? Was it her trust in him that she'd never known with any other man that made her not want to back down?

Renzo's smirk was full of devilish teasing. "No, *bella*. Unless you're shy about these things and want the cover of darkness?"

This was what he meant when he said his control was thin

tonight. He meant to demand her surrender in a way she'd never given any man. "I'm not…a virgin," Mimi said, full-on blushing now. She needed to get this out, though. "But I don't have a lot of experience. I mean…"

"I guess we could do this under the covers then." Something dark danced in Renzo's eyes, and every inch of her trembled in response. "It's not what I want for tonight, but I guess I shall make do."

She bristled and straightened her shoulders. "You're pushing me, knowing how much I hate to look incompetent."

He laughed then, and it was full of a…strange emotion she seemed to provoke in him. A shiver zinged down her spine as she wondered if it could be fondness or even affection. "Competence has nothing to do with this, Mimi."

His hands danced on the band of her silk shorts, pulling at the soft elastic and then letting it go, so that it snapped over and over. And then, in that little gap between, he brushed his fingers over her skin. Going a sliver lower each time.

Such fleeting contact, and yet she felt it as if he were branding her with a hot poker. The tips of his fingers could be leaving scorch marks on her flesh for how seared she felt.

Slowly, fisting her fingers tight in his shirt, Mimi pushed herself back. The muscles in her belly strained, but she kept going.

Dark, hungry eyes watched every movement, and she wondered if this was their own version of a trust fall. She had no doubt that he was testing her and expecting, almost wanting, her to fail. The latter she didn't understand.

So that he could refuse her invitation without offending her? Or because, for once in her life, Renzo needed someone else, and he couldn't bear it? Did he need her as much as she needed him?

Finally, her elbows bumped into the glass table behind

her. Holding his gaze, she let her head fall back all the way too.

Her front felt like it was on fire while the cool glass kissed her back. Renzo's hand moved to her upper thighs, and she spread them like he told her to. "I never back down from a challenge."

Everything in her protested at how she was spread out before him. And yet for Renzo, she wanted to do this.

The light from the chandelier was bright against her eyes, hiding his shadowed expression from her. Instead, she looked down over her own body. Her nipples stood out hard and throbbing, while her silk top pulled up, baring a silky swath of her midriff.

"Plant your feet on the armrests of the chair."

Mimi bit back the automatic protest that rose to her lips. She would be completely open to his gaze like that. Something about his stance told her he was waiting for her to back down, to walk away from him in his dark mood. To play it safe and by the rules. Stay between the lines that Pia and her mother had drawn for her, like she'd always done all her life.

He wanted her to prove to him, and herself, that she could be what he wanted, or needed, at a time like this.

That little wildness she'd always caged inside her, afraid of failing measured against her mother and her stepsister, fluttered its wings against the bars. She planted her feet firmly and made sure to dig her toes into his hard thighs.

Renzo's hands lingered on the seam of her shorts. Then in one swoop, he pulled them off.

Mimi didn't want to think too much about how smooth his actions were. After the clunky, unsatisfactory attempts at sex, she wanted a partner who actually knew what to do.

She wanted Renzo's confidence and his skill to undo her as his eyes had been promising from day one. But she was also afraid of the aftermath. Of how he would change her, because nothing in her life had prepared her for a man like him.

She barely processed the cool sensation of the glass against her buttocks when his fingers delved into her core. Sensation skewered her. His fingers were cold, the tips rough against her intimate folds. His movements, though…were gentle and slow, not lingering long enough at any one spot.

That small ache she had been feeling all evening, for days even, flared into an impossible flame, begging to be put out. Panting, already writhing, she bit her lower lip to keep any sound from escaping.

And those eyes of his…they held her in a challenge, in a thrall. Even as his wicked fingers learned every inch of her.

A soft mewl escaped her anyway when he dipped the tip of one finger into her slit. The mindless way he dipped and drew back tightened her belly muscles like they were taut springs. "*Dio mio*, all this for me, *bella*?"

"Yes," she said in a near shout, every inch of her protesting when his fingers retreated. "It's for you, Renzo. If you're forgetting how we got here—" her voice was a ragged whisper "—it's because I've thrown myself at you, okay? I'm horny for you. I sniff at your shirts like an addict. I rub your body wash over my body because I like the smell of you on my skin. I…sneak glances at you when you return from the gym downstairs, dripping in sweat, because your body turns me on. Everything about you, the way you look at me, the way you look after me, the way you…" Her breath hitched. "Everything turns me on, and I've never felt this way."

He chuckled, but the sound was hollow. Even self-deprecating, while the hunger in his eyes dialed up to devouring. "You don't have to sneak glances at me, *bella*. I'm all yours."

"You say that and yet you…" Whatever else she had been

about to say floated away as he bent his head and his tongue unnervingly found her clit, as if she'd given him a hand-drawn map.

Mimi jerked, her spine arching into his touch as if she were a puppet and he held her strings. Not that she cared one bit. He could turn her inside out if he touched her like this.

She barely processed the first lazy, languorous stroke when he changed it up to little circles. On and on, over and over, he tapped, licked and stroked at her clit while his fingers brushed in and out of her, going deeper every time.

The pleasure coiled, intense, breath-stealing, spiraling, and Mimi buried her hands in his hair, both terrified and excited.

When he stopped licking and instead sucked at her with those sinuous lips that she couldn't get over kissing, with a scandalous, erotic sound, she went off.

Her orgasm crashed through her, shaking her from within, thrashing her around, making her shiver from head to toe. A moan slipped from her as she caught the sight of her husband's arrogant head squeezed between her trembling thighs.

With a smacking kiss on her outer lips, Renzo looked up. Lips damp with her arousal, hair mussed by her hands, and a wicked smile bringing out all those little imperfections that she adored so much...her heart gave a jarring thud against her chest, and her channel fluttered.

The orgasm should have wiped her out, and yet she felt achingly empty. Voraciously hungry for more. He hadn't fully penetrated her, and suddenly she was obsessed with knowing how he would feel inside her.

She tried to push up, but her body was mostly made of pudding right then.

Pulling back from the cradle of her thighs, Renzo adjusted her shorts and then gave her a hand. A sudden shyness engulfed her as she took it, her eyes level with his. "That was…" she started, then stopped. "Do you want that review now?"

"Not really," he said, patting her cheek. She could smell her arousal on his fingers, and that did strange, wicked things to her insides. "The sounds you make when you come apart are mine and only mine, *sì*? That's reward enough."

She grasped his palm and brought those very fingers to her lips. She wanted to shock him like he had done her. But even more than that, she wanted to let her deepest, darkest desires out to play. What better man than Renzo DiCarlo, her husband by law, to indulge herself with?

She could live a hundred lives, and he would still be the man she would trust to not mock her or belittle her or wish she was someone she wasn't and never could be. Opening her mouth, she licked at the tips of his fingers before sucking one inside her mouth.

His sharp exhale was all the encouragement she needed. Wrapping her tongue around the digit, she sucked at his long finger. His jaw tightened, and a curse fell from his lips. Then she released him with a popping sound. "Now, am I allowed to devour you too? Or are you one of those men who demand surrender from their partner but can't give an inch?"

CHAPTER TEN

THE BREATH PUNCHED out of Renzo at his wife's pure challenge. With her tart taste still on his tongue, her lush body in his hands, he felt giddy as if he had drunk way too much. Which he never had, even as a young adult.

Because he'd had to be the responsible one.

Suddenly, strong arms and soft curves wound around him in that sweet torment. "Come back to me, Renzo."

He sank his fingers into her hair, his willpower in shreds.

Cristo, he wanted to own this woman so badly that he was shaking with it. But it was more than just simple lust.

It was the way she challenged him, sought to understand him, saw him as more than the ruthless, powerful billionaire who could give her whatever she wanted. And now this…passionate, bold creature met his gaze with a tilted chin and glistening lips.

"I'm afraid your hand or your mouth would not do tonight, *cara*. I want to be inside you. And I want to know how you feel when you fight it so much, as if you have to earn the pleasure, and then inevitably fall apart."

Color streaked her cheeks, and damn if it didn't get him all hot and hard. Then her eyes widened, as if with dawning realization. "I mean, I have never…so hard that I nearly blacked out, but I thought that was just how I was…"

He liked that she was shy about sex and intimacy and yet

bold enough to come to him. To admit to wanting to devour him. To reveal that she wanted him so much that all those little inhibitions fell away.

Now he realized what it had cost her to not only come to him but to offer to soothe him in any way he liked. It wasn't simply a sexual favor she'd offered but her trust, her hope that she could make a difference in his mood.

He clasped her cheek and took her mouth in a soft kiss. She tasted of her own arousal and something fundamentally her. A taste he couldn't define but already knew he would never get enough of.

They surfaced from the kiss, arms tangled around each other, their breaths harsh, the tips of their noses touching. Renzo rubbed his fingers over her lower lip, incapable of not touching her even in that state. "I mean, I will make do with your hand, *bella*," he whispered at her temple, then slid his mouth to the delicate shell of her ear, "if it's too much. I don't want to hurt you or cause you discomfort."

"I will tell you if it gets…" she blushed again. "The only thing the doctor warned against was to not feel forced emotionally. I told her that wasn't a worry with us. And then I embarrassed her by admitting that I probably would have to seduce you. I also had an IUD put in. I'm allergic to latex."

As always, her efficient response both startled and fascinated him. And aroused him no end.

Renzo scooped her off the table. With a squeal, she wrapped her arms and legs around him and buried her face in his neck. The rough strokes of her exhales, the press of her breasts against his chest, the drag of her belly against his cock made his skin burn with need.

He dropped her onto the bed and instantly crawled over her, straddling her hips. The gold highlights in her brown hair glinted in the light. Hair spread like a halo around his pillow, breasts rising and falling, she looked…enchantingly beautiful.

But it was the trust in her eyes, the absolute naked need for him, that made her a goddess in his own.

Pushing her knees apart, he let his lower body press hers into the bed. Her thighs fell away on a breathless gasp, and the heat and dampness of her core seeped into his trousers.

Her hips thrust up in a quick tilt just as he canted his own down. Their groans rent the air, joining in a rough melody. "That…feels amazing," she said, a dizzy smile curving her lips. "Please. I want to feel more of you. I want…" again that lip-bite as if she was giving away too much "…all of you."

"Not yet," he whispered, swatting away her hands when they moved to his abdomen. "You tormented me for weeks, your hands all over me, your curves pressed against me. I mean to avenge myself, *bella*. Plus, there's too much of you I haven't kissed or touched or licked yet."

He laughed when she pouted and took her in a rough kiss she met with equal ferocity. They licked and nipped at each other, their teeth clanking in a fierce duel.

Then he filled his hands with her smooth skin and lush curves.

The thrust of her clavicle to her shoulders, to the smooth skin between her breasts and then to the lush mounds that filled his hands to overflowing…he rolled the hem of her silk top up and kissed the undersides of her breasts. And when the fabric got into his way too much, he grabbed it with both hands and ripped it apart.

Her breasts fell into his waiting hands. Eyes closed, Mimi arched into his touch as he kneaded them and then kissed around the aureoles, taking his time.

He continued, never touching the aching buds with his

fingers or lips. Slender fingers dove into his hair with a rough grasp and pulled. "Please Renzo. No more teasing."

Just as he was about to lick the hard peaks, a drop of milk appeared.

Mimi stiffened instantly, embarrassed color pouring into her cheeks like hot lava. One slim hand came to cover up her breast. "I pumped before the shower, but—"

Renzo gently pushed her hand aside and licked up the stray drop. It was sweet on his tongue. "Don't tell me you're ashamed of something your body does to nurture our son, Mimi. I thought you too sensible for that."

"Not ashamed." She licked at the beads of sweat dotting her upper lip. "All this, you, it's too raw, too much sometimes. It almost feels like I'll drown in all that you make me feel, Renzo. And that I'm alone with it."

"You are not," Renzo said before finding her mouth.

Mimi sank into his kiss, as if his assurance was a vow. Her hands moved over his back, and she tugged at his shirt. "Want to feel your skin."

"My wife's wish is my command," he said, pushing to his knees.

Wide eyes took him in as he shed the shirt first. He undid the fly of his trousers and waited. That blush he adored stole up her neck and cheeks before she said, "Yes, please. All of you."

Renzo kicked off his trousers and boxers in one sweep. Her gaze skidded over every inch of him, never staying, never lingering. And his skin burned at the intensity of her openly greedy perusal.

Pushing up gently, breasts heaving, she raked a nail down his nipple, then followed the thick trail of hair down past his abdomen and stopped. "You're beautiful," she whispered.

"Lie back and touch me," Renzo said, straddling her hips.

She licked her lips in that nervous gesture of hers, but the way her fingers flexed and grasped his cock was firm. A soft gasp huffed out of her. "God, I can't wait to feel you inside me."

He threw his head back and exhaled, fighting the ravenous urge to pump into her hand. But he was too greedy for the sight of her like this—sprawled over his bed, deliciously naked and spread out for him, and her slender fingers fisting him tight—to look away for too long.

And just as he imagined, her brow was tight in concentration, lower lip caught between her teeth. "Keep squeezing me, Mimi. As hard as you can." Already he was panting, his control nearly nonexistent around her.

If she applied herself a little more rigorously—which, knowing her, he knew she would—he was going to spill all over her lush breasts and thick belly.

Like he had promised her, like they had been both waiting for apparently for some time now, he wanted to be inside her. He wanted to make her his wife completely, tonight. Now.

Which meant he wanted her to fall over with him, one more time. He wanted to feel her channel flutter and fall apart around him.

Leaning forward, keeping his full weight off her, he kissed her mouth softly. Instantly, her grip on his cock released, her fingers moving to his nape. She moaned and writhed under him, trapping his erection against her belly.

"I love the taste of you everywhere, *bella*," he whispered, licking the long line of her neck, kissing a trail between her breasts. He made a stop and teased her nipples into hard peaks again with his lips and tongue.

On and on, he went on a journey of discovery down her body. Every little patch of her skin, every little divot and crease and fold, he tasted all of her. Left his own marks. Claimed every inch of her.

Her breathing shallowed, her body undulating like a cresting wave under his caresses as he built her toward the peak again.

His name was a chant, falling over and over from her lips as he played with her clit and folds again. Wetness coated his fingers, and he smeared it all over her folds.

"Tell me anytime if it becomes too much," he whispered, pressing his forehead to hers, gritting his teeth, nudging the head of his cock against her slit, "and I'll stop."

A soft sob broke through her lips as he pushed the broad head in. Her fingers clasped his biceps, nails digging into him. Her gaze, though, clear and certain as always, held his. "More, Renzo. Please, I'm dying of anticipation here."

He chuckled and pressed in a little more. "You're tight, *bella*, and resisting me. Always resisting me," he said, kissing her temple. "Relax for me."

Her spine arched into him, and her feet came to rest on his buttocks. "I just… I want this to be good for you, Renzo."

"If it got any better, I would probably expire," he said, and thrust in all the way.

She jerked and stilled.

Sweat dripping from his forehead, Renzo sought her mouth again. He kissed her hard, all the tension in him rippling out into the kiss. She let him ravage her, giving it back in equal measure. "Tell me, Mimi. Tell me how it feels."

"Full and achy and not enough." Her brown eyes held a spark of mischief that sent heat to his balls. "Whatever you're doing, it's not enough, Renzo. I need more. I need…" that pretty pink blush stole into her cheeks as she dragged her nails down his back and onto his buttocks "…faster and harder. And I want to come again."

"Yes to everything, *bella*," he said, pulling her hips up and canting his down at the same time. This time when he stroked into her, the movement dragged against her popped clit.

She reacted instantly, her pelvis muscles choking him and clasping him harder and harder.

He took her in long, deep strokes but at a slow pace that he thought might kill him soon. "I'm close, *cara*. And you squeeze me so well that I can't stop myself. Touch yourself. Get yourself to the edge."

Eyes wide as pools, the tip of her tongue peeking out, she ran her hand down between their bodies. The tentative graze of her fingers against the root of his shaft drove him wild, relentless heat running down his spine.

Their gazes dove down their bodies to where they were joined, and then sought each other.

Her soft cries added to the rough symphony of their bodies coming together and pulling apart. Leaning down, Renzo caught her nipple between his lips and gave a rough tug.

Instantly, she shattered around him, her muscles milking him for all he was worth.

His own release thundered down on him, and he pumped his hips wildly, eager to ride the wave, roughly using up her delicate flesh.

The intensity of it doubled when Mimi arched up and reached for his mouth. She took him on another ride with a rough, greedy, grasping kiss. Damp eyes full of wonder and trust clung to his as if she hadn't expected it to be this good. As if she had needed this more than she needed her breath.

As if nothing existed for her except him and this feverish intimacy between them.

He was the one who wanted to own her, who had his

name falling from her lips like a chant. Yet strangely, Renzo felt owned by his wife, like no one had ever owned him.

Mimi ran her hand over Renzo's forearm, relishing the solid feel of him under her fingers. Her body was still humming from the aftershocks of their frenzy, and her heart felt like it had grown too big for her chest and was dancing a jig.

She might have guessed that sex with her husband might be a soul-wrenching experience that would change her composition, as it were. Already, she felt freer and bolder and easier in her body than she had ever felt. And more confused, more possessive and more selfish too.

She grimaced as she moved her legs to scissor through Renzo's, and her core twitched with soreness.

With his powerful body draped over her from behind, she felt...protected. It was an alien thing to her, and she didn't know how to feel about the emotion itself.

If she wasn't careful, she might even end up craving it. And yet was it so wrong, so selfish, to want this intimacy with him after a round of such passionate sex?

"You're in pain?" Renzo said, stiffening behind her. "I've hurt you."

Mimi tightened her grip over him, loath to lose the cocoon of his body. She didn't want to move from the bed or face all the feelings she'd have to process the moment they stepped out of it. "If you get out of this bed, I will be very mad, Renzo."

She felt his tension releasing a little. His breath danced over her nape. "Tell me how you feel."

His command would have grated on her any other time. But now she could hear the undercurrent of his uncertainty, of his dark mood still hovering over them like a black cloud. And that earlier urge to soothe him, to share whatever it was that bothered him, was magnified by a hundred times. "Like I've had two mind-blowing orgasms. Like I've satisfied my very sexy, very studly Italian husband with my body. Like I've been remade." She couldn't help giggling at the last.

"Mimi..." he said, his voice far too grave.

Mimi frowned, and as if to soothe herself, she pulled his hand up to her face and kissed the center. The shape of his fingers, the lines on his palm, the rough mound of his hand...when had he grown so familiar to her?

She couldn't get over the plain fact that she could touch Renzo DiCarlo like this. Freely. Whenever she wanted.

"It was quite the workout, Renzo. And while I've been slowly getting back to walking and other forms of exercise, this was a lot of...rigor." She laughed at her own word choice, hoping he would join in too. No such luck though. "Of course I'm sore. And no, you didn't hurt me. At all."

The press of his lips over her upper back made her shiver. As did his broad hand cupping her hip in a possessive grip. As did the outline of his already hard shaft pressing against her bottom. "If you want to go again, my earlier offer stands," she said, making a popping sound with her mouth.

"No more tonight, *cara*," he said, nudging closer to her.

"Let me turn," she said sharply, having had enough. With a sigh, he loosened the fortress he made around her with his arms and legs.

A buffet of tiny twitches and pains greeted her as she turned to face him. His arm came to rest on her waist loosely as he studied her. She studied him in return, awed yet again that this...wonderful man was hers, in that moment at least.

His stylishly cut hair stood in all directions, his thin lips were swollen from her nips and bites, and there were scratch marks on his shoulders and chest.

He looked like he was…hers. Only hers.

And then it swept through her, like a storm ravaging a town.

Renzo DiCarlo was more than just his wealth or his power or his arrogance. There was a wealth of goodness and caring beneath the facade he showed the world. A man capable of feeling deep emotions and deeper pain.

He had been hurt tonight by his family's boorish behavior. He had been furious on her behalf, even though she had held her own. He had made her feel so protected that just having him by her side had made her strong. Bold. She had stood up for herself, something she'd never done, not even with her own family.

And she had seen the very same loneliness in his eyes that she had known for so long. But together, they could be so much more than what they were alone.

And if she was willing to take the risk with her own heart, if she could trust him and trust herself to get this right, they could have something real. Something Mimi had never thought possible for her.

Something like…true love.

A pained gasp escaped her as she realized that she was retrofitting rationale and good sense to something that was already out of her hands. Trying to exert control over a situation when it was too late…

She was in love with her husband. Irrevocably. Completely. Like a steel fist clutching her heart in its grip. The knowledge of her love for him filled her bone and sinew, truly remaking her now.

How could she not love him when he had helped her see who she could be when she was wholly herself? When she didn't doubt her own self-worth? When she simply let herself be?

"That is my least favorite sound in the world."

His caustic tone brought Mimi back to the present, to the reality of him. To the clawing, painful truth of loving him and knowing that he might never love her in return. That had been their agreement, hadn't it?

Neither of us wants anything to do with love, he'd said when he'd proposed marriage to her. More than once he'd made it clear that the thing he admired about her was that her head and her heart were firmly planted on cold, hard ground.

"I'll check with my database and try not to produce any sounds that might offend my lordly husband," she said, her response tart and sharp, as if it could stop her love from flashing across her face like a neon sign.

God, could he see in her face how hopelessly in love she was with him? Would he mock her, cut their deal short?

His chuckle brought her gaze to his mouth. She sighed. When he laughed like that, her entire being seemed to light up as if that laugh was powering every cell.

"I do not like it when you hide yourself away, *cara*. When you're sad. I take my duties very seriously."

She knew that much about him for sure. "I'm not sad," she said morosely.

Fingers clasped her cheek, and he tilted her face this way and that as if he were searching for the truth. Throwing an arm around his neck, she pressed herself to him, her face landing in the hollow of his throat.

Joy and fear duked it out inside her, and she trembled from the effort of struggling with both. The drag of her bare breasts against his chest, though…pure, glorious sensation. She anchored herself to it.

"You're trembling, Mimi," he said, lifting her chin.

Like a wanton creature in heat, she rubbed herself against

him from head to toe, hoping to distract him. Hoping to drown herself in so much sensation that she could escape the truth sitting on her chest like an anvil.

He caught her lips with a rumbling groan that she swallowed happily. But contrary man that he was, he didn't let her deepen the kiss. Didn't let her give in to the frenzy. And she didn't have the confidence yet to push him into his own.

It was a soft kiss. Almost an apology of sorts. Something else too, something deeper that she wished he would put into words. And it nearly broke her resolve to keep the admission that burned on her lips to herself.

When he released her, she clung to him. Her mind whirred in a thousand directions. Luca was going to come home soon. And from everything she had learned about her husband so far, their bond with Luca would only deepen their bond with each other.

And yet she knew nothing about why he was so against love. Was it having been exposed to his father's constant infidelity growing up? Then there had been Pia and Santo's marriage—another disaster.

He had been upset with his family earlier tonight, but the emotion beneath had been a pulsing anger. Even hurt.

"That woman Chiara invited tonight… Rosa, I think," Mimi mumbled, impressions from the evening coming back to her now.

Instantly, Renzo tensed. "What about her?"

Mimi pulled back casually, though she kept her cheek on his arm.

"You could barely stand to look at her."

"You read me well, *cara*." He turned to lie on his back, though one arm stayed wrapped around her. "I *couldn't* stand to look at her."

"May I ask why?"

"Rosa was my best friend once. My first lover. The woman I loved. The woman I thought I would marry and build a family with." There was no bitterness in his words anymore, though. Only a strange resignation, even emptiness.

"Oh," Mimi said, as if the one word could convey her quaking insides. Clawing fingers of jealousy gripped her. The sensation was so alien to her that she rubbed a hand over her chest.

And then she remembered what she had just said. Renzo hadn't even looked in this woman's direction. He hadn't left her side even for a minute. He was nothing like his father, she reminded herself.

And yet it was his highly developed sense of duty, his version of honor that would forbid him from even looking at the woman when he was married. Didn't matter if his feelings had been revived for her or not.

"I'm sorry I asked about her then," she said, trying so hard to not probe further.

"Don't be. Your curiosity is natural. She's Chiara's close friend. She got divorced a couple of years ago. My sister's been trying to set us up again."

"And she invited her tonight even though you're now married and have a son," Mimi said, her own fury creeping into her words. It was one thing for his sister to tell Mimi that she didn't like her. A whole other to ambush him by inviting the girl he'd loved once. "And Chiara dared to call Pia manipulative."

As fast as it came, her fury tapped out, leaving her with more questions. To hell with Chiara. All she wanted to know was why Renzo had been so angry at the sight of that girl.

She scooted up into a sitting position and dragged the duvet to her chest, suddenly feeling far too restless. Damn her sister-in-law for ruining her first post-orgasmic haze with her husband.

Renzo followed her, his movements far more graceful than her jerky lumbering. "It will not happen again."

"I'm angrier on your behalf than mine." Mimi bit her lip, hating that she needed to ask the question. That she needed to know beyond doubt if he had any remnant affection for Rosa. "I… Did you consider getting back with her, Renzo, before Luca and I ruined your plans?"

Dark anger flashed in Renzo's eyes as he turned to face her. Even amid the muddle of her thoughts, Mimi couldn't not notice the sculpted musculature of his chest. Or how his olive skin gleamed and rippled when he moved.

God, she wanted to worship him with her lips and tongue and fingers and all of her. She wanted to whisper her admission of love into every sinew and bone, until he was overflowing with it.

"You are asking the wrong question, *cara*."

The darkness remained in his gaze as she hurriedly pulled up hers. Though the anger transformed to a self-satisfied smirk. "You don't have to preen that I'm drooling over you, Renzo. This is the first time in my life that I'm so completely and utterly…horny over a man. Give me a break."

Grabbing the duvet toga-style, she tried to get off the bed when instead she found herself in his lap, his arm a steel band under her breasts. She squirmed, felt his hardness poke at her behind, heard his near-pained grunt and settled in with a huff.

"Stop moving, *bella*." His desire colored his words with rich texture.

Sinking into him, she thought back to his comment. Past the new current of anxiety and awareness in her belly that reminded her she was so vulnerable against him now. *Wrong question*, he'd said… "Why did you and Rosa break up?"

He chuckled softly at her ear. The sound traveled through her, settling deep into her core, planting roots. "Have I ever told you that I find your mind as arousing as your body?"

Mimi turned, kissed him and mumbled, "No. Tell me, please. I will never mention her again."

He dipped his head until his chin rested on her shoulder. "When I was twenty-one, it came out that our family was in massive debt. The business was crumbling. Investors were pulling out. My father, whether through sheer stupidity or negligence, ran everything to ground. Rosa's father found out and told her. She sent me a message through her brother that she was canceling our engagement."

Mimi turned in his arms again and pressed her cheek to his bare chest. His heart thudded under her ears in a steady beat while hers…ached for him. No wonder he'd been so predisposed to dislike Pia too. While her sister hadn't worshipped status and wealth particularly, she had cared about the superficial stuff more than her own or Santo's happiness. "I'm sorry."

"Don't be. Rosa taught me a valuable lesson I never forgot, motivated me enough to clean up my father's mess. It took me more than a decade, but I fixed everything. Rebuilt the resorts into a luxury brand."

"I don't understand it," Mimi said, her confusion seeping into her words. "From what Massimo told me at the party, it seems Rosa's and Chiara's husbands went into business together, and it all sank. You literally had to rescue your brother-in-law. Weren't you at least a little happy to have her see you like this? To rub your success and power and wealth in her snotty face?"

He laughed so hard that Mimi shook along with him. "What a bloodthirsty little heart you have, *cara*. I like you more and more."

Mimi shrugged, even as every inch of her thrummed at his praise. At the glint of admiration in his tone. "Instead, you were...distressed to see her. You're sure you have no lingering feelings for her?"

His teeth bit down on her earlobe, sending a lick of flaming sensation down to her sensitized core. Mimi gasped and writhed in his lap as he followed it up by licking at the hurt he caused.

"No feelings for her, *cara*. I will not have you doubt my word or my commitment to this."

"I don't, Renzo," she said, mouth falling open in a long gravelly moan as he cupped her breasts. "But I—"

She never got to finish her thought or the sentence as he spread her thighs wide open on his lap and dipped his fingers into her core.

"The way you're dripping, I'm not sure this can be termed as punishment, Mimi." One swipe of a long finger followed, from her clit to slit, and Mimi sobbed at the sharp avalanche of sensations pooling there. This time, his teeth dug into her shoulder. "Maybe I should stop."

"Please don't," she said, grasping his wrist, making his palm fall flat against her mound.

"Then we're agreed that there will be no discussion about that woman?"

Mimi knew, in the back recesses of her mind where a figment of rationale persisted, that he wasn't answering her question. That he was seducing her into forgetting the small niggling doubt she had raised.

But, God, she was helpless against his voice, against him, against the skillful strokes of his fingers. Against loving him so completely that all she wanted was the moment to go on forever.

His fingers pulled away with a tap against her clit that had her angling her hips into his hand. "I didn't hear your answer, Mimi."

"No talking about her ever again," Mimi whispered, falling back against him. Every cell in her, every inch of her being seemed to dwell at the point where he stroked her again. In clever, mindful circles that drove her out of her skin. So skilled already at what would push her to the edge.

Her climax shimmered out of reach, teasing her, taunting her. "I don't know if I can, Renzo."

"Yes, *bella*, you can. Your body sings for me, Mimi. Do you know what a turn-on that is? Do you know what it does to me when you don't hide your desire for me? When you respond to my every touch like you were the most sensitive instrument ever crafted?"

With each searing word, he played her like a maestro. And Mimi followed him up the spiraling steps, her mind, her body, her soul all his to control.

His to protect.

His to…love. If only he wanted to.

Raking her fingers through his hair, she sobbed at the intrusive thought. Reality ruining her jagged climb toward completion. "More, Renzo. Please."

He gave her everything she begged for and more. A heady cocktail of sweat and sex filled her nostrils. "Come for me, *bella*. Because then, I'm going to take you up on your offer and use your hands. Right on this bed. You'll be too sore for the rest of the night, *sì*? So maybe I'll paint your breasts with my—"

Mimi clutched his wrist, arched up and off him like a bowstring pulled taut, and shattered into a thousand fragments of nothingness. And the man she utterly adored held her through it, praising her, soothing her comedown, kissing her.

As if she were precious to him too. As if she were the woman he had chosen for himself and not by a cruel twist of fate.

CHAPTER ELEVEN

LUCA CAME HOME the next day while Renzo was out of town.

He had been gone the next morning when she'd woken up in their bed. A scribbled note lay fluttering on the nightstand in his quite illegible scrawl.

Urgent, unavoidable issues at ski resort at the Alps.
—R.

Nothing about when he would return or that he would miss her and their son.

Okay, yes, they weren't teenagers trading secret love notes in the classroom, but still…her foolish heart ached for something more personal.

Especially after the night they had shared, after he had so thoroughly debauched her. He had been insatiable even at dawn, waking her up to ask her if her mouth was still on offer. Of course she had whispered yes. What followed had been both revelatory of her own sexual boundaries and how easily she could cross them for him, and how savage her love for him could be. That session had ended with his powerful body shaking, praising her for her "competence" yet again.

It had nearly crushed her to wake up alone in the large bed. To find her body sore and exhausted in the best way, but to be unable to reach over and kiss him. To be unable to see the man she had fallen in love with, in the bright, fresh light of the morning with this new, keen awareness.

Tears smarting the back of her eyes, she had gotten ready for her day. When she arrived at the clinic, the neonatal specialist had informed her that she could take Luca home immediately.

A cheerful Massimo and their mother had arrived within minutes of her calling.

Mimi knew she could have waited for Renzo to return. But coward that she was, she was trying to escape all the feelings her husband evoked in her by drowning herself in her son.

Or maybe it wasn't cowardice but stubborn self-preservation. She needed to prove to herself that one passionate night with her husband hadn't rendered her foolish or incapable of doing what needed to be done. That her mind, her very nature, hadn't been rewritten by Renzo's passion for her.

Passion, not love, she reminded herself.

They had been waiting for so long for Luca to come home. Her precious baby boy was the reason she and Renzo were even together.

So she brought him home, aided by Renzo's mother, his brother, and an army of nurses and nannies that Renzo had already hired.

He had married her precisely because she was no-nonsense, capable and didn't believe in love. He had shown her immense kindness and comfort and even passion precisely because he expected her to not turn into this…lovesick, maudlin creature.

And really, what was even the guarantee that all these strange new feelings wouldn't set her up for more heartache? More rejection? And God, she had had enough to last a lifetime at her mom's hands.

So she would not change herself one bit, she told herself, burying her face into her son's belly. She would not let this love she felt for her husband make a fool out of her.

If her tears leaked out and she had to change Luca's onesie, she pretended like they were tears of happiness at his coming home.

Renzo crept into his bedroom on soft feet, moonlight his only aid in the dark room. He felt like a thief sneaking into someone else's house under the cover of night.

Frustration and anger at himself coiled like twin ropes inside him, driving the breath out of him. He saw only now that it was the intensity of his feelings for Mimi that had driven him away, causing him to miss his son being discharged from the hospital. He had been gone for two days, and it felt like two eternities.

His heart scuttled into his throat like a crab on sand as he reached the foot of the large bed.

A soft night-light had been left on his side of the bed, casting an ethereal glow. The sight that greeted him made his heart fall back into his chest with a thud.

Luca was fast asleep, cocooned tightly in a blue blanket, tiny fisted hands thrown above him as if in a cheer. Wisps of jet-black hair fluttered beneath a woolen cap, the jut of his straight nose prominent in his chubby face.

Next to Luca, with the tips of her fingers grazing his belly, as if she couldn't bear to not touch him, was his wife. Lying on her side, with her head tucked on her folded arm. It struck Renzo that she was just as pure of heart as their son.

Two innocent, bright-as-sun lives that had come into his orbit by sheer chance. Taunting him with the fact that he hadn't even known he would want this in his life.

Leaning over, he brushed a wavy lock of hair from her

face, wishing she would wake. And set those perceptive eyes on him, maybe challenge him as to why he had fled like that. Even help him figure out this confused tangle of emotions within him.

Because he *had* run away, like a coward.

After using her all night, after slaking his desire on her still-recovering body over and over.

Cristo, he hadn't expected to lose himself in her like that. Hadn't expected to find both his salvation and his destruction in her soft smiles, in her hard kisses and her willing, warm body.

But then, he shouldn't have been surprised that Mimi would be as giving and passionate in bed as she was anywhere else. Her passion had been a demanding sword and a comforting embrace all at once. He had been so out of control, so needy that he had even woken her up at dawn, demanding she give him her mouth.

But he refused to regret it. She would hate him if he regretted it because she had met him as an equal. Then he had woken up in the morning, tangled in her arms.

Bright sunlight had streamed into the room, lighting up the dark shadows under her eyes and all the marks he had left on her neck and chest. He had realized then what had disturbed him so about seeing Rosa the previous night.

His real trajectory in life had begun with her rejecting a future with him, rejecting his love.

It had become his identity—to be the provider of all things for the people around him. If he hadn't stepped up all those years ago and fixed their crumbling finances, none of them would live in the easy luxury they did now.

But in the long slog he'd put in for years, in his refusal to stop even a day for his own rest or recreation, he had become only that—a man who fixed things for others. A man whose only value lay in his wealth, in his power and reach. A man who didn't want or understand deeper connections.

He was surrounded by people who needed things from him. His beautiful, bright, brave wife had stood out in sharp contrast at that damned party for one very particular reason. A reason that stole the ground from under his feet.

What was it that Mimi needed from him? What could he give her that she would willingly bind herself to him forever?

It had been arrogant of him to assume that he would simply keep her. Because now, he wanted her to want this life with him.

If their frenzied night of lovemaking had clarified one thing, it was that he was falling for her and this little family they were building. And that he didn't have anything to offer to make her stay.

She had been reluctant about marrying him, had only given in because he'd forced her into understanding the reality of carrying his son. He hadn't exaggerated.

She and Luca did need his protection. But soon, the media's interest in them would fade, and the year would be up.

The prospect of letting her go, of learning that there was nothing he could give her to bind her to him when that day dawned…nearly brought him to his knees.

So he had gone away, using the problems with the ski resort as the perfect excuse. To think and strategize and plan, though he was realizing that there was no blueprint for this. All he could do was stall and arrest the complete descent.

Moving slowly, he climbed into the bed on the other side of his son and carefully touched his cheek with the tip of his finger, loath to disturb his sleep. Then he brushed the same finger across her cheek over the top of his son's head and left it there.

His breath settled for the first time in days. He couldn't bear to part with either of them for tonight.

Tomorrow, he would keep himself at a distance, until he figured out how to make this ache a little more bearable. Tomorrow, he would ration himself on how much of his wife he could have.

The next evening, Mimi's steps slowed and she paused in the doorway, letting her gaze sweep slowly over the room. As if she were seeing it for the first time but really bracing herself for the sight that would meet her eyes.

The nursery was a haven of understated elegance—walls painted a soft dove gray accented with white crown molding. A pale blue mobile shaped like delicate Venetian gondolas hung above a polished white crib.

A tufted armchair sat in one corner, beside a bookshelf stocked with colorful storybooks she had started collecting long before Luca's birth. Warm, honey-colored wood floors gleamed faintly under the glow of a muted table lamp.

Near the large picture window that offered a glimpse of the shimmering Grand Canal, Renzo lay propped on his elbow on the thick wool rug. He had returned late last night, and she had stepped out of the penthouse before he had been awake, sticking to her own work schedule.

He was barefoot, the casual jeans and snug black sweater fitting him with effortless perfection. Two months into their marriage and her heart still stuttered at the sight of him— all that sexy masculinity sprawled around wherever she turned—as if it were all a dream.

His dark hair was slightly tousled, a stark contrast to his usual meticulously groomed appearance.

Luca, wrapped snugly in a soft knit blanket, blinked up at his father with wide, sleepy eyes. His hands, still so small and fragile, twitched slightly as if testing their strength. Renzo's deep voice was a soothing murmur, speaking Italian lullabies that melted the edges of Mimi's lingering tension.

He had been gone for only two days, and yet in the aftermath of bringing Luca home, she had realized how lonely she had been.

The wool rug was soft beneath her bare feet as she leaned against the doorframe, her chest painfully tight at the scene. If there were a picture of her heart beating outside of her, it would be this—the man she loved and their son together. "You two look comfortable," she said, infusing a teasing warmth she didn't feel into her words.

Renzo glanced up, his gaze instantly darkening as he swept it over her. She could live to be a hundred, but the thrill of his eyes landing on her would never pass. "You look…exhausted."

Mimi chuckled, stepping fully into the room and dropping onto her knees beside them. Instantly, a cocktail of scents greeted her nostrils—her son's baby powder and her husband's cologne. She felt dizzy, a rush of overwhelming love for both filling her. "I hate working out even as the trainer begins. It's only after that I feel the rush." She sighed and rubbed her face in Luca's belly. "It would be nice if we could feel the adrenaline rush before we do the hard things in life, wouldn't it? A little reminder that it would be worth it."

Renzo remained silent. She wondered if it was because he understood what she meant or if he didn't care. A hot prickle of tears greeted the backs of her eyes, and she blinked rapidly.

He had dragged her kicking and screaming into this marriage, given her a taste of how wonderful their relationship could be, and then distanced himself. She wanted to scream at him, demand he explain himself. Only he hadn't done anything to break the conditions of their agreement, had he?

It was she who had changed utterly. And even though it was her fault, she couldn't live with the unbearable ache of loving him and knowing he might never love her.

Lying down next to Luca, she grabbed his chubby hand and rubbed her nose in it. "What are you two talking about?"

Renzo shifted slightly, propping Luca up into his arms. Instantly, her son let out a long gurgle, excitement making his dark eyes shine.

God, he was tiny on that corded forearm, and yet Mimi never doubted that Renzo would temper his strength.

It was how he handled her too. Though she lived for the times when he lost control, when his raw need trumped his protective instincts and he let himself take what he needed from her. When he let her see how demanding he could be.

"I was telling him about Venice," he said. "How the city sounds different as it gets colder. You hear fewer boats at night and fewer footsteps on the bridges."

Mimi smiled, her gaze fixed on Luca. "Think he understood any of that?"

"Of course," Renzo said, not meeting her eyes. "He's very advanced for his age."

She laughed softly, this time brushing her fingers over Luca's feet. "I think he's just happy to be warm and fed. Aren't you, baby boy?"

Luca's mouth moved slightly, and Mimi swore his eyes lingered on hers for a moment longer than usual.

"I didn't realize what a big difference a few days makes in appearance," Renzo said, his tone tinged with awe. "Every day, I notice something new. Like how he looks at us now. Like he knows we're his."

Mimi's throat tightened as she glanced at her husband.

The light from the lamps caught on the sharp planes of his face, softening the usual intensity in his expression. There was something so tender, so unguarded, about the way he looked at Luca. And every time she caught that look, it made her realize that it was reserved only for their son.

No one else. But she wanted him to look at her like that too. She wanted so badly to be more than his son's mother, his sensible, competent wife or his lover when the mood struck. She wanted to be everything to him.

"I think he recognizes you already," she said, her voice soft.

Renzo chuckled, the rich sound filling the room. "He probably wonders why I talk so much."

Mimi smiled, shifting closer until their shoulders touched. The air between them felt warmer now, a subtle connection threading through the quiet moment.

But the warmth, the shared connection, would disappear the minute they were out of Luca's presence. And Mimi knew suddenly, despite wondering if she was shortchanging her son, that she couldn't bear to live like this anymore.

CHAPTER TWELVE

"WHAT'S THIS?" MIMI SAID a couple of hours later, staring at the official-looking envelope sitting on her pillow with her name scrawled on top.

It had taken them a long time to get Luca settled into his crib. She wondered if her own restlessness had triggered his crankiness.

The connecting door clicked behind Renzo. She turned to find him undoing the buttons on his shirt. Tension arced between them, sexual and otherwise.

He looked tired, with deep grooves settling under his eyes and around his mouth. In a moment, her frustration with him melted away.

She longed to go to him, to cradle his cheeks and brush her mouth against his, to feel his solid strength around her. She longed to offer him solace in whatever way she could.

But she wasn't sure if her efforts would be welcome, and that hurt immensely. She didn't know if he would welcome her admission of love either, or scoff at her for being such an easy fool. Nothing in her life had prepared her for facing him with that admission.

When he remained silent, she bristled. "Please don't tell me it's another gift."

"I had a lot of meetings with my lawyers this past week, *cara*. It was convenient to take care of this too." His own frustration resonated in his words now. "And I don't get what is so strange about a husband arranging things for his wife. You're the one who calls them gifts."

With that parting shot, he went into the closet.

Mimi followed him, her patience dwindling with this cat and mouse game they were playing.

The colorful designer clothes hanging on her side of the closet, along with multiple boxes of expensive jewelry, brought her problem with him to the forefront. All the things Renzo insisted on buying for her, despite her protests.

She was Renzo DiCarlo's wife, as much as she didn't like to wear that as some kind of mantle. As such, there was always a certain amount of interest in her.

So yes, it made sense to upgrade her wardrobe and obtain some jewelry pieces and accessories.

She told herself that it was all part of a costume for a play she sometimes participated in. Especially since, whether she was dressed in designer duds or her usual black leggings and loose sweatshirts, the way he looked at her never changed.

It had begun with the equipment he had delivered to her, even before Luca had come home—expensive, state-of-the-art cameras and other accessories that she was afraid to even touch. Equipment that had made her drool like a child in a pastry shop.

She had refused at first, even though every inch of her had protested. And the rogue had persuaded her to keep it by kissing her, by telling her that if she was serious about her career, then she needed to invest in proper equipment.

Then had come the search for a house. An estate they had finally found near Milan to Renzo's satisfaction—on the edge of Lake Como, to be precise—because Renzo insisted that at some point, Luca would need more space to play, and a sterile, monochromatic penthouse was the last place for a child.

And yet when his personal lawyer had come to have her sign some papers, Mimi had realized that the mansion had been deeded in her name. And another place in London, because her work might take her back to the city, and they needed a stable place for Luca.

Again, she had hotly protested. Again, he had convinced her that it made sense to have some properties in her name, that it was the wedding gift he had never given her. A place where they would build a bigger family, if they wanted to, at some point in the future.

The only thing that had stopped her from shouting that she wanted that with him was the flash of something in his eyes. And suddenly, she began to see the pattern.

Renzo bought her things—expensive houses and jewelry and video equipment.

Renzo was setting up properties for her, ostensibly, that were far away from where he would be most of the time, away from Venice, which was his main base.

Was he slowly trying to build a long-distance, perfectly polite marriage? Was he already bored with the domesticity Luca, and she, had forced on him?

For all that his family treated him as if he was an eternal fount granting their desires, he was only a man. There was no doubt that he was burnt out after Santo's death.

Did he resent her and Luca too, as being too needy, too dependent on him after all the responsibilities he had shouldered all his life?

The questions came at her fast, nearly knocking her off her feet.

She turned to demand he tell her the truth. And stilled.

He'd shrugged off his shirt, and the light from the overhead chandelier kissed every plane and ridge of his chest.

Even now, Mimi felt that near-manic urge to throw herself at him—to claw her fingers over that olive skin stretched taut over hard sinew, to lose herself in his rough, biting kiss, to urge him to bury himself inside her until all her doubts melted away.

Because when they were tangled up in each other's arms, there was no doubt that he wanted her in his life. That he wanted her. It was outside of the intimacy that she lost all her footing.

Now that she could see past her own misery, though, she noted the tension clamping his shoulders. "What's wrong? Is it Massimo? Is he in trouble again?"

A soft smile split his mouth. "No, apparently you were right about him. He apologized for being so…out of control in the last few months. He said he missed Santo. Neither of us realized that we should talk to each other about how much we miss our older brother."

"You have a thousand responsibilities to shoulder," she said, instantly coming to his defense. "What's his excuse?"

"You're a witch, *bella*. Because Massimo did have one." He unbuckled his trousers, pushed them off his tapered hips along with his boxer shorts. Utterly confident in his body. Utterly magnificent in his nakedness.

Then he pulled on gray sweatpants, and Mimi forced herself to focus. "Which is what?"

"Apparently, he has always been intimidated by me."

"Oh. That's not…impossible. You are a man with ruthless, exacting standards in every aspect of life, Renzo. Mere mortals could find it hard to please you."

"You've never failed, *bella*."

Mimi flushed, her skin nearly vibrating with the need

to go to him. "By those exacting standards, you allow me a lot of leeway. And honestly, it's hard to read you, Renzo."

"Not for you," he retorted again.

"Again, only so much as you allow me," she said, busying herself with opening the new clothes she had ordered for Luca. "You very much control what I or anyone else perceives about you. You're a damned master at it."

She didn't care look at him, but she knew her words had landed. For a while, he didn't say anything. The expansive closet with its full-length mirrors and pristine marble floors suddenly felt too small and too cold to hold the tension crackling between them.

"So his not even trying to behave like a mature adult is valid because I have high standards?" Renzo sounded so aggravated by this, by her defense of Massimo, that Mimi stared at him. Something about his tone nagged at her, but she couldn't put her finger on it.

"No. I never said that. Massimo's good at trying to get out of a fix even when he's admitting that he's messed up. He's a charmer through and through. And honestly, with Santo so wrapped up in his own life and you buried in your business, I don't blame him for feeling lost."

"We should have had you there, refereeing our discussion."

This time, his disgruntlement was as clear as the cold draft of air kissing her skin. Mimi grabbed an old sweatshirt of Renzo's and pulled it on when he set that dark gaze on her.

"He pays attention to you," Renzo said. "I think he has a little crush on you."

Heat crept up her cheeks. "That's…ridiculous. We share some interests. As much as you mock him, I think he's serious about photography. You wanted him to change, Renzo. Give him a chance now."

Gaze thoughtful, Renzo nodded.

"What about Chiara?" she said, knowing he needed to talk about his family. Only then could she address their own relationship. "Your mother has been visiting regularly, but she doesn't mention Chiara. And neither do I," Mimi admitted, suddenly feeling guilty. "I mean, I know I should try to make amends with her, but with Luca coming home and everything else, it's just been a lot, and I..."

Renzo took her hands in his and squeezed. When Mimi thought he would pull her to him and wrap those strong arms around her—her entire being nearly ready to fling herself at him—he let go.

Hurt crashed through her, and suddenly it felt unbearable. Why did he touch her only in a sexual context? What happened to the Renzo who had teased her, made fun of her and provoked her? Why was he spending so much time away from her and Luca when he was the one who insisted on this marriage?

Had it all been to control the situation and her?

"I haven't spoken to her either. I did pay off her husband's debt, in case you thought I acted on my threat. Mama said they might be filing for divorce. Chiara has made her bed, though, and she needs to make a decision—whether she wants to lie in it or not."

He paused and then raised a hand as if to stop her next question. Something like resignation settled into his stark features. "I've given up trying to manage their lives. If they get in trouble, I will help. But no more expectations that they will behave, that they will fix their mistakes, or that they will understand me."

Mimi's heart ached for him as she followed him to their

bedroom. And then her gaze fell on the damned envelope again.

"Open it," he said with that arrogant tilt of his head that she had come to recognize as a tell of his uncertainty.

She almost protested, but the last thing she wanted to spend her energy on was a silly fight.

Mimi opened the envelope and quickly skimmed the documents. It was a lot of legalese, but she understood enough to feel as if she had been burned. She dropped them onto the bed, anger sparking and lighting up her flashpoint.

"What the hell? Why are you settling this much money on me?" She scoffed at her incapability to do mental math. "I can't even convert that number into pounds. I didn't ask you for any of this."

"You're overreacting."

Mimi was so angry at this statement that she simply sputtered at him.

"You know I set up trust funds for Chiara's children, for Massimo. I did one for Luca, and this is for you."

"Why? Are you planning to divorce me soon? Are you worried that I might ask for too much?"

"Of course not. You are the one who made up the one-year plan, not me."

Mimi folded her hands and glared at him. "Did no one tell you that the last thing you should say to your wife is that she's overreacting?"

"You do overreact when it comes to me buying you anything. We've been through this, Mimi. I am a rich man. I like to buy my wife certain things. One would think you'd learn to accept them with grace."

"Not when it feels like you're buying me out for some reason, Renzo. I told you when you proposed this whole arrangement—" she still couldn't bring herself to say *this marriage* "—that I don't want anything from you. Except your support in raising Luca when we separate."

He remained stubbornly mute.

"So, are we separating? Is that what you want? All these new residences you have been buying me in different cities, these overnight trips you take, the way you're never here to—"

"I never what? You're telling me I'm failing in my duty as a husband and a father?"

Duty…there was that word again.

She had never hated a word in the language so much as she did then. And it also gave her the answer for the questions that plagued her day and night like vultures pecking at her tender flesh.

She would always be another responsibility to him, nothing more. Another burden he had taken on. And maybe because she was a novelty to him right now, or because she provided easy, convenient, hassle-free relief in the form of sex, he gave her and demanded physical intimacy.

But how long would that last if he saw her as another item on his to-do list? How long would it last if they had nothing else outside it?

As hard as she fought, a tear slipped down her cheek. Because she didn't understand how to get back what they had once had. She didn't even know if it had been anything more than a mirage of a connection brought on by their shared grief for their lost siblings and love for the innocent life they were bringing into the world.

"I want to go to London for Christmas and take Luca with me," she blurted out, having reached the end of her tether.

His head jerked up as if someone had punched him. And he continued to stare at her for several long moments without a question or a statement.

Mimi wrapped her arms around herself and looked out the large window. The world outside seemed to be going on at its usual rhythms while hers…was tilting upside down. "One of the documentaries I made when I was pregnant—about prenatal healthcare for women from lower economic backgrounds—got nominated for an award. The banquet is a few days before Christmas, in London. I want to—I have to attend. And I want to bring Luca with me. There's a bunch of friends who want to see him, and I…need a break."

"A break from what?" Renzo finally said.

"From being cooped up here," she said, meeting his eyes. *Please, ask me not to leave*, her foolish heart murmured. *Ask me to stay. Tell me you'll fix whatever's gone wrong between us.*

The lines of strain around his mouth deepened as he regarded her. "How long are you talking about?"

"I don't know. I think you have a lot to deal with right now, with that new resort being built. And I need to go back to my life for a little while." She bit her lip, arresting the bitterness that wanted to spew forth. "Luca's the most important thing in my life now, and…there are things I need to sort out with my mother too. I've been running away from my own home for too long."

"And you're not now?" he demanded, his question sharp as a knife. But he didn't give her a chance to respond. "Whatever you want, *bella*. Just do me the favor of staying at the London flat I bought you recently." His mouth twisted wryly. "Seems like I have foresight."

And then he walked out.

No arguments. No threats. No discussion.

Leaving Mimi alone with their son.

CHAPTER THIRTEEN

THE SLEEK BLACK chauffeur-driven Bentley pulled up to the entrance of the Mayfair Grand DiCarlo, its golden lights spilling onto the rain-slicked pavement. London glowed, festive and alive, twinkling in the drizzle.

Inside the car, Mimi sat frozen, her fingers curled around the cold glass of her award.

She had won.

Best Documentary.

She should have been elated. She should have been riding the high of the applause, the champagne toasts, the congratulations. And yet all she could think about was *him*.

The moment they announced her name, the small banquet hall had erupted.

Thunderous waves of applause had rolled over her, shaking the air, stealing her breath. Strangers had stood for her. Her peers and friends and her parents had cheered.

It was a small achievement in a small career, but she was proud of herself. Because her best work had come when she had persevered through the roughest year of her life.

And yet she wasn't…happy.

She felt as if she were bodily present but absent in spirit, as if she were playacting in someone else's life. It had been the same in the last week since she had left Venice.

Because the only person she had wanted to share her achievement and her joy with wasn't there.

Renzo wasn't there.

It had been his voice in her ear in those fractious weeks when Luca was still at the hospital. Asking her to tell him about her latest project. Then, low and certain, urging her to apply for the award when she'd nearly talked herself out of it. When she'd sat at her laptop, doubting every word of the essay she'd written for the application, wondering if the documentary she'd worked on during her pregnancy was too bleak, it had been his belief in her passion that had made her press Send.

You're not just talented, cara, *but hold a unique perspective. Let the world see it.*

She had ached to turn to him, to see his face in the crowd, to rush into his arms and hear that deep, gravelly voice in her ear again. To hear him call her his clever, competent, sexy-as-sin wife again. To see the glimmer of pride in his eyes.

But he hadn't been there.

And in the days since she had left, he hadn't called her even once. Their nanny made sure he chatted with Luca every morning and evening.

Her chest twisted in a tight, painful knot when she heard the deep lilt of his Italian as he greeted their son. Her soul ached to lay eyes on him. She had resisted.

And yet when she'd accepted the award and looked into the glare of flashbulbs and cameras in the crowd, for just a second, she'd thought she'd seen him.

Tall, unmistakably handsome, watching her with that quiet, unreadable intensity that always made her pulse skitter.

She had felt it in how her nape prickled, how her body sang. She had felt him close.

But when she had stepped off the stage, searching, there had been no sign of him. Of course, Renzo wasn't there.

It was just another trick of her own foolish mind, another cruel mirage her hopeless love offered to soothe her.

God, she was going mad. Seeing him in places he wasn't, hearing his voice in echoes that didn't exist.

The driver cleared his throat, and she realized the car had stopped.

Right. The hotel.

Tomorrow was Christmas Eve. And while every inch of her wanted to hide under a weighted blanket and not emerge until the New Year's, this was her son's first Christmas.

She owed it to him, and herself, to celebrate their togetherness, to start new traditions. She had lost too much recently to not see what she did have. Even if her heart felt like it was dented in a hundred places.

The air was crisp, carrying the scent of damp pavement and expensive perfume. Heels clicking against the marble, she stepped into the grand lobby, only to come to a sudden standstill. Her breath danced in her throat, almost choking her.

Was that Massimo stepping out of the grand elevator? Or was her mind creating mirages again?

With that long-limbed stride and easy laughter, his gaze caught on the phone in his hand, he strolled out the other exit, utterly at ease.

If he was here, why hadn't he contacted her? Why was he in London at all? It wasn't as though their mother would let him out of her sight during the holiday season. Only Renzo could convince her to let him travel with him…

The realization hit her like a blow to the chest.

That meant Renzo was here in London. It *was* her husband she'd seen at the awards ceremony. He had been present in the audience, hiding in the shadows, but hadn't shown himself.

How dare he hide away like a thief? How dare he play with her feelings?

A host of emotions crashed over her, all hot and sharp and unbearable.

Anger. Longing. Heartbreak.

Anger won out, propelling her forward. Her pulse thundered as she pivoted toward the front desk, jaw tight.

"Hi, I have a question," she said, voice sharp.

The receptionist barely looked up before reaching under the counter. "Good evening, Mrs. DiCarlo. Did you need a new key card?" His voice was smooth, professional, with the polite indifference of someone who dealt with VIPs daily. He simply slid a key card across the marble counter as if this was routine.

Mimi's breath caught.

Mrs. DiCarlo.

Because the poor man assumed that she would know her goddamned husband was already here. At his own hotel.

Her hands trembled as she took the smooth white key-card, her blood boiling now.

The private elevator ride felt both too slow and too fast. Matching the uneven rhythm of her own heartbeats.

She pushed it open, stepping into the darkened expanse. The only light came from the city skyline, gleaming through the floor-to-ceiling windows. The room smelled clean, expensive, undeniably like her arrogant, suave Italian husband.

Her pulse went haywire as she finally spotted him.

Standing by the window, jacket discarded, sleeves rolled up, a glass of whiskey in his hand. He didn't seem surprised that she was standing there.

"You were at the gala, weren't you?" she demanded without preamble.

"Buonasera, cara."

The whiskey-deep timbre of his voice made her knees shake. "Answer my question, Renzo."

"Yes, I was there." He didn't turn to look at her, though. Instead, he swirled the amber liquid in his glass, exhaling slowly. As if he couldn't bear to meet her eyes. "Congratulations, *bella*. You were glowing up there. That quick speech you gave...everyone could hear your passion for what you do."

"What the hell kind of a game are you playing, Renzo? How long have you been in London?" Her voice cracked with betrayal. "You're toying with me, with my feelings."

Finally, he looked at her. His dark eyes were unreadable, and tension radiated from him. "I didn't mean to hurt you. Not today, not before."

She took a step closer, her heart slamming against her ribs. "So what? You were spying on me?"

"For what reason?" A flash of anger broke through the surface.

Mimi welcomed it. She hated it when he looked...tired. Or burnt out. Or as if he was losing a battle. Which was exactly how he had looked that night in their bedroom.

Ten odd days of distance from him, from her own confused thoughts, gave her crystal-clear clarity. There had been a kind of resignation when he talked about his family, but there had been acceptance too. Like setting down a burden that he had carried for so long. So, his unhappiness had been because of her? Because of where they stood with each other?

Should she have had more patience, more courage and faith in their relationship? In him and herself?

He'd even taunted that she was running away again. But she hadn't paid attention, miserable in her love for him.

How had she not even told him? How had she failed herself without even trying?

"I didn't want to ruin your moment," he said, bringing her to the present. "I didn't want to make it about us."

"Ruin it?" Her voice broke. And her self-control lay in shreds at her feet, knowing that it was her own fault for not verbalizing what she needed from him. For failing him and herself both. "Renzo, you being there was the only thing that would have made it feel real."

A muscle ticked in his jaw, but he said nothing.

She swallowed hard. "Why did you come? Why not tell me that you're here? Why…"

His eyes flickered, something raw passing through them. The intensity of it stole her anger and her words. "Because I'm a coward who's still trying to figure out how to tell you that I'm in love with you, *bella*."

The breath whooshed from her lungs, and she swayed on her feet, the entire day catching up with her.

Renzo set his glass down with a thud and caught her.

Renzo kicked the door of the bedroom shut behind him with a kick. Not that anyone from the staff would dare disturb them. But with Massimo around, he didn't want to take any chances.

He gently deposited Mimi on the bed and sat down by her side.

Like a prickly cat, she pushed away from his hold and scooted up to sit against the tufted headboard. The hem of the pink silk dress she wore bunched up against her knees and higher, exposing long, smooth limbs to his greedy eyes. The sweetheart neckline fought against the heaving thrust of her breasts, revealing the upper swells.

He gritted his teeth—it was hardly the time for him to drool over her—and met her gaze.

Color dusted her cheeks. Her hair, smooth and silky like a rainfall in the pitch-black of the night, danced around her bare shoulders. She looked…so beautiful that it was an ache to look at her and not touch her.

"Did you…" she licked her lower lip nervously "…say what I thought I heard?"

He nodded.

Tears filled her big brown eyes, overflowing instantly. "You're not playing with me?"

It cleaved him to see her so hurt, so disbelieving. "I've never said anything to you that I didn't mean, *bella*."

"But all those gifts…"

A self-deprecating laugh escaped him. "After that party, I realized I was already falling for you. Seeing Rosa…" he thrust a hand through his hair "…made me realize you were the only person in my life who didn't want my power or wealth or influence. I had nothing you could possibly want. So I decided, with my twisted logic, that I would drown you in so many lavish things that you would see the value of having me in your life."

"That *is* twisted," she said, honest to the last. "I wouldn't have minded those…gifts so much if you hadn't retreated from me. One minute, you're engraving yourself into my flesh, my heart, and the next, you're treating me as if I'm another burden you couldn't escape. You stopped teasing me, provoking me, touching me… I felt desolate."

"Not touch you?" Renzo said, shaking his head. "I couldn't keep my hands off you."

"Sex is not the only intimacy we shared. In fact, it was the last thing that fell into place. The grand finish that told me how perfect you are. But suddenly, outside of sex, you didn't…touch me at all. Here I was, sitting with the realization that I was in love with you, and you couldn't bear to look at me."

Renzo stilled. Every inch of his body pulled toward hers as if she were using her very own gravity on him. "You love me?"

She swiped at her tears with the backs of her hands. "It feels like forever already."

"Why didn't you tell me?" Even he could hear the awe in his tone.

"You know my mother and I have issues, right?"

He laughed at her dry tone.

"I know that your family and mine always seems to be front and center of our lives, but this is the last time I bring her or Pia up, I promise."

He took her hand in his and traced the knuckles gently. "I'll listen to whatever you tell me, *bella*. Especially if it means it will remove the shadows from your eyes."

"I…she raised me when she was single, and my deadbeat father had already fled. But she wasn't…the maternal sort. She loved her acting career the most, and I…" She swallowed and looked at her hands in her lap. "Even as a child, I hated being the center of attention. She wasn't cruel or negligent, Renzo. She was just…not overtly loving."

Renzo grabbed her tightly clasped hands and kissed each knuckle. "Stop excusing her behavior toward you, *bella*."

"I'm not. The last week I spent with her, I reexamined it all. With the perspective of an adult and as a new mother myself. She had no support of any kind, and she did her best. We would have muddled through somehow…"

"Except she married John, and Pia came into your lives."

Mimi laughed. The tip of her nose was red, and her eyes were still damp, but she was the most beautiful sight he had ever seen. "Pia..." she whispered and sighed. "I adored her from the beginning, you know. She was everything I wasn't. Beautiful, bright, witty...and petty and manipulative as hell."

Renzo laughed too.

"She and Mom got along like a house on fire from day one. I didn't mind it one bit. John was lovely and kind to me. Until Pia told me that he was her father and not mine, and she wasn't going to let me steal him from her. And yet I never doubted that she loved me too. She was the one who bought me my first camera, did you know?"

Renzo shook his head.

Mimi smiled. "I...see now that for all that she was, she was also very insecure. It made her needy and manipulative. She wanted Mom and John and even me all to herself. We weren't supposed to want or love each other or anyone else. But I didn't understand it as a teenager. When I..." her throat bobbed "...found her kissing my boyfriend, my best friend of years... I lost faith in myself. And yet I'm not sure if I would have believed her if she had told me that he had been hitting on her for a long while. She made me see the truth even though it broke my heart in the process."

"You're making her out to be better than she was, Mimi."

"No, I'm seeing her clearly for the first time. I'm seeing her not as this girl I desperately wanted to please and love, but as a whole person. I needed to sort this all out in my head, for myself, for Luca. I needed to realize that she loved me in her own way, and I loved her. Because one day, far into the future, I want to tell him about her and Santo. They deserved to be known to him, don't you think?"

His own eyes damp, Renzo nodded. How expansive and strong his fragile wife's heart was, and he had tried to buy his way into it.

"I had to see the past clearly for the last time, see how she and Mom shaped me, so that I can be free. And you…tasting what life could be like with you gave me the courage."

"Free for what, *bella*?"

"To dare to want you for myself, Renzo." Fresh tears drew tracks over her cheeks. "To have the courage to tell you that I fell in love with you, despite my every effort to resist you. I love you so much that it's like carrying around an ache. To trust in myself and you, enough to know that after helping me see myself in this new way, you love me too."

Nothing in the world would have stopped him then. Renzo climbed into the bed and pulled her to him.

Their kiss was salty and swift and clunky but *Cristo*, he didn't want to live another moment without tasting her. Without holding her.

He pressed her back into the bed and let her feel his weight, his need for her. He trailed frenzied kisses over her forehead, her eyes, her temples, her cheeks, and finally he found her lips again.

This time their kiss was soft, slow, even as her hands wandered restlessly over his back. "I love you, *cara mia*. With all my faulty heart. The idea of you leaving me at some vague point in the future twisted me out of my head. I… distanced myself from you because I knew I was failing. And all along, all I had to do was tell you that I love you."

"Please, never do that to me again. Never pull away after you've shown me what love can be, how colorful and happy I can be with you."

Renzo pressed their foreheads together, his own breath shallow now. "Never again, *bella*. You're mine. Your smart brain, your tart mouth, your curvy body, your generous heart, your sparkling soul…you are all mine, Mimi. And I'm never letting you out of my sight ever again."

* * *

It was a while later—although not too long, since Renzo had been in frenzied need—that they went to collect their son from John and her mother.

Legs thrown into his lap in the back seat of the Bentley, Mimi clung to her husband as he talked about how they would return to Venice that very night and celebrate Christmas by themselves.

No one was allowed to interrupt them, he decided.

"Maybe just Massimo?" she asked, knowing how attached her son was becoming to his uncle.

Renzo growled that he would not share her with anyone, not even his charming brother.

Mimi called him a jealous, overbearing brute, and he kissed her.

And she decided she didn't care how Renzo acted as long as he kissed her and held her and loved her like he did.

Like she was the sun, and the stars, and the sky all combined.

* * * * *

Were you blown away by the drama in
Baby Before Vows? *Then why not explore these other dazzling stories by Tara Pammi!*

Fiancée for the Cameras
Contractually Wed
Her Twin Secret
Vows to a King
His Forgotten Wife

Available now!

PREGNANT AND CONVENIENTLY WED

ROSIE MAXWELL

MILLS & BOON

CHAPTER ONE

THIS WAS THE part of the evening that Serena Addison loathed the most. The part when her friends went off in one direction and she had to go another.

Tonight, it was worse than usual because she wasn't just missing out on after-work drinks at the pub around the corner from where they worked in London, she was missing out on a once-in-a-lifetime experience in Singapore. Missing out on a nightclub that was not only the hottest club in the city, but one of the most talked about nightlife venues in the world right now. And she knew the soundtrack to tomorrow morning would be her friends excited chatter as they relived their exploits in annoyingly exhaustive detail, and she would have to listen and smile with interest, all the while pretending she wasn't seething that she was missing out yet again, hearing about their experiences instead of living her own. And that was so goddamned maddening, Serena wanted to scream with the force of her frustration.

'You could come with us, you know,' Evie, her closest friend, had whispered to her earlier. 'We're seven thousand miles away from London and from evil Marcia. She'll never know what you do tonight.'

It was tempting to believe that, but living in a world dominated by social media rendered those seven thousand miles meaningless, and Serena knew it. She had said as much to Evie too. It would take only one photograph of her drinking and dancing with her friends for her stepmother to follow through with the heinous threats she loved to issue and banish Serena from the family home and, even more devastatingly, sever her contact with her younger brother and sister, which as their adoptive mother she had every right to do. But that was not a price Serena was willing to pay.

Being separated from Kit and Alexis wasn't an option. It never had been. Having helped to take care of them from the first day of their lives after the heartbreaking loss of their mother during childbirth, their bond was far beyond that of normal siblings, and after the unexpected and upending death of their father almost six years ago, she was the only blood family they had. And they were hers, so it was imperative they stay together.

Not just because Serena grew heartsick at the thought of breaking the promise she had made to her mother during her pregnancy—that she would always be there for her younger siblings—but because she'd already endured all the loss she could stomach.

Her mum, then her dad and then the baby she'd been carrying when she was eighteen years old. She'd only been ten weeks pregnant and the situation had been far from ideal, especially after the boyfriend she'd thought she could count on had fled, but Serena had formed such a strong attachment to her pregnancy that the loss of it had been a body blow, and without loving parents there to support her, it had been the hardest loss by far. It was in that moment that she'd known she didn't want to endure any more of that pain and had vowed to never again put herself in the position where she would lose someone else.

But even knowing that didn't stop a hotter than usual frustration burning through her blood as she watched Evie and the other girls disappear into the glowing darkness of the nightclub. Didn't stop her heart from pounding with heavy, sickly thuds because she wanted so badly to be with them. To sip colourful cocktails and dance the night away. More than anything she wanted to have some fun and not spend another evening alone, excruciatingly aware of everything she was missing out on. But that was not an option. Not as long as she had her stepmother's beady eyes scrutinising her every move, she thought with a thick surge of resentment.

There had never been any closeness between them. In all the years of being in her life, her stepmother had never shown Serena a shred of love or support or understanding. Not even when her father had died, and definitely not even when she'd suffered her miscarriage. Bewildered as to what had happened and why, Serena had been desperate for a set of comforting arms to hold her and would have welcomed that even from her cold stepmother, but all she had offered was the unfeeling sentiment of *it's probably for the best,* as though Serena would have made a hopeless mother. She'd had to find the strength within herself to pick up the pieces and pull herself up, and she had, only for Marcia to strike again. Untrusting of Serena to not bring scandal and shame to their name again, she had stymied her plans, *dreams,* of attending art school. Serena knew she hadn't been an angel, especially not after her father had passed away and she'd sought escape from her grief in letting loose with her friends, but the punishment hardly seemed fair. Unless she'd wanted to lose Kit and Alexis, Serena's only choice was to endure it.

And endure it she had, along with all of Marcia's other ridiculous and oppressive rules, for five long years.

No revealing clothes. No late nights. No bars or night-clubs. No freedom. No fun. The list went on and on and on…

Although it had been worth it to remain close to Kit and Alexis, the sacrifices had never been easy, and lately Serena felt more exasperated than ever before with all the limitations, frustration bubbling away deep inside and pushing ever closer to the surface. More and more often she caught herself longing for the day when she would finally escape her stepmother's clutches and be free to live as she wanted.

Soon, Serena reminded herself on a steadying breath, because she could feel the aggravation building afresh. The twins would turn twelve on their next birthday, and with another year or two, when they had more autonomy over their lives and Marcia couldn't prevent them from seeing her, then she could seize and embrace her free-dom. But until then, she had to play by Marcia's rules. If she wanted to remain in Kit's and Alexis's lives, she had no other choice. And she'd survived all this time. She could put up with it for another few years. At least that was what she kept telling herself.

It wasn't as if it was all bad. Living within Marcia's tight boundaries had prevented her from getting close to anyone, from searching for love in the wrong place as she had done with Lucas. She had not been able to expose her-self to any more of the heartbreak and loss that had been delivered to her in two cruel blows—his desertion and then her miscarriage. For that, at least, she was grateful.

But they've stopped you from experiencing anything else either.

That thought sounded so loudly in her head that it inflamed every bad feeling she already had. Aware that she needed to act to keep her mood from plummeting any lower, Serena spun on her heel and started to walk purposefully towards the elevators, knowing exactly what she would do. If she was at home, she would lock herself away in her little attic annex and vent her frustration through creation, spewing her feelings across her canvases with thick, emotional sweeps of the bright oil paints she loved so much. That was how she had navigated the emotional quagmire of her father's sudden death and the loss of her baby. With no one other than Evie in her life to turn to—and Serena hadn't ever fully opened up to her about everything she'd been through—it was still the way she dealt with the onset of any hard emotions. But since she was unable to do that, she would go to the gym in her hotel instead and exercise out her rage. Lately boxing had become her workout of choice. She would punch the bag until her hair was damp and her arms were aching and her body was rid of the frustration weighing it down.

She'd only taken a few steps, however, when she crashed into something solid and, with a yelp of surprise, stumbled backwards. It was only the sudden grip of a strong arm around her waist preventing her from toppling backwards that made her realise it was a *someone* that she had crashed into.

'Oh, my goodness, I am so sorry. I wasn't focusing on where I was going and I...' As Serena lifted her head, the collision of her gaze with a set of smooth silvery-grey eyes drove the words she had been about to speak right out of her mind.

Her body quaked with the immediate attraction that pulsed sharp and hot behind her breastbone, and she found herself unable to stop the spread of pleasant heat across her cheeks. Powerless to do anything except stare up at the owner of those mesmerising eyes and as her gaze clung to his impressive features, her heart chimed once, twice, three times. Each strike was more forceful than the last, because he was without question, the most devastatingly sexy man she had ever set eyes upon.

The cut of his face was sharp and distinct and his chiselled features were tanned. His jaw was strong without being square and was dusted with a light stubble that he wore with style. His hair was cut close to his head and dark brows that were straight and imposing sat above those unusual, intriguing eyes of the softest grey. And Serena was intrigued, in a way she had not been in an awfully long time, and in a way that was threatening to set her ablaze right then and there.

There was a small siren of warning somewhere in her brain, instructing her to look away or, even better, to walk away, but she couldn't summon the necessary willpower to do either. And then he flashed a smile that had even more plumes of desire unfurling in her stomach. 'It's fine. I probably wasn't paying as much attention as I should have been to where I was walking either.'

As his accent—South African? Australian?—brushed across her senses and stirred them into an even more heightened state of awareness, Serena felt more colour bloom in her cheeks. It startled her, that heady rush of attraction for the second time in less than a minute because it had been so long since she'd felt anything that even remotely resembled desire, and she knew she really should look away before it wrote itself even more blatantly across her face and she thoroughly embarrassed herself. Only she couldn't. Because he was staring back at her just as intently and his magnetising gaze was holding her captive.

'That's kind of you to say, but I think we both know it was my fault,' she breathed out in a rush, as the heat clamouring beneath her skin intensified. 'Are you sure I didn't hurt you?'

'No damage at all.' His gaze made a quick yet thorough sweep over her face and he immediately spoke again. 'But I'd be happy to invent some minor injury as a pretext for you to stick around a little while longer.'

The irreverent suggestion had a smile tugging at Serena's lips. 'That would be a pretty shameless thing to do, don't you think?'

'Without a doubt.' His gaze grew even livelier, sparkling with a rich masculine appreciation that made Serena's breath catch and her pulse quicken. She couldn't remember the last time a member of the opposite sex had looked at her like that. She certainly hadn't been looking for it and would probably have run a mile had anyone shown a real interest, but every now and then that little boost to her confidence would have been welcome. Because underneath all of Marcia's rules it had been hard not to feel like she was fading, becoming invisible. Every time a set of eyes had bypassed her in her dark clothes and sparsely made-up face and locked onto Evie or one of the other girls, she'd felt it that bit more. But he was seeing her and liking what he saw. And that was more powerful, more disarming that she would have expected. 'But I don't mind engaging in some shameless behaviour every now and then, especially if it helps me to get what I want,' he confessed with a quirk of his lips that sent a charge zipping along her spine and made her wonder exactly what else his lips could do and how they would feel moving over her skin. The musing was as shocking as the warm ripples that moved through her in helpless response to it.

'And what is it that you want?' she asked, the flirtatious riposte falling from her lips before she could stop it.

Her heart rapped out another beat of warning, not that Serena needed it. She could feel herself edging closer to the dangerous territory that she normally avoided at all costs, but she couldn't seem to stop herself. Something about him was pulling her further and further in, encouraging everything she knew she shouldn't be feeling. Everything she hadn't wanted to feel since suffering her miscarriage, because she knew exactly where those feelings led. To pleasure, but also, potentially, to pain. The worst pain she'd ever known and never wanted to experience again.

'What I want,' he began, and his eyes as they swept over her again, were hot—shameless and decadent, 'is for you to have a drink with me.'

The thrill that streaked through her sent her pulse beating desperately against her skin, but she shook her head quickly, before her traitorous lips could strike again. 'I can't.'

'You can't?' His eyebrows arched, taken aback by her words. And she wasn't surprised. There was an aura of power about him, which suggested that he was unaccustomed to hearing the word *no* from anyone—in either a personal or professional capacity—but most especially from women.

She gave another shake of her head, her throat growing dry. 'I was actually just leaving to go back to my hotel. I had dinner with my friends and they headed into the club, but I have an early start. My boss likes a rundown of her daily schedule first thing in the morning and…'

He moved a step closer and Serena instantly fell silent. Her body started to hum as his grey eyes glowed down at her, glittering as if they'd been made from stardust. Their bodies were almost touching again, his tall and lean physique just a fingertip away, and she could detect the scent of his skin; hints of lemon and vanilla dancing beneath her nose, forcing her to take only the tiniest of breaths even though she wanted to take a deep inhale of him, to catch that scent and hold it close. Drown in it. 'One drink. I promise not to keep you out too late.'

Serena's throat dried even more, and the lowest part of her stomach tightened too, because that wasn't the only promise glittering in his eyes. There was heat and seduction swirling in them too and, God help her, Serena wanted to say yes. More than she'd ever wanted to say yes to anything.

It wasn't just that he was making her feel more than she'd felt in a long time, he was making her feel as she'd never felt before, all fizzed up inside like a shaken bottle of champagne. And she wanted more if it. She wanted more of this intoxicating and vibrant sense of being alive, of being on the edge of something unknown and exciting. She wanted to feel more of the delicious, dangerous heat that unravelled within her when his smoky eyes swept over her, more of the fierce beating of her pulse, the way he was making her feel beautiful and sexy and wanted when she so often felt the complete opposite.

But the consequences...

Drinks with handsome men with wicked smiles and sexy eyes were even more forbidden than nightclubs and short skirts, and should she find out, Marcia wouldn't hesitate to exact her punishment, and that awareness had Serena's heart fluttering fretfully. But even more frightening was the risk she'd be taking with her own body and heart if she did leap into that fire, as part of her very much wanted to. She had her own reasons for avoiding intimacy of any kind—because she didn't want to risk falling pregnant again. Even the thought of it was enough to crack her heart apart, and it was that fear which flowed through her blood, intensifying with every second.

The only thing Serena could do, what she *had* to do, was repeat her refusal. But then she imagined her handsome stranger tuning away and disappearing from her sight forever. A sense of lung-squeezing loss gripped her, and she knew that she couldn't say no.

Would there really be any harm in one drink with him? In letting herself, for a little while, enjoy an exhilarating flirtation with a very handsome man? It didn't need to go any further than that. And she was seven thousand miles away from home, after all. There was no reason for Marcia to ever know it happened. But Serena would. It would a be a break from her normal monotony, a delicious memory to tuck away and take out to look at on her loneliest and dreariest days, of which there were many.

'Alright, one drink,' she agreed, fireworks exploding in her stomach as she seized the moment and chose to forget, just this once and just for a little while, the many reasons why she absolutely shouldn't.

The first thought in Caleb Morgenthau's head when he looked down at the woman who had crashed into him was that she was beautiful. With red-gold hair falling in a gleaming wave down her back and the creamy complexion of her slender face that boasted prominent cheekbones and bright eyes, she was captivating. His second thought was to wonder if she had walked into him on purpose.

He'd known women to do far crazier things to get his attention. His third thought, hot on the heels of his second, was that he didn't really care whether the collision had been a construct on her part or an accident. The result remained the same. He was interested. Very much so. But having learned from past mistakes, Caleb was careful to only engage with women who had a similar mindset as his own, women uninterested in anything other than a night of pleasurable abandon, and before he took things any further, he needed to make sure she fit that mould.

He studied her with an assessing gaze and, reading the heat in the eyes that clung to him and sensing the same hunger for a night of uncomplicated pleasure beating through her blood, Caleb, to his delight, intuited there was no danger at all in indulging his temptation and invited her to join him for a drink. Her initial refusal didn't concern him—he'd never felt in any real danger of being rejected—and now he was leading her up to the rooftop lounge, where they would linger for one drink, maybe two, before hopefully ending the evening in his bed.

His mind was already racing ahead to that moment when he could slide the dress from her body and see the delights that lay beneath. He could picture her long red hair spilling across his pillows, her creamy skin glowing beneath the white fire of the moonlight as she stared up at him with breathless rapture while he brought her to orgasm over and over again. The sexy image had an irresistible anticipation roaring through his veins, unlike anything he'd felt for the longest time.

When was the last time he'd been so impatient for a woman? Lately his sexual encounters had become indistinguishable from one another, the experiences all shades of the same colour. But there was something about this woman whose name he didn't yet know. Something about the way her eyes had held his, how that slow curving smile seemed to hint at something different. Something unexpected. He felt drawn to her in a way he couldn't put words to.

He was so deep in his musings that it was only her small gasp of delight as they emerged on the rooftop that alerted him to their arrival.

'Wow. I thought the city was beautiful from down on the ground, but from here it's even more spectacular.' Her eyes swept side to side several times to take in the wonder of Singapore's glowing skyline; the pale lights of the business district and the colourful illuminations of the Gardens by the Bay. 'I'm surprised it's not busier up here though,' she commented, as he led her to a vacant table in the corner with views across the vibrant city. 'I thought the rooftop lounge was fully booked tonight. My friend, Evie, wanted to come up here for a drink before dinner and was so disappointed when we couldn't get in.'

'This is the members-only rooftop lounge,' Caleb informed her as a waiter arrived at their table with two flutes of champagne, depositing one in front of each of them. 'It's solely for VIP guests.'

Her eyes went round with surprise, looking first at him and then around the intimately lit surroundings. The tables were well spaced out, and many of them were occupied with parties of varying sizes. He watched her eyes pop with shocked recognition as she spotted the cluster of Hollywood superstars sitting with minor members of the British Royal Family and then graze the world-renowned tennis champion at the table behind, celebrating his latest championship title.

'Well, I certainly feel foolish for not having realised that

before now.' She reached for her glass and was halfway
to lifting it to her full pink lips when she froze, her eyes
turning back to him. 'That makes you a VIP guest too?'

'Technically I'm the owner.' He held out his hand,
seeing further surprise abound through her expression.
'Caleb Morgenthau.'

It was a novel experience for him to not be known. In
Australia, the Morgenthau name was widely recognised,
and as the son of such a professionally prominent and socially powerful father, Caleb's profile had always been
high. His personal business success, along with his unat-
tainable, untameable bachelor status, had generated even
greater attention around him, attention that followed him
wherever he went, and six months of living in Singapore
hadn't changed that. He knew women were often drawn
to him because of that notoriety. It didn't bother him. He
wasn't looking for anything to last longer than a night, so
the motives of the women who sought him out were imma-
terial, but it was refreshing to know that it hadn't played
any part in her interest and that she was there for the same
reasons as him—pure physical and sexual attraction.

Slowly, almost shyly, she slid her fingers against his,
and the feeling of her soft, delicate hand encased in his
had the strongest sensations rippling across his skin. Her
skin was as smooth and warm as he had imagined and
the desire to touch more of her flared through him like
a rocket, because her hand fit so seamlessly inside of
his that he knew their bodies would lock together just as
perfectly, as if they were connecting pieces of a jigsaw
puzzle. 'Serena Addison.'

Beneath his fingertips her pulse fluttered at twice the
normal speed and that same explosion of feeling was mirrored in the eyes that boldly held his gaze.

'Serena,' he repeated, liking how the syllables rolled around his mouth. It was a name he wanted to say again and again and again. 'That's beautiful. It suits you.'

'Thank you.' Their eyes continued to hold in a way that had Caleb's blood thickening and a series of low throbs beating pleasantly in his groin. 'My mother was Italian, and even though she married an Englishman and settled in England, she wanted to honour her heritage with the name that she gave me.'

As Serena spoke, she rearranged her legs in front of her, drawing Caleb's eyes down to their spectacular slim shape and length, and he couldn't keep himself from imagining them curled around his waist. They were the only part of her body that her silky navy dress show-cased, but she was definitely right to show them off. It took a giant surge of willpower to angle his gaze away from them quickly.

'Italian?' he asked, reaching for his own glass and taking a sip to moisten his mouth, because even by his standards, it was too soon to start taking it further yet. 'Do you spend much time in Italy?'

She gave a light shake of her head. 'No. I haven't been there in a long time.'

'How come?'

'There aren't many reasons to. My mother left the country because she had didn't have any family left there and wanted a fresh start. We used to visit when I was younger, but she passed away when I was twelve and I've never been back.'

She made that final admission quickly, as though it caused her physical pain to speak that fact aloud, and Caleb could hear her sadness and the loss she felt. It changed the tenor of her voice, momentarily casting a shadow across her beautiful face, and he found himself longing to reach out and smooth it away, which surprised him as he wasn't usually given to such tender impulses. But he was familiar with the deep ache of not having a mother. For Serena, however, to have lost her mother after knowing her and being loved by her...well, that was a cruelty he couldn't speak to. His mother had absconded before Caleb could even begin to remember her, and a person couldn't miss what they'd never had, could they? At least, that was what he always told himself in the moments he caught himself approaching some form of pathetic, melancholic sentimentality.

'It's a shame that you lost her at such a young age,' Caleb sympathised, focusing on Serena instead of the dart of poisonous feeling arrowing across his chest that accompanied any consideration of the woman who'd given him life. The woman whose decision to leave and never return had carved a void in him that had never been filled and created a wedge between him and his father that was yet to be bridged.

'It is. She was a very vibrant character and a lot of fun, so her loss left a big void.' Sadness haunted the rim of her eyes as she continued, 'But it's much worse for my younger brother and sister. They never even had the chance to know her. I, at least, have my memories.' Her eyes grew wet and she blinked rapidly, angling her face away. 'I'm sorry. I don't know why I'm getting emotional. This is terrible drinks conversation.'

'It's fine conversation.' Gently placing a finger under her chin, he turned her face back to his, but the sparks that ignited from that brief moment of contact seemed to still them both, their gazes meeting and holding, the air seeming to charge as they did. 'You have nothing to apologise for.'

With a swipe of her inky lashes, she banished the sadness from her eyes and smiled again, a smile of determination. 'Your turn now, Caleb Morgenthau. Tell me about you,' she invited, leaning her head on her hand and looking at him through such bright eyes and with such a soft smile that he was captivated all over again, and he found himself leaning in to her as close as possible, as if being pulled by some invisible thread.

'What would you like to know?'

'You're Australian, yes?' At his nod of confirmation, she smiled. 'Whereabouts in Australia is home?'

'I was born and raised in Melbourne, but nowadays home is wherever I'm establishing a new venue. In the last few years, I've lived in Sydney, Bali, Hong Kong and here in Singapore.'

'You have places like this in all those cities?' she asked, looking more than a little impressed.

'Not exactly like this, but yes. And few more besides.' Caleb grinned. 'Now that this place is running successfully and there's a good management team in place, the next stop is Europe. After that, the plan is to expand into North America.'

'So, you're looking to conquer the world?'

'Perhaps I am.' He smiled, but in that moment, he was far more interested in conquering her. Taking her over kiss by kiss, touch by touch, until she was completely and undeniably his.

The smile dancing at the corners of her mouth made him think she knew exactly what he was thinking, that she was thinking it too. She took another sip of her champagne. 'Where are you opening in Europe?'

'Saint-Tropez. Mykonos. Rome and London,' he answered, waiting for the hint to be dropped that she would love to visit those venues and pleasantly surprised when it didn't. Usually, the women he met couldn't wait to exploit the connection for access to his luxurious nightlife experiences.

Instead, her eyes shone. 'You're so lucky. Getting to live and work in all those different places.' Wistfulness infused her words and made him think of his younger self, of the days that he'd spent chafing at the ties that bound him, dreaming of an escape, of freedom, and he wondered what it was that she was dreaming of escaping. Responsibilities at home perhaps? She had mentioned having younger siblings. 'Was this what you always wanted to do?'

'I wouldn't exactly say that,' he admitted with a wry smile. 'It's an inherited family business. My grandfather owned a small restaurant in Melbourne fifty years ago. My father joined the business at sixteen and when he eventually took over, he expanded across the state. By the time I was growing up, we had places in every major city across Australia and it was just expected that I would join the business and one day take over. I was never asked if it was what I wanted to do, and I struggled with that choice of how I wanted to live my life being essentially taken from me. I felt...' Caleb searched for the best way to describe it, even though he had never been good at drawing feelings out of himself or putting his emotions into words. He had figured out at a young age that it was better to bury whatever he felt, rather than be consumed by it.

'Boxed in,' Serena supplied knowingly, and it took him aback that she could so easily identify what he had felt. As if she too knew that feeling. As if they were connected.

'Yes. Exactly,' he breathed, staring at her with a strange lump forming in his throat, because when had he ever felt such a strong bond of kindship with anyone else, especially a woman?

Was that what had compelled him to share so much in that moment, when expressing his feelings quite so openly about anything wasn't something he ever did. He was certainly asked his fair share of probing questions, but Caleb always denied the requests to drill into his life, holding everyone, especially women, at arm's length. Life, he'd learned, was safer that way. Tidier.

'I get it. Having your life mapped out for you before you have the chance to claim it as your own is not easy.' Something moved in her eyes that told of her own experience with that, and he felt his breath catch again, the same strange feeling hooking in his chest. 'But you obviously managed to get past it somehow?'

'Eventually I realised I was lucky to be part of something, to be part of that legacy and that it was time I started contributing to it. And I knew how much it meant to my father too, to have me be part of it.'

'Both he and your grandfather must be incredibly proud of all you're achieving.'

'I think my father would be happier if I slowed down long enough to have a family and provide the next generation of Morgenthaus, but since that's not going to happen, he'll have to be content with global expansion.'

Caleb couldn't fathom where those words had come from either, other than his earlier conversation with his father was still playing on his mind. It was the same discussion they'd had a dozen times already—his father exerting paternal pressure on him to fulfil the rest of his obligation and provide heirs to continue the family legacy—and it had ended the same as every other time, in a stony stalemate. His father didn't want to hear his refusals, and Caleb wasn't willing to offer the reasoning behind his unyielding stance. The events, scorched into his brain, were not moments of his life he had any interest in talking about, especially not with his father. They had never been close like that, not after his father had spent the majority of Caleb's formative years battling his heartache over his wife's desertion and finding solace in burying himself in work and never in his son—the son he held responsible for that loss.

'You're don't plan on getting married and having a family?' Serena queried.

'No. I like my life as it is. I have no desire to change it,' he answered, with a frankness that left no room for doubt. He liked to always have those cards face up on the table so any woman who crossed his path knew what to expect. And what *not* to expect. That was key. Not that it was necessary, not when he was so careful to only entertain women on the same page as him. 'Now, I think it's your turn again,' Caleb said, his eyes mapping the striking planes of her face. 'Tell me what brought you to Singapore?'

'Work. My boss is looking to expand her overseas business, so we're here, taking lots of meetings and exploring new opportunities.'

'Do you like your job?'

She nodded impassively. 'I've been doing it for a few years.'

He smiled, recognising avoidance when he saw it. 'That isn't what I asked.'

She sighed, funnelling her fingers through her hair and releasing the sweetest scent into the air between them.

It quickened Caleb's heart and caused his pulse to thud with even more eagerness. He wanted to bury his face in that scent, in her neck and her hair. 'If you're asking if I dreamed of being an executive assistant as a little girl, then no.'

'Why didn't you pursue your dream?' She didn't seem like someone lacking in courage or confidence, so he was curious as to why she had settled for something she didn't want.

More curiosity, Caleb. Really?

It was unusual for him, he had to admit, but he couldn't help it.

A sadness, or perhaps a weariness, came into her eyes, and she momentarily turned her gaze away, looking off into the starry sky. 'I kind of got boxed in too.' It was then that he saw it flash in her eyes, everything he had once felt. The constraint, the powerlessness, the frustration.

'By what?'

She shook her head gently. 'It's really too long of a story to go into,' she murmured, drawing her eyes down and away from his, and when she looked back at him, they had shuttered, and he didn't like that at all. 'And I think it's time I should be going anyway.'

The words caught him off guard. She wanted to leave? 'You should?'

'Yes. I said one drink and that drink is finished. Thank you. It was nice meeting you, Caleb.'

Caleb stared at her as she got to her feet, a slight frown pinching between his brows. Women had walked away from him before. Not often, but it had happened. He'd never been all that bothered. There were always other women. But he was bothered now, watching her prepare to leave with a rapidly beating heart. Because she was beautiful and he wanted to take her, yes. But, also, because he wanted to know more of her. Because the past while with her was the most connected he'd felt to another person in a long time. It wasn't a feeling Caleb had been seeking, or that he had ever sought, nor was it something that he'd particularly felt he was missing because he knew the chaos that emotional connections caused. Yet in spite of how strange it felt pulsing within his chest and how worryingly out of character that was, he wasn't ready to let it go.

And where was the harm in indulging it for a little while longer? It wouldn't linger. His interest never did.

'Are you sure you can't stay another while?'

Serena swallowed the emotion at the back of her throat. Was she sure? No, she wasn't.

She knew she couldn't stay, that she needed to leave. Not just because of Marcia, but because the more they talked and shared and the longer she lingered in his sphere of dominance, spellbound by his glittering eyes and undeniable charm, the greater was the temptation to throw caution to the wind, let all else drift from her mind and into the starry stratosphere above and give in to what she wanted.

Him.

To let herself, for one night, be and feel without restraint. Without *fear*. Her defences had already melted away and she could feel the tendrils of temptation stroking, beckoning. She was only a single step away from crossing that all-important line and diving head first into reckless abandon, and goodness knew where that would lead her this time. It wasn't as though Caleb was offering anything; on the contrary, he'd made it clear he wasn't looking for anything serious or permanent. It was a risk that she just couldn't take. So, leaving was imperative.

Yet the compulsion to stay was just as strong. Every cell in her body longed to sit back down and bask under his attention, the delight of being seen and considered. Being visible. And it wasn't as though Serena wanted a promise of something more, or would even believe it if one was made, not with the memory of Lucas's flimsy promises still strong in her mind. But she did want Caleb, and whatever sense and strength she had found to stick to her original promise of leaving after one drink was fading under that beseeching look in his eyes that whispered her agreeing to stay would make his every dream come true.

She'd never felt so torn in two, as if there was no wrong answer, rightness in both choices, staying and leaving.

'I'm sure,' she said on a deep breath, feeling the crash of relief and disappointment.

He nodded, something that looked a lot like disappointment flaring in his eyes. Seeing how he felt about her, when he could have any woman he wanted, made her heart sigh. 'I'll come down to the lobby with you. Arrange a car to take you back to your hotel.'

Serena waved away the offer, certain than every extra second spent with this man was a moment that threatened to change her mind. 'You don't need to do that.'

'I want to,' he insisted, placing a hand at the small of her back as he walked her towards the elevator. He wasn't actually touching her and yet Serena's skin burned as if he was. *Imagine how good it would feel if he did actually touch you.* She chased the dangerous thought from her mind. She'd made her decision, the safe and smart one. 'You're alone and don't know your way around the city, and I'll spend all night worrying about you otherwise.'

Serena quite liked the thought of him spending all night dwelling on her. It would mean she wasn't alone in brooding over him, because she knew that was what was going to happen. She would relive her encounter with him over again, fall asleep dreaming of him, dreams that would no doubt leave her hot and achy.

'If you insist,' she acquiesced, praying the ride down would be fast because her mind was already starting to swim with the potency of his scent.

But as they stepped inside, it was even worse than she had feared. Trapped in such a small, enclosed space, with the scent of him infusing every breath she took, her heart went berserk. Racing. Leaping. *Wanting.* Serena fixed her eyes to the floor, reminding herself of all the reasons why she couldn't. Mustn't. But the heat bubbling beneath her skin continued to soar because he was so close, close enough that she could reach out and touch him.

Suddenly the lights flickered and the car jolted so violently that Serena lost her balance and tumbled into Caleb. He caught her, preventing her from falling any further with the solid wall of his chest and by securing his arms around her waist. His hold tightened as they jolted again, and this time Serena couldn't keep the gasp of alarm from squeaking from her mouth. Caleb pulled her even more securely against his body.

The lights snapped back on and the car steadied. Still holding her, Caleb looked down at her, concern written across his face. 'Are you OK?'

She nodded, her heart in her throat. 'Yes. What was that?'

'A power surge, most likely. Are you sure you're OK?'

She could only nod, words deserting her again as those silver eyes glowed down at her and she became aware that the throb of fear that her life was going to end was ebbing away and being replaced by a different, more pleasant and intoxicating throb, emanating from where his fingers were warm and firm against her body. Her heart rapped out a fast tattoo of warning. *Tell him he can let go of you now.* But Serena's lips wouldn't move, and the words wouldn't materialise. Because she didn't, in her heart, want him to let her go. She liked how it felt being held in his arms, liked the heady vibration of her heart and her blood. All of the feeling that had been jostling in her begged for release even more desperately and before she was even really aware of what she was doing, before she could summon the sense or power to stop herself, Serena was pressing to her tiptoes and reaching for his mouth. *Just one kiss*, she promised herself, *just so I know how it feels, and then I'll stop.*

One kiss, however, was all it took to ignite an even more ferocious fire in her blood. The press of Caleb's mouth vibrated through her whole body, unlocking the bars around those feelings so they flowed free and unchecked for the first time in so, so long—rivulets of pure, potent, sparkling sensation streaming upwards and outwards and in every other direction as he kissed her back with such exquisite tenderness and skill that Serena thought she might die of pleasure. *And wouldn't that be a perfect way to go*, she thought, feeling so replete and yet hungry for so much more that she consented to a second swipe of his lips, and then another, and by that time she was sliding her arms up to loop around his neck, securing herself to him, and any thought of stopping was obliterated from her mind entirely.

CHAPTER TWO

SERENA'S MOUTH TASTED even better than he'd thought it would. Sweet, like honey. So sweet it was quickly becoming addictive, and Caleb knew that for the rest of his life he'd never again be able to enjoy the nectar without thinking of her and that moment, the eagerness of her mouth beneath his and her yielding body.

Her lips parted beneath his and he didn't waste a second seizing that opportunity to slide his tongue into the wet heat of her mouth and back her up against the wall of the elevator. The spread of heat through his body, sure and sexy, inflamed in intensity, and sent a heavy beat drumming through his blood. Kissing her, being kissed by her was the most pleasurable assault he'd ever known, and for all that Caleb was used to this interplay between male and female—the warm scent of a woman's skin, the soft noises of assent and delight, the press of the feminine shape—with her it all felt new. Thrilling. A dream he wanted to sink even deeper into.

Maybe it was the way she responded to each sweep of his hands, as if his touch was electrifying her. Or maybe it was the way her shape fitted so sleekly against his, as though their bodies had been cut from a shared mould. Destined for one another.

It was a ridiculous thought, and not one that he would

have countenanced in any other moment, but right then and there, being driven crazy by the duelling desires to savour and devour her, it seemed to make perfect sense, to explain this new vortex of sexual potency he was being sucked into. Serena was his match, her body made explicitly for his, designed to draw from him all that he could offer and to receive a pleasure that only he could deliver.

Trailing a line of fire down her neck, Caleb didn't stop until he located the spot of her hammering pulse. As he settled his mouth on that spot, the taste of her skin driving him as high as the play of his lips was sending her, that scorching convergence wound a new blistering heat around them, binding them together even more strongly.

Lifting her leg, she curled it around his thigh, and his erection, already painfully tight, throbbed at the explicit invitation, at how beautifully his pelvis nestled against the heart of her. Caleb responded instinctively, pressing even harder against her and, driven by the need to feel all of her, to take her to the highest possible peak of pleasure, slid his hand along the smooth skin of her thigh. Eager to see her bright eyes shatter with delight, to see her pleasure wash over her, his fingers ventured higher until the slight quiver of her flesh stirred an awareness that should have surfaced prior to that moment.

Because whilst he was in no doubt as to what he wanted, could Serena say the same? Mere moments ago, she'd been set on leaving, and had the jolt of the elevator not thrown her into his arms, she'd likely already be gone. And he would have let her go. He'd never had to plead with a woman to go to bed with him and never would. Nor was he a man who'd take advantage of a woman who was carried away.

'What is it? What's wrong?' she asked, her lips beautifully swollen and hair mussed from where his hands had tangled in its glossy lengths.

'Nothing. You're perfect,' he said quickly to erase that flash of insecurity in her eyes. 'And I would gladly whisk you to my suite to continue this, but I don't want you to feel that has to happen. You can still leave. I want you to be sure this is what you want too.'

Her hands were resting against his jacket, and as she smiled, they curled into the fabric, ready to pull him closer. 'I'm sure,' she replied quickly.

Too quickly? But whilst a sense continued to whisper through his mind that perhaps he should put a stop to it anyway, his body was more than convinced, his hand swiping the control panel with his access card to get them to his suite as his mouth reclaimed hers with a hunger that continued to transcend all he had ever felt before. A want that was feeling more and more like need.

Compelling, desperate, irresistible, insatiable need.

Serena was relieved when Caleb lifted her into his arms and carried her from the elevator, because she didn't know how much longer she'd be able to remain standing upright, not when every single inch of her body was trembling. Every touch, every kiss was penetrating so deeply, if felt as if her soul was shaking too.

He had asked her if she was sure, and with feeling as powerful as that, snaking and curling through her, how could she be anything but sure?

Her world had narrowed to him, to the feelings he'd set spinning inside her. The life she had known before this evening, before him, had faded, retreating from her mind almost entirely, pushed aside to make room for all this glorious newness. She knew, however, that she had never done anything like this before, never been tempted into being ravished in an elevator, to letting a man she hadn't known before that night slide his hand between her legs. But that didn't seem to matter. There was no longer a single doubt in her heart or her head. Any reservations had been burned away by the fire blazing between them, and for this one night she would ignore what she should do and do what she wanted. Take what she craved. Needed.

There would be slowing, no stopping. She wanted the opposite. She wanted more.

As if reading that wish, Caleb's kisses grew less restrained—not that they had been restrained before—but as he lowered her to the bed, pressing her back into the covers with his weight, it was as if there was a new urgency driving him. An even deeper hunger opening up inside of him.

Serena felt it too; her body was achy and hot and only growing hotter. Restless. She'd never known a feeling like it, a desperation so pure she wasn't sure how she could stand it. Her hands went to his chest, her fingers scrabbling with the tiny buttons of his shirt, impatient to bare the hard chest beneath, and she felt his lips curve at her hurried fumbling, enjoying it. His hands were far more skilled, pushing up her dress, curling into the thin band of her knickers and sliding them down her legs to the floor in one easy move.

If there was a moment for Serena to be beset by any kind of uncertainty or hesitation, that was probably it, but, for one of the only times in her whole life, she was being ruled by impulse and impulse alone. She was trapped in the eye of a wild, heady storm, and it felt exactly right.

This moment, this place, this man. It felt more right than anything had in a long time. Perhaps ever.

Locating the hidden fastening on her dress, Caleb nudged the fabric apart, a hiss emerging from between his teeth as first his eyes and then his mouth made contact with her breasts. He kissed the top of them, before dragging one lacy cup down and fastening his mouth around the nipple, laving it with his tongue until she was arching beneath him.

Nothing had ever come close to what he was making her feel, and Serena throbbed with all the glorious, pounding sensations, a restless tattoo inside her that she had never experienced before but could suddenly feel everywhere, and she arched upwards again, pressing against him.

Seeming to know exactly what she was asking for, exactly where and how she needed to be caressed, Caleb slipped his hand between their bodies, sending his fingers straight to the pulsing heart of her. That first stroke of his finger to the taut cluster of nerves zagged through her like lightning, jolting her, blinding her. Even as she cried out, he didn't stop, touching her with the perfect amount of pressure to undo her even further. He whispered words to her, words she didn't hear as she rose and fell with the ministrations of his hand, her breath so close to dying altogether. And then she was crying out again, whispering his name, begging him to stop and not stop in the same breath, as her body was rocked by one long explosion.

Immediately she wanted more. She reached for his trousers, unfastening them, and together she and Caleb pushed them down his legs. For a second, she allowed her eyes to indulge in the beauty of his naked body, but only for a second, because her hunger was too relentless to be paused for long.

'Do you have a condom?' she gasped, and he nodded surely, having already reached for his wallet from the floor. Tearing open the small foil packet with his teeth, he rolled it along his length, his hands not entirely steady, and Serena was so filled with anticipation she could barely breathe.

He covered her again, the eyes holding hers alight with pewter sparks as he nudged her entrance. That brief flicker of contact had her arching, ready to accept him, and as she did, Caleb thrust smoothly into her. Whatever tightness or strangeness there was lasted only the barest of seconds before she was filled with an overpowering sense of completion and connection. Caleb growled out a noise of contentment, shuddering from deep within his chest, and it was enormously gratifying that it felt as good for him as it did for her.

With each thrust he seemed to take pride in taking even deeper possession of her, drawing out each movement to maximise every drop of pleasure and to send the sweetness surging to the tips of her extremities.

With every thought that she was capable of, which wasn't much, Serena thought it couldn't get any better, only it did. As he hitched her leg up to lock around his waist and claimed her lips, he drove into her with a surge of such desire that her hands clawed down his back, needing to remain anchored to something because she could feel everything—her sense of self and life—shattering around her. And then she was gone, soaring past pleasure, past sanity, past all she'd believed was possible and landing in the abyss. Only it wasn't dark and lonely; it was a bright, sparkling land where pleasure followed pleasure and for the longest time she drifted, floating amongst those beautiful, starry sensations.

But then those quakes of delight began to ebb away and the stars started to fade and everything that had been shunted aside by the needy impulses that had flowered so powerfully, so violently, inside of her, rushed back.

Slowly, so slowly it felt a hundred times worse, it dawned on her the risks she had taken, the jeopardy she had put herself in, her body and her heart. It settled over her like a chill. Horror bottlenecked her throat, and the thuds of her heart echoed like crashes of doom.

There was only one thing she could do, and it was what she should have done long before now—get out of there as fast as she could.

Caleb was still riding the wave, his breath burning his lungs and his body feeling as though it had been struck by a supercharged bolt of lightning. He'd always enjoyed sex but nothing before had ever come close to that. He wanted to savour it, bask in each and every sensation rippling through his body, but he was also greedy to start all over again. The night was long, but nowhere near long enough for him to enjoy and explore Serena in all the ways he was already vividly—very vividly—imagining before they had to go their separate ways.

Feeling the mattress shift, he turned his head to the side, frowning when he saw that she was sitting up and covering her lovely body with her dress.

'Are you OK?'

'Yes,' she replied, too fast and in an octave too high for her voice, so that he was instantly alert. 'I just need to leave.'

'Is something wrong?' Concern launched him into a sitting position so he could see her better.

'No. I just… I should get back to my hotel. I shouldn't be here.' Those words sounded all wrong, especially as it was his view that she was exactly where she should be and where he wanted her to spend the rest of the night. He was on the verge of reaching out to her when she bolted off the bed, practically running to the door of his bedroom without looking at him once, and he was sure he heard her say *I shouldn't have done this.*

'Serena?' he called after her, his chest thumping hard with emotion he couldn't fully comprehend.

His brain whirring with confusion, Caleb searched the floor. Locating his trousers where they'd been hastily discarded, he pulled them on and followed her into the suites living space, where she located her bag and then turned so hastily for the elevator that she nearly knocked into an end table. Caleb hurried to intercept her, catching her arm. 'Serena, stop.'

He spun her around to face him, and as her face lifted to his, he saw the panic darting through her eyes, but it was the unshed tears that triggered his own awareness and it hit him like a punch to the gut.

He only had one rule and he had just broken it.

He released her arm, scalded as much by the force of his own feelings as he was by the look on her face. The horror surging through his bloodstream thickened until it felt as if it would clog his veins and his lungs, even his throat. His heart pounded in his ears, a torrid drumbeat of sound before he ordered himself to take a breath, and then another, so that his voice would be somewhat steady when he spoke. Because he had to speak. He had to ask the question. As much as he didn't want to breathe any more life into this nightmare, he needed to know. 'You don't normally do anything like this, do you?' he demanded, his voice not without sympathy because he could see that she was as out of her depth as him. Just for a very different reason.

Her throat quivered. 'Anything like what?' she asked, bravely lifting her head to meet his eyes.

The answering look he sent her was piercing, but she didn't flinch. 'Going back to a hotel room with a man you just met and having sex with him?' He snapped the words out, as with each second his patience was fraying too much to keep his tone measured, and her skin turned an even paler shade of white.

She swallowed, making him wait before she answered. 'No.'

'Never?' he demanded, hoping that maybe she wasn't as innocent as his worst thoughts were telling him.

'Never,' she clarified, spitting out the word as though it had refused to come willingly, the last thing she wanted to admit.

Her face faded from his view. All he could see was bright red flashing lights of alarm, feel panic surrounding him like cement walls closing in. He had his rules for a reason, and he abided by them for a reason. Because he didn't ever want to hurt a woman the way he had hurt Charlotte.

She hadn't been one of his usual carefree, sophisticated lovers either, but he hadn't cared about that when he'd brought her into his life. He'd wanted her and had pursued her with no thought for those differences, never thinking that perhaps their affair had greater meaning to her than it did to him. Never caring enough to find out.

And he had devastated her in ways that were carved into his mind—the memories a stain that would never fade.

That was why he only engaged with women like him now, women who understood how he operated. Women who he couldn't devastate, because the only thing they wanted from him was something he was more than willing to give. Pleasure. Distraction. He had thought Serena was, or had he just wanted to believe that because of how urgently he'd wanted her from that first moment? Had the signs been there and he just hadn't wanted to acknowledge them? He feared so. He had wanted her too much. And that was unforgivable.

'You weren't…' His voice deserted him, the thought that had just occurred to him out of nowhere ripping the breath from his lungs. 'Please tell me this wasn't your first time,' he pleaded, because taking an innocent would be too much.

'What does that have to do with anything?' she demanded on a breath that managed to be both anguished and furious.

'Answer the question.'

Their gazes warred. His desperate. Hers blistering with reproach. 'No,' she finally snapped. 'I wasn't a virgin.'

'That's something at least,' he breathed, a fraction of the two-tonne weight lifting from his chest. 'But, regardless, you are right—this shouldn't have happened. You should not be here right now.' Her gaze reflected pain and anger at receiving those words, but he didn't allow himself to feel bad. She needed to understand so that she didn't walk away with any hope that this meant more than what it had been. Or that he was someone he wasn't. 'It's my fault, not yours. I should have…' *Been more careful. Stopped. Heeded my thoughts.* He should have done all of the above, but what was the use of going backwards? Nothing he said or did now could change what had happened. He had learned that lesson the hard way a long time ago. 'I'm sorry. I'll have a car pick you up downstairs and drive you back to your hotel.' What *you should have done an hour ago.*

Serena barely managed a nod, her mouth tight, her eyes focused on the floor rather than him and her arms wound tightly across her chest as she walked to the elevator. It was a desolate sight, and one that nipped at his insides for reasons that he had no interest in unravelling. 'I'm not trying to be cruel, Serena. But I don't…the women I usually take to bed are more experienced, more like me. They are as uninterested in a relationship as I am. They understand…'

She stepped hastily into the elevator as it arrived, lifting her head at last and spearing him with the sudden angry flash of her amber eyes. 'You can save the speech, Caleb. I understand perfectly well that this was just a one-night thing, and as hard as you may find it to believe, I wasn't looking for it to be anything more than a brief interlude. So, you have nothing to worry about. I get it loud and clear that you're only interested in bedding and forgetting women, and since you've already successfully completed the first part, now you can start on the forgetting part. That's exactly what I'm planning to do.'

Her words rooted him to the spot. The truth was his sexual encounters didn't take up any space in his mind, and it didn't bother him in the slightest if the women he'd slept with never thought of him again, so why did hearing Serena say that she would forget him make him clench with anger, make him want to reach out, take her in his arms and force her to take the words back? And why as the doors of the elevator slid to a soundless close and whisked her out of his life for good, was he left with the searing feeling in his chest that he was losing something, when she'd never been his to begin with?

CHAPTER THREE

SO MUCH FOR forgetting that night had ever happened, Serena thought eight weeks later, the heavy bumps of her heart echoing all the way up in her throat as the small strip in the centre of the plastic white stick she held in her trembling hand turned a bright and unmistakable pink.

She swallowed, the panic that she had so far managed to hold at bay erupting in her chest as the truth sank through her like a chill. *Pregnant.*

She'd been feeling unwell for weeks now, but had attributed it to the stomach virus running rampant through her office. Even as those around her had recovered within a week, Serena had clung to that explanation, willing it to be that simple, because the thought that the universe had dealt her the fate she most feared after a single act of intimacy in five years was too much to bear.

She hadn't thought about that night since. She hadn't wanted to remember the humiliation as Caleb had probed her level of sexual history, or the sting of rejection as he'd dismissed the night as a mistake because of her lack of experience, and it had seemed safer to not recall how heavenly it had felt in his arms. She had just put it from her mind and continued on as though it hadn't happened.

But now...

Dropping her head into her hands, Serena cursed herself for stupidly believing that she could seize that one night of pleasure and not suffer any consequences. Life had never been that kind to her, and now that uncharacteristic moment of abandon had invited the past to repeat itself with a pregnancy that she was terrified to want in case it all went heartbreakingly wrong again and she was left to lament her failure once more. Because the miscarriage had to have been her fault, didn't it? Something she had done or had failed to do? That was the only option. The doctors hadn't been able to provide any other definite answer.

Serena had still been reeling from the shock of discovering that she was pregnant and the agony that her boyfriend had deserted her within twenty-four hours of learning the news, when she had miscarried. Knowing that something was wrong, that the sharp pains stabbing her stomach were abnormal but that there was nothing she could do to stop it had been excruciating. It had been one of the worst moments of her life when the sombre-faced doctor had entered the room and explained to her what was happening—having to contend with yet another loss and to do so without anyone there to support her. But like everything else she had been through, Serena had survived and it had made her stronger. Helped her to learn to stand on her own two feet and rely on herself for support and salvation. She would need all of that and more now.

She would find no grace or support from her stepmother. All she had proven was that Marcia's accusations and criticisms of impulsivity and carelessness were spot on, and more than anything that was a vindication she couldn't bear giving the older woman. But she would have to, wouldn't she? Her stepmother made it her business to know everything, and by Serena's reckoning she was nearly eight weeks pregnant. She'd thrown up every day for the past fortnight. How long before her stepmother put the pieces together? And when she did, Serena knew what would happen. Marcia had been horrified by the scandal of her first pregnancy and, fearing for her own reputation, had made it clear that Serena and her illegitimate child were not welcome in her home. This time would be no different.

For a moment Serena was paralysed by the familiar feeling of powerlessness, of life being swept out of her control again, and she had to remind herself that she wasn't a child this time, nor was she helpless. She would be fine on her own. Emotionally she'd been on her own since her father had died, but it was what it meant for Kit and Alexis that troubled her most deeply. The chances were, Marica wouldn't allow her to still see them, but perhaps Serena could sit down with her stepmother and appeal to her better nature… Oh, who was she kidding? Marcia didn't have a better nature, definitely not where Serena was concerned, and Serena knew she was partially to blame for that.

Although it had been over two years since her mother's passing when her father introduced Marcia, Serena had struggled with having a new woman in their lives, especially one so different from her mother. It hadn't helped that whilst Marcia had made every effort to bond with the twins, her treatment of Serena had been more lukewarm. Serena had realised why when she overhead Marcia talking to her friends, lamenting how closely Serena resembled her mother and how difficult she found that. Her father had insisted that with time they would get used to one another, but time didn't make things easier. Serena's struggle only intensified once they married and

Marcia adopted the twins—a fate she flatly refused for herself—and it seemed that making room for Marcia in their lives meant erasing nearly all trace of her mother. It was only through the refereeing of her father that their relationship remained relatively peaceful, but once he was gone there'd been nothing to temper their resentment of each other, and relations had deteriorated quickly. Had it not meant leaving Kit and Alexis behind, she would have left and not looked back, but walking away from them was unthinkable.

Only now she was facing exactly that.

As hard as Serena looked, she could see no way to keep it from happening. The only way would be to quickly and quietly terminate the pregnancy, but Serena recoiled from that thought as soon as it formed.

She may be terrified, but she wanted her baby.

It wasn't what she'd planned—she hadn't been sure she'd ever want to try for a child again after what happened last time—but there was no question how precious the little life nestled inside of her was. Her only wish was that it didn't have to upend everything else and once again she cursed herself for getting so carried away by Caleb's touch…

Caleb.

His name reverberated through her like a punch. She'd been so preoccupied with the consequences closer to home that she hadn't even considered him, but of course she would have to tell him about the pregnancy. He had every right to know. Only the thought of sharing that news with him sent her blood pressure skyrocketing, because how was she supposed to tell a man she'd only met once that their passionate encounter had resulted in a baby? A man who had been very clear that he had zero desire for a family or to make a commitment longer than a night to anyone.

A man who had made it clear that he regretted making love to her at all.

That shouldn't have happened. You should not be here right now.

The brutal words sounded in her mind, bringing the sting of tears to her eyes and causing her stomach to lurch with the same violent rejection she'd felt in his suite, the very same feeling as when she'd realised Lucas had deserted her. Would Caleb tell her that the child they'd created was a mistake also? That thought made her angry enough to do something she would never have expected and question if she needed to tell him at all. She hadn't hesitated all those years ago to tell Lucas that she was pregnant, but he'd been her boyfriend. She'd thought they were in love and would weather everything together; never had she anticipated that he would run from her and his responsibilities.

Caleb Morgenthau was another story. She had no reason to expect him to be pleased about the news. Wouldn't it be a kindness to spare herself another brutal rejection? Or the crushing disappointment of another man making it blindingly clear he had no interest in the child he fathered? Never mind that the worst could happen still and it would all be for nothing…but no, that wasn't a possibility that Serena would give any willing headspace to. She would think positive thoughts only. The doctor at the time had reassured her that there was no reason to believe she wouldn't conceive and carry successfully in the future, and she really wanted to believe that.

As for telling Caleb, it was the right thing to do. She'd never be able to face herself in the mirror again if she didn't. After scouring the internet, she located a public email address on his website and composed an email. Serena was surprised at how easily the words came and how few were needed to share the news. But she wasn't asking him for anything, so that made it straightforward. Hitting Send, she turned off the laptop and sank onto her bed, seeing no reason to wait for a response because there wasn't a single part of her that expected one. Not after seeing all the tabloid gossip surrounding Caleb online, referring to him as Australia's Untameable Bachelor and documenting the exploits that never included the same woman twice.

After Lucas left the way he did, Serena had sworn she'd never again waste time waiting for what others had no intention of giving. It hurt to remember how pathetic she'd been back then, so sure that he wouldn't have abandoned her and desperate to hear from him, checking her phone for a message as soon as she woke up, leaping every time she received a new notification. Only none of them had been from him. She had only prolonged her own agony and wouldn't make the same mistake with Caleb. No, her eyes were wide open this time.

It would be a lie to say there wasn't a small part of her that was sad about that, for ideally, she would love for her child to know their father, but she needed to focus her emotion and energy on the more practical plans, such as finding somewhere to live and finding a way to stay in Kit's and Alexis's lives. Right now, she had little idea of how she'd manage either, and along with the prospect of single motherhood, she did feel somewhat daunted as she lay in bed unable to sleep, but Serena trusted she would figure it out. She had to. And given all the ways that life, and the people she'd been unfortunate enough to know, had taught her that the only person she could really rely on was herself, it was probably better that she was doing it alone anyway.

'Is that everything?' Caleb asked of his assistant, handing the relevant files back to her and arranging the papers that needed his signature.

'There's one more thing,' Nicole replied, pausing ever so slightly. 'An email has come through to the public account, but it's addressed personally to you. From a woman named Serena Addison.'

Serena. The mention of her name had Caleb's body stirring in ways that it hadn't in weeks. Not since the night he'd met her. Ever since that encounter he'd struggled to summon a shred of sexual interest for any of the women who had made themselves known to him, women of beauty and sophistication and experience, women with whom a night of debauched sex would be greatly enjoyed and wouldn't trouble his conscience. But now, that flash of her face in his mind, with that sexy tumble of red-gold hair and those bewitching amber eyes, promoted a landslide of torrid recollection—her tight hot heat and the ecstatic feeling in his blood as he'd thrust eagerly into her, the bite of her hands as she clung to him in delight, begging silently for more—and his body fired to life. Heat, rapid and relentless, swarmed in his blood and his groin hardened to an almost painful degree.

Whilst it was a relief to know that he was still capable of feeling desire, Caleb found it unbelievably frustrating that it was prompted by *her*. Because he didn't long for repeat encounters with women he'd already bedded, and it still burned that he had bedded her in the first place. It was an error he'd had no business making, and delving into why only reminded him how utterly he'd lost his head over her, and losing his control over a woman was not something he regarded with any pleasure at all. And whilst he had no problem still berating himself after eight long weeks, whatever he had felt for her that night should have dissipated entirely. Her name certainly shouldn't have the capability to charge his body with such a fierce, erotic longing that he was having to battle to shut it down. It shouldn't please him that she obviously hadn't forgotten him after all. And it certainly shouldn't be on the tip of his tongue to ask what she wanted, because it didn't matter. He wasn't going to see her again. Yet the question was pushing at his mind, testing his boundaries.

'You know how I feel about unsolicited communications from women,' he said, his jaw clenched with the effort required to force out the words. 'Delete it.'

Nicole hesitated again. 'I think you should read it.'

Without waiting for his agreement, she laid the tablet on the glass-topped desk before him, and unease leapt in the pit of his stomach. Nicole, who he appreciated so greatly because she followed his every instruction to the smallest requirement, would only insist if it was serious, if there was something in the correspondence that he *needed* to know.

There were very few things that Serena could have to impart that would directly affect him, and none of them were good.

The unease morphed into a tempest of foreboding that swirled ominously as he lowered his eyes to the device, absorbing the words of the brief message once. And then again.

Atop the desk his hand curled into a fist as his heart pounded. *Pregnant.*

She was claiming that she was pregnant with his child!

Emotion pulsed at the crown of his head—a frenzied, frantic feeling—and there was so much breath backing up in his lungs that his chest puffed outwards so hard that the buttons of his shirt strained.

'I take it that what she's saying is possible?' Nicole queried gently when he didn't speak.

'It's not impossible,' Caleb admitted with difficulty, his stomach turning over with the words. But exactly how *probable* was it, he questioned with the kind of cool and ruthless logic that reigned over all of his dealings.

He and Serena had only had sex once, and he had used protection. He always did, specifically to avoid a situation like this. So, the odds that she was actually pregnant, and if she was, that the child was his, were not favourable.

Suspicion buzzed loudly in his ears. Was she hoping to trap him into the type of relationship that he'd been explicit about not wanting? Had she researched him and realised the wonderful opportunity that he presented. He was socially astute enough to understand the powerful lure of his wealth and status. He knew others who'd been the target of similar abhorrent schemes. Serena had spoken about being boxed in, about her job not being her dream existence, he remembered with a burst of memory that was discomfortingly clear, so had she decided that he could be her ticket to a better life, a convenient escape from mundanity and responsibility?

Anger scorched its way along his veins, and yet part of him resisted the notion that the woman with alluringly amber eyes who had responded to him with such earnest eagerness could be capable of deceit.

And Caleb always heeded his instincts; they rarely steered him wrong. But he had already been wrong about who Serena was once, and this was not a matter that he could approach without question or caution. Not when there was such a high stake. *Fatherhood.*

Something he'd never sought. Something he wouldn't be any good at.

Something he didn't want to believe could be happening.

And he certainly wasn't about to allow himself to became ensnared in a ploy that was as old as time itself. He couldn't just take her word for it; he had to get to the truth of the matter himself, and if she was lying, well, he'd have no more trouble erasing her from his mind.

But if she is telling the truth? If she is pregnant with your child?

The questions were only a whisper in his head, but they were impossible to silence...

Serena was leaving work for the day when she heard her phone ringing and she dug into her pocket to snatch it up quickly in case it was either Kit or Alexis.

'Hello?' she asked, so eager to hear either of their voices that she failed to glance at the caller ID.

It had been ten days since she'd seen them, the longest they had ever gone without contact. The few video chats they had managed didn't count, as they'd been brief and conducted in whispers to ensure Marcia didn't overhear.

As Serena had feared, it hadn't taken long for her ever-watchful stepmother to realise Serena's stomach virus was in fact not a virus, and she had wasted no time in venting her disappointment and disapproval and banishing Serena from the house, much to the twins' dismay. She hadn't had any luck finding somewhere else to live that was close to the twins and within her budget, but fortunately, Evie had offered to let Serena stay with her. The separation from her siblings, however, was less easily fixed.

She was missing them and worrying about them desperately. Sensitive Kit had been distraught at the upheaval and the loss of Serena from the house, and even Alexis, who was normally the more placid and adaptable of the two, was struggling to accept the situation. And as much as Marcia doted on them, she was far too conservative to be able to offer much help with modern-day tween concerns. Serena was the one they turned to with those troubles, and it was killing her that she was shut out of being there should they need her, and that she was falling short of the promise she'd long ago made her to her mother to always remain close to them.

Each day that passed without that changing only deepened her feelings of failure and helplessness, but what made it even worse was that, buried beneath that anguish, was a buoyant relief that she was finally free from her stepmother's clutches. Free to do what she wanted, go wherever she pleased, wear what she liked. Serena couldn't enjoy it, not with so many uncertainties hovering over her and breeding anxiety in her heart, but just knowing that life was once more her own, and that most of what happened going forwards was in her sole and entire control, was like breathing fresh air after being stuck underground.

'Serena.'

She froze mid step. The voice belonged to neither Kit or Alexis, but it was still far more familiar than it should be and sent a shock wave straight to her heart. 'Caleb?' she gasped, when she finally found her voice.

'I'm in London.' Her grip on her phone tightened, because those words were even more unexpected than the velvet familiarity of his voice and sent panic wheeling across her chest. 'I want to meet up.'

'Why?'

'*Why*?' he repeated in an astounded pitch. 'Because we have something fairly important to discuss, don't you think?' *Did they?* Everything she had wanted to say to him, she had said in her email and couldn't imagine what would be weighing so heavily on his mind when she'd made it clear that she required nothing from him. Not his participation, his support, his money—not a single thing. Surely, that was the ideal outcome for him…so why on earth was he here? 'Are you free right now?'

Serena's heart thumped with annoyance. Did he really think that he could just show up and demand a piece of her time with no forewarning and that she would jump? 'No, I'm working late this evening,' she lied, feeling not even the teensiest bit bad about doing so. It wasn't as if she owed him anything. She'd done her duty by telling him about the baby and, if she did agree to sit down with him at some point, and that was a big *if*, then she wanted more preparation than a few seconds, wanted her thoughts to be ordered and eloquent and she was feeling neither of those things in that moment.

The sound of his voice had undone her, propelled her back to that night in Singapore, to all that she had felt that she didn't want to remember. How much worse would it be if she actually had to see him? How would she be able to meet those quicksilver eyes and not feel, not remember it all in exquisitely painful and hypnotising detail?

It had been hard enough squelching everything he'd awoken in her, forgetting the joy of their connection and how it felt to not be lonely. She didn't need that box opened.

'Is that so?' Caleb drawled. 'Because someone who looks exactly like you seems to be exiting your office building at this very second.'

Serena stiffened. *He was here, watching her?*

Her heart thudded again and frustration had her gritting her teeth together, not because she'd been caught out, but because he had obviously been testing her, and it was a test she had failed.

Casting her eyes left and right, it was then that she noticed the black Escalade, parked only a few feet away. Before she could say or think anything else, the door was opening and a long, strong body was emerging to stand on the pavement before her. He was dressed in a dark suit and coat, both of which screamed designer and only enhanced his towering six-foot-three, unrepentantly masculine appeal.

Through either the monstrous efforts of self-preservation or the passage of time, Serena wasn't sure which, the memory of what a breathtakingly formidable presence he was to behold had dimmed to something more palatable, but as he faced her down, there was no hiding from the truth of him. His full spectacular force filled her vision, and her heart thumped again. Harder.

'Hello, Serena.'

The face that regarded her was hard, and unnervingly cool eyes observed her with even more implacability. The strain on her senses intensified, and the sense of foreboding inched even higher up her spine, yet still she stood, devouring him with her eyes, wary, and yet also very, very *aware*.

Of how the coat hugged the width of his shoulders.

How his eyes, even in evident displeasure, still seemed to glow. How he commanded the air surrounding him. And that was when she felt it, that slow-moving ripple across her skin, which made her tingle all the way down to her bones and which she wanted to quell at all costs.

'Why didn't you say from the outset that you were outside my office waiting for me?' she demanded, crossing her arms over her chest and staring at him with as much coolness as she could muster, which was exceedingly difficult when heat continued to rise in her like a lethal tide.

The brief movement of his sharp features offered no kind of answer. 'Why did you lie about working late?'

'Because I'm tired,' Serena shot back without taking a breath, her nerves rattling very close to the surface now. 'I've had a long day and an even longer week, and I really don't feel like having this conversation right now.'

'Well, now you have no choice in the matter.' He checked his watch. 'I reserved us a table at a place nearby. We should be going if we're to make it on time.'

Serena didn't move. 'I meant what I said, Caleb. I'm tired.'

'As am I,' he said, closing the short distance between them with two forceful, impatient strides. 'I've spent twenty hours flying halfway across the world, but the sooner we have this conversation the sooner we can both go home and get some rest.'

Stalking back to the car, Caleb held the door open, expectancy glowing in the steely eyes that glared over at her. Stubbornness kept Serena planted exactly where she was. She had never responded well to being told what to do and liked it even less since Marcia had thoroughly abused the power, and she resented the hell out of Caleb for airdropping into her day and issuing his arrogant commands. But now that he was here, unease would eat away at her until she knew exactly what he wanted, and she didn't need that extra strain, not when she was trying so hard to keep her stress levels low to avoid the same fate for the pregnancy as last time. Huffing out a sigh, she stepped forwards. 'I'll give you one hour of my time,' she said, sweeping by him without making any eye contact and with care not to touch him as she slid into the warm interior of the car. 'Not a minute more.'

Serena watched the waiter carefully set down their drinks on the polished table, her chest tightening with every extra second that he took. Not a word had passed between herself and Caleb on the short car ride. They seemed to have tacitly agreed not to speak of the matter at hand until they had reached their destination, but now the air between them was stretched so taut that every breath she took was tainted with the bitter taste of tension. It also didn't help that her body felt...*electrified*. As if every nerve and every sense had sprung into quivering life. Not with fear, but with something else...something she didn't want to name or think of or feel as acutely as she did. What she wanted was for this—whatever it was— to be over so she could get on with her evening. Her life.

'You seem nervous, Serena,' he commented as she clattered her spoon against her cup.

Slowly, she lifted her eyes to look at him, feeling thrumming through her as their gazes clashed. 'Wasn't that the whole point of your ambush outside of my office? To catch me off guard and throw me off balance?'

Caleb was a man who liked to always have the upper hand. Even if Serena hadn't already deduced that from their brief interaction, one look at him, with his towering stance and determined jaw, would have confirmed it. The problem right now was that he didn't have control—after all, she was the one carrying his child and making decisions that could impact his life—but it was clear that he wanted the power back where he believed it rightfully belonged—in his hands. And that he would make whatever moves he could to get it back.

'I think *ambush* is a little extreme,' he responded levelly. 'I would have been in contact, but prior to setting off I wasn't one hundred percent sure of my plans. Once I was here, I thought it was more expedient to come to you straight away so we could talk about the situation.'

Something in her coiled as he referred to her pregnancy as a *situation,* but she was grateful for the anger as it singed away some of the nerves, infusing her instead with the strength required to force her way through this laborious conversation without giving away anything she didn't want to. Her power, for one.

That was something she was never surrendering again. Ever.

'So, talk.'

He fixed his grey gaze on her, as stormy as the skies beyond the window. 'You are pregnant?'

'I am.' His eyes seemed to drill deeper into her. 'If you were hoping to see some proof of that on my body, you're a few months early.'

He leaned forwards. 'I don't understand how it could have happened.'

'I would have thought you'd understand the basic facts of life.'

Annoyance flared in his slate gaze and Serena felt a small dart of childish pleasure that she was getting under his skin. 'What I mean is we only had sex once, Serena. *Once.* And I used protection. I always do.'

'Clearly it wasn't as effective as either of us would have liked,' she muttered, taking a small sip of her tea.

'You weren't taking a contraceptive pill?'

'No. I had no reason to be.'

A muscled flickered in his jaw. 'You seem very calm about all of this.'

'If my choice is between being calm or hysterical, I choose calm.' She hadn't been hysterical last time, but she hadn't been far from it. Being eighteen and pregnant, her emotions had been all over the place, and those feelings of fear and overwhelm had only spun more out of control when Lucas had deserted her. She carried a lot of guilt over that, certain that her fraught emotional state had contributed to her miscarriage, and she was determined that couldn't happen again. This time, she would keep herself in check, take care of herself. 'And it's not as though being worked up about it will change anything, is it? Nor would it do any good to me or the baby.'

It was impossible to miss the flare in his eyes at mention of the baby. 'So, you are planning to continue with the pregnancy then?'

'Yes. That's not up for discussion,' she added warningly, noting the spike of emotion in his expression. Was it panic? Frustration? Dread? It occurred to her then, with a rush of distress, that perhaps that was why he had made the long journey to London, to try and compel her to abort the pregnancy. The thought rattled her, and she settled an arm protectively across her stomach. 'So, if that is what you came all this way to talk about, you had a wasted journey.' She only just managed keep her voice civil.

'You think I would fly more than halfway around the world to pressure a woman into terminating a pregnancy?' he demanded, his horrified expression appearing to be genuine in its offence. 'That's the type of man you think I am?'

'How would I know?' Serena posited, refusing to feel quelled by his response. 'I don't know you, do I?'

She knew how his skin tasted on her tongue, she knew the strength contained in his chest and arms and how it felt to be locked against his body and trapped in his silvery gaze. They were things she hadn't been able to forget however hard she'd tried—things she wasn't sure she'd ever be able to forget—but that was physical. Irrelevant. Emotionally, she had no idea who Caleb Morgenthau was.

For a brief moment, Serena had thought she did. She'd thought that they understood one another in a way that had been rare and rich. As much as a she'd known nothing could really come of it, that moment of connection had been like finding a rare jewel, one that she could take out and admire on her hardest days, but then he had turned so cool and remote, so perturbed by her lack of sexual experience that everything that had come before had been proven false and it had hit her like a freezing wave that she really didn't know him at all. Just as she hadn't known Lucas. The resulting disillusionment had been even more chilling than the realization, and that had only made her want to flee even faster. She wouldn't be making the same mistake twice, presuming to know what kind of heart guided his intentions and motivations. She had to be guarded. There was no other choice.

'*Exactly*,' he exclaimed, seizing upon the word with a vehemence that warned his emotions were far closer to the surface and far more volatile than Serena had first reckoned. 'You don't know me.'

'But I do know what you told me that night in Singapore, which is that family and commitment hold no appeal for you.'

He had been upfront about that, and Serena hadn't expected it to suddenly change. That was why she had been so unprepared for the sight of him. If her actual boyfriend, someone who had professed to love her, had run away from her and their baby, why would Caleb, a man she'd spent only a single night with, go to the special length of crossing the globe to be involved? In a perfect world, maybe, but Serena knew the world wasn't perfect. It could be unfair and unkind.

Losing her mother so young had taught her that, and just when she'd been finding some kind of equilibrium, life had taken her father from her. Again, she'd picked herself up, found a way forwards, and when she'd thought happiness was in striking distance, that she could build a new life with Lucas and their baby and the twins and finally have a whole and happy family life again, cruelty had struck once more. So, she had to tailor her expectations to reality to keep from being broken all over again.

Looking him in the eyes, she took a steadying breath. 'Look, Caleb, the reason I told you about the pregnancy is because I believe you have a right to know, and so that if one day, twenty years from now, this child wants to find you, it won't be a complete shock. But that's the *only* reason. I wasn't trying to induce some reluctant involvement on your part when I know that's the last thing you want. I certainly wasn't expecting you to interrupt your life and fly all the way here...'

'I was coming to Europe anyway. I have business in the South of France,' he interrupted. 'I continue there tomorrow.'

She was just a pit stop, then. It was hard to decide whether to be relieved or insulted by that, but Serena settled on relieved, the admission making some kind of sense to her, given what she knew of him. He had ventured in her direction only because he was in the vicinity and he wanted to see how big of a problem she was to be solved, and that was something she could set his mind at ease on right away.

'My point is, I never had any expectation that your feelings would miraculously change overnight. I made this decision aware of that. So, this—' she gestured with a wave of her hand between them '—you being here, checking in, whatever it is you're doing, isn't necessary. At all.'

If anything, her words seemed to have caused even darker storm-clouds to gather in his eyes. 'On the contrary, *if* you are pregnant, and *if* I am the father, then I have certain responsibilities. Surely you would agree on that point?'

'*If,*' Serena scoffed, trying not to be offended and failing, because it was impossible to misunderstand the ugly intention behind his question. He was all but accusing her of being an opportunist, or even worse! 'You think I'm making this up?'

Briefly, the expression in his eyes seemed to shift, *soften,* and she thought he was going to reassure her that he did believe her, but in an instant, they'd regained their hard glitter. 'In the same way you don't know me, I don't know you well enough to make an assessment on what you would or wouldn't do.' Even as he said that, Serena knew that he had already made an assessment—and one that hurt. 'So, to start with, I'm here for my own confirmation that this pregnancy is real.'

As much as Serena would have liked him to take her

word for it, she supposed it was a fair and pragmatic request and one she shouldn't judge him too harshly for.
As a man of wealth and prominence, he had every reason
to seek his own clarification. Not that she was sure why
he wanted it when she didn't anticipate him doing much
with it. He hadn't exactly refuted her suggestion that he
didn't need to be involved, had he? Yes, he'd made mention of responsibilities, but what ones exactly? Nothing
about him screamed hands-on parenting was anywhere
in his future. His custom designer suit certainly wouldn't
hold up well around the bodily functions of a baby. Serena could only surmise that he was thinking of financial
responsibilities, offering a lump sum in lieu of anything
else. She didn't have to wonder too hard about why that
option would appeal to him.

'OK. I can arrange to have a blood test and have you
copied in on the results. I'll call my doctor, but it may
take a few days to get an appointment.'

'I have a doctor who has agreed to fit us in and do the
test this evening,' Caleb announced.

'Of course you do.'

'At my request, and with your consent, she will also
perform a DNA test.'

Serena tensed, a fear-poisoned arrow shooting to her
heart. She had heard about amniocentesis, the needle and
possible side effects, and with panicked breath building
in her chest, she started to shake her head. She was absolutely not risking her pregnancy just so he could have…

'There's no need to look alarmed,' Caleb said, almost
too kindly. 'I've been assured its non-invasive and perfectly safe. Blood is taken from both of us and provided
you are over eight weeks pregnant, which if I am the fa-

ther, you should be, fetal blood should be present with yours and be a match for mine.'

Although he hadn't moved an inch, his eyes seemed to regard her with even more probing intensity, as though trying to discern her every flicker of answering emotion. As the threatened beats of her heart began to subside, Serena nodded slowly. 'Alright.'

A small furrow cut into the space between his dark brows, as though he hadn't expected such easy agreement and Serena quickly realised that he had been watching— hoping for?— the opposite reaction.

'And when these tests prove that I am pregnant with your child, what then?' she asked, because it was clear that he preferred the idea that this was some crazy scheme rather than that she was actually carrying his child, and that he would in all likelihood walk away, even once he had his confirmation.

'Let's just take this one step at a time, OK, Serena,' he said, through lips suddenly tight with tension.

His unwillingness to commit to anything disappointed her, even though it was what she'd known would happen. 'Shall we get going then?' she said, getting to her feet, eager to move on.

The sooner they got this over with, the sooner he could go on his merry way and leave her to carry on picking up the pieces of her life and putting them back together to create a new and hopefully far happier one.

CHAPTER FOUR

'WE SHOULD ARRIVE at the airfield in about forty minutes, sir.'

'Good. Thank you.' Caleb nodded his gratitude to his driver as he settled himself into the luxurious interior of the car, his departure from London not coming a moment too soon. He couldn't wait to put this whole sordid pregnancy ordeal behind him and never think of it again.

Never think of Serena Addison again either.

And how are you going to do that? You've been trying to put her from your mind for weeks without any success, and seeing her again in the flesh certainly hasn't helped!

Tenison buzzed through Caleb's veins, too much truth within that burst of thought for him to dismiss it as easily as he wanted to. Seeing Serena again yesterday had stirred a greater reaction than he had been prepared for, igniting a fire in his blood that had continued to smoulder long after they had parted ways...

Watching from the darkened window of the car, his intent had been to observe her unvarnished reaction to his presence, but the moment she had exited her office building, unmissable with her striking long legs and slim body and that sexy tumble of strawberry hair, he hadn't wanted to do anything except stare. Devour the sight of her because she was even more beautiful than he had remembered. Heat had kindled low in his stomach, and the tug of awareness deep in his groin had been fierce, so potent that the anger churning through him ever since reading that damned email and burning so hotly he hadn't slept at all on the journey to London, had been stilled into near submission.

The wave of desire had been so strong that for a moment he had forgotten—*actually forgotten*—his reason for being there as his mind flooded with heated imaginings of those long legs locked tightly around his waist and his face buried in the sweet-smelling, and even sweeter-tasting, hollow of her neck as he drove himself deep into her body. Wrenching himself from the sensual daydream had taken supreme effort, and even then, tendrils of smoky heat continued to curl through his bloodstream, threatening to pull him back under should he lose control for even the barest of seconds. The frustration he'd felt with himself for that lapse, and the continuing weakness where she was concerned, had only made him even more unyielding when they had finally stood face-to-face. Because as much of a nuisance as his undying desire for her was, it was an even greater aggravation hat he was burning up inside for someone who could be trying to dupe him.

However, the longer he'd spent with her, the harder it had been to keep his suspicions burning. Nothing about her seemed deceitful, and she had agreed easily to all that he'd asked, as though she truly had nothing to hide.

The conundrum of it had kept him awake into the early hours, uncomfortable with his assumptions about her. Yet he just couldn't accept the other option—that she was being honest and he was going to be a father.

A notification alert on his phone drew his attention,

and withdrawing it from his inner pocket, Caleb was happy to see it was the results of the pregnancy and DNA test. Finally, the matter could be put to bed for good, and before he reached the South of France so he would be able to proceed with the urgent matters on the new Saint-Tropez beach club without any distractions. Except…

His heart thumped uncomfortably and the air in his chest grew thin. Tight.

Serena *was* pregnant.

And the test confirmed that he was the father.

Caleb shook his head. It was impossible. It couldn't be. It couldn't…and yet it was, he accepted, glancing again at the test results, which he had been assured were 97 percent accurate.

He was going to be a father. There was shock and disbelief spreading at an alarming speed across his chest, but amongst that turbulence there was also an unassailable clarity and, although he was suddenly in a situation he'd never wanted to find himself in, Caleb knew exactly what he had to do.

'Turn the car around.'

The driver startled, eyes flicking to the rearview mirror. 'Sir? I thought you had a flight you needed to…'

'What I need is to go back into the city,' Caleb snapped impatiently. 'Turn the car around now!'

The queue of traffic heading into the capital was far greater than the line heading out, so the car crawled for long stretches of time, but Caleb barely noticed, too lost in his own web of thoughts.

There were many reasons why he'd never entertained the notion of fatherhood. He was selfish, for starters. He worked ridiculously long hours and rarely spent more than a year in one city before moving on again. He had no stellar example to emulate. His father had often worked so late into the night that he'd slept at his office and left the rearing of his son to a rotation of highly qualified nannies. And having spent the majority of his life studiously avoiding getting close to anyone and feeling anything, to prevent the mess of emotion and pain that had stained his childhood, it was now less of a habit and more of an ingrained way of being that Caleb wasn't sure could be changed. Or that he particularly wanted to change.

However, all of those reasons paled in comparison to the main motive, the one that was never far from his mind, that whispered its fearful prophecy in his ear whenever his father instigated another of his imploring conversations about continuing the family line and securing their future legacy—the chilling knowledge that, should he let someone into his life, someone who could grow to care about him, he would only end up hurting them.

Just as he had hurt Charlotte.

He may not intend to, but it was inevitable that he would. Hurting Charlotte was the last thing he'd wanted, but it had happened. Just by being himself.

You ruined her. Our beautiful daughter and you ruined her. She loved you and you didn't deserve it.

Caleb's heart never failed to race whenever he recalled those words that Charlotte's parents had hurled at him in the corridor of the hospital when he'd attempted to visit, armed with flowers and an apology, the apology he should have offered her hours earlier, the apology that could have prevented the horrible, tragic mess that had unfolded. Only he hadn't been able to get anywhere near Charlotte to tell her how sorry he was or how awful he felt. Faced with her family's anger and his own suffocating sense of responsibility, he'd fled, but he'd never been able to erase the image of their devastated faces, ravaged by rage and pain...so much pain for their beloved daughter and her lost future—the future that, before him, had been so bright and full of opportunity.

Charlotte had been in Melbourne for a prestigious summer internship when they'd met. Unacquainted with the city or its social elite, she'd had no knowledge of his reputation for cycling through women, and he hadn't taken the time to tell her, because he didn't explain himself to anyone. He was a Morgenthau and he did whatever he wanted, whenever he wanted, with whomever he wanted. It had never crossed his mind that she would fall in love with him because love was the last thing on his agenda. Caleb had no intention of feeling that, not for her, not for anyone, not after the emotional carnage of his childhood. When Charlotte had finally realised that, she'd been devastated.

She had raged at him. Sobbed and shouted and eventually stormed from the club, and in her tearful, brokenhearted state had rammed her car straight into a wall, shattering her body the way Caleb had shattered her heart.

It wasn't until late the next day that Caleb learned what had happened, but once he did, he'd been racked with guilt. Who could doubt that it was his fault when it was his cruelty that had caused the accident? Had Charlotte not been in such an anguished state, she would never have lost control of the vehicle, wouldn't have gotten in the car at all. And he'd seen how distressed she was. Why hadn't he gone after her, stopped her? The heavy pounding of guilt had consumed him, and the angry reaction of her parents had confirmed the fault he bore.

And Caleb had known then, with a certainty as clear as water, that he couldn't allow anyone remotely close to him again. Because they would only end up hurting too, and he couldn't bear to inflict that magnitude of pain of another unsuspecting, innocent heart.

And it would happen again. He knew that. Because Charlotte wasn't the first person to be devastated by him. Years earlier, Caleb had destroyed his father when he'd driven away his mother, leaving Adlai Morgenthau a desolate, grief-stricken shell of himself. But after Charlotte, he was determined there would be no others.

He'd stuck to that resolve ever since, careful in ways he'd never been before about the type of women he spent his nights with, strict about limiting their involvement to a single encounter, a period of time too brief for any feelings, for *anything real*, to develop. The only misstep he'd ever made was with Serena…a misstep that still sent chills down his spine because with her inexperience and emotionality, there were so many ways he could have hurt her.

And now that she was carrying his child, there were many more.

Despite his knee-jerk reaction to return to the capital, instinct was once again urging him that the best thing he could do for Serena and for the child was to leave them alone. Generously provide, of course, but from afar, where they would be spared the harm that he would eventually cause and he could spare himself the burden of having to live with disappointing them.

But how could he just turn away from his child, his own flesh and blood, the way he turned away from everyone else?

Especially when he knew what it was to grow up with

only one parent. He knew the persistent ache of abandonment, the questions that filled that yawning empty space—questions destined never to be answered. He knew it was a void that could be painted over and ignored, but still, somehow, remained. Could he really condemn his son or daughter to that fate?

There were other considerations charging through his mind too. Practical ones. This child would be the sole heir to the Morgenthau name and empire. Whilst he had been unwilling to bring an innocent child into the world just to satisfy his father's wish to safeguard the future, now there was a child, so it was a different consideration altogether. It wasn't about creating a life. That had already happened; now it had to be about protecting them as best he could, ensuring they received all the privilege and security their blood entitled them to. He was the only one with the power to guarantee that. And he had to. There was no certainty of what kind of father he would be, so he had to give his child every protection possible.

From deep within his chest his heart kicked, his stomach twisting as he approached an uneasy decision. Instinct might still be screaming at him the same old message, that the best thing he could do was stay far away from both Serena and the baby, but he could feel the tug of other instincts now too, paternal ones, and they would countenance nothing of the sort.

CHAPTER FIVE

SHOCK PINNED SERENA to the spot as she pulled open the front door and found herself staring into a set of smoky grey eyes. 'Caleb,' she breathed, her heart quickening as he filled the doorway. In another of his bespoke suits, this one a perfect match for the shade of his eyes, with a crisp white shirt beneath, he was a devastating sight. 'What are you doing here?'

'I got the test results back a short while ago,' he answered, his gaze heavy. 'The DNA is a match. You're carrying my child.'

One hand clung to the door for support because her knees had turned to water, but Serena managed to pull herself up taller and meet his eyes fearlessly, even as flickers of apprehension licked at the sides of her stomach. Wasn't he supposed to be on his way to the South of France? 'You came here to tell me something I already know?'

'No. I'm here to discuss our next steps. Preferably not on the doorstep.' He scowled, brushing past her, and Serena didn't even try to stop him, stumbling as she was over his use of the word *our*—as though this was a situation they were in together. Which, yes, biologically they were. But in every other way, they absolutely weren't.

'What exactly do you mean *our* next steps?' Serena

asked urgently, trailing him into the living space and scanning his face for some clue that would help her ward off her rapidly descending sense of alarm—but he was as inscrutable as ever. 'Because I told you yesterday that I'm perfectly happy to raise this child alone...' she reminded him, striving to keep her voice steady even though she felt as if she was suddenly hovering over a minefield and, with any step, there would be an explosion.

'And I'm telling you today that whatever you thought yesterday is not acceptable to me.' His eyes glowed down at her in a way that made her far too aware of the unfettered leaping of her heart and pulse. 'There is no world in which any child of mine will grow up without my name, or without me being in their life. So, you and I are going to get married.'

The word detonated in Serena's ears and it was a moment before the disorientation cleared enough for her to form words. 'Married?' she repeated, hoping he would tell her that she had misheard him, but that hope sank as he made a single, controlled gesture of his dark head. She shook her head, backing away from him and from the treacherous frissons that were firing through her at the thought. 'I don't...no. You and I are not going to get married, Caleb. That's insane.'

'Actually, it's highly pragmatic,' he countered emotionlessly. 'You're pregnant with my child—it's the logical next step. The *only* next step.'

'No. No, it's not. Because this is the twenty-first century. A pregnancy no longer mandates a ring.'

In some situations, perhaps, but definitely not theirs. They didn't know the first thing about one another. *That's not entirely true though, is it?* a voice in her head asked, stirring recollections of the night in Singapore, spine-tingling memories of how they had connected so quickly, so easily. Except they hadn't, she argued back. She only *thought* they had connected, wanting to believe it was more than it had been and that was a folly she had no excuse for. She should have learned from her experience with Lucas, because she'd done the same thing with him. Believing that they shared a special connection and that he would always be there for her. She didn't want to be that same stupid girl, making the same stupid mistakes, as she tried—hopelessly—to recreate the life and family she'd loved and lost. She wouldn't be!

Because that life that she'd known was gone—and trying to bring it back would only cause more heartbreak, which wasn't a risk she was willing to take.

'The baby can have your name without us being married, if that's so important to you. And you can be involved too. I'm sure we can figure something out,' she said, trying to keep hold of the control over her life that she'd only just regained. But she didn't quite manage to hide the edge of scepticism from her rush of words, because she wasn't sure she trusted that Caleb's commitment to being involved was quite as robust as he made out. Not when a day ago, hell, probably even an hour ago, he hadn't even been willing to accept his responsibility in the pregnancy. Not when he had stated clearly and with certainty that he didn't want any commitment in his life, and a child was the greatest commitment of all. A lifelong relationship. Lucas hadn't wanted that. So why would he?

'Serena…' Her name emerged from his full lips as part reasoning and part censure. 'Be reasonable.'

Her mouth almost hit the floor. How could he say that to *her* when he was the one suggesting something as absurd as marriage? 'You don't even want to be a father, Caleb. You don't want to get married.'

'True, on both counts,' he agreed calmly, moving in place and taking over even more of the damnably small living space with his dark, sex-edged, oozing masculinity. There wasn't anywhere that Serena could look and not feel him in her gaze, nowhere to stand where she could be unaffected by the power that vibrated off him. 'But things have changed. Now I am going to be a father and that necessitates other changes and compromises. Especially if my child is to inherit all that is rightfully theirs.' Serena must have looked as nonplussed as she felt, because he sighed. 'The child you're carrying is the sole heir to my billion-dollar company, and I will not have them denied any of that because they were born illegitimate.'

'So, you only want to get married so they can inherit and run your company in twenty-five years?' she demanded, thinking that was hardly a sufficient reason.

'That's not the only reason, no,' he responded, obviously reading her lack of enthusiasm. 'But it is a pressing one. They are entitled to it, Serena. All of it. It's their birthright.'

That made her mind spin because it wasn't an aspect she had considered, or even realised was at stake, and that made her aware of just how out of her depth she was with Caleb. 'No. I won't do it. I can't. I'm not marrying you.'

His expression hardened with displeasure, but also with determination. 'Give me one good reason why not.'

'I'll give you two. I don't love you and I don't trust you.'

He dismissed her feelings with a motion of his hand. 'That's of no consequence. I don't require either your love or your trust, or for us to have any substantial relationship of any kind. All I require is your hand in marriage for all the world to see.'

This time her mouth did fall open at the dearth of emotion in his words, so at odds with the determination smouldering in his eyes. So, he was proposing a marriage in name only, with no feeling, no friendship even, between them? How could he so blithely give his life away to someone he didn't at least care for in some small way? And how dare he expect her to?

'There's no need to look so indignant. What I'm suggesting may not be to your personal taste, but it makes perfect sense.'

How did it? Marriage wasn't a solution to a problem. It was a solemn vow between two people who adored one another, just as her parents had. Having watched their marriage, Serena had always believed that it should only be considered when a deep and abiding love and trust were present. And as she'd said, she didn't love or trust Caleb. He was so high-handed that he'd be the last man she'd want to marry. He'd been there less than a minute and was already trying to take over her life, and as for trusting anyone ever again...after Lucas had stomped all over her heart in his haste to desert her, that was definitely unlikely to happen. Why would she sign up for more heartbreak?

'Not to me it doesn't,' she riposted.

In surviving all that she had, Serena had learned the valuable lesson that the one and only person she could, and should, truly rely on was herself. It was safer and smarter that way.

'That's because you're thinking with your heart, and not your head,' he said with mild condemnation, his eyes sweeping over her and rousing tingles that she fought not to feel.

He was silent a moment, as though expecting her to change her mind, and when she didn't, his sensual lips firmed into a flat line of displeasure, a storm whipping to life in his gaze that had pulses of frenetic nervous energy zinging from one side of her body to the other. But crossing her arms over her chest, partly to hide the merciless rhythm of her heart that hadn't once ceased in his presence, Serena held her ground.

Was he really endowed with such arrogance that he'd expected she would jump at the chance to be his wife? Or was he just too used to everyone he surrounded himself with falling in line with his wishes that he'd forgotten that people had minds of their own? Both, she decided, as she watched his jaw sharpen with a fresh burst of resolve.

He moved towards her, a hard smile smoothing over his wicked mouth, a mouth she remembered all too well. How it moved. Tasted. How it had claimed her moans again and again and again. She fought to stay in the moment and not drift back to that night spent in his arms, but that had been a difficult enough task when he hadn't been in London. Now that he was here, and so tantalisingly close, it was all too easy to sink into the memories, forget how he had hurt and humiliated her and remember only the exquisite bliss he had delivered…

'Just consider for a moment the life I can provide for you. The security and comfort,' he added, making a point of looking around the room. 'Far more than you'll know here. You have to admit it's a little cramped—what will it be like when you add a baby to it?'

His line of questioning cut too close to her own fears

and concerns for her not to react. 'I'm only staying here temporarily—until I find someplace of my own.'

It was only as she watched his quick mind seize upon that information that she realised her error in snapping back.

'Why only temporarily? What happened to where you were living previously?'

'I… I had to move out,' she explained falteringly, loath to say any more than that because she knew that the truth would only weight the case in his favour.

'Because…?'

'My stepmother doesn't approve of the pregnancy,' she said when the silence became unbearable. 'Or how I came to be pregnant.'

His eyes narrowed, reading between the lines of what she'd said. 'She threw you out?'

Serena could only manage a small nod of her head, the pain of it still raw, the way she had failed her siblings still a barbed lump rolling around her chest, as well as her failure to find a way to fix it.

'Your father didn't have anything to say about that?'

'My father passed away six years ago,' she shared, her heart sore.

Caleb's expression changed; so too did his body, angling more fully in her direction. In an instant, she was under the intense spotlight of his gaze, and that made her feel unaccountably breathless. Trapped. Especially as his expression was suddenly so full of sympathy. 'Serena, I'm so sorry. That must have been—must still be— awful for you.'

'It was a long time ago. It's fine.'

Wrenching her gaze away, she tried to think about something else, *anything else*, because that show of heartfelt sympathy was pushing on something that she didn't want to be touched. Couldn't afford to be touched. Because she needed to remain strong, just as she'd always had to be, and if she were to dwell on how much she longed for her parents right now, or how alone she felt in the dark of night and how truly, deeply worried she was for the future, for Kit and Alexis, for her baby, she might just fall apart and she couldn't do that.

And why was it sympathy from this man, of all men, that was threatening to undo her? Threatening to unleash a torrent of emotion that would drown her, when for years she had mastered the art of squashing and compressing and storing it neatly away.

'It's not. Losing both parents at such a young age isn't something anyone should have to live through.' There was such sincerity in his voice that her fight only grew harder. 'And not having family support must be difficult. I know I'm not offering anything traditional, but I can provide plenty more. A home. Security. Support. Anything—*everything*—you could want. And our child will grow up with both of their parents in their life.' He levelled her with eyes that suddenly seemed to be made of steel. 'Which is as it should be, Serena. You know that. It matters to you that our baby grows up knowing who their father is, or you wouldn't have told me about the pregnancy at all.'

She cursed his logic. And when had he moved so close to her? His sudden nearness sparked an attraction that flared too hot and fast for her to have any hope of resisting. Or, much to her annoyance, concealing. She could feel his heat and power and strength winding their way around her like the threads of a spell, rendering her immobile. She could only stare up at him, saying nothing but feeling everything. If Caleb saw or felt those shimmers of reaction streaking through her, he didn't show it.

'I'll give you some time to think it over. I'm sure that with a little consideration, you'll see it's the right thing to do. I'll see myself out.'

His eyes flashed down at her a final time before he turned away, stalking to the door, which he closed softly behind him. Only then did Serena realise how badly she was shaking, reeling from both his proposal and his presence.

The last thing she'd expected was for him to show up. She thought he'd be so eager to get to the South of France that he'd sprout wings and fly there himself, never to be heard from again. Just like Lucas. A brief pain pulsed in her heart as she remembered the agonising moment she realised he'd gone. And after that hurt had come the bruising disappointment. In him, but mostly in herself. For believing in Lucas so ardently that she'd ignored the warning signs that he wasn't who she wanted him to be and dismissed words of caution from others, including her stepmother, that he wasn't the right guy for her.

But she had been so in need of someone in her life. Someone to love her and hold her and fill that enormous empty space the loss of her parents had left. At least when she'd lost her mum, she'd still had her father. But when he died, there was no one. It was that aloneness that had been the hardest and scariest thing to deal with, and when, after only a matter of months, Marcia had started changing the house to suit her tastes, it had felt as if there was nothing left of the life she'd once known. Outside of her brother and sister, the only solace she'd been able to find was her friends, in the noise and laughter and fun that surrounded her when she was with them, drowning out the reality that she was suddenly an orphan. It was at that time that she'd met Lucas and he'd made her feel so much good that the bad had been pushed away.

But then he'd disappeared, forcing Serena to navigate another loss, followed quickly by the hardest one of all—her baby. The loss, which in her heart, she'd never stopped blaming herself for, and Serena didn't want to make any more mistakes—*couldn't*—and the only way she knew to do that was to stay separate, rely only on herself.

She'd been doing it so long already that it didn't faze her—much. Financially it would be challenging, but emotionally it would be far safer. Not being tempted to open herself up, not getting attached to someone only to then lose them and have the bottom drop out of her world again.

But is that the best thing for your baby?

Caleb was offering support and security, a life where their child would want for nothing. A life with two parents, and she knew how precious a gift that was. She wanted that for her child. And as much as she feared she had messed up once again, becoming entangled with someone as charming and careless as Lucas had been, Caleb had shown up. And he was determined to be involved. That made him different.

Serena paced to the opposite end of the room. Had Caleb been right? Had she reacted with her heart, been led by her fears?

But how could she not be afraid?

Life had slapped her in the face time after time. Every time she thought she'd found some stable ground, it had shifted under her. She'd lost almost everyone she'd ever loved, except the twins, but even they were lost to her now too—unless marrying Caleb could solve that also?

But if she agreed—and it all somehow went wrong? And how would she manage her strange feelings for him? How would she manage *him*? He was impossible and arrogant and high-handed, waltzing in as he had and expecting her to go along with his plan just because he'd decided it was for the best.

She'd only just gotten her life back. The thought of surrendering it again was hideous, and she really didn't want to. But if it was in the best interests of her baby, and Kit and Alexis, then could she really say no...?

Caleb would have preferred if Serena had agreed to his proposal straight away, but after his many years in business, he was used to dealing with difficult parties. He knew how impactful walking away from a negotiation could be, how it nearly always spurred the other side into a quick agreement to his terms, so as he made the journey to Serena's flat the next day, he was sure that after a night to consider her options, she'd be eager to accept his proposal. Almost sure, anyway. After witnessing her stubborn resistance yesterday, he'd learned there was nothing predictable about Serena. Any other woman would have leapt at the opportunity to marry him, especially one in her predicament.

An orphan. Banished from her home. No family support. It was hard to comprehend how much she had been through. It had hurt him to hear it, and he'd been overcome by a surge of protective instincts he hadn't known he possessed, wanting to provide the security and support that she'd been denied and to make everything bad in her life better, which was crazy, because when had he ever made anything better for anyone?

But he knew that their marrying would benefit Serena

greatly, even if she was unwilling to see it. For one thing, she'd have a home that she couldn't be evicted from, and one with more square footage then a shoebox. She'd also have financial security for the rest of her life, but more importantly than all of that, she wouldn't have to raise their child on her own. She'd known enough struggles in her life already; he didn't want her to have to navigate parenthood alone too.

As he prepared to press again for her hand in marriage, those emotional considerations were as strong in his mind as the practical ones. No longer was he only thinking of pleasing his father with the continuation of the family line, or of guaranteeing his child's lifelong financial security, but of ensuring a better future for Serena too, free from any further angst. Caleb wasn't sure how he felt about that.

He reassured himself that it was for the good of their child as much as anything. A contented mother would be a better mother, and he wanted his child to have their mother in their life. To never know the bitter pain that had lived in him.

That was the most emotion he was willing to acknowledge because the last thing he wanted was for emotions to be part of the equation. And they weren't. He'd proposed marriage because he'd known instinctively it was what the situation demanded, *not* because of any desire to rescue her, or because knowing for certain that his child grew in her stomach had unleashed a fierce urge to claim her as his.

He didn't like the thought of marrying any more than he had before. His stomach writhed with unease at bringing Serena into his orbit, where hurt was not just a possibility, but a reality, especially after everything she'd already been through. Paradoxically, that was the best way for him to protect her and their unborn child. That was the reason—the only reason—he felt such desperation for her to agree to be his wife.

And he had considered the situation at length, with his customary focus and attention to detail, figuring out how it would work, how he would paint clear and thick boundaries between them. Even once she was his wife, he would hold Serena at arm's length the same way he did everyone. They would only interact wherever and whenever was necessary, and if it granted his child the emotional security that he had been denied, then that was what mattered most. The greatest thing he wished was for them to be whole and happy and loved and to know they were wanted. All of the things that he himself had yearned to know but never been sure of.

It was why he had awoken that morning even more aware of the importance of Serena agreeing to the marriage, and even more resolved to do whatever it took to ensure that outcome. It was with that determination powering his body that he alighted from the car and strode up the path to Serena's flat, his movement faltering as he saw the front door was ajar and he detected raised voices from within. His first and only thought was of Serena's safety, and without hesitating, he shouldered his way inside, every inch of his body primed to intervene in whatever was happening, before he slowed to listen to the heated argument in progress.

'They are my brother and sister. You have no right to keep us apart. They *need* me,' Serena cried. 'They've already lost their mother and father, the last thing they need is to lose me too. You have no idea what kind of negative impact this could have on them.'

'I don't see any negative effects of them being spared your vile influence,' hissed a cold female voice in response. 'Really, what kind of example are you, Serena? As if being pregnant out of wedlock *again* isn't bad enough, but to be pregnant from a fumble with someone you barely knew... It's shameful. It is definitely not the example I want Kit or Alexis to be exposed to, and it's not something I want to be associated with either. You knew the rules, Serena. And you chose to break them. You brought this on yourself. I wish I could say that surprises me, but you've always been headed for this kind of disgraceful, scandalous existence, and I will not let you drag Kit and Alexis down with you. I tried my best to steer you towards a better path, but...'

'Nothing you ever did was to try and help me,' Serena fired back, just as Caleb, having heard enough to understand exactly what was going on, stepped into the room, his protective instincts firing even harder. His sudden presence disturbed the taut, hostile air, and both women turned abruptly to look at him.

'Caleb...' Serena paled, blinking rapidly. 'Now isn't really a good time,' she pleaded, the emotional tremble wracking her voice causing even more unfamiliar feeling to strain within him. Not just to protect, but to comfort. To reassure her that she hadn't done anything wrong.

'I can see that.' He stepped to Serena's side, casting his eyes across her face quickly and reading the full depth of her distress. Something sharp seared across his chest as he did, the instinct to raise his hand to her cheek and stroke away all the pain rising within him. He resisted, *obviously*, swivelling his eyes to fix his attention on the other woman instead. 'You must be Serena's stepmother.'

'Marcia Addison,' she replied imperiously, and with

more courtesy that he knew he would have received had she not immediately been struck by his aura of power and wealth. She had been absorbing every detail of his person since he'd stepped into the room. He hadn't missed her eyes dusting over him, noting his custom-made suit, Italian handcrafted shoes and limited edition watch.

'It's lovely to meet you at last.' Supressing the anger still bubbling over the cruelty she had shown Serena, he sent her his most charming smile. 'I'm Caleb Morgenthau. Serena's fiancé.'

Her eyes widened, her eyebrows flying up into her hairline. 'Her... I'm sorry...her *fiancé*?'

'Yes,' he confirmed silkily, slipping his arm around Serena's waist to draw her tightly into his side. Serena tensed, but his secure grip neutralised her attempts to wriggle away, and the pleasure of how snugly she fitted against him infiltrated his mind and body with far too many sparks. Unbidden, memories of their night together flooded his brain—heated flashes of their seeking, open-mouthed kisses, their bodies kneading hungrily together, her flesh welcoming him—and an inferno of heat exploded in his core, but he clung to his focus. 'Please accept my apology for you only just this moment finding out, but I insisted on Serena and I sharing the news together in person, and business kept me from London until yesterday. That may, however, have been a mistake as it seems our happy news has caused some friction within your family.' He made sure to meet the woman's eyes, summoning all of his commanding power into his gaze. 'I'm sure it's nothing more than a misunderstanding, as surely you, and anyone else who cares to look, can see there's no scandal here. Just a young couple who've fallen in love in a whirlwind relationship and are starting their life together.' He gazed down at Serena the way he imagined a besotted man might, and it was far easier than he'd thought as his eyes indulged in her bright amber gaze and full, inviting mouth and a smile drew naturally across his lips. *Mine*, he thought, shocked by the possessive force of the thought. 'There's certainly no reason for anyone to have questions over Serena's propriety. And whilst I completely understand and respect your desire to protect your children from harmful influences, there are none here. Unless you consider joy and happiness to be harmful.'

'Well…of course not…' Marcia replied falteringly.

'Excellent, so there's no reason for there to be any further talk of Serena being a bad influence, and definitely no reason for three siblings who love and rely on each other very much to be kept apart any longer. Is there?' he demanded, daring her from behind his charm to defy him.

Her mouth thinned, tightened. 'If you are in fact getting married and starting a respectable family…then, no,' she agreed, reluctance underwriting her every word. 'There is no problem.'

'Perfect.' Caleb beamed, enjoying watching her almost choke on the words and catching a hint of a smile on Serena's lips too. 'Now, we would love to share this news with Kit and Alexis ourselves, so how about we arrange a visit for once they've finished school this afternoon? And as for the wedding,' Caleb continued, not offering her any chance to respond, 'it's planned for this weekend, in the South of France. It's set to be an extraordinary day, but please don't worry about the arrangements, I will take care of everything.'

'I look forward to it,' murmured Marcia, her skin losing colour rapidly. 'Now I had best be going.'

'I'll walk you out,' Caleb offered, gesturing for Marcia to precede him out into the hallway. 'I'd like to think I can rely on you to quash any further talk of scandal, Mrs Addison? I would hate for my fiancée's reputation to be impugned for no reason, and should I find out that people were talking of her in such a way, I would have to take quite drastic steps in response. That is a husband's prerogative, after all, to protect his wife from anyone who means her harm. *Anyone* at all,' he added, firing a pointed look that there was no chance of her misunderstanding

'I'm sure that won't be necessary,' she demurred.

'I hope not,' he said, seeing her into the street and smiling as she walked away, deflated and defeated, because victory was such a sweet taste, and a double victory… well, that was double the sweetness.

'What the hell was that?' Serena demanded, rounding on Caleb with temper blistering in her eyes as soon as he walked back through the door.

From his superior height, Caleb regarded her calmly, almost smugly, from eyes that blazed victorious. 'I think that the words you're looking for are *thank you*.'

'Thank you?' Serena parroted on a giant breath of disbelief. 'Thank you? You actually expect me to be grateful for the way you just railroaded me into a marriage that I hadn't agreed to.'

'I think you should be grateful that I just put your stepmother back in her box and enabled you to keep having a relationship with your siblings and to see them as soon as this afternoon.'

That took the wind right out of Serena's words because he had done exactly that and it was no small feat, mastering her stepmother in the way that he had. It wasn't something she'd ever been able to manage. Serena had never seen Marcia back down so quickly or be at such a loss for words, but she'd been no match for Caleb's lethal charm offensive. Watching it unfold had rendered her speechless and weak-kneed at his show of power. However, the fire raging in her chest was less easy to dampen because of *how* he had done it.

'By telling her that we're getting married. And this weekend!'

Caleb tipped his dark head ever so slightly, the steel in his eyes softening to silver. 'I'm afraid I saw no other way around it. You heard her, Serena. There was no way she was going to let you back into your siblings' lives, not whilst you were, at least in her eyes, disgraced.'

Arms crossed tightly across her chest, she glared back at him. 'Do not pretend that you did that to help me. You are not some knight in shining armour who just slew a dragon and rescued me from a tower.' Although there was some part of her that did feel rescued, and she hated that. Because she couldn't even start to believe he was someone she could rely on in that way. In any way. 'You saw an opportunity to get exactly what you wanted, and you seized upon it.'

'Perhaps I did. But I never claimed to be someone who wouldn't do whatever I have to, to get what I want, did I?' Shivers ran over her because he was so unapologetically arrogant, and it was dazzling. 'And it doesn't mean I didn't want to help you and your siblings. And why didn't *you* tell me that in addition to kicking you out, she was stopping you from seeing your brother and sister?' he asked, watching her from his gleaming gaze. 'How can she even get away with that?'

'Because she adopted them when they were little, right

after she married my dad, so she has final say on everything. And I didn't say anything because it has nothing to do with you.'

She hated that she sounded like a petulant teenager, but the way he had crashed into her life and thrown out commands and now backed her in a corner from which she had no escape had sent her spinning back to all those other times where she'd felt utterly, horribly powerless, as if every drop of power she possessed was slipping from her grasp, and the harder she tried to catch and hold on to it, the more she lost. And now it was happening all over again. And it was worse, because as much as she wanted to loathe Caleb entirely—she didn't. Couldn't.

Because he had helped her. Without any hesitation. It had been so long since she'd had anyone on her side, anyone to fight for her when she felt weak. Her father had almost always taken her side in her scrapes with Marcia. With hindsight she could see how that had aggravated their tenuous relationship, their closeness only making Marcia harden towards her, but in spite of her stepmother's coolness, she'd known such safety, knowing her father was there to catch her if she stumbled or fell. But then, in a blink, he'd been gone and she'd been so alone… So, to finally have someone on her side felt good. Too good, so she had to snap herself out of it because he wasn't offering that kind of partnership. He'd done it in service to himself.

'We both know that isn't true. As long as you're carrying my child, your life is my business.'

The words sounded so full of sense that her feelings only spiralled even deeper. 'That doesn't give you the right to sweep in and start making decisions that affect the rest of it.'

He inched towards her, making her blood fizz and pop all over again. Serena could still feel where his arm had banded around her waist, as if the strength and heat of his skin had imprinted deeply, and she remembered how being pressed up against the hard, hot muscle of his body had made everything else she was feeling slip away and brought desire to the fore, as if she'd been turned upside down, yet had suddenly felt righted.

'I didn't hear you interrupting to tell your stepmother that I was jumping the gun, that we're not getting married,' he pointed out with a smartly arched brow, pausing for the observation to sit between them and rankle her further. Because it was true. She hadn't stopped him. 'And I think the reason you didn't is because you know that marrying me is the only solution available to you.'

Serena spun away from the all-knowing expression on his handsome face with an anguished exhale, knowing he was right on all counts. She didn't have any other options. She had consulted a legal expert. They could help, but it would be a protracted and expensive battle, and whilst it was a fight she would happily undertake, she couldn't afford to, not financially, nor, she suspected, emotionally. Not whilst she was pregnant and not when it was *now* that the twins needed her. Not in the years it would take for the battle to be waged and won.

No, if she wanted to be back in her siblings' lives, marrying Caleb was her only choice. Marcia would be far less troublesome if Serena had Caleb by her side. As much as anything else, she would enjoy having a stepson-in-law of such wealth and bearing. Was that why, as Caleb had pointed out, she hadn't interjected to correct him, even though the words had been on her tongue, hadn't pulled away from his snug grip around her waist, even as it had stirred memories, *yearnings*, that she would have preferred remained undisturbed? Not because his touch had penetrated every level of her being and rendered her helpless, but because for the first time in days she'd seen a chink of light on the horizon, felt a kindling of hope that she could right the wrongs and reunite with Kit and Alexis. Even if it meant compromising on the future she'd envisioned again and binding herself to this impossible man, wasn't it worth it to feel whole again? To be able to fulfil the last promise she'd made to her mother? Not to mention all the other advantages to her unborn child that she'd agonised over all night, wavering the more she'd considered...

'Fine. We'll get married,' she said, forcing the words out.

'I knew you'd come around,' he drawled with a smile that was so wolfish that Serena's stomach quivered ominously, because at least when dealing with her stepmother, she'd known what she was letting herself in for. With Caleb, she had no clue.

But there was one thing she was absolutely certain of—she would not be giving up her freedom. He'd proposed a marriage in name only and that was what he would get, because the days of her living under anyone else's control were well and truly over.

CHAPTER SIX

IT DIDN'T, HOWEVER, take long for Serena to realise that she had very little control over what was happening. Only twenty-four hours after her reluctant agreement, she found herself in the South of France, having left London that morning on a private jet and landing a few hours later at a private airfield, where a car waited to transport them to the hilltop villa Caleb informed her would be home for the following weeks. A small contingent of staff greeted their arrival, ready to cater to Serena's every need and whim, but in spite of the beauty and luxury of her new surroundings, all Serena felt was overwhelmed. Powerless. The speed with which she'd been uprooted from her life and dropped into a whole new one had set her head spinning and her emotions struggling to catch up, feelings certainly not helped when in the same breath he informed her that he was leaving to attend to business matters, Caleb also told her he'd arranged for her to sit down with an event planner to discuss wedding details.

Serena had bristled at that. He had no right to make plans on her behalf and, really, she was in no mood to plan a union that she didn't want to happen. But had he asked her what she wanted? Of course not. And what details needed to be discussed for a wedding that was a formality anyway? Given the circumstances, Serena had assumed that it would be a discreet affair, with minimum fuss. However, within minutes of sitting down with the wedding coordinator, she discovered how flawed that assumption was. Per Caleb's instructions—words that made her bristles bristle—their wedding would be a showstopper, an event to proclaim their love for all the world to witness. Each detail had been more extravagant than the last, culminating with the arrival of the world-renowned couturier who had been hired to dress her for the big day, another of Caleb's executive decisions, even though it was customarily the bride's prerogative to choose her own gown. But the message was clear—she was in his world now, living by his rules and his expectations.

Out of the frying pan and into the fire.

It ignited an angry fire in Serena's stomach, and in spite of taking to the infinity pool in the hopes of relaxing, she tensed all over again. There was sense in marrying him, she knew that, but Caleb didn't seem to understand her agreeing to marry him didn't mean he had control over her life. Maybe she should have been clearer on that from the outset. That was something Serena would fix as soon as she saw him again, which she didn't imagine would be soon, as he'd told her he was in meetings until late. And that was how their marriage would unfold, she expected, with him running his global business whilst she lived her life at home. Serena hesitated on that thought, because Caleb hadn't actually specified how he planned on their conjoined life unfolding. He hadn't shared much of anything, really.

They'd passed the journey to France in relative silence. As soon as they'd boarded, Caleb had settled down to work, the head bent low over his computer emitting a very strong *DO NOT DISTURB* signal, and Serena had been happy to leave him to it, her feelings about him having become troublingly ambivalent overnight. As angry as she wanted to be at the way he had manoeuvred her to right where he wanted her, that emotion was hard to maintain when it had reunited her with Kit and Alexis. Instead, she felt a gratitude to him, and remembering the effort he'd made with her siblings had softened her feelings even more. She hadn't expected him to have any skill with kids, but not only had he charmed Alexis, he'd gently coaxed Kit out of his shell, and that had made her wonder at the father he would prove to be. It was a softer side of him that had reminded her why she had broken all the rules with him that night in Singapore, when she'd rarely been tempted to before.

So, she was glad at the resurgence of her anger. She didn't want to like him. Their situation would be easier if she didn't. Easier to keep from feeling anything remotely tempting or dangerous…

Like the sudden charge of crackling electricity that had her insides tightening and heat whispering over her.

Caleb.

He was back. She could feel the burn of his gaze awakening the parts of her that only he seemed capable of touching, stirring them into a fever. She ordered herself to ignore it, but found herself turning, regardless, seeking him out. Her eyes locked with his, and as they did a current shimmered through the air between them, so strong that she vibrated with the force of it. So strong that it scared her and she broke the connection, swimming to the edge of the pool and climbing out, reaching hastily for the robe she'd left on a nearby lounger.

'You didn't have to get out on my account,' he said,

eyes on her, and she wished he would look away. Or even better, go away.

'I didn't.' She pulled the tie as tight as she could. 'I was done.'

'How did it go with the wedding planner?'

'Fine,' she replied, pausing to see if there was an apology forthcoming for the way he had thrown her into the situation with no warning and without asking her, but of course there wasn't. 'She seems to have a handle on everything. I, however, was a little surprised that we aren't just getting married quickly and quietly.'

'As in eloping?' he drawled with that maddening slant of his eyebrow that so eloquently conveyed his distaste. 'Eloping is all about secrecy, which implies that we have something scandalous to hide, which is the very image we're trying to avoid. A big, extravagant wedding is necessary for our purposes.'

Serena hated to admit, even to herself, that it made sense, because she really would have preferred something small and quiet, something that didn't resemble a real celebration. Because she hadn't just felt overwhelmed earlier, or aggravated. As she'd stood in a gorgeous, flowing white dress and saw herself as a bride for the first time, something else had stirred in her too, something soft and hopeful, almost *yearning*, something that had been dormant since Lucas and which she hadn't expected to ever feel again. Didn't want to feel now. And that had caused an upwelling of worry, because she needed her emotions to stay out of this, yet everything about this wedding was designed to draw out emotion.

Only Caleb hadn't asked what she would have preferred, had he?

He'd just taken it upon himself to make the decision

about what was best and pressed ahead with it. Irrespective of what she thought.

'Then I'm sure you'll be happy with her work,' she said, feeling grateful for that fresh spike of frustration. 'But I would appreciate it, if in future, you would check with me before arranging a meeting on my behalf.'

'If possible, of course,' he replied airily. 'Since my meetings finished earlier than expected, I was able to pick this up for you.' Reaching into his pocket, he withdrew a small velvet box and placed it on the table that stood between them.

'What is that?'

'Why don't you open it and see.'

Apprehension bubbled beneath her skin as she reached for the box, her fingers trembling because she had a fairly good idea of what nestled inside. As much as she wanted to be able to breeze through the moment as if it was nothing, Serena was scared of the rush of emotion that could happen once she popped that lid open. She couldn't seem to manage the same emotional impartiality that Caleb conducted himself with, and as expected her heart jumped when she saw the diamond ring glittering up at her from a bed of black cushion. *Wow.*

It was so stunning that tears hit the back of her eyes, but she quickly blinked them away because the moment was as much of a pretence as everything else. And she didn't like that that bothered her. Didn't understand at all why it did, when the last thing she wanted was the vulnerability of love and marriage.

'Do you like it?' Caleb prompted when she failed to speak.

'Of course.' She could barely take her eyes off it, but forced herself to. 'It's beautiful. Any woman would love it.'

She was wary of saying anymore, of allowing her emotions too long a leash, especially in comparison to his cool practicality. However, the answer clearly didn't satisfy whatever response he'd wanted, as his jaw hardened and mouth firmed, eyes glittering with shards of angry obsidian. She could *feel* his displeasure too, even with the distance she was meticulously holding between them; it radiated off him in sizzling waves. 'Then put it on. It's not just to admire. You are required to wear it.'

Another command. Serena bristled at the instruction, but jammed it onto her finger, fixing him with her gaze. 'Happy, now?'

'Ecstatic.' Eyes narrowing, he subjected her to a protracted perusal, frustrated shadows cutting into the smooth planes of his face. 'I understand this situation isn't ideal, Serena. It isn't where I expected or wanted to find myself either, you know.'

'You think I don't know that? You made your regret about what happened between us very clear that night in Singapore.' His nostrils flared as she threw that at him, and a line of intense colour scored its way across his cheekbones. 'And as if that wasn't enough, you then didn't even believe I was actually pregnant. You came to London intent on exposing me as a liar.'

Serena hated that it still hurt, that his opinion held such power over her. That she wanted him to see her as someone good. Someone who wasn't a regret.

'Put yourself in my position, Serena. With my wealth and status, I only questioned what any man in my situation would.' He sighed heavily. 'But you're right. I didn't handle the situation well, and you didn't deserve to be met with that. But when I got your email, I went into self-protection mode, and it was easier for me to believe that it wasn't true and to focus on that anger that made me feel, than it was to deal with all the feelings that accepting the truth would conjure.'

It was a moment of such startling and unexpected honesty that Serena's heartbeat faltered. It was her first glimpse of the man who lay beneath the impenetrable façade, and she wanted to see more of him.

'Feelings about how a family was never something you wanted?' she ventured tentatively.

He nodded stiffly, and the uneasy emotion spiking in his gaze seemed to hint at a wound that had never quite healed, a scar that he would go to any lengths to prevent inflicting on any child of his own. Her curiosity intensified.

'Did something happen to make you feel that way?'

He looked over at her, and Serena held her breath, her heart racing with anticipation to learn more, to know *something real* about him, but with a blink, his gaze shuttered once again, and the abrupt change sent a chill across her skin.

'It's not important.' The words fell like bricks, reconstructing that wall between them that had, for a moment, felt like it was beginning to be dismantled. 'What matters now is that there is a child and we are going to be a family and that I do the best I can for both of you. It's not what either of us expected, but it's the situation we're in. I suggest you accept that. The sooner you do, the better off we'll both be.'

Her eyes narrowed, the words scraping against her overwrought senses, the disappointment at how quickly he had shut her out making her annoyance even more potent. 'You may be able to control everything else, Caleb, but you do *not* have command over my thoughts or emotions.'

He arched a brow, clearly disliking his command capabilities being questioned. 'Is that so?' he drawled, gazing down at her with such emotion brewing in his gaze that her bones actually shook.

Until that moment Serena hadn't realised that they'd been drawing closer and closer and now stood only an inch apart. They were so close that every frantic breath she drew in contained a heart-stopping trace of him, and in the glitter of his eyes she could read the intent to prove that, should he wish to, should he *choose* to, he could very easily exert mastery over all of her, just as he had that night in Singapore. Her breath locked in her chest at the prospect, as thrilled by it as she was scared. The light in his eyes deepened as they dropped to her mouth, eyes which seemed intent on devouring, and curse her, a part of Serena hoped that he would. Craved it desperately. Because she knew that the moment his lips touched hers, all else would cease to matter. Her frustration, her fear, her reality—all of it would be silenced by the exquisite texture of his sensual skill, by the possessive slide of his hands over her skin. There would only be oblivion, and right now, that was so very tempting to her.

An inch. That was all that was separating Caleb's mouth from Serena's. He would barely need to move his head to feel her lips yielding beneath his. And Caleb had no doubt that she would yield. The same flare of white-hot intensity that licked at his insides was dancing coaxingly in her eyes and humming in her blood. He could hear it. See it. The flutters of her pulse were so hard they were visible and it was *because of him*.

The intoxicating knowledge nudged him even closer to the kind of reckless behaviour he knew he needed to stay far away from. But, despite knowing that, in that moment, he found it difficult to care or believe in its imperativeness. He knew that the force of his longing was all the greater because it had been so long since he'd found sexual release. The only woman he'd wanted was the woman now standing temptingly close to him, her presence some kind of dangerous dare. And to finally slake that deep and vast hunger, to finish what they had started but not fully satisfied, all he needed to do was lower his head a single, tiny inch. But whilst that was what he wanted to do most of all, he hadn't entirely forgotten that it was the last thing he could allow to happen.

So, he summoned the discipline that had never been in such short supply as it was around Serena and took a step backwards. And then another. His blood continued to burn with the proximity of temptation, and even more alarming was the way he could feel that something between them had tilted. Not for better or for worse, but something that had been simmering since their reunion on the street in London, but which had not been acknowledged, had just flared too powerfully for either of them to be unmoved. To keep pretending it no longer existed. Even if it was the last thing he wanted to exist between them because there was no place for it in their relationship.

Their marriage was going to be an unemotional endeavor, and he needed to be sure Serena understood that. That he made the parameters clear now, at the outset, so that she didn't build pretty, romantic plans in her head and end up with her life in tatters, as Charlotte had. So that she didn't interpret any moments of unforgivable weakness on his part as anything other than exactly that—the very real needs of a red-blooded man around a beautiful woman, a woman who made him burn hotter and higher than any who had come before. Even after all this time, and all his efforts to put her from his mind.

He needed to keep it front and centre in his own mind too, especially now they were sharing the same home, because every moment spent in Serena's presence was a moment that threatened a loss of control that couldn't, *mustn't*, happen.

Only moments ago, he'd been felled by the sight of her in the swimming pool, the elegant shape of her back and the pale peach tone of her skin inflaming a desire that had stopped him in his tracks. His eyes had feasted on her, and he'd wondered if she was naked in the water and blood had surged south with the thought. He'd been hit with the thought of stripping off his suit and diving into the water to join her. But he knew better. And yet he hadn't been able to make himself continue on to his room, so he'd stood, drinking her in like a man starved of water, until the weight of his gaze had become too heavy and her head had turned and their eyes had caught and the connection that had zinged between them had been electric.

However, it had disappeared as quickly as it had struck, and instead of the fire and hunger that Caleb had wanted to see in Serena's eyes, there had been annoyance. Even the diamond ring hadn't sparked any pleasure, and it aggravated on a male level that whilst he had been affected, she hadn't. And he was being affected too often, and in too many ways. He'd let her believe that his dismantling of her stepmother had been done to press his advantage, which it had, but not entirely. He'd wanted to protect her too. She'd looked so fragile, so broken down by her stepmother that he'd wanted to be her white knight—not that there was anything to recommend him for the role—and rescuing her had felt good. Far better than it should. Which was far too much.

'You should shower and change. Chef Pierre will be arriving soon to prepare dinner.'

She blinked in surprise. 'You didn't mention anything about having dinner together earlier.'

'Well, I'm mentioning it now,' he snapped, his patience running low.

'And what about my feelings on the matter? Do I not get a say in how I spend my evening?' she demanded, the fire of her Italian heritage rising again as if from nowhere, and he hated that he found it so sexy, that it made him want to plumb the depths of her even more.

'No, you don't. There are matters we still need to discuss,' he riposted, seeing anger flash like lightning in her eyes again before he turned on his heel and walked away. Let her think of him as arrogant and controlling. It was better that way, better if she loathed him. It would help keep distance between them, distance he was struggling with. 'Be ready in an hour.'

CHAPTER SEVEN

SERENA LOOKED ANYWHERE other than at Caleb as they sat opposite one another at the table exquisitely set for two. Her body was still vibrating and her lips tingling with the want that had coursed through her and been left unsatisfied. She was so angry with herself for wanting the kiss so badly, and angry with him, for being able to step back so easily and then demanding she sit down to eat with him. Because with every interaction with him, Serena felt less in control of the situation, and even more worryingly, of herself.

'A contract is being drawn up and will be delivered to you before the wedding for your review and signature,' Caleb began, after their first course was laid before them. 'But I thought it would be a good idea for us to go over in person some of the main details of what our marriage will entail.'

'A contract?' The word caused unease to prickle along her skin, making her think of rules and consequences, reminding her too much of life under her stepmother. 'Is that necessary? This isn't a business deal.'

He dealt her a quelling look. 'That's exactly what this is, Serena. A short-term merger so to speak. The contract just lays out all the particulars.'

She started to feel hot all over, trapped again. 'What if I don't like the "particulars" in this contract?'

'Since that's what we're going to discuss now, I don't foresee that being a problem. Now, the contract will state that we will remain married for a minimum of five years and then divorce at some point of our choosing after that, at which time we will share custody of our son or daughter equally and move forwards co-parenting.'

'Share custody?' Serena repeated, her hand settling protectively over her stomach.

'Unless you would like me to take primary custody.'

'No. If anyone should have primary custody, it would be me, the mother.' She had already lost one child and felt similar pain slicing through her at being separated from this one.

'But as already stated, I refuse to be apart from my child, and since you seem to feel the same, shared custody is the only option. Now, in terms of where we'll live as a family, I assume you won't want to leave London.'

'Of course not. Kit and Alexis are there.'

'Which I fully anticipated, and that suits me fine. With the European expansion, I had planned on relocating to Europe, and London is an ideal base. I've had my team researching properties and I feel this is the best. I'm sure it will be to your liking too.'

He held out the tablet for her to view the images of the chosen property, and although recognising that he'd shown a certain consideration in selecting London as their base because of her family ties, Serena still frowned at his instinctive autocratic ways. He said they'd be *discussing* things—only he didn't seem to know the meaning of the word!

'What do you think?'

'It's fine, but...'

'Very good,' he said, lifting the device from her hands and not letting her finish before continuing on with his agenda. 'As I mentioned, I'll travel often for business. The majority of the time I'll go alone, but on occasion you will be required to accompany me—and it goes without saying, play the role of loving wife. For example, the opening of the beach club here in a few weeks. You'll be by my side. There will be other events that you'll attend too—banquets, charity galas, social parties. My assistant will coordinate your calendar so you'll know in advance when and where you'll be required. Obviously, we'll take into account the pregnancy, especially as it progresses. No one is expecting you to exert yourself.'

No, just to pass over control of her calendar, as well as the next five years of her life to him, apparently. The disquiet spiking her blood grew hotter, and her head started to spin, overwhelmed by his high-handedness. 'Have you forgotten that I work full time?' she reminded him, determined to be heard this time. 'I can't be taking time off to travel and attend parties whenever you summon me.'

He looked back at her, untroubled. 'I'm sure we can work it out. You don't even need to keep working if you don't want to.'

'You expect me to give up my job?'

'No. But it's an option. I'll be providing for you financially now.'

'Caleb, that's generous, but I'm not sure I'm comfortable giving up that aspect of my independence. It's important to me that I'm able to take care of myself.'

'Even once the baby is born?' he queried. It made Serena wary to look that far ahead, not when there was so much time for things to go wrong. 'Because I don't love the idea of our child being raised by an army of nannies.'

Serena couldn't clamp down her annoyance at his he-who-shall-be-obeyed tone. 'So, you *do* expect me to stop working?' she demanded, reeling. 'Why did you say you wanted to *discuss* all of this, when you seemed to have made all of the decisions already, without so much as a conversation with me?'

'We're having a conversation now,' he responded, his coolness only making her feel worse because she was so overwhelmed. 'And I haven't made any decisions, I'm only expressing...'

'You're telling me *how* it will be,' she interrupted hotly, feeling like she was eighteen again and back in her bedroom, being told by her stepmother the rules and behaviours she was expected to adhere to, her world narrowing with each passing second. '*What* I will do and *when* I'll do it.'

Her frustration burned so hotly that her heart battered against her ribs as she saw her future unfold without her having any voice or autonomy in it. Again.

For a brief moment it had actually been within her power to write her own future, but now this.

Him.

She couldn't help but think of all of the things she'd lost and missed out on as her life had been steered by another hand, and her throat thickened as that feeling of powerlessness descended again. Truthfully, she didn't want a nanny raising her child either, but she wanted that to be *her* decision. Or an actual discussion between them. Not a law laid down that she was expected to obediently follow.

But he was so...domineering. She couldn't even loathe

him for it, because he had used that resolute power to subdue her stepmother. Without him being the way he was, who he was, she would still be stuck in that hell of yesterday. She fought to remain calm, to stabilise the punching of her heart, but emotion was building, stacking higher and higher until there was only panic.

'Serena…'

'No. Stop talking. Please.'

But it didn't help. She pushed herself to her feet.

'Where are you going?' he demanded.

'I need a minute. I'm not asking,' she warned him as his mouth opened and she swept past him, taking the path down to the beach, called by the openness of the sea and sky, the way it stretched even farther than she could see, full of possibilities and no limits.

She'd never forgotten the stories her mother had told her of her time as a young artist in Rome and Paris and London. Serena had dreamed of following in her footsteps, even more so after she'd died, knowing it would keep the memory of her mother close, and she would have had the opportunity to live and work in Paris or Florence as part of her degree. It was that which had kept her focused, kept her grief over her father's passing and miscarriage from swallowing her completely. But right when she'd been on the cusp of it, Marcia had intervened, forcing her to choose between herself and the twins.

There had been no choice to make. Leaving Kit and Alexis was unthinkable, but letting go of her dreams had been so hard. It had been like letting go a piece of herself, and a piece of her mother. She wasn't losing anything as profound this time, but the emotion was the same nonetheless.

Serena didn't realise she was crying until she felt the

teardrops drop to her chest. Lifting a hand to her face, it came away wet, but the release felt good, the pressure on her chest easing substantially. She had held everything in for so long, having to be strong, that this moment of privacy in which to break down was a gift, and she felt better for it.

'Are you ok?'

Serena sucked in a breath. The last thing she wanted was for Caleb to see her in tears. 'I'm fine.'

She had survived her stepmother and would handle this too. Because she wasn't a young girl anymore, frightened and fragile, and she wouldn't let this be the same. Wiping her face dry, she squared her shoulders and turned across the sand towards him.

'Let's go back to dinner and finish our conversation.' Calmer now, she had terms of her own to assert.

But as she passed by, Caleb's hand snatched out and seized her arm, halting her. His eyes raked over her face. 'You've been crying. You're upset. What's wrong?'

She tried to tug her arm free because his touch was scorching her skin and as that heat sank deep into her blood and her bones, her pulse skittered. But what shook her even more was the concern she read in his eyes, a concern that had long been absent from her life.

When she'd miscarried, Serena had had to take herself to the hospital. There hadn't been anyone to hold her hand or stroke her hair as she'd tensed in battle against the indescribable discomfort. There had been no one's shoulder to cry on, no arms to comfort her when the doctor had delivered the bad news and no one to take her home and tuck her in bed to rest and mourn. She'd had only herself to rely on, and going forwards, that was exactly what she had done.

It had been sink or swim and she'd refused to drown. To give her stepmother the pleasure of watching her flounder. That was how she'd lived the last five years, not looking for care and affection from others, because she knew she couldn't count on it being given. It had been hard and lonely…but less painful. So, to see it now, in the last place she would have expected to find it, in Caleb's face, was disarming, and even more surprising was that she wanted to tell him—everything. To not have to be strong and guarded and just…be.

'Serena? Tell me.'

'OK,' she said, following the feeling, even though she had no idea where it would lead. 'I thought I was finally going to get to live my life on my terms. To be in control of my life, at last, but instead…there's you. With your commands and expectations and contract. Telling me what I will and won't do. And I don't want to be told what to do and who to be anymore.'

'I'm not telling you what to do,' he blustered, but a quick look at her tear-streaked face had that conviction deserting him. 'Or at least, I'm not trying to.' He looked bewildered by the accusation, horrified that she had even for a second imagined that he was trying to control her. 'Serena, if that's how it seems, I'm sorry. I appreciate that I can be somewhat domineering…'

'Somewhat?' she quickly cut in, her brow arching.

'OK, a lot domineering,' he amended. 'It's what my life, my role, demands of me. But I don't ever want you to think that I want to control you. That's the last thing I want.' He stared down at her, his gaze weighty, working to assimilate this new, explosive information. 'It was your stepmother, wasn't it? The person telling you what to do before?'

Serena nodded. 'It was the only way I was able to stay in Kit's and Alexis's lives—by adhering to what she wanted, living by the rules and standards that she set. Everything from where I worked to how I dressed, to who I was friends with was dictated by her.'

Horror leached into his expression. 'Serena, I would never try to tell you how to live. Not at all. I hate that I've made you feel that way. I'm sorry. God, I...' Drawing in a breath, he ran his hand over his face. 'All I was trying to do was to banish some of the uncertainty from this situation we're in and make sure we're on the same page moving forwards. Not for a second did I think you would feel dictated to. That's the last thing I intended. Please tell me you believe that.'

His dismay was so apparent, so genuine that it was easy to believe his taking charge emanated from a conscientiousness and not a will to control. 'I believe you.'

His relief was palpable. 'I still don't understand why your stepmother would treat you that way?'

'Because...' Serena stopped as soon as she started. There was no way for him to understand without knowing the whole story. But it was a story that out of fear and shame she had never shared with anyone, keeping it bottled so tightly within her. But how could he understand otherwise? And, much to her surprise, she wanted him to understand. And surely, he had a right to know. Taking a breath, she began again. 'Because she didn't trust me to behave and not create another scandal like the one I caused when I got pregnant at eighteen.'

Shock rippled through his silver eyes. 'You were pregnant before?'

She nodded, anticipating his next question. 'I miscarried at nine weeks.'

'Serena…'

'That's why she did it. Because she didn't think I could be trusted and that I could be a bad influence on the twins. And given that I did fall into your arms within hours of meeting you and fall pregnant again, maybe she wasn't wrong.'

'First of all, you have no reason to feel any guilt or shame about what happened between us,' he asserted strongly. 'It was natural and wonderful. And when I said it shouldn't have happened, I meant me taking someone less experienced than me. *You* were never a mistake. And secondly, I don't care about your stepmother right now. Only about you.' His throat worked, and she could see how affected he was by her admission. 'Serena, you lost a baby.'

'Yes.' And now that she had uncorked that bottle, she could feel it all rising up within her, that tide of feeling she had always been so afraid of. Scared to speak of in case others shamed her as Marcia had, or blamed her as she blamed herself. But, looking into Caleb's expression, so full of compassion, she felt safe to speak. 'It was awful. I was alone in this hospital room for hours and I just felt like… I'd failed.'

'Yor stepmother wasn't with you?'

'No,' she scoffed. 'Things between Marcia and I got worse after that, but they'd been bad before. Not just because of her,' Serena admitted. 'I never made it easy. I didn't want her in our lives where my mum should have been. I accepted the marriage because my father asked me to, because he said Kit and Alexis needed a mother, but I never wanted her there and we never got on. I never felt like she liked me. She loved the twins from the moment she met them—I think she liked that she could make them hers, that she would be the only mother they knew—whereas I was my mother's daughter through and through. And I looked so like her—the woman my father had loved first and still loved. Whilst he was alive my dad was our go-between, advocating on each of our behalf's and smoothing over the tension he could see. But once he was gone…that tension just ballooned. Nothing I did was right. And when she learned I was pregnant, she was furious. Scandalised and ashamed. And when I miscarried…all she had to say was it was probably for the best.'

Tears rolled from her eyes and she was taken aback when Caleb pulled her into his arms. 'She should have supported you better. She owed you that.' His voice contained a trace of anger. 'Regardless of how you behaved, you were a grieving girl. She was the adult. She'll never hurt you or shame you again. I promise.'

The words were delivered with such conviction that Serena couldn't do anything but trust them and, held so tight against him, she even felt secure enough to peel herself open more 'I'm scared that the same thing is going to happen again—with the baby,' she admitted in a whisper. 'I try not to think about it, but it's in my head. There was no reason for why it happened last time… which makes it worse. If there was something I could do or avoid doing…but I just feel like I failed. That I somehow caused it to happen.'

'I don't think it works like that,' he murmured, detangling from her, but continuing to holding her by the arms as he looked down into her face. 'It just wasn't meant to be, as hard as that is to accept. Did you like Dr Newman?'

'Yes.'

'Good. We'll make an appointment for you to see her as soon as we return to London, and after that you'll see her as often as you want to, OK. Whatever it takes for you to feel comfortable and reassured. And if you're ever worried that something is wrong, tell me. I don't care if it's the middle of the day or the middle of the night. We'll do whatever it takes to keep this pregnancy safe.'

'Thank you,' she murmured. It was the exact reassurance she needed, and she didn't know how he'd known that, but as she looked up at him, she recognised the haunted look in his eyes, the urgency of not wanting to lose anyone and feel that sting of loss again. Had he lost someone too, she wondered. That could explain why he'd never wanted a family, because loss went hand in hand with love. Maybe that was that why he kept such a tight hold on everything as well, trying to prevent a repeat of whatever he had suffered.

Caleb presented such an impenetrable front, but the past few hours had shown that he was vulnerable too.

'And moving forwards I'll try to be less domineering. But I really did just want us both to know where we stand going forwards.'

Boundaries were important to him, Serena realised, as much as her freedom was to her. He liked clear and defined lines that didn't get smudged. It was what had unpinned him in Singapore, that he had strayed from his norm with her, crossed some invisible line, and he needed those lines to be comfortable. But why? What was he so afraid of happening?

'I get that now.' She sent her eyes up to his face, feeling thrumming through her as she did. 'I know it hasn't seemed so, but I am grateful that you're here, that you want to be involved and grateful for what you did with Marcia. I have Kit and Alexis back because of you.'

'It's admirable—all you sacrificed for them.'

'I could never leave them. They were only seven years old at the time. They'd already lost both our parents. They couldn't lose me too. And I promised my mum, when she was pregnant with them that I'd always be there for them. I couldn't let her down.'

'You haven't.' He was quick to issue that assurance. 'Your brother and sister are lucky to have you, Serena. And our baby is lucky to have such a strong mother.' His expression grew serious, and caught between the sunlight and growing shadows, Serena saw a whole new plane of Caleb's face, saw the whisper of vulnerability that flashed and then slowly faded. 'I have no idea what kind of father I'll be, so I'm glad they have you.'

Her heart caught. 'Are you scared? Of being a father? Is that why you were reluctant to accept that I was pregnant?'

He was slow to answer. 'I'm scared of making mistakes that I've already made before.'

The words were so stark, and his expression, as he emitted them, so bleak that her stomach knotted. 'What could you have possibly done that was so bad?'

He looked away, out into the encroaching darkness. 'I hurt someone once. In every way a person can be hurt.'

'Who?'

'Her name was Charlotte. We were…involved.'

'I thought you didn't have relationships,' Serena murmured, her heart faltering with a spike of envy.

'I don't.' A warning seemed to shoot from his eyes. 'I didn't then either. It was a casual thing, at least to me. But since then, since her, I don't even do that.'

'What happened?'

'I was young and reckless. Impossible.'

'You're still impossible now,' she murmured with a

small smile, being granted one in return, but it was only half-hearted.

'I was worse back then. I lived a charmed life. I was used to getting everything I wanted, and the moment I saw Charlotte, I wanted her, so I did what I always did—pursued her until I got her. She was only in Melbourne for the summer. She had no knowledge of my lifestyle, how I cycled through women, and I never explained it to her. I was just having fun, but she was falling in love with me, talking to her family about us living together and getting married.' He paused, regret writing itself into every line across his face. 'When Charlotte realised that I had no notion of a future with her and never had, she was crushed, as she had every right to be. She lost it right there in the club, screaming at me that I'd led her on. Then she stormed out.' He exhaled and closed his eyes and, seeing how arduous it was for him, Serena reached out, touching her fingertips to his knee, letting him know she was there. 'I should have followed her. I should have run after her. Every time I replay that night in my head, I do. I chase after her, stop her. I get her home safe. But I was careless and selfish, and I just let her leave. She went to another bar, had too much to drink and then got in her car to drive home. And then she rammed the car into a tree.'

Serena's breath stuck somewhere in her throat, but she kept her eyes fixed on Caleb.

'She broke her back and a few other bones. She needed to have surgery on her spine and then months of rehab. The company she'd spent the summer interning for had been so impressed that they'd offered her a permanent position, but she couldn't take it, not with her injuries. Her future, everything she'd worked so hard for, was set back years. Because of me.'

The words fell like a hammer blow and he looked away, a line of deep-seated shame scoring its way across his cheeks, and Serena marvelled at that burden that he made himself carry.

'No, not because of you. What happened to her was awful, but it wasn't your fault, Caleb.'

'Of course it was,' he insisted sharply. 'She was too smart, too level-headed to have done anything like that before getting involved with me. But I hurt her so badly that she forgot herself entirely.'

'Yes, you hurt her. But the decisions that caused the accident were hers.' How could he not see that? 'You weren't responsible.'

'I wreaked havoc on her life, Serena. And her family's life. You should have seen the worry and pain on their faces at the hospital. Because of me. And the things they said...they were right.'

'They were angry, Caleb. Upset and scared. They needed someone to blame and lash out at. But you're not to blame. You shouldn't be punishing yourself for what happened.'

He looked away again, and Serena inched closer, even though what she really wanted was to hold him as tight as she could, the way he had held her. He had condemned himself for what had happened, without seeing that a man without a conscience wouldn't care. He would have moved on, absolved himself and forgotten. The fact that he carried what had happened meant that he'd never been, not even for a second, the reckless man he believed himself to have been. But he'd consigned himself to a prison of his own making as punishment for a crime he was determined to believe he was guilty of.

'It's as you said—you were young. You made a mistake. But you're not the worst thing you've ever done.' Did he not think he was deserving of love or a happy future? Of course, she realised, this was why he limited his involvement to the briefest period possible, painting thick lines around himself. Everything he hadn't done with Charlotte. 'That's why it's important to you that everything is neat and clear between us? So, there'll be no misunderstandings?'

'Yes.'

Serena nodded, wishing she knew what more to say, but as she searched for the right words, Caleb glanced at his watch and shifted. 'It's late and you've had a long day. You should get some rest.'

She didn't want to agree. She wanted to stay locked in the moment with him, both of their guards down so that it felt like the beginning all over again, but she was exhausted, not to mention emotionally drained, and the fact that she wanted to stay meant she definitely needed to move. Because she had liked getting to know the man that Caleb was beneath his strong surface a little too much. So, distance was necessary now, to reset after such an emotional evening and pull her emotions back to safe ground. Because the last thing Serena needed, or wanted, was to get caught up in him, in their relationship, and Caleb had been clear on not wanting that either. *I don't have relationships.*

He'd marry her, but he wanted nothing else. And Serena was determined to want nothing else from him either.

CHAPTER EIGHT

THE MUSIC FROM the quartet changed, signalling the arrival of his bride, and Caleb's shoulders tensed, the magnitude of the moment striking him squarely in the chest despite his efforts to pretend this was just another day.

It will be fine. You have this all under control, he assured himself in response to the apprehension thudding through his veins and thwacking against his heart like a drum as he thought back to the starlit moments he and Serena had shared on their beach just a few days ago, and how close they had drawn together in those moments.

Closer than he should ever have allowed...

But her confessions about her traumatic miscarriage and difficult relationship with her stepmother had touched a part of him that was normally untouchable, and once again, he'd felt sore at how much she'd endured, whilst also marvelling at her resilience and strength in refusing to give up. Feeling so much for her had shaken him, and before he'd really known what he was doing, and before he could silence himself, he'd been telling her about Charlotte. *Why?* He'd asked himself that question over and over again since, and as much as he'd tried telling himself it had been as a cautionary tale, a warning to Serena about wanting too much from him, he couldn't make himself believe that. No, it was almost if he'd wanted to share it with her, to be as open and brave as she had been with him and offer up a part of himself, deepening their connection instead of halting it, which was bizarre to him because that was never something he'd wanted before. So, what had come over him in that moment?

And when she'd said he wasn't to blame…for the first time Caleb had wondered if that could be true. Her assurance had felt stronger than his guilt, and for a moment he'd wondered if he wasn't destined to always cause pain, if he didn't have to carry all that guilt with him into his future as a father. And husband.

Not that he wanted a real future, not with Serena, not with anyone. That was a decision he'd made long ago, long before Charlotte, after witnessing and experiencing the destruction that love could unleash.

The proud beaming man sitting in the front row with his wife of eight years by his side was not the father that Caleb had grown up with. Back then, his father had been broken and distant, tormented by the loss of his wife and unable to offer his son anything because there was nothing in him to give. Hollowed out himself from being deserted by his mother, Caleb had longed desperately for something, *anything*, from his father, and the ache when he hadn't received it had been messy and tormented. Agonised, hopeless feelings had rattled in his body all day and night long—feelings he had worked hard to suppress and lock away and which he had no interest in unleashing again, and until now, until her, they'd never felt in any danger of being unlocked.

But Serena evoked more feeling in him that anyone else had ever managed to. And not because she was carrying his child and he felt a sense of responsibility towards her—he'd already tried dismissing it as that—but just because of who she was. That was what was most disconcerting—that for no apparent reason she exposed the soft spots that still existed within him. The pieces that could be made to feel.

To hurt.

Parts of himself that he didn't want to exist, and keeping himself so busy in the preceding days had been as much about closing down those weaknesses within him as it was about preventing a repeat of anything that had arced between them on the beach—that sense of closeness and connection and the yearning for more of it—*especially* that.

Because there was no place for it, not in their marriage and certainly not in his life. The last thing he wanted was closeness and confidences. He was happy holding everyone at arm's-length and didn't want Serena to override his usual emotional reserve.

It had happened twice now…there couldn't be a third time. He wouldn't let there be. Their marriage was a practical endeavour after all, and after a lifetime eschewing emotion, it shouldn't be difficult to heed the warnings filtering down from his brain that counselled—*urged*—caution. Distance.

He had managed it successfully the past few days, resetting their relationship to what it should be, and saw no reason for the lines to blur again.

Sensing Serena's approach from the buzz running through the guests, Caleb turned his head, eager to prove that the past days distance had worked and he could look at her and remain detached… Only for the sight of her to punch every last whisp of air from his lungs.

She was…exquisite. Breathtaking.

Beyond retaining the services of a renowned French fashion designer and instructing them to provide a dress that endorsed his narrative of a whirlwind, fairy tale falling in love, he hadn't much considered how Serena would look. Now he wished that he had in some way prepared himself, because then maybe his heart wouldn't be beating quite so fast and the fabric of his custom suit wouldn't feel quite so tight as his body swelled with sexual hunger.

The dress, whilst every inch the romantic and elegant creation he had specified, clung to her like a second skin, revealing to his appreciative eyes the changes wrought by the pregnancy. Her hips had more curve, and her breasts were unquestionably fuller. Whilst aware of his promise to maintain distance, physically as well as emotionally, suddenly he craved the taste of her in his mouth more than anything else, craved the intimacy of her essence lingering on his tongue. Caleb imagined drawing the material of the dress down and sucking her nipple in his mouth and an answering heat sliding sinuously in the pit of his stomach, before shooting south with all the force of a bullet.

Later, he thought excitedly, and it took a moment for awareness to strike that there wouldn't be a later. Because this was not a real wedding. How had he forgotten that, even momentarily?

Serena reached him, her caramel eyes meeting his with a nervousness that she was clearly trying to fight, and he reached for her hand, squeezing it tight, belatedly telling himself he did so as part of the show.

The officiant started to speak, and Caleb tried to listen to the words, but was prevented by the feeling pulsing steadily beneath his skin. It only intensified as Serena pledged herself to him, her voice rattling ever so slightly with nerves, and he returned the sentiment with a possessiveness that he knew should not have been beating quite so fiercely in his chest but which refused to calm.

It was acceptable for other men to feel that way on their wedding day, but not him. This was not a real wedding, after all. Not a real marriage.

'With great happiness, I declare you husband and wife. You may now kiss your bride.'

Caleb smiled down at Serena, ignoring the surge of delight the officiant's words had prompted, and curled his arm around her, drawing her in slowly to deliver the gentle kiss that would be appropriate and risk-free. However, the moment his lips met hers and he was struck with her intoxicating scent, all thoughts of slow and steady faded.

Instead, there was hunger and need and those flagrant forces conspired to drive his tongue into the warm cavern of her mouth. He devoured the taste of her, thinking only of staking his claim so completely, of doing what he hadn't allowed himself to do, to even really think of doing. Serena shuddered against him, but didn't resist. One of her hands flattened against his chest, the other sliding around his neck and with that tender touch, the flames roaring in his gut raced along his veins, the kiss gaining heat with each second. He angled her head for better access, drawing more of her elemental response from her as he hugged her even closer to his pounding body. Then he heard it, the sound of applause exploding around them, and finding some remaining vestige of control, Caleb eased his mouth from hers.

Keeping hold of her trembling body and avoiding her dazed gaze, he turned to face their cheering guests. But as they walked back down the aisle, showered by thousands of flower petals, behind the smile etched on his face, Caleb's brain whirred with troubled whisperings. Suddenly he was wondering if this marriage was going to be as manageable as he kept telling himself.

* * *

'It's time for our first dance, Mrs Morgenthau.'

Serena glanced at the hand that Caleb held out, fear skittering along her veins at the heat that would take hold when her skin brushed against his, when he pulled her against his body and held her close. But Evie was right beside her, watching, and everyone else was watching too, so Serena summoned a smile and, drawing up as many barricades as she could, placed her hand in his, letting him lead her to the centre of the dance floor.

The hand that settled on her back scorched, burning through the thin fabric of her stunning gown, and she fought with all of her might not to melt with instant desire. But that was a battle that she'd been losing nearly all day long.

Serena had started the day a nervous wreck, her stomach cramping as she sat through hair and make-up, antsy with the thoughts of what lay ahead even though she knew it was the right thing. But, in spite of that, more than once she'd wanted to turn and run as she'd waited to begin her walk down the aisle. Had still been thinking about it as she made her way to the altar, but then her eyes had locked on Caleb—seeing him properly for the first time in days—waiting beneath the abundant arch of fragrant white flowers, and her feelings had shifted.

Nerves continued to ripple beneath her skin, but they were threaded with heat, and the longing to run was no longer to run away, but *towards* him. Because in the tailored suit superbly fitted to the tall musculature of his body, and looking more darkly, impossibly handsome than usual under the beam of sunlight, he embodied every dream her head had once been filled with, everything she had once wished would be waiting for her in her future, and remembering how he had held her as she'd cried out the pain and shame that she'd been carrying for years, she'd felt inexorably bonded to him. Serena's heart had quickened even more as he'd settled his striking eyes on her, watching her as if she was his every dream come true too, and for a tiny second, she had fallen under the spell of the moment, believing that it was real, that in spite of all the hardship she'd been dealt, she had finally found her way to happiness. But that had snapped her out of it, because she knew happiness never lasted. Whenever she'd thought she was approaching a happy and settled place in the past, the bottom always dropped out of her world with more hurt or loss. In that way, her arrangement with Caleb was ideal, because she knew exactly when the end would be and wouldn't have anything invested emotionally to feel that loss like a physical wound.

Or so she told herself. Yet, since their conversation on the beach, her feelings for Caleb had been evolving.

He'd been so understanding, and so open in return, and for the first time it had really occurred to Serena how he must be struggling with the enormity of what they were doing too. Logistically. Emotionally. He invested so much energy in keeping people at arm's length, afraid of hurting them the way he'd hurt Charlotte, but he'd hardly hesitated at bringing her into his life and that had to be costing him something.

Hard as she had tried to not think about him, to not watch for his return to the villa, Serena did. Too many times she'd caught herself wondering about the man that he was and the scars that he bore, wanting to know even more. Which was completely illogical, because she'd agreed to give him her hand, not her heart, and yet the thought of him never failed to make her heart beat faster.

But still, the thought of her heart becoming involved filled her with dread. She didn't want to give someone that degree of power over her, and she was reminding herself of that a lot, and that their relationship wasn't real. And that she didn't want it to be.

And that heat building and pulsing at your breastbone—is that not real either?

Pushing that awareness, and the questions it raised, out of her mind, Serena concentrated on keeping her smile in place, keeping her eyes on Caleb, starry and dreamy, as if this was everything she had ever wanted as they progressed through the ceremony, even as she worked to root herself as firmly as she could in reality, plant her feet so deeply she wouldn't lose herself to the charade again.

But then…that kiss.

Her eyes had widened as the officiant invited them to seal their vows with a kiss, having conveniently overlooked that part of the ceremony, but she had no time to dwell on it as Caleb lowered his head. She'd assumed it would be something brief and sweet. After all, he'd made it clear, with words and actions, that there would be nothing between them. But there had been nothing chaste about what had exploded between them.

The second his mouth had touched hers, heat detonated in her like a firework. Prising her lips apart, his tongue had curled against hers, stroking the inside of her mouth, and she'd been helpless, unable to fight her instinctive response, that hungry neediness that surged from deep within her to see her fist her hand around his neck and hold him close, pleading with her body, her fingers, for him to never, ever stop what he was doing.

But of course, he did. Because he was only acting and

so ended the kiss easily, whilst she had felt every single pulse of it in every inch of her body.

Events were something of a haze after that. She remembered Caleb leading her back down the aisle to applause, his hand tight around hers. She remembered the wedding planner stealing them away for photographs and being painfully aware of Caleb's every touch, and of the panic when each touch penetrated that much deeper, evoking an even deeper quiver of longing. Though she continued to smile and pose, Serena had grown more anxious by the second, fretting that she had tied herself to someone she had little hope of resisting, and no amount of rooting herself in reality would be enough to combat that vital and visceral attraction.

It hadn't been problematic when she was annoyed by him, but now there was nothing to prevent those feelings from flooding her, and Serena became even more blisteringly aware of that as his body brushed purposely against hers, and her face rested close to the nook of his neck, inhaling that bergamot scent straight off his skin, skin she was close enough to touch. To...

Her thoughts scattered as his fingertips caressed the bare skin of her back, and she felt the bones in her knees threaten to give way. She didn't know how she was going to get through this. How she would survive the next five minutes, never mind the following *five years*?

They stretched ahead, long and ominous, day after day of longing for the husband she shouldn't want and couldn't have. And what about the nights? Sharing the same home, same space as him, teased every day by his scent. It had been hard enough the last few days, even though Caleb had rarely been present, but now with this new fervent desire pulsing in her veins—a beat that felt as if it would never stop, it would be impossible.

'You're tense,' he observed, breath as warm as fire brushing her ear.

'Sorry,' she murmured, trying to wipe her mind clear. She was thinking too much about feeling too much, and she needed to stop doing both.

'Is it your stepmother? I saw the two of you talking. Did she say something to you?'

He tensed, primed to leap to her defence and Serena found herself smiling at that even as she shook her head. 'It was just a brief conversation. I thanked her for coming and for bringing the twins. She complimented the wedding and the dress and you. I think I've actually done something she approves of.'

'After the way she treated you, it should be her worrying about earning your approval, not the other way around,' he ground out, his anger on her behalf igniting sparks in his eyes. 'I still can't believe how she treated you for all those years. But maybe…maybe in her own mind by being so tough on you she was trying to protect you.'

'I doubt it,' Serena retorted sceptically. Just because good intentions had underpinned Caleb's domineering delivery didn't mean the same was true of her stepmother. But then she really considered his words and saw the slight possibility in them. She remembered how Marcia had tried to warn her about Lucas; at the time Serena had assumed she was just being Marcia, but maybe she had been trying to protect her. 'But then again, maybe you're right,' she acquiesced. 'I've never really thought of it that way. It was always so uneasy between us that I just assumed everything she did came from a bad place. And, come a certain point, I started to think that I…'

'Thought what?' His gaze probed hers. 'That you deserved it?'

'Yes,' she admitted tearfully, realising just how much she had internalised it all. She had to take a breath, feeling unsteady. 'I did mess up. I didn't show the greatest sense, or that I deserved to be trusted.'

'Serena, you were a young girl who lost her mum and then her dad and you were grieving. You suffered so much in a short space of time. It was your stepmother's job to understand that and be there for you and support you. It was her who failed you, not the other way around.'

The moment felt like a release, as if something she'd carried for far too long had just whooshed out of her. It was so powerful that tears slipped down her cheeks, and Serena made the decision in that moment to choose to believe that some of Marcia's tough treatment of her had been in an effort to protect her, and now she was ready to move on from it as best she could. She'd carried pain and frustration for long enough and wanted to begin this new chapter without that baggage. And as long as Kit and Alexis were in her life, Marcia would be too.

She smiled up at Caleb. 'Thank you.'

'For what?'

'For being kind. And supportive.'

He brushed away the falling tears with his thumb. 'I told you—this may not be the most traditional set-up, but we can make it work.'

She nodded, believing in that. 'I'm not sure I'll ever like being dishonest with people about our relationship though. Lying to Evie today has been awful, especially because she's so happy for me.'

'I'm sorry. I know that it's hard. Hopefully with time it will get a little easier.'

'As easy as it is for you? Because you don't seem to be struggling at all.'

A light smile touched his mouth. 'It's not without effort, I promise.'

Oh. The words stung and it must have shown on her face.

'I didn't mean that way,' he breathed quickly, pulling her harder against his body when she wasn't sure he'd meant to. 'There's no hardship in touching you, or holding you. Only in stopping myself from doing more of it.'

The words struck her heart like a bolt of electricity, and as her eyes lifted to his with surprise, she saw the same shock in his. Although she knew she'd be wiser to let it go, she couldn't. Because as much as she didn't want to give him her heart, her body rejoiced at the thought of being seized by him.

'I didn't think you were interested in…more,' she said carefully.

'I'm trying not to be.' The fact that he didn't deny wanting more with her made her blood fizzle. 'But you're not making that very easy,' he added, casting her a glance filled with longing. It was the most unguarded she had ever seen him and seeing that power she possessed over him too sent a thrill snaking through her. 'Don't worry. I don't plan on acting on it, or renegotiating our arrangement. It's better if it remains as it is.'

Serena didn't disagree, and yet there was a part of her that wondered *why*? Which was a bad thought. An unwise one. It was hard enough exercising control of her thoughts without further confusing them with sex, and yet there was always the possibility that giving into their chemistry would bring clarity and not confusion. If they leant into the sexy, edgy energy and satisfied the beating needs of her body, maybe she could stop fretting that her feelings were more than desire. She knew Caleb wanted to keep the waters between them clear, and she did too, but provided they both agreed it was about attraction and pleasure only, would it be the worst thing if the lines blurred a little?

Yes, it would, a voice in her head screeched, and Serena quickly shook the crazy notion from her mind, questioning frantically where it had come from.

For the remainder of the dance, she guarded her thoughts carefully, relieved when the song ended and she was able to step away from the temptation of her husband. At least temporarily...

When they arrived back at the villa, Serena was exhausted. Not from the celebrations, but from the effort of resisting Caleb and controlling her own thoughts and reactions to him, especially after his revelations about desiring her... That had shaken everything in her, and even though she'd kept a tighter rein on her thoughts, ever since then their interactions had felt even more charged. Even now, when the pretence was over and she should have been able to relax, she was still achingly aware of the sensual tension oozing in the air between them, making it heavy and hot as it brushed against her skin. It wasn't helping that with their arrival back at the villa, she kept thinking of what would be happening were this a real wedding night, her throat thickening as she did, because a part of her was aching for that pleasure-filled release.

'I guess this is goodnight then,' she said, breaking the heavy, crackling silence as they hovered in the open plan living space, their bedrooms at opposite ends of the villa.

'It's not that late,' Caleb mused. 'Stay up for a nightcap with me?'

It was the last thing she'd expected him to say, and

though the invite was delivered innocuously, it somehow seemed laced with…danger. Breathing quickly, Serena contemplated an answer, letting her eyes slowly journey towards his, and as they met, the truth of where the night would end if she agreed shimmered between them. Her heart launched into her throat. It was only a handful of hours ago that he'd said he had no intention of acting on his feelings, but she sensed they'd gone beyond what he could control now. She didn't know how it had happened, or when, but she could taste the inevitability of it, feel the pulsing life force of their mutual desire. It needed only a single spark to catch alight and send them both up in flames, and she wasn't sure she was ready to be caught in that inferno.

Are you prepared to not experience it either?

'I'm not sure that's the best idea,' she admitted with a quivering smile, unable to forget the many reasons to resist. The safety in resisting. 'I think I should just go to bed.'

'You're probably right,' he conceded with a wry smile of his own, his eyes lingering on her, as if savouring his last look of the day. 'Goodnight, Serena.'

'Goodnight Caleb.'

On trembling legs, she turned and walked to her bedroom. Even once alone, her body continued to jostle and she had no idea how she was going to sleep, not with such ferocious want beating in her blood. Quickly, however, Serena realised she had a more immediate problem. She couldn't reach the fastenings at the back of her gown to take it off, and no amount of manoeuvring of her arms was helping. Asking Caleb for help was her only choice, but she had only just managed to walk away before and wasn't sure she'd be able to do so a second time.

Why do you need to? You're both feeling and want-

ing the same things. And neither of you are looking for it to mean more.

Serena was tired from the effort of denying herself. She had spent so much time being held back, and not just by her stepmother's rules, but also, she could see now, by herself. The events in her life had taken a toll on her, knocking the fearlessness out of her and impressing on her the advantages of caution. She'd been scared of making more mistakes and bringing on further hurt and disappointment. But something had happened today. She'd let go of the belief that she had screwed up and the walls that had been holding her in had shattered, releasing all the pain and fear that had plagued her, and she could see more clearly now.

Serena wasn't the young vulnerable girl she had been, desperately seeking love and family. She wasn't going to make the same errors. She was older now. Wiser. She'd craved a future in which she lived for herself, decided for herself, and if she was completely honest, she knew what she wanted. All she had to do was trust that she could handle it. Reach for it...

Taking a breath, she pulled open the bedroom door and returned to the living area, only to find it empty, but carried forwards by the new, empowering certainty within herself, she ventured to the other side of the house.

The door of Caleb's room was slightly ajar, and with another breath, she knocked lightly. 'Caleb?'

'Yes? Come in.'

The richness of his voice sent nerves skittering across her skin as she pushed open the door to his private space. A sole lamp lit the spacious room, the low lighting creating an intimate impression and that was before her eyes found him. When they did, Serena stilled. He was midway through getting undressed, his black trousers riding low on his lean hips and his chest bare, all hard muscle and gold skin for her eyes to gorge on. She remembered all too well the feel of him, but the sight of him…that was something else entirely. An even hotter heat exploded in her middle, engulfing her from head to toe, and all the moisture in her mouth evaporated as her eyes traced the faint line of hair bisecting his torso all the way down to where it disappeared into the band of his trousers.

'You need something?' he asked when she didn't speak.

Levering herself out of her stupor, Serena nodded. 'I can't reach the fastenings at the back of the dress, and I was hoping you could help.'

She couldn't control the warble to her voice, not when she could taste the danger of this moment, feel her feelings ready to catch fire with one single touch that she craved so desperately…

'Of course.'

As Caleb came towards her, she turned to offer him her back. Her breath shifted, quickening with the anticipation of his touch, and her stomach was tightening, almost to the point of pain, with the longing that ascended from so deep inside of her. Gently, he brushed her hair to the side, and as he did so his fingers brushed the sensitive skin of her neck. It was like being electrocuted, sparks of feeling arrowing in each and every direction. Shivers travelled across her skin as his fingers moved to undo the tiny buttons, his warm breath fanning over her, his body so close that she could feel…*everything*.

Strength. Heat. Temptation.

Surrender.

As his fingers moved lower, it got harder and harder to breathe. The dress was unfastened enough now for her to complete the task, but she made no effort to move and Caleb didn't remove his hands; instead, they slipped confidently beneath the fabric, settling on her waist and Serena swallowed a gasp at the blissful meeting of flesh. *Yes. Touch me. Take me.*

His fingers spanned outwards, creeping upwards to brush the base of her breast and this time she was powerless against the shudder that rippled through her. She had never wanted to be touched so desperately in her life, for her breasts to be cupped and caressed, stroked and sucked.

'Caleb...' She sighed, pressing back against him in invitation and turning her head for his mouth to claim hers, a kiss that, when it began, was unrestrained.

His tongue stroked the seam of her lips and then delved into her mouth, and with a sigh that seemed to be ripped from the deepest recess of his body, Caleb pulled her tightly against him. The gown slipped to the ground and his hands roved down her body in a slide that was pure possession. Excitement bubbled beneath her skin, liking it, wanting it. Needing it. To be claimed by him. To belong to him in every way possible. There was no one else she could imagine committing such surrender to. And this was...essential. Imperative. There was no other way to describe how it felt between them. She had to seize this gloriousness with him whilst it was here, because happiness never lasted, did it?

His firm mouth demanded more, demanded everything she had to give, and Serena offered it without hesitation, turning in his arms and clinging to him as the current building between their bodies threatened to sweep them both away. With another rumble from deep in his chest, Caleb scooped her into his arms and carried her to the bed, his mouth never leaving hers.

He tumbled her on to the softness of the covers, and

Serena curled herself around him as snugly as she could, her blood beating with an unknown rhythm, whimpering as he pulled away, but only briefly and only so he could rip at his trousers and then he was covering her again, naked, his skin hot to the touch and as he fitted himself onto the cradle of her thighs, her body filled with so many wants and wishes, so many feelings, she wasn't sure how she didn't explode.

'You're so beautiful, Serena,' he breathed, the rise and fall of his chest heavy, as though she was too much to truly take in. 'So beautiful it's driving me crazy.'

The final words were delivered on a breath of desperation, and then he was lowering his head in worship, burying his face in the valley of her breasts so the embers simmering low in her stomach exploded into a full-on wildfire. His hands moved to palm her breasts, but they had become so sensitive that at the tiniest amount of pressure, she gasped, and Caleb pulled back, alarmed.

'It's OK,' she assured him breathlessly. 'They're just really sensitive right now.'

A soft light burned in his eyes. 'I'll be very gentle then.'

And he was. Beautifully, exquisitely gentle. He caressed her almost reverently, stroking her with fingers as soft as a butterfly's wing and where he would have used his thumb, employed his tongue instead, licking and sucking her into the warm heat of his mouth and the tenderness of his ministrations only seemed to send their power arrowing deeper into her so that she was quivering beneath him.

'Caleb,' she pleaded, the stars flashing before her eyes with such brightness she was half-convinced she could reach out and touch them.

His only response was the flash of a smile as he drew

his line of teasing kisses even lower down her body, blazing a path over her stomach and lower again to where she had never been touched. Even if Serena had possessed the breath to protest, she wouldn't, because his mouth on her most secret cavern felt like the ultimate way of giving and belonging, and there was a relentless tattoo striking right there, which only throbbed with greater insistence as his mouth neared. And then his mouth was on her, his lips and tongue moving with synchronised perfection and in a matter of moments Serena was soaring, spinning higher and higher out of herself and it didn't once enter her mind to be scared of the plummet back to earth, because she knew that Caleb was there to catch her.

Caleb had never seen a sight more beautiful than Serena trapped in the grip of her quaking release. She sparkled with the orgasm tearing through her, and as the ripples subsided long enough for her to open her eyes, and they locked on him, her smile was as dazzling as rays of sunlight.

'That was incredible,' she breathed, reaching for him to press, fast, eager kisses to his lips.

'I am nowhere near finished yet,' he promised, his chest flooding with the pleasure he'd given and all that he still intended to bestow and with a single move pinned her beneath his weight.

Surrender had never felt so good. Thinking only about this moment and nothing else. For the first time in a long time, it was the impulses of his body leading the way instead of his brain, and his body wanted this—closeness, pleasure. *Serena.* He had known the moment they returned to the villa that he didn't want to fight anymore. *Couldn't* fight anymore. He had been fighting all day, and after too many moments holding her close and being teased and tempted by her softness and her scent, his hunger for her was too great to be denied. Another night without her seemed…impossible. And had he known how spectacularly eager and responsive she would be beneath him, he would have lost his battle hours earlier.

Caleb drew his lips across her mouth, before moving down her neck and chest, over her stomach and then to the arch of her thighs, dropping open-mouthed kisses back up her body. He would have kept on kissing her, tasting every inch, but his impatience was insistent, and with the way she was arching and pulsing under him, Caleb couldn't wait a moment longer to sink his hard length inside her, and the welcome he received, her muscles stretching and tightening around him like a hug, was beyond his greatest longing. He wanted to hold steady, to relish that moment of reunion after craving it for so long and so fervently, but he simply couldn't. He had to move, compelled by the emotions powering through him. More than everything he had already acknowledged feeling for her, more than protectiveness, more than lust.

She shuddered out his name as he started to move, slow and deep, and with each surge, the sensations unfurling beneath his skin and throughout his chest tautened and deepened. It felt like drowning, in the best way possible. Pleasure saturated him, and as she craned her mouth to reach his, the sweetness of her exploding on his tongue was an aphrodisiac unlike any other he'd ever known. His climax began to build, too soon but unstoppable. And as Serena hit her peak, her cry the most joyous, breathless sound he'd ever heard as he delivered her to a world that was uniquely theirs, Caleb's climax ripped through him, his roar of release drowning out the sounds of her fulfilment before he collapsed on top of her like a ship wrecked on the shore.

CHAPTER NINE

SERENA WAS THE first thing Caleb saw when he opened his eyes the next morning. Her face soft and beautiful in sleep, her lips curved with contentment. He would have been content to lie and watch her a while longer, but the warmth filling his chest and the stirrings that had absolutely nothing to do with sex were making his mind uneasy, so he turned away and slipped out from beneath the covers, careful not to wake her.

He didn't regret last night, not at all, but entertaining thoughts of lazing away the morning in bed with her was not OK. Giving into them even less so. Just because she was now his wife didn't mean he could abandon all of his usual practices; in fact, it probably made them even more important, especially with the way Serena could so easily get under his skin. He couldn't do anything that encouraged her to believe that their marriage was now, or ever could be, *more.*

He didn't want to feel deeper yearnings within himself either, not when those kinds of feelings only caused emotional chaos, the kind that had reigned over his childhood. He'd never been able to forget the long days and longer nights of agony that came from being deserted by his mother and all but ignored by his father—a pain that had felt it would never end.

He'd found a way to live that was chaos-free and he wasn't going to abandon that now, not when the stakes were higher than ever with a child of his own coming into the world. So, he took himself for a swim, cleansing himself of all yearnings in the clear, warm water before settling into his office and turning his focus to work, ignoring the uncomfortable thoughts of Serena waking up alone after such an incredible night together.

He didn't know how long he'd been burying himself in work when there was a small knock on the door, and looking up, he found Serena standing in the doorway, her sleep-tousled hair tumbling around her shoulders. She was wearing only his shirt. His heart thudded. 'Are you busy?' she asked before he even found his voice, his eyes too busy lingering on the line where the hem of his shirt met her slender thighs, his eyes drifting down her endless legs.

'Just sending emails.'

'They must be very important to be sending out the morning after you get married.' She strolled towards him. 'Considering you're the one concerned with our marriage appearing real, I would have thought you'd realise that looks a little suspect. Working is definitely not what a man besotted with his new wife would do' She came around to lean against the desk, her legs directly in his eyeline, and he had the sense she knew exactly the temptation she was. 'Unless you're really in here hiding?'

'Why would I be hiding?'

There was a flash of insecurity in her eyes that he knew had been put there by him. 'Because you regret what happened between us last night?'

'No. Last night was incredible,' he assured her, wanting so badly to touch her, but knowing that one touch would lead to another and another…and then he'd never be able to stop, so he dug his hands into his pockets instead.

'So, you left bed at the crack of dawn because…?'

He took a breath, the answer an easy one because it was the truth. 'Because we agreed to this being a marriage in name only, and I don't know that blurring those lines any more than we did last night is the best idea.'

She absorbed that with a steady expression. 'Because you're worried that I won't be able to separate sex and emotion, and I'll get the wrong idea and end up hurt the way Charlotte was?' she questioned astutely. 'Or because you're worried that *you'll* end up hurting again?'

'What do you mean?' he demanded, startled that she'd come so close to the truth he'd never exposed.

'You were hurt by what happened too,' she said softly. 'Not in the same way, but you've carried the guilt and pain of it for years. It's understandable that you wouldn't want to feel that way ever again.'

'You're right. I don't,' he admitted. He didn't want to feel anything. That was preferable to the everything he'd felt as a boy, the constant agitation of his heart, the huge cavern in his chest and the endless yearning that had driven him crazy until he'd shut it down by cutting himself off and removing love from the equation. For good.

'Then let me assure you that's not going to happen.' She met his eyes with firm insistence. 'I'm not going to let it happen. My eyes are open to what this is, Caleb. What our marriage is. What last night was. And it's enough for me. I don't want anything more, anything real.'

'You don't?' he asked, surprised, because he knew that at one point in time Serena had known such a happy life. He'd seen it when she talked about it, and in his mind, it was natural that she'd want to have that again. It was what most women wanted, wasn't it?

'Maybe at some point I did. I can see how tempting it would have been to recreate what I'd known when I was small and I had my parents. But a lot has happened since then,' she said with a sad tilt of her lips, 'and I know now that anything real comes with risk, and I don't want that. I don't want to lose anyone else. I can't go through that again.' He watched as she touched her hand to her stomach without realising it. As familiar as he was with loss, and as much empathy as he had for her, Caleb knew he really couldn't comprehend how great her fear of loss must be, not after experiencing so much of it, but this was the first time he'd ever heard her allow it to define her. As pleased as he was to hear it, because it suited their arrangement—even meant he could bend the rules a little—it also made him sad. 'Not after my parents and Lucas and the miscarriage. Those days worrying that I'd lost Kit and Alexis reminded me of how much I don't want that risk in my life.'

'Lucas?' he questioned, the name having stood out to him. 'Who… Was he…?'

'The father of the baby I lost, yes. Also, my boyfriend.'

'You didn't mention him before,' he said tightly, not liking the thought of the faceless stranger from her past.

'For good reason.' Serena sighed. 'He took off after I told him I was pregnant, crushing my heart in the process. It was a week later that I miscarried.' The anger that Caleb felt on her behalf was extreme and overrode all need for distance, and he reached out to her, sliding an arm around her waist. 'I think that's why I was so hard on you when you first showed up. I was projecting, expecting you to do the same. But I was wrong. You're a thoroughly better man than he ever was.' Her hands splayed against his chest; her amber eyes warm as they looked into his. 'I know you've spent a long time not believing that, and I know that I don't know who you were back then—maybe you were everything you say—but I know who you are now. Someone good and generous and protective. A man who does the right thing, who takes care of the people in his life.'

'Always. I'm not going to walk away, Serena.' He was vociferous. Wanting—needing—her to believe it, to never be plagued by that fear with him. 'I want you to know that and trust it. We've both had to endure the pain of that and I'll never do that to our child.'

Caleb's words caused Serena's heart to stutter. 'Someone left you too.' She saw his frustration that he'd spoken without thinking. His hand dropped from where it had settled and he retreated a step, but she wasn't going to let him push her away. He'd tried that once already this morning, leaving her alone in bed, and for a moment it had worked, before her understanding of him had kicked in and she'd realised he was trying to reset after breaching his own lines. She knew how important boundaries were to Caleb. He told himself it was about keeping others safe, but she sensed it was as much about protecting himself. And maybe this was why. 'Who?'

'My mother. She walked out the door one day and never came back.'

Serena's mouth dropped open. She knew his mother hadn't been at the wedding. He hadn't told her, but she'd realised it on the day, and whilst she had intended to ask, there'd been so many other things clamouring for attention.

'How old were you?'

His smile was sad. 'Three'

Serena gasped. 'Three?'

'It's a blessing really. I don't remember her, or her leaving.' But the look on his face spoke of a curse and not a blessing. From his body language, it was obvious he wanted to shut the topic down, maybe even regretted telling her, but Serena had so many questions. This was a trauma they shared. Was this why he'd been so understanding and supportive of her, because he knew the emotional scars she bore? But, then, why hadn't he let her support him in return? She knew the struggle it was to find people with similar experiences who could understand. She'd felt so alone with hers until Caleb. She didn't want him to feel alone either.

'Why did she leave?'

He shrugged, shaking away the shadow that had descended over his expression. 'I don't know. I don't think motherhood made her very happy.'

'She never tried to reach out to you?' He shook his head and her heart jammed somewhere in her throat. 'I'm so sorry, Caleb.' She reached for him, sliding her hand up and over his arms, the muscles bunched tightly.

'You don't need to be sorry,' he said curtly, before gentling his tone. 'I told you, it's not something I remember, so it didn't affect me a whole lot.'

Except he was talking about it, and the memory had been roused by her own tale of abandonment, so he clearly felt something. 'You may be able to get away with spinning that line to other people, but not me. I know how it feels to not have a mother. And I know the toll it's taken on Kit and Alexis, not remembering our mum. The scars it's left'

'There's a big difference between my situation and

theirs. Their mother died. She was taken from them, and you. Mine made the choice to leave.' He said it with such a heart-wrenching starkness that she wanted to fold him into her arms and hold him as tight as possible for as long as possible.

'That's why it was so important to you to be involved,' she realised, the wound she'd sensed in him but not been able to see. 'Why you insisted on us marrying, so our baby would grow up with two parents.'

Caleb barely acknowledged it, but Serena knew she was right. Knew that regardless of what he said, it had affected him, only maybe in ways he didn't want to acknowledge, ways he didn't know how to express. She wished he'd told her sooner. It would have gone such a long way to explaining his earlier insistence, maybe making it easier for her to accept, to understand his actions as protective and not controlling.

'It's also why you avoid relationships, isn't it?'

His eyes were veiled as they lifted to her. 'I think that's enough sharing for one morning. We have plenty of time to get to know these things.' But it was obvious he didn't want her to know them, didn't want to dwell on his mother and the scars it had left. Or how to heal them. *And it's not your job to heal them,* she reminded herself. *You're his wife in name only.*

But that didn't mean they couldn't be close, or friendly. Surely their situation demanded it, and if helping him enabled him to be a better father to their baby, it wasn't only about him. It was about all of them. But he was right—there was time for that.

'If we're not going to talk, we'll have to find something else to do. I have one idea,' she mused, burning with the thought of him taking her again. Last night hadn't been anywhere near enough. She wanted more time to explore his body, to explore the heat shimmering between them. Last night, Caleb had shown her what it was to matter, to be wanted and hungered for. Worshipped. She wanted her chance to revere him too. 'Unless…' It occurred to her then that maybe he didn't want her body as much as he didn't want her heart. Maybe as enjoyable as last night had been, it hadn't blown his mind the way it had hers, and he was using this as a convenient excuse. She was inexperienced after all—maybe she hadn't satisfied him. Maybe that was why she had woken to an empty bed.

'Unless what?' he prompted, raising an eyebrow.

Serena swallowed the insecurity bobbing in her throat. 'Nothing.' She lacked the bravery to expose that much of herself to him. And if he tried to deny it, that would be…too awful. But he advanced towards her, taking her chin between his fingers and tilting her head back until she was trapped in his gaze.

'You question if I really desire you? Even after last night?' She couldn't answer, there was too much emotion crowding her brain. 'Serena, if you knew how hard it is to see you in only that shirt right now, to see the outline of your body, to breathe in your scent and not bury myself inside you…if you could feel what being this close to you is doing to my body, you would know how very much I do want you.'

His voice was low and rough, sexy, and Serena trembled beneath his words, her blood humming as if she was being subjected to his touch. 'What are you doing?' he asked as she reached out.

'Feeling what I do to you.' He didn't let go so much as he loosened his grip enough for her to free her hand herself, and she laid it gently against his bare chest, right above his heart. The rapid beats pulsed against her palm, hard and insistent. It stole her breath, and with her heart leaping in her throat, she slowly slid her hand lower, tracing over the ridges of his stomach and slipping beneath the waistband of his pants and onto the erection that was throbbing with heat and steel. His breath hissed out, but that only encouraged the slow strokes of her hand.

'Enough.'

'No. Not enough.' Flicking her thumb across the tip of his erection, she watched his control shatter, watched him fight it. His eyes darkened to gunmetal. She couldn't tell if his resolve was weakening or strengthening, but she knew her own will was strong, as strong as it ever had been. This was her marriage as much as his, and having found her voice again, her confidence, she wanted to keep using them.

With a growl, his mouth crashed down on hers, his hands on either side of her face, holding her captive as his tongue plundered mercilessly, soaking up every ounce of her hunger. He growled again, not getting enough, and hauled her against him, lifting her shirt and pressing his burning hands to her hungry flesh. The more he touched and tasted, the greater Serena's hunger grew. With hands and tongue, she urged more, faster, and Caleb obliged, pinning her against the nearest wall and lifting her up, and with a single thrust of impatient possession, buried himself inside of her. Her climax hit hard and powerful, the long and glorious shudder wracking him too, and he buried his face in her neck, breathing loudly.

After a few minutes, he moved, carrying her with him. 'Where are we going?'

'To bed.' His eyes glowed like obsidian. 'And I'm warning you now, we won't be leaving it for a while.'

* * *

'This is beautiful.' Caleb watched Serena's delight with enjoyment as they sailed into the sheltered bay, their destination the picturesque harbour ahead. 'Where exactly are we?'

'Villefranche-sur-Mer.' He smiled, extending his hand to help her off the yacht once they had docked.

It had been five days since the wedding, and this was the first time they'd left the villa—the first time Caleb had let Serena get clothes on—but she'd mentioned her desire to explore the region, and Caleb had been more than happy to make it happen. It wasn't behaviour he would normally have engaged in with a woman, but with Serena's assurances that she understood the lines between them and wasn't going to develop feelings for him beyond the desire they shared, he saw no harm in the deviation. He liked seeing her happiness, particularly knowing that she had known too little of it, and whatever pangs of unease he experienced about breaking another of his norms, he dispelled with the argument that being seen enjoying typical honeymoon activities would only help their marriage charade. Additionally, building a good relationship now, from the outset, would enable them to co-parent better in the long term, even once their marriage was over, except looking ahead to that point in time sent discomfort drilling deep into his chest.

Pushing the thought away and keeping hold of Serena's hand, he guided her up from the harbour, past the waterside restaurants and into heart of the town.

'It's like stepping back in time,' she mused as they strolled the medieval streets, the sun warm on their skin, the day stretching easily ahead. Caleb relished that feeling of freedom, of not having to distract or restrain himself. 'How did you find the town?'

'I explored the region pretty extensively when I was looking for the perfect South of France location.'

'You don't have a team who do that?'

'I do. But I like doing my own research too, ensuring that everything fits with my vision. And with this being our first European location, it was important that everything was absolutely perfect.'

'And is it? Absolutely perfect?'

'Almost,' he smiled. 'It will be by the time we open.'

She turned her face up towards him, the light catching in her hair so she shimmered. 'Do I get a sneak peak of this beach club before it opens?'

Caleb looked back at her in surprise. 'Do you want to see it before the opening?'

'Of course. You've been working so hard—I'd like to know what you do every day.'

Her interest sparked more pleasure than it really should, but he was too preoccupied with the thought of showing it to her, sharing it with her, to truly care. 'Then, of course. I'll take you one day.' And because felt a little too happy about doing so, feeling himself edge into deeply personal territory, he qualified it as part of their charade—that, of course, a husband would give his wife a preview of his work.

'Is your father excited about the European expansion?'

'He is. That and the new generation of Morgenthaus have conspired to make him a very happy man at present.'

Serena stopped to admire an ancient church. 'Will you expect our son or daughter to take over the company one day?'

'I'll want them to be part of it, if that's what they want.

But I wouldn't want to ever bully them into it, make them feel as though they can't explore other avenues.'

'The way you felt?'

'Yes. So please, if you ever see me doing that, feel free to step in.' He only realised what he'd said after he said it, looking forwards that many years and seeing them together. *Wanting that?* He dismissed the thought. Of course he didn't want that. He never had. *But* if the situation worked to their advantage, then there was no reason the five years couldn't be extended. 'But I do like the thought of having our child to pass it all onto, and share it with. Lately, there's felt a greater purpose to all the work I do. It's always felt somewhat about the past, continuing the legacy of my father and grandfather. Now it feels more about the future—about what I can leave to our child.' He realised he was smiling as that feeling of purpose filled him.

'I know your father has stepped back now, but did you enjoy working with him?' asked Serena.

The question, such a complicated one, caused strain to his chest. 'My father and I have never had the easiest relationship.' She didn't look surprised, but she was no stranger to parental tension, was she? She would understand it better than most, and maybe that was why he continued speaking when it was a vault he never normally opened. 'It's been that way for as long as I can remember. We never quite recovered from my mother leaving. Or *he* didn't, I should say. He threw himself into work to deal with it, or *avoid* dealing with it, and was rarely around, so we never established any kind of father-son bond.'

Memories rose quickly, of how his father would never quite meet his eye, and on the few occasions he did, seemed to look right through him. So aware of the ab-

sence of his mother, Caleb had been so desperate for his
father's attention and affection that he could still feel the
memory of that desperation squirming within him and
quickly worked to lock the memory away, disliking the
feelings ready to spill free and cause havoc within him.

'Was that why you resented him pushing you into the
business?' she asked as they turned into another narrow street.

'Probably,' he admitted. 'To suddenly see me and demand my capitulation after fifteen years of ignoring me
was a little hard to swallow.'

'He ignored you?' Serena breathed, shocked.

'Like I said, he struggled a lot after she left. He…
blamed me somewhat, I think.'

You. She left because of you, Caleb.

'Why would you think that?' Caleb couldn't bring himself to say the words, but the answer was conveyed in his
silence. 'Did your father say that?'

'Only once,' Caleb responded quickly, feeling protective of his father in spite of it all, because he knew how
pained he'd been by his mother walking out, so it had to
have been ten times worse for his father, who he knew
had loved her deeply, 'and he'd made quite a dent in a
bottle of Scotch by that point. I don't think he even remembers it.'

'You never asked him about it again?'

'It wasn't a conversation I was in a hurry to revisit.'

'You don't believe that's true, do you?'

He shrugged lightly, keeping his gaze fixed ahead.
'I've wondered. I saw photos of them together and they
seemed happy, so something obviously went wrong once
they had me.'

'Caleb, there could be a hundred reasons why your

mother left. None of them to do with you,' Serena said urgently. 'I know how easy it is to let stuff like that go inward, but you can't think like that. Not when the chances are your mother left for her own reasons.' She ran her free hand up his arm, dissolving the tension in his biceps with just her touch. 'You really don't remember anything about her?'

'No. And after she left, my father removed everything that was a reminder of her.'

Her fingers curled around him. 'I'm sorry.'

'You must have plenty of memories of your mum,' he said, neatly redirecting the conversation because he had no desire to dig any deeper, and Serena nodded. 'Tell me about her?' he asked, knowing from the way her voice changed that she loved speaking of her mother and hadn't had enough opportunity to do so.

'She was beautiful. Vivacious. The most fun person in any room, with the biggest smile and most stunning laugh. Sometimes, I still think I can hear it.' Her smile was wistful. 'She could make even the dullest day fun. And the way my father used to look at her...he adored her.' She paused, hesitated, looked up at him. 'I think that was the worst thing about living without her, that the house seemed so quiet, so lifeless, as if all the happiness had gone, which in a way it had.' She looked down at the cobbled ground. 'We muddled on, my dad and I and the babies, but it was never the same. It's probably why whenever I do feel happy now, I'm always waiting for the bottom to fall out of it.'

'You can be what she was to you, to our baby though.'

'I hope so. She was a really good mum. I know Marcia always thought she sounded too spontaneous and lively to be a good parent—which I think was always why it hurt so much when she accused me of being the same way, because she really was the best. She had a joy that not many people have. I was actually thinking that if we have a girl, we could name her after my mum. Not necessarily her first name, maybe a middle one…but it would mean a lot to me.' Her nervous flow of words ended with a look of hope.

'What was her name?'

She smiled. 'Francesca.'

Caleb nodded. 'That's beautiful. It's a perfect idea.' Her smile was brighter than the sun, and Caleb could only stare, captivated, delighted at making her beam so widely.

Leaning down, he stole a kiss from her lips. 'What was that for?'

'I just wanted to.'

And he wanted to do it again, and again, to have that sweetness of her mouth permanently on his to lips to savour. Instead, he threaded his fingers with hers and resumed their stroll, uneasy thoughts buzzing around the edges of his mind, because he'd told himself he would get her out of his system, had justified their intimacy on those grounds, but the ways he craved her were only intensifying. And that wasn't the worst of it. The worst was that in certain moments, he was no longer sure that getting her out of his system was something he wanted at all.

Serena hadn't thought the day could get more enjoyable after their morning exploring the charm of the medieval town, but as midday approached and they continued on their journey around the coast, they sailed into a secluded cove to enjoy a luxury picnic lunch on the narrow curve of sand. They were sheltered from any view by the most spectacular wall of rock, and azure waters glittered ahead of them as far as the eye could see.

The picnic had been provided by one of the restaurants back in Villefranche-sur-Mer, boasting rustic baguettes with pâté, quiche Lorraine, a pan bagnat, a selection of fruits and miniature lemon meringue tarts, the taste of which exploded on her tongue. She couldn't have painted a more idyllic day and was touched that Caleb had gone to so much trouble to arrange it. However, Serena took care to remind herself that it wasn't done solely for her or from the goodness of his heart. He had, no doubt, considered a sighting of them on a typical honeymoon outing would consolidate their fictitious love story. She wasn't under any illusions as to how important it was to him that the world perceive their marriage as real, that they ensure that protection for their child, and now that she knew about his mother leaving him as a small boy, she understood it a lot better. He wanted to ensure that their child never experienced any of the insecurity or vulnerability that he had felt. Knowing that he had ever felt that way made her heart sore.

Serena had wanted to ask him more about that time in his life, to uncover just how significantly his mother's leaving had impacted him. In those circumstances his relationship with his remaining parent would have become all the more significant, but it was clear from his words, that his father had been too lost in his own agony to have any time for Caleb's. Was that why Caleb didn't want anything real? His view of love and relationships had been coloured by the breakdown of his family, seeing only loss and anger and pain where there should have been love. Had he felt too much negative emotion himself to want to risk opening up again? And to have blamed himself…it was little wonder Caleb had felt so guilty about Charlotte when in his mind that was the second time he'd been responsible for a tragedy, and even less surprising that he'd shut down even more afterwards. But maybe, with a little time and encouragement, he could get comfortable opening up again, for the sake of their child if nothing else. Serena hoped that he'd heard her when she said it wasn't his fault, but she wasn't sure. And she knew any further questions would be out of bounds, and the last thing she wanted was to upset the closeness they had created.

Caleb was not a man who yielded easily, but he had yielded on that, and she definitely didn't want that to change, she thought, watching him emerge from the sparkling aqua waters from his swim, looking like a deity who'd descended from another world. Her eyes clung to him as he ran up the sand towards her, sleek, bronzed and muscled with droplets of water clinging to every ridge of hard muscle. Her mouth ran dry as feeling exploded along her veins and gathered low in her stomach.

How was it possible that a man, mere flesh, blood and bone, could be so spectacular? Her body grew hotter, that single glance conjuring a need, a hunger, that was unlike anything she'd ever known. Her body yearned for his touch, for the feel of him above her, just as her mouth ached for one of his deep, devouring, kisses, and thinking it, her nipples pulled tight and taut, her core *throbbing*.

Almost as if he knew the effect he was having, his eyes gleamed as he dropped down on top of her, tempting her with his closeness and lightly kissing her lips, smiling as he did, teasingly pulling back as she leaned in for more.

'Come in the water with me—it's beautiful,' he said in between light kisses.

'I'm rather enjoying the view from where I am right now. Maybe in a little while.'

'Now,' he commanded. 'You can either come willingly or...' He let the slow smile imply the rest.

'Or?' she prompted laughingly.

'Or I'll just do this.' Scooping her up in one effortless move, Caleb sped back towards the water, not stopping until they were chest-deep. Her laughing ceased only when his mouth covered hers, and he didn't break the kiss until she was gasping for air. With her legs wrapped around his waist, she felt the hard press of his erection and almost groaned, the feel of it sending shock waves crashing through her and igniting the same scorching need as always at her core. Serena hadn't known that desire could be so beautifully painful. Nor could she quite believe that he wanted her as much as he did.

At least for now. She knew there was no promise of permanence. At the most she'd have a few years of the sensational pleasure he could deliver. At worst—until his desire waned.

It shouldn't hurt so deeply. It was what she had agreed to and all but instigated, after all. But perhaps, at times, she hadn't been as watchful of her thoughts as she should have been, gazing into the future and seeing life in a way she hadn't been capable of for the longest time. Seeing herself and Caleb and their child, a little family. Growing together, happy together. But it wouldn't be that way forever, would it?

Comforting rather than scolding herself, Serena accepted that it was understandable, but cautioned herself against indulging those daydreams going forwards. She had to keep a tighter rein on her thoughts, and perhaps her feelings also. Happiness was a beautiful thing, and she was enjoying this period of it, but it never lasted. The bottom always fell out eventually, and she had to remain pragmatic to be sure she didn't end up crushed when it did. Because she'd been broken before, in so many ways, and had meant it when she said she had no interest in that happening again.

'If the plan is to make it to Monaco at some point this afternoon, shouldn't we be getting back to the yacht?' she prompted, with that in mind.

His eyes drifted to her lips. 'Fifteen more minutes isn't going to hurt,' he said, seizing her mouth eagerly as beneath the water his hand slid between her legs, under her bikini, and she arched, clinging to his shoulders even tighter, resistance impossible as she became his whole focus.

Fifteen more minutes definitely, she conceded as his fingers stroked her to realms of incredible pleasure. But would that be enough? Would there ever be a time when Serena could say enough? Now that she knew Caleb's touch, how deeply it could penetrate and move her, would she ever be able to stop wanting him? She'd meant every word of her promise when she'd made it—to both him and herself—but Serena was no longer so sure it would be quite so easy to keep.

CHAPTER TEN

'THERE THEY ARE—the newlyweds.' As Serena and Caleb made their way through the front door of the property, they were greeted by the welcoming smiles of their hosts, Thierry and Mathilde Clement, faces that Serena vaguely remembered from their wedding. 'We're so pleased that you were able to come and celebrate with us, interrupting your honeymoon, no less.'

'We wouldn't have missed it,' Caleb smiled smoothly, showing none of the nerves that were writhing in Serena's stomach as they embarked on their first public appearance as a married couple. The evening was important to Caleb, and she didn't want to do anything to disappoint him. 'Would we?' Caleb asked, gazing down at her with eyes that sparkled like starlight, and her heart leapt in response.

'Not at all. I cannot wait to see all the work you've done here. Caleb told me you've been renovating for two years, so I'm sure it's going to be spectacular.'

'Your wife is as generous as she is beautiful, Caleb,' Thierry remarked smilingly. 'There's no question why, after a lifetime, of bachelorhood you wasted no time putting a ring on her finger.'

'What can I say? Serena got under my skin the moment we met and I just couldn't let her go.' Serena glanced up at him, warmed by his words. She knew they were a key part of their narrative, but there was a sincerity to them and an ease to their delivery that made her wonder if they could be more than just a soundbite. If they contained some kernel of truth. She knew it was true for her, that Caleb had affected her, in spite of her dogged pretence to the contrary, right from the start, but was it possible that she burrowed just as deeply under his skin? The thought thrilled her, sparking hope that was dangerous, but too potent to be extinguished. 'I was always told it would happen one day and I never believed it, but…here we are.'

His eyes stroked over her again, rousing tingles everywhere, and as their gazes caught, a deeper and richer light started to smoulder, something that seemed to speak only to her, the deepest, most secret part of her. A message that only she would see and understand. Everything in her responded. Was that another sign of his feelings changing, deepening in spite of what he had said about not wanting anything real or was he just a far better actor that she was? Playing the performance of his life for their hosts to eat up?

Serena didn't know. But she wanted to know. It *mattered*. And yet it shouldn't matter. She shouldn't care. She certainly shouldn't be feeling cold and wobbly at the thought that he was only pretending when it was what they'd agreed. But when he looked at her like that, when his fingers moved against her waist in that subtle, tender, exquisitely powerful way to soothe her nervousness, because he knew without her having to say anything that she was nervous, everything felt confused and she couldn't keep her mind, or her heart from forming questions that she'd be safer and smarter not asking, not wanting to ask.

But the thought that he could possibly feel more for her, that it wasn't all a pretence—that was dizzying. Electrifying. Heart-stopping.

'Serena,' Caleb prompted and she realised she'd been so deep in her thoughts that she'd lost the thread of conversation.

'I'm so sorry. I was too busy admiring everything, and I stopped listening for a second. Forgive me.'

'Please admire away,' Mathilde encouraged. 'That is why we invited you. Admiration and compliments, as many as you wish, none too grand.' Serena smiled at the other woman's playfulness, liking her immensely and feeling a little more at ease. 'How about a tour, my dear? You and I can get to know each other better, since you'll be regular visitors out here with the new beach club. You can tell me all about how you and this glorious man met.'

As Mathilde drew her away, she was aware of Caleb tensing and keeping hold of her. 'Do I not get the tour too?' he asked with a laugh.

'If you are unable to part from your bride for all of thirty minutes, then by all means join us,' she offered airily.

He pretended to consider for a second when Serena knew by the look in his eye his mind was already made up. 'I think I will. Thirty minutes is far too long for us to be apart.'

Mathilde flashed them an indulgent smile. 'Young love. So beautiful.' Her eyes moved to Thierry with fondness. 'I remember when that was us, *ma chérie*.'

'I would say it still is us,' he drawled, dropping a brief kiss to her lips before she beckoned them to follow her.

Caleb stayed close, his chest pressing against her back, his hand resting on her waist as though he couldn't bear for their contact to be severed. Serena's heart soared with the thought, but remembering her pledge to keep a tighter rein on her thoughts, she brought herself back down with the caution that it could be nothing more than foolish, wishful thinking to indulge in the romantic notion that he couldn't bear to part from her, when really it was all for show, Caleb playing role of a besotted and attentive husband? And if she let that notion take root, she could be leading herself towards heartache again, the same kind of heartache she'd opened herself up to with Lucas, ignoring all the red flags around him and seeing only what she wanted, *needed*, to see.

But I'm not that desperate young girl anymore, Serena reminded herself.

But if that was true, why was she hoping Caleb's feelings were growing as much as hers?

Her head suddenly aching with confusion, it occurred to Serena then that she should insist on going on the tour with Mathilde alone and send Caleb to mingle with Thierry. That way she'd be able to find some perspective amongst her jumbled thoughts and get herself back on the page she was meant to be on. The page she *needed* to stay for her own protection. And she was never going to find that composure, or rationale, fizzing with delight at his nearness and with his every touch frying her nerve endings. But as she looked back at Caleb with that intent, she found she couldn't say the words.

How was she meant to chase him away and enforce that much-needed distance when all she wanted was exactly what she had, his closeness?

Caleb couldn't remember ever being as proud as he was of Serena that evening. She shone like the treasure she was, drawing everyone to her and alternately charming them with anecdotes about her siblings and impressing them with her extensive appreciation and knowledge of art. He hadn't been worried at all, but he knew she had been nervous about fitting into his world. Her body had been twanging with nerves as they'd arrived but she had overcome them to show off her beautiful self—just as she had overcome so much else. There wasn't a day that passed when he wasn't in awe of her strength, of the grit she had displayed to survive the traumas she'd suffered and remain a steady port for her siblings in the face of adversity from her stepmother. But he loved that she was now regaining her life, and herself.

Stealing her away the first moment he could, he led her outside to the gardens, a manicured paradise of lantern-lit stony pathways and low succulents. As soon as they were alone, he pulled her against him, satisfying as much as he could the need to have her taste on his tongue.

'I've been desperate to do that for an hour, but there were too many other people around,' he breathed as he pulled back and read the happiness and confidence radiating from her eyes. 'I think you've been an even bigger success tonight than the hotel. I told you there was no reason to be nervous.'

'I just didn't want to let you down,' she confessed.

'That would never happen. I didn't know you knew so much about the art world though.'

She shrugged. 'Marcia may have kept me from studying it at university, but I kept up learning as much as I could.'

'You caught Roberto Paloma's attention, and that's not easy," Caleb said, making reference to one of the other guests at the party, a renowned art gallery owner whom

Serena had recognised the moment she set eyes on him from across the room. 'I watched him as you were speaking in there and he was impressed,' Caleb shared, hoping that she would draw further confidence from having gained the attention of a man she respected.

'I cannot believe you know him. Or that I was in the same room as him. I've admired him for years, Caleb.'

He smiled at her excitement. 'I think you mentioned that earlier.' Along with how she'd dreamed of visiting his galleries across Europe and loved the variety of artists he worked with. 'His next big venture is opening a gallery in London.'

'He told me.' The enthusiasm in her face dimmed, and she became very interested in smoothing down the lapels of his jacket. 'He actually said that if I was interested in a new career, he would like to hire me.'

'Really? I told you he was impressed.' But he wondered why she didn't look happier, why, if anything, she looked uneasy. 'Are you interested?'

She hesitated, conflict written all over her face. 'I mean...working in the art world has always been my dream, but I'd resigned myself to it not happening. And now that we have a baby on the way... I want to be there to raise them and I know you want that too...'

His brow drew together. Was he the reason she was hesitant? Did she think he would prevent her from taking a job she so clearly wanted? But then again, after all those years of her stepmother, how could she not...

'What I want,' he began, speaking around the lump that had formed in his throat, because he hated that she even considered it a possibility that he would hold her back, 'is for you to be happy and to have everything you desire. I meant it when I said I didn't want to control you.

And you've missed out on too much already to not take advantage of this opportunity.'

Her eyes searched his. 'Do you really mean that?' she asked, looking so hopeful and yet so frightened to hope.

'I do.'

Caleb hadn't even got the words out before she threw her arms around him and held on so tightly that he could feel the exaggerated beats of her heart. He smiled at her happiness, thrilled to be the source of it...but when exactly had her happiness become quite so important to him? More important, it seemed, than all else.

CHAPTER ELEVEN

CONTENT.

That was what Serena felt when she woke the following morning. It had been so long since she'd felt anything close to it that it took a moment to identify, but she smiled as she did. Because she was happy—as happy as she could ever remember being. Over the years she had learned to draw fulfilment from what she was fortunate to have in her life, like her brother and sister, and her evenings painting, but she hadn't been happy. But now it seemed as if her life was falling into place. Kit and Alexis were happy and cared for, her pregnancy was on the verge of entering its second trimester where the risk of miscarriage lessened, Caleb was proving to be a wonderful partner and she had just been offered her dream job.

She'd wanted to tell Caleb about the offer as soon as Roberto had made it, but she'd been wary—what if he didn't like the idea, after all she knew it mattered to him that their child wasn't left in the care of others? But he had been so supportive and encouraging, and that had touched her heart in ways she couldn't even explain.

Stretching out to find his warm body, she was disappointed when she didn't, only then remembering that the beach club was having an inspection and so he was leaving earlier than usual. He emerged from the dressing room, straightening the cuffs on his jacket, and Serena threw back the bedcovers, rising to wish him luck, but Caleb had gone still, his eyes fixed on something on the bed.

'What is it? What's wrong?'

She turned to see what had frozen his expression and felt ice course through her own veins as her eyes took in the red stain on the sheets. *Blood.* Her heart lurched and slowly, terror twisting its way around her, she lowered her eyes to her legs, gasping at the streaks of blood there too.

Her heart listed in her chest.

It was happening again.

The wait to find out what was happening was interminable.

Fear rattled in Serena's chest with every breath that she drew, the worst-case scenario unspooling in her mind on a loop as the jagged memories that had finally been fading from her mind returned with furious vengeance. Was this another baby she was destined to never know, another loss to be etched on her heart?

The only thing stopping her from falling apart completely was the pressure of Caleb's hand around hers, the knowledge that she wasn't on her own and didn't have to navigate the nightmare alone, as she had last time.

He hadn't wasted a second to spring into action back at the villa, guiding her to the car and driving to the hospital as if hellhounds were on his heels. He hadn't left her side, hadn't once let go of her hand, even as all she could do was stare at the blank wall opposite, her mind trapped somewhere between the past and the present and too scared of what the imminent future could hold to want to get there. For a moment there she had been really, truly happy. Excited for all of her tomorrows...

But wasn't this why she was so wary of happiness? Because she knew it never lasted. That eventually it always came crashing down.

A tear rolled down her cheek, and before she could swipe it away, Caleb did, moving from his chair to sit on the edge of the bed, taking her face in his hands. 'Hey. We don't know that there is anything wrong. There is every chance that everything is fine...'

'Please don't say that.' She couldn't hear those words. Couldn't let that injection of hope into her mind or her heart, not when she knew how hope turned so easily to ashes. 'Please don't tell me that everything is going to be OK, when you can't possibly know that.'

'OK.' He nodded, his eyes serious. 'How about I just tell you that whatever is happening, we'll deal with it together.'

Would they though?

Even as she sank into the warm, cocooning embrace of his arms, comforted by his strong presence and grateful for it, she couldn't help but fret over how long she would have him if the worst was happening. They had only married because she was pregnant, so what would happen if there was no longer a baby? Would the fact that they had grown so close hold any power? She knew he cared for her. She'd felt it...but as much as he gave with his body, he'd offered no words or promises to back up the actions. He had been clear their marriage was not an emotional affair and was primarily to safeguard their child's future. So, if there was no longer a baby...

It was on the tip of her tongue to voice her fears when the door opened and the doctor entered. Caleb held her hand tightly in his as she was examined, holding her eyes with his own, promising that she wasn't alone. *But for how long?*

'You and your baby are perfectly fine, Madame Morgenthau,' the doctor announced after a series of tests.

'You're sure?' Caleb demanded of him urgently, leaving no doubt that he had been as fearful for the well-being of their baby as she had.

'Perfectly.'

'But how?' Serena questioned, stunned to hear those words, because she had convinced herself the news would not be good. 'How is that possible? I was bleeding.'

'Bleeding is actually very common during the early stages of pregnancy,' he explained patiently. 'One in every four or five women experience it, and the majority go on to have a healthy pregnancy. At this time, I'm seeing nothing to suggest that cannot be the case for you too.' The words prompted a flicker of joy in her heart. She was relieved, most of all, that the baby was OK, but also that her relationship with Caleb was not under imminent threat. 'You can see for yourself, if you like,' he offered, angling the sonogram screen that he had been studying intently moments ago so that it faced them. 'That right there is your baby.' He smiled, pointing to a small curled shape in the centre of the screen. 'And this pulsing is his or her heartbeat, which you can hear is steady and strong.'

'Oh, my goodness.' Serena launched herself into a sitting position to better see the image, mesmerised by the tiny shape and the sound of its beating heart. Relief and delight poured through her, the image of her baby—safe and there—scattering the remainder of her fear the way light banished shadows. 'There you are.' She touched her fingertips to the screen, the tears that now fell solely of delight. 'My precious little one.'

'That's incredible,' Caleb whispered. 'Our baby.'

'I never got this far last time,' Serena told him quietly. And it was all the more wonderful to share it with him, and smiling into his eyes, it hit her how deeply she had fallen in love with him.

She didn't know how she hadn't realised it sooner. She'd certainly been aware of her feelings for him deepening. Her favourite time of day was when he returned home, and her heart fizzed and stomach overflowed every time he looked her way and delivered that slow smile before drawing her close for a kiss. She loved how he always asked about Kit and Alexis when he knew she'd spoken with them, and she loved how he made her feel so safe and cared for that she didn't always feel as if she had to be superstrong.

Only weeks ago, the thought of falling for Caleb had filled her with dread, but now she felt *stronger* for loving him. For having opened up her heart and letting him into it. He'd healed her, in so many ways, given her back so much of her life, showing her that it was OK for her to need someone and to lean on them.

But would he be willing to give her what she most wanted? A life with him.

Because he had told her explicitly that he didn't want love in his life, and Serena had promised that neither did she, so how could she now tell him that she had fallen more in love with him than she had ever thought possible?

But how could she *not* tell him?

Serena had *agreed* to a half life at eighteen because she had been vulnerable and scared, and doing so had kept her with Kit and Alexis, so she didn't regret it. But she'd had to repress so much of herself, her desires and dreams. She didn't want to deny herself again, and with her fears conquered and her past behind her, now was the time for her to start living a beautiful, full life.

Settling for less was no longer an option

Satisfied that Serena was resting after the ordeal of the morning, Caleb left the darkened bedroom and shut himself in the quiet privacy of the study, leaning back against the door and exhaling the ragged breath that he'd been holding all morning.

Never in his life had he been as scared as he was in that hospital, seeing Serena so pale and frightened, and unsure if he would get to meet his child, and his relief had never been as profound as when he watched the life force of his child pulsing steadily on the small screen. All of that and more still thudded through his chest.

It wasn't a surprise to Caleb that he cared. Of course he did. How could he not? Living in such close proximity, it was impossible to not develop human feelings, and he had already recognised his arrogance in imagining that he could manage his emotions for Serena and the pregnancy in the same clinical way he handled all else in his life. Even the pretence of a family required some degree of attachment. But caring for them, *her*, was one thing. It was acceptable. Just.

But the feelings pounding through him were more than that. They were violent and chaotic, desperate and fearful—everything Caleb had never wanted to feel again. The emotion he had spent his whole life avoiding after the pain of his childhood. The agony and the yearning. He didn't like it. He didn't want it.

He was happy feeling nothing...happier than when

he'd felt everything. As a boy, the loss of his mother and indifference of his father had set loose emotional forces that had tormented him, and he refused to go back to that place of despair, where his feelings had complete control over him and his ability to function—to eat, sleep, live. He wouldn't allow himself to turn into his father, to become the wreck that he had become, controlled and defined by his torment. His father was pulled back together now, but that recovery had taken the better part of Caleb's life. He wouldn't live like that. He'd found a way as a boy to shut down the feeling, to end the agony, and would do so again now.

Forcing himself to sit, Caleb quickly formulated a plan and contacted his assistant with instructions and awaited her confirmation, ignoring the pinches of guilt to his gut. It had to be this way.

He had been so focused on Serena not developing feelings for him that he'd failed to keep watch over himself. He had sensed last night that something was amiss, when he'd prioritised her happiness to take the job...

He had been too liberal with his time and emotions around Serena, and if he carried on in the same vein, he'd be no type of father to his child. He would be no better than his own, trapped in the storm of his own body and of no use to anyone. And how could he support Serena like that? She needed him to be strong so that she could be scared, as had been the case today, and he couldn't be strong for her if he was roiling inside, agitated with emotion that couldn't be soothed or contained. Emotion that led to only one place—destruction.

And it wasn't as if he was reneging on anything, just setting things back to how they were always supposed to have been, with him and Serena living their own lives. Not that telling himself that made him feel any better.

But by the time Chef Pierre was serving their evening meal, the plans were in place and all that was left to do was tell Serena. She was already seated at the table when he emerged, and he was pleased to see the colour had returned to her face. He forced himself to push away the thought that she would lose it again once he'd said his piece.

'How are you feeling?'

'Good. Better than I did earlier. And hungry,' she added, as a plate was set before her. 'I'm sorry that you missed your meetings today. I know how important they were.'

'Don't worry about it. Meetings can be rescheduled. Our baby was more important.' She smiled at him as she dug into another forkful, but Caleb's appetite was gone because he knew the moment had arrived. 'Speaking of that, I've arranged for you to return to London tomorrow.' He ignored the shock that came over her face. 'I spoke to Dr Newman and explained the situation, and she has time to see you tomorrow afternoon.'

'Is that really necessary? The doctor here said there was no reason for alarm. And I feel fine.'

'Dr Newman is the best in her field. I'd be happier if you saw her and got her opinion. And she is your primary physician.'

'OK,' Serena assented. 'I'll go to London, spend the night, see Kit and Alexis and come back the next day.'

'You don't need to do that. Once you're back in London, you should stay, get settled into the house. I've been assured its ready for us.'

Serena turned her eyes on him like twin spotlights that

Caleb had to steel himself against. 'Are you coming back too?' He heard the tremor of unease enter her voice and guilt tightened his stomach.

'No. I'm going to stay here a while longer, whilst the final developments and inspections are happening. I'll return to London then.'

Her eyes hadn't left his face. He could feel them burning through his skin. 'Then I'll come back too. It could look strange us being in separate places so soon, no?'

Caleb shook his head. 'I don't think so. Everyone at the wedding saw your siblings. They're enough of a reason for you to be back in London without me. And this was always the plan. You in London, me wherever I'm needed,' he reminded her, summoning the detachment that had always come so easily to him and mentally snipping the threads that had grown between them. One day, hopefully, she would see that this was for the best.

'Yes, but that was before...' She cut herself off from whatever she'd been on the verge of saying, hurt creeping into her expression as she absorbed the detachment in his. She set down her fork and looked at him, almost pleadingly. 'I don't understand what's going on right now. Why don't you want me here? Why are you sending me away? Is it because of what happened earlier...'

'I told you. It's so you can see Dr Newman...'

'If your concern for me and the baby was all this was about, then you would be coming with me,' she asserted with conviction. 'What's really going on, Caleb? Tell me.'

'Nothing is going on...' But still he got up and walked away, unable to stand her expression any more, the way it tugged at him. He wished he could close his ears to the bewilderment in her voice as easily as he could avert his gaze.

'I don't believe you.' She followed him, searching his face with her anguished eyes. 'You're doing this for a reason. You're pushing me away. You're scared of something. I can see it. You're scared of what you felt today. *How much* you felt. Tell me I'm wrong.'

He wished he could.

'This marriage isn't about feelings, Serena. You know that,' he gritted out, keeping a tight hold on his emotions because she needed to see, as well as hear, that he didn't feel anything. And maybe with enough time, that would be true again.

'I know it wasn't meant to be. But that isn't something that either of us can control.' She pulled in a breath, reaching for him and the blaze of her fingertips against him…

Caleb resisted and savoured in the same moment. He knew he would never touch her again.

'Today, at the hospital, Caleb, I was so scared. I was scared about the baby, of course, but I was also scared about what would happen between us if I did lose the baby. Because as much as I know we got married to protect our child and keep me in my brother and sister's lives, the truth is I would want to be married to you even if those reasons didn't exist.' Her eyes filled with fear and with hope. 'Because I love you.'

For a second the words seemed to warm him, before the expected coldness struck, as if his chest had been packed with ice. 'You promised that wouldn't happen.'

She nodded. 'I believed that when I said it. I thought I'd endured too much loss and couldn't stand the risk of anymore. The last thing I wanted was to put my heart in harm's way again. But being with you, opening up to you…it's changed that. Taken me back to who I was before it all got so hard, and as frightening as it still is to know that I could lose again, it's not scary enough to stop me from wanting to try. Not anymore. Not with you.' All the feeling he was trying so hard to suppress threatened. 'I spent so long living a life that wasn't what I wanted, Caleb. I don't want to do that again. You're the one who told me that I didn't have to, that I could have everything I wanted, and this is what I want. Happiness. Family. Passion. Love. With you.'

Love. She was asking for the one thing she knew he couldn't give. Didn't want to give. He cared for her, more deeply than he'd cared for anyone, and he'd happily give her all else that he could, but love? The word alone was enough to make him lock down. What had loving ever brought anyone in his life? Desolation and despair. He wouldn't ever invite that in.

'I can't give you what you want, Serena. I'm sorry.'

'Can't?' she demanded. 'Or won't? I know you're scared, Caleb. It's frightening for me too. But won't you even try? I know what we have matters to you. I *know* it. Isn't that worth trying?'

'I have been honest with you from the beginning, Serena,' he stated, holding on to his emotion by a thread whilst keeping her at bay with his cool tone. 'I never lied about what this could be, or what I was willing to offer. Not once.'

'That's it? That's all you have to say? She looked so despairing, and so disappointed in him. *See,* he wanted to say, *this is what love does. What love is.* She stepped back, looking as though she'd taken a punch to the stomach. As wrecked, if not more, than she had looked earlier, and it tore at him to be the cause of it. But that was what happened when you let love in. It was why he never would. She turned away so he couldn't see the tears that shook her shoulders, but when she turned back, it was anger, not pain, boiling in her eyes, and he loathed himself for forcing her back to her guarded stance, to that place where she refused to let anyone see her flounder. 'I guess I will go back to London then. But tonight. And not as your wife.'

In a single, deliberate movement she removed the rings from her finger and put them on the table, and the act landed like a grenade in his gut.

His heart banged so powerfully; he was sure it bruised his insides. 'Serena…'

'No.' She held up a silencing hand. 'We've said everything that needs to be said. This is where we are. You're not willing to offer me more and I refuse to settle for less. So, this is the only way forwards. Goodbye Caleb.'

Half an hour later, he watched silently as she walked out of the door, and though his despair grew with every step away from him that she took, he let her go because he had to, because he was too afraid to do anything other than that.

CHAPTER TWELVE

CALEB'S EYES WERE gritty with tiredness as he glanced at the clock and saw that it was nearly midnight. *That explains that.* He'd been working for almost eighteen hours, and on barely any sleep. But instead of reaching for his jacket and returning to the villa, and his bed, he began scrolling through his emails, filling his mind with more work.

Just like your father.

The comparison landed like a blow, the uncomfortable truth forcing him back in his chair. He was doing exactly as his father had, wasn't he? Burying himself in business in an attempt to forget about his feelings, pretend they didn't exist.

Only they did exist.

And he was tired of pretending not to feel them. To not feel the ache and agony.

He'd thought he would feel better, more like himself, once he had wrested back control of the situation and his emotions—and he had. At first. But very quickly that sense of victory at mastering his feelings, his heart, had fled, and far from feeling on safe ground, he felt more lost than ever before.

Lost and lonely and empty.

Because he hadn't just pushed Serena away emotionally, he had pushed her all the way out of his life. So much of him had revolted at letting her walk out the door unchallenged, but forcing her to stay hadn't been an option, regardless of what she'd promised, or what agreement she had signed her name to. It was bad enough that he'd cornered her into the marriage in the first place; he couldn't force her to remain in a situation that didn't provide the emotional sustenance that she needed. Deserved. It would be nice to think that if he'd known then what he knew about her life now, he would never have strong-armed her into the stupid arrangement, only he couldn't say for sure. But he was a better man now, and after everything she'd been through, Serena had earned the right to have the life she wanted. And since the only way for her to find that happiness was for him to let her and their baby go, that was what he'd done.

But he throbbed with how badly he missed her. She was still the first thing he thought of each day, and each evening he searched the villa for any trace of her; her scent, a missed belonging.

Did I make a terrible mistake?

Caleb prowled to the window, staring into the darkness. He had always maintained that it was preferable to feel nothing, to keep his heart safe and separate, but forcing himself to be honest, Caleb had never felt more content or settled in his life, more at peace than during these past weeks with Serena.

He'd been scared from the beginning of how much she had made him feel, thinking it was a bad thing, that it would lead him back to a place he wanted to avoid at all costs, but it was only when he had feared that he was losing her, and the baby, that the chaos had returned. It was only now, without her, that he couldn't eat or sleep. Function.

It was letting her in, *loving her*, that had brought him peace. Just as it was finding a new love with Ellie that had healed his father. Helped him find peace after so many years of hurt. Caleb just hadn't realised that until now.

He drew in a sharp breath at the realisation, but didn't hide from it or try to fight it off. Because it was true. He loved Serena. He suspected he had for a while.

For as long as he could remember, love was something to be avoided, something that would only invite chaos into his body and soul, but it was the opposite that was true.

Serena said that he had given her life back to her, but she'd brought him back to life too, he realised with a jolt of his heart. It was because of her that he'd started to heal, to forgive himself for his past mistakes with Charlotte and see himself in a different way. The only reason that he believed he could be a good father to their child was because of her, because of her faith and trust in him, the love she had given so freely and fearlessly.

But when she'd been brave enough to ask for what she needed and wanted, he'd been a coward. He'd denied her, pushed her away, let her believe that she wasn't loved, and that made him sick to his stomach, because if there was one person on the planet who deserved to be loved, it was Serena.

He needed to fix it. Whatever it took, he would fix it. Because he'd been wrong. So wrong. And he didn't want to waste a minute to make it right again.

She had done the right thing.

That was what Serena kept telling herself. What she had to keep reminding herself. Each morning when she woke and another day without Caleb stretched endlessly ahead. Each time she looked at the sonogram shot of their baby and thought of all the moments she wouldn't get to share with him. Each night as she lay in bed alone and aching, missing his warm presence beside her.

She hated being all alone again…

But leaving had been the only thing to do.

She had held out her heart for him to accept, and he hadn't wanted it. Which was the outcome Serena had feared, and yet some part of her had still hoped that the closeness they'd built would be enough to change his mind about not wanting love in his life. Because she really thought their relationship had changed him. Serena knew he had felt as much terror and joy as she had in the hospital. She knew it wasn't only her heart that had become invested in the relationship… Caleb just wasn't willing to accept that.

He didn't want it to be the truth. He didn't want to love her.

And Serena couldn't force him to.

She could have stayed and waited to see if, with a little more time, Caleb did change his mind, but that would only have been short-changing herself, and she'd already lost so much time that to spend another minute of her life not living it the way she wanted, without the love that she was now brave enough to admit that she craved, was impossible. Especially now that she remembered how exhilarating it was to love. How fulfilling.

Even though it had ended in the way she'd most wanted to avoid, with her heart tearing apart, she wouldn't be flattened by that pain. The scar on her heart was a mark of bravery, of how she'd risked herself for love, and despite the pain being worse than anything she had endured before—deeper and sharper, persisting through all hours of the day and night—Serena knew she could survive it. Would survive it. The time she'd spent with Caleb had shown her that. She was a fighter, a survivor, and she would never forget that again. Never doubt her own power again.

She would make it through this, without closing herself off to the future. She would build a good life for herself and her child, chase happiness because she deserved it and without the fear of losing it, even if there remained a part of her that was always sad that she hadn't been able to find that happiness with Caleb…

That was why, after days of lying curled up on Evie's sofa, she'd taken the step of going to the new house, because she had to move on and move forwards. It was a beautiful Georgian house in Holland Park, only a short walk from where Kit and Alexis lived with her step-mother. She had just finished unpacking and exploring the space that was now her home, when there was a knock at the door.

'Caleb…' It was the strangest moment of déjà vu, to find him looming on her doorstep once again, and despite the elation filling in her heart, she quickly tensed, not interested in letting history repeat itself. 'If you're here to twist my arm into coming back and keeping up the pretence…'

'I'm not,' he said, holding up a hand as though swearing to that, and it was then she noticed the crescent shadows beneath his eyes, his stubble an inch thicker than normal, and his paleness beneath his tan. But his eyes glowed with his characteristic determination. 'All I'm asking for is five minutes of your time because there are some things I need to say.'

She knew he could accomplish a lot in five minutes,

and yet it was such a small thing to ask for that refusing seemed petty. And she couldn't avoid him forever—not when they had a child to raise. 'Alright.'

But Serena was wary as she stepped back to let him inside, and as he followed her into the living room, she chose to stand as far from his magnetic force field as possible, trying to keep her heart from rioting out of control.

'I'm sorry,' he said, startling her because they were the last words she had expected to hear. 'I'm so sorry, Serena. For pushing you away and for saying nothing when you told me you loved me. I shouldn't have let a single second go by without telling you the same, but instead I pushed you away even more, because I was scared. Scared of how much I loved hearing you tell me that and scared of how much I felt for you.' He came a step closer, and she knew she should maintain a safe distance between them, but was too stunned to move. 'Serena, for as long as I can remember, I've thought of love as something destructive, something that causes chaos and weakness and would weaken me if I let it. I watched what loving my mother did to my father after she left, and even though I didn't remember her, I know what it did to me. There was this gaping hole that nothing could heal, and it made me yearn for something so badly that I thought I'd die from the force of it. I *never* wanted to feel that again. That desperation and chaos inside me, so I pulled back from everyone, from wanting anything from them. But then came you, and I don't really know what happened. Just that it happened easily, but when you asked me to name it, all I could think of was all that bad from my childhood. But I do love you, Serena. I love your heart and strength and how hard you fight. I love how much you love Kit and Alexis, and how much I know you will love and protect our child. And, if there was no baby, I would still love you. I would still want you at my side.' Serena didn't know when she'd started crying; only realised her face was wet as her pain and longing fought through her control. Hearing him explain the effects of his childhood was heartbreaking. It wasn't hard to understand that boy—rejected and scared to love and ask for more, to accept more, in case it made him vulnerable again—still lived inside of him. No wonder he'd been frightened of the love building between them, and been so unwilling to acknowledge it. 'I know what I did was awful, but I wanted you to know the truth. To know that you are loved. And to tell you that if you could find it within you to forgive and let me back into your life, I would never make you doubt it again. I would never let you down again.'

The words were perfect, everything she'd wanted him to say to her all those days ago. But he hadn't, and that silence had wounded her more than words could express, and as badly as she wanted to sink into him now, could she trust him?

'You let me walk out of the door, Caleb. Out of your life and our marriage.' Guilty colour slashed across his cheeks and his head bowed with the weight of his regret, but the weight of her pain was heavy too. 'You didn't even try to stop me.'

'I wanted to. At least a part of me did. But I was too scared.' His eyes pleaded with her. 'I wasn't ready to accept how I felt. I regret it, Serena. More than anything I've ever done before. I'll regret it forever. But I want to fix it. That's why I'm here. To make it better. You deserve to have exactly the life you want, Serena. A life full of love and passion and happiness, and I want to give you that life.'

'And what happens the next time you feel scared?' she demanded, trembling with the force of her feeling. Her hope and her fear. 'When you get overwhelmed by all your emotions? Are you going to push me away again?'

'Never. Never again.'

'Because it's not just me, Caleb. It's Kit and Alexis too. They have lost just as much as me, and in another few months there will be another little person, and I won't do that to them. I won't put them through it.'

'It won't happen, Serena.' He stepped closer again, his eyes blazing. 'I promise. I am here. I am in this. Every day, I will be here. With you. For you. In love with you. Trust me. *Please trust me.* I know I haven't done much to deserve it, but trust me. I won't let you down. I love you. And I won't ever let you go ever again.'

'Say that again.'

He took a breath. 'I will never let you go…'

'No. Not that part.' Serena offered him a little smile. 'The part about loving me.'

Taking her face in his hands, Caleb looked deep into her eyes with his own honest gaze, where she saw nothing but the truth. Pain. But also love. 'I love you, Serena. I love everything about you, with everything that I am. You, and this little one, were the last thing I thought I wanted, but you're the best things that have ever happened to me.'

It was impossible to last a moment more without throwing her arms around him and sinking into the heat and safety of his body. 'I missed you, Caleb.'

'Nowhere near as much as I've missed you,' he breathed, pressing kisses to her mouth, her cheeks, her eyelids. 'My life was empty without you, Serena. I never want to go back to that.'

'You'll never have to,' she promised, holding tight and smiling. Because whilst she had no idea what life would throw at them, Serena trusted—no, she *knew*—it would be alright because she had him.

Because they had each other.

EPILOGUE

WHO KNEW THAT a toddler's birthday party would create such widespread detritus?

As they did their usual divide-and-conquer routine, and Caleb put their three-year-old daughter to bed, Serena tackled the mess downstairs, clearing the rooms, tidying the new stack of toys, stacking the dishwasher and wiping down the counters. By the time she heard her husband descending the stairs, their living space was gleaming again.

'Did Frankie go down okay?'

He smiled indulgently, sliding his arms around her from behind. 'She was fast asleep in my arms before her head went anywhere near her pillow. She was worn-out.'

'She did have a big day.'

'I cannot believe how much she relished being the centre of attention at her party. I know she *always* loves being the centre of attention,' he added quickly, 'but she revelled in it even more than usual today.'

Serena smiled, resting her head against his shoulder. 'When we decided to name her after my mum, I hoped she would have a little of her spirit, but we definitely got more than we bargained for. I wouldn't change her though, not a single thing.' Even if she was *exhausting*!

'Me neither,' he agreed, pressing a warm kiss to her cheek. 'She's perfect, just like her very beautiful, very sexy mother.' Serena spun in his arms, feeling his arousal, and without delay heat swept through her body, delighted by the thought of surrendering to him. 'Please tell me everyone has left,' he breathed, seizing her mouth for a burning kiss.

'Mm-hmm. Kit is staying at his friends down the road. Your father and Ellie have gone back to the hotel, and Evie is dropping Alexis off at Marcia's.'

Marcia had been invited to the party, but preexisting plans meant she hadn't been able to attend. She had sent a gift though, a gesture that Serena appreciated. The years hadn't brought them any closer—too much had passed between them for there to be closeness—but they had learned to respect one another and had built a civil relationship for the sake of Kit and Alexis. It was peaceful, which was enough.

'Excellent. I think we should make the most of this rare moment of peace and quiet—no toddler running around, no teenagers wandering in and out—and start practicing to make another perfect human all over again.'

Serena arched her eyebrows, smiling. 'That's really what you want? Another baby?'

'Yes.' He nodded, barely able to hide his eagerness.

He'd been talking about extending their family for a while. He loved being a father to Frankie and a surrogate father-cum-big brother to Kit and Alexis. And Serena loved watching him do it. He was so sure and steady, never holding back in his affection or guidance. Watching him, it was hard to believe he'd ever been worried about being a good father.

Becoming a dad had also helped his relationship with

his own father. It was in the high emotion surrounding Frankie's birth that Caleb had finally found the courage to broach the matter of his childhood with his father. As Caleb suspected, his father had no recollection of blaming him and had been horrified to hear about his actions. His apology had been swift and sincere, and his explanation of his heartache had been met with understanding from Caleb. His father had spent every day since working hard to heal the rift between them and to be the best father and grandfather possible, and it hadn't taken long for them to overcome all the guilt and pain they both carried from that long-ago time in their lives.

'I'm glad you feel that way because I found out today that I'm six weeks pregnant.'

She watched his reaction; his eyes widening with disbelief and then glowing with delight 'You are?' Emotion shimmered in his gaze as he looked quickly down at her stomach. 'Wait. Six weeks?'

Serena had to laugh. 'I know. It's crazy.' Six weeks ago, they had been on the way back from their biannual trip to Australia and had stopped in Singapore for a few days. 'There's just something about you, me and Singapore that seems to be a very potent combination.' She laughed, smoothing her hand over his short hair.

'I love you so much, Serena,' he said earnestly, claiming her lips for one of the deep kisses she loved, because it seemed to say he couldn't get enough of her. 'And I love our family so much.'

She knew he did. There was never any doubt about that in her mind, not with all the ways he'd changed his life to make them his priority, but it was always so much fun when he demonstrated it too.

'Show me how much,' she breathed, leaning in to him to curl her arms around his neck and touch her lips to his, and it wasn't a request she had to make twice.

* * * * *

Did Pregnant and Conveniently Wed
have you enthralled?
Then don't miss Rosie Maxwell's other
dramatic stories!

An Heir for the Vengeful Billionaire
Billionaire's Runaway Wife

Available now!

MILLS & BOON®

Coming next month

SECRETLY PREGNANT PRINCESS
Lorraine Hall

Evelyne saw Gabriel's eyes widen. She tried to recover, but it was too late. He'd seen.

He pointed at her—at her stomach. 'What is that?' Gabriel demanded.

She had dreamed of this in her weaker moments. Telling him that he was to be a father. In her fantasies, she was calm, casual, disdainful almost. She did not give him the satisfaction of thinking that she needed him, wanted him, or was afraid of being alone.

She was determined to make fantasy a reality.

So, she beamed at him, made sure she sounded cheerful. 'In the States they call it a baby bump.' She ran her hands over the roundness, moved to give him a profile view. Refused to let the nerves fluttering through her show—she'd had ample practice at hiding those. 'Isn't that cute?'

He said nothing. Didn't move. She wasn't sure he breathed.

When he finally moved, it was with clear-cut precision. 'Explain yourself,' he said quietly, dangerously.

She chose to maintain her flippancy. 'Is it not self-explanatory, Gabriel? I am pregnant.'

Continue reading

SECRETLY PREGNANT PRINCESS
Lorraine Hall

Available next month
millsandboon.co.uk

Copyright ©2026 Lorraine Hall

COMING SOON!

We really hope you enjoyed reading this book.
If you're looking for more romance
be sure to head to the shops when
new books are available on

Thursday 15th January

To see which titles are coming soon, please visit

millsandboon.co.uk/nextmonth

MILLS & BOON

FOUR BRAND NEW BOOKS FROM
MILLS & BOON MODERN

Indulge in desire, drama, and breathtaking
romance – where passion knows no bounds!

2
BOOKS
IN ONE

STOLEN BY A SICILIAN

Jackie Ashenden   Caitlin Crews

Babies to Bind

2
BOOKS
IN ONE

Tara Pammi   Rosie Maxwell

2
BOOKS
IN ONE

TO HIRE AND TO HATE

Michelle Smart   Annie West

2
BOOKS
IN ONE

KEEPING THE Enemy Close...

KIM LAWRENCE   BELLA MASON

OUT NOW

Eight Modern stories published every month, find them all at:

millsandboon.co.uk

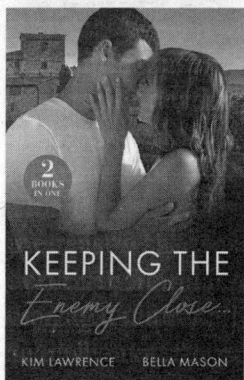

TWO BRAND NEW BOOKS FROM

Love Always

Once Upon
a Second
Chance

2
BOOKS
IN ONE

Kate Hardy · Michele Renae

Juliette Hyland   Clare Miles

Matches
in a
Million

2
BOOKS
IN ONE

Be prepared to be swept away to incredible
worldwide destinations along with our strong,
relatable heroines and intensely desirable heroes.

OUT NOW

Four Love Always stories published
every month, find them all at:

millsandboon.co.uk

OUT NOW!

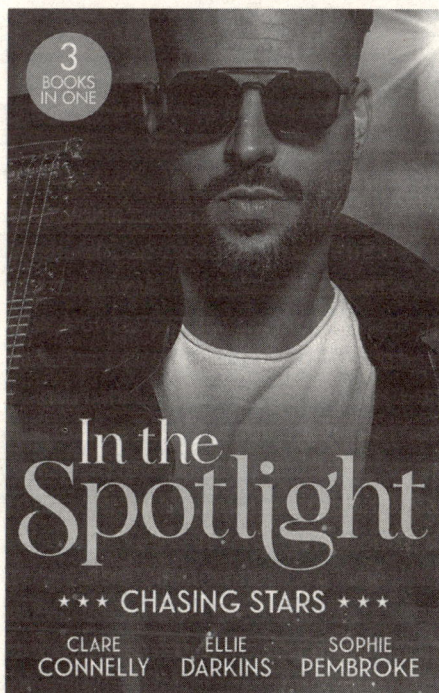

3 BOOKS IN ONE

In the Spotlight

★★★ CHASING STARS ★★★

CLARE CONNELLY   ELLIE DARKINS   SOPHIE PEMBROKE

Available at
millsandboon.co.uk

MILLS & BOON

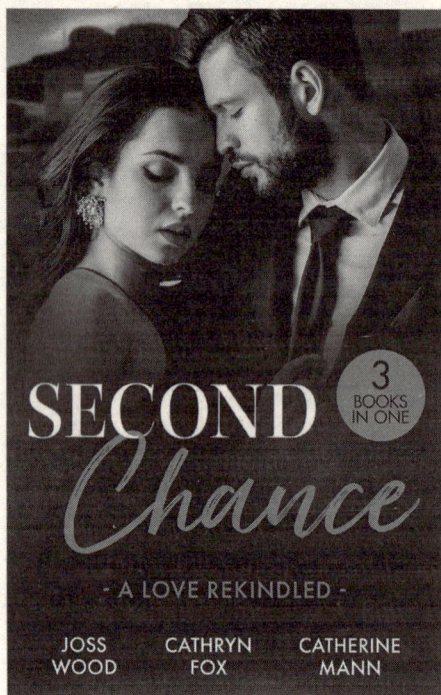

OUT NOW!

SECOND
Chance

3 BOOKS IN ONE

- A LOVE REKINDLED -

JOSS WOOD   CATHRYN FOX   CATHERINE MANN

Available at
millsandboon.co.uk

MILLS & BOON

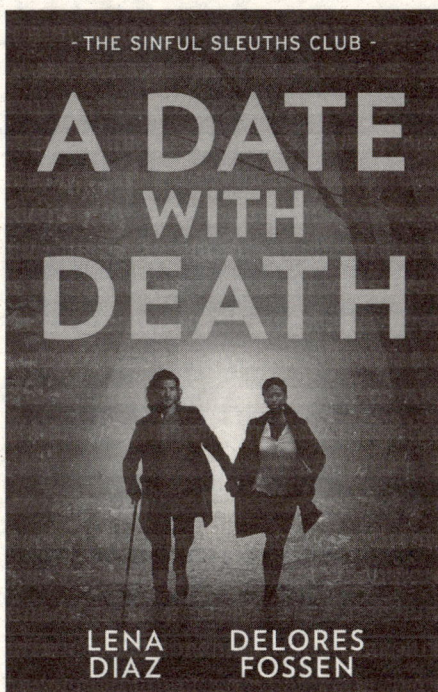

OUT NOW!

- THE SINFUL SLEUTHS CLUB -

A DATE
WITH
DEATH

**LENA
DIAZ**

**DELORES
FOSSEN**

Available at
millsandboon.co.uk

MILLS & BOON

LET'S TALK

Romance

For exclusive extracts, competitions and special offers, find us online:

- **f** MillsandBoon
- **X** @MillsandBoon
- **O** @MillsandBoonUK
- **♪** @MillsandBoonUK

Get in touch on 01413 063 232

For all the latest titles coming soon, visit
millsandboon.co.uk/nextmonth